RAVAGED SOUL

ANACONDA TALES - BOOK TWO

J ROSE

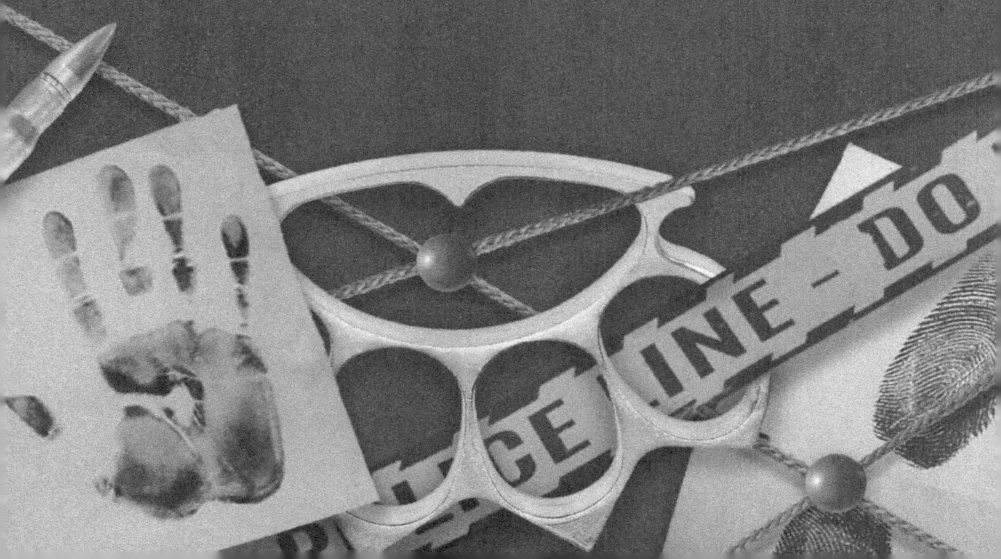

For those who grew up too fast and survived alone.
Letting people in isn't a weakness. When they cradle the broken
parts of you without turning their nose up in disgust… You'll
realise that you survived for a reason.

You survived to feel their love.
To build a new life.
To find your home.
You survived to belong.

1
DO NOT CROSS

"I have my boot on the throat of hell right now. Watch me beat my demons into submission. Surviving's ugly work and here I am, so hideously alive."

- Trista Mateer

TRIGGER WARNING

Ravaged Soul (Anaconda Tales #2) is a slow burn, why choose romance, so the main character will have multiple love interests she will not have to choose between.

This book is dark and contains scenes that may be triggering for some readers. These include strong mental health themes, human trafficking, allusions to sexual assault, psychological/physical torture, chronic illness and graphic violence.

If you are easily offended or triggered by any of this content, please do not read this book. This is dark romance, and therefore, not for the faint of heart.

1
NOT CROSS

J ROSE SHARED UNIVERSE

All of J Rose's contemporary, dark romance books are set in the same shared universe. From the walls of Blackwood Institute and Harrowdean Manor to Sabre Security's HQ and the small town of Briar Valley, all of the characters inhabit the same world and feature in Easter egg cameos in each other's books.

You can read these books in any order, dipping in and out of different series and stories, but here is the recommended order for the full effect of the shared universe and the ties between the books.

More Information: www.jroseauthor.com/readingorder

A
TYPE I (NORMAL) POSITION
INDEX
Play
me
CONFIDENTIAL

PROLOGUE

BLAINE

MAKES ME WANT YOU – SOMBR

8 MONTHS AGO

Tucked away on the wire mezzanine floor of the warehouse's office, I watch operations unfold beneath me. Countless workstations are occupied by laughing thugs, packaging little white pills to be pushed across the city this weekend.

We're a fraction of the size we used to be, but contrary to popular belief, my family's criminal empire didn't burn entirely. I was happy for the world to believe it had so my people could move our work underground while I served time.

The fact that the assholes from Sabre Security thought they dismantled my entire operation when they arrested me is laughable, really. An organism this huge can't merely be dismantled.

It has to be killed.

Fucking obliterated.

Each limb must be poisoned, allowed to rot, then sloughed away like dead skin cells in need of exfoliation. They did a shit poor job of that. Surface level at best.

The one thing they didn't do a shit poor job of? Scaring the worthless piece of scum who fathered me into fleeing this city. I can't find the motherfucker anywhere.

Legs propped up on my desk, I lazily tilt back in my office chair to blow smoke up towards the ceiling. The sight of my own bare, scar-littered chest awakens a hateful whisper in my mind.

You were born into a great dynasty, Blaine.

Yet you continually disappoint.

Gaze fixed on the glowing tip of the joint, its fragrant smoke does little to alleviate the bad memories. I don't smoke cigarettes like he did before he put them out on my flesh, but a blunt is pleasurable once in a while.

Father used to light up before all of our 'business meetings' where he'd list my failures for that particular week. Even for a grown-ass man in his thirties, I still found myself afraid of the torture he'd dole out.

Childhood scars were soon replaced by adult ones, forming a motley patchwork of burns, slices and slashes that will forever remind me of the past. Dead or alive, I can't ever forget my father's violence.

"Where the hell is he?" a female voice screeches.

Is that...?

"Blaine!"

Jolting upright in surprise, I let my thumb pad lift from a particularly gnarly burn mark on my lower belly.

"Blaine motherfucking Madden!"

"Raye?" I call out.

"Where are you?"

"Up here."

Without a door on the raised metal level, Raye is free to storm straight in from the factory floor. Her pierced face is set in a scowl, navy-blue pixie cut spiking in all directions above a stare that drips with aggravation.

Despite spending the past few months running our latest overseas venture, she's unchanged. Still as sour-faced as ever. I've missed her take-no-crap attitude around here, if I'm honest.

"You're back."

"No shit!" Raye blusters. "Fuck, Blaine. Answer your phone for once."

Shrugging, I gesture towards the switched-off device with my joint. "I'm thinking."

"You and your thinking is what got us into this shit in the first place."

"This shit being?"

Scrubbing a hand over her pale face, she rubs beneath her shadow-marked eyes. "I'm too tired for this."

"You haven't checked in since last week. I was starting to worry."

"Because I had to be smuggled onto a cargo ship, sail across the Atlantic Ocean, then pay off some sleazy freight handlers to get back into the country unseen!"

A dark chuckle spills from my lips through a cloud of smoke. "It's good to have you back, Raye."

"Yeah, yeah. Don't bullshit me. You're incapable of worrying about another human being."

"And you are?" I cock a brow in challenge.

"Fucking dickhead. Missed you too."

"Alright, enough of that." My hand rotates in a hurrying motion. "Don't hold me in suspense."

Kicking a half-empty box of plastic pill baggies, Raye throws up her hands. "You sent me to Mexico to track down the Lawson girl."

"And did you?"

She scoffs hatefully. "Next time, send Spyder!"

"Raye…"

"He'd fit right in with the exploitative—"

"Raye," I repeat, my patience splintering. "Did. You. Find. Her?"

She drops into the armchair opposite my desk. "Sort of."

My spine lengthens, solidified by anticipation-laced concrete. I quickly stub out the remaining length of my joint to give Raye my full attention.

"What the hell does that mean?"

"I didn't find Lawson, but I heard rumours about some big fight. Decided to check it out."

Huffing, I lean sideways to tug open the bottom drawer of my desk. Inside, I keep a bottle of single malt whiskey for emergencies. Raye nods when I fill two chipped tumblers then offer one to her.

"Explain."

"I was poking around a few of the underground fight clubs." She knocks back her measure of amber nectar. "Figured working girls may be targeting the circuit, so it was a good place to look."

My internal muscles clench tight as I roll smooth, smoky whiskey over my tongue then swallow. I'm hardly one to discuss the morals of anyone's illegal operations, but the skin trade turns my fucking stomach.

I'll push pills and weapons until my dying day and reap the rewards, but I'd never touch the worldwide trafficking of innocent lives. Not a chance. That's a market reserved for the worst of the worst.

In every single country on this rotating rock, an underground market of stolen flesh exists. Every continent is guilty of it. So many victims, trapped in a mechanism they'll never escape.

They're left with no choice but to obey the commands of their captors, including prostitution and far worse. I know exactly how degrading it is to be imprisoned by someone else's greed, just the thought of it makes my blood boil.

Sure, I've never been forced to sell my body. But I've torn off bloodied chunks of my soul and sold them to the highest bidder just to earn my father's mercy enough times.

"Wasn't paying much attention to the fight until I heard it end." Raye sets her empty glass down. "Imagine my surprise when I recognised the woman doing a goddamn victory lap."

I feel myself recoil in shock.

"Are you saying what I think you are?"

"Yeah," she confirms solemnly. "It was Ember Lawson."

Confusion seeps through me, intermingling with the fiery threads of liquor seeping into my bloodstream. "Ember Lawson was kidnapped over five years ago. We're looking for a working girl or a body, not a damn street fighter."

"It was her." She shrugs, leaving no room for doubt.

"You got proof?"

"What do you take me for? I saw her myself. Lawson broke some Puerto Rican dude's cheekbone… before she broke his leg for good measure."

Hand thrusting into her pocket, Raye fishes out her mobile phone. I wait in tense anticipation as she brings up her photos then shoves the device towards me so I can see the screen.

"Look."

Well, fuck me gently.

Thumbing through a series of decent shots, the delicate sweep of Lawson's oval-shaped face, paired with two grey-blue eyes that seem to violently pierce her opponent, are unmistakable once I zoom in.

Through our research, I've seen enough old photos to know that Lawson was originally a redhead. The bleach-blonde job on her missing persons' photos is long gone now, replaced by fiery, natural auburn.

She's lithe and muscled, her taut body rippling with iron-like strength. My fingers tighten on Raye's phone as I study the way her supple curves, defined calves and tight, pert ass seem to dominate the screen.

"Believe me now?" Raye challenges.

Tongue held, I merely nod.

"Good. I'm told she won nearly half a mil in illegal bets that night. Everyone knows her as 768 now."

Disgust forces my muscles to clench. "768?"

"Apparently."

"Little more than a number."

"That may be so, but her reputation speaks for itself. She's the crown jewel of the cartel's collection."

Passing the phone back to Raye, I flex my hands to crack my knuckles. I don't owe this bitch anything—she's little more than a pawn to me—but the inhumane treatment still sours my stomach. I dislike needless suffering.

Still, this isn't a personal endeavour for me. I want the leverage that Ember Lawson's safe return from overseas will provide. Our little jailbird has some very powerful familial connections. Ones that I intend to exploit.

"Well, shit."

"Precisely my reaction," Raye agrees drily.

"This just got a lot more complicated."

It's taken almost eighteen months of work to make it this far. Fuck knows how she's survived this long. Especially if the cartel has her working a shady, street fight circuit.

"So she was spared the flesh market and turned into some kind of business asset instead." I lean back in my chair, kneading the stress that's strangling my neck. "How unexpected."

"Tell me about it. If we knew where to look, we could've saved ourselves a whole lot of time instead of looking for her in sleazy strip clubs."

"We have her now." My bare shoulder lifts then drops. "The rest is irrelevant."

"Irrelevant?" Raye scowls so hard, I wonder if she's attempting to melt my skin. "I was smuggled on a fucking ship, Blaine!"

"Your paycheck shall reflect your hardships."

"You're damn right it will."

Ignoring her disgruntlement, I try to gather my windswept thoughts. My mind is whirring uncontrollably, tossing out different scenarios and options. Complicated doesn't begin to cover the clusterfuck Raye has uncovered.

This was meant to be easy. Locate Lawson, pluck her out of whatever hovel the cartel had her working in, or perhaps locate her corpse, then deliver her to those dickheads at Sabre to secure myself the favour of the century.

That's a little hard to do when our mark is a bonafide assassin raking in millions for a powerful criminal empire. She'll be near impossible to locate, let alone free.

"Where is she now?" I demand. "Fuck, you should've stayed in Mexico! We need eyes on her."

Snatching the bottle of whiskey, Raye dumps an oversized measure into her own glass, disregarding mine. I watch her angrily toss it back with barely a wince.

"First of all, fuck you. I did my job. I found her."

"Well, you—"

"Second of all," she plows on. "768 is in the wind. No one knows when or where she's going to pop up to fight next. Whoever's controlling her… they've got her location locked down tight."

"Someone must know!"

"Her fights aren't exactly public knowledge, Blaine! She pops up, beats the shit out of whoever she's battling, then vanishes with the fucking cash. The cycle repeats."

"Then we need to get ahead of her."

Rising to stand, I give Raye my back while I locate a clean, black t-shirt from the chest at the back of my office. We've gotten used to bouncing around with no real home or possessions, so I always keep spares on hand.

Competing ideas continue to flit around inside my skull as I eye my other shirt, laying in bloodstained tatters on the metal floor where I ripped it off when I stormed up here.

Our enemies have gotten bold in my absence. Sending a member of their syndicate here to wave a knife around was a poor choice. Lucky for him, his heart gave out before I could finish plucking his severed fingers off.

It isn't that hard to do once you know how to slice the cartilage just right. Those fingers have already been sent to our rivals as a warning. Nobody messes with the Madden dynasty.

"Blaine! Care to clue me in?"

"I'm still thinking." Tugging the t-shirt over my head, it covers my ugly quilt of scars. "How well-protected is she while fighting?"

Raye wrinkles her nose. "From what I saw, she doesn't need protection. Bitch is a fucking hellhound. Those men are her captors, not her guards."

"And you have no idea where she'll be fighting next?"

"It's a big country," she snarls acidly. "I can't keep track of every last underground club. If you want to find her, you need a professional tracker."

"That can be arranged."

Floral tattoo-covered arms folded, Raye pins me with the stink eye. It's not my favourite look on her. She's loyal to a goddamn fault, but nine times out of ten, she's a massive pain in my backside.

"What are you plotting? Why do you care about her?"

"I don't care about Ember Lawson," I quickly deny.

"Then what's the deal? Why is she so important?"

"Because she's the key to everything."

Moving to face the dirt-speckled, floor-to-ceiling warehouse windows, I gaze outside. The metal, crisscrossed slats offer snapshots of the capital's lawless streets.

This deep into London's seedy underbelly, we're surrounded by the industrial beating heart of the glitz and glamour that most associate with this city. Reality is far less romantic.

The United Kingdom is no different than any other country. We have our own underground subculture of criminality and exploitation. For years, I benefitted from it. Until my own family turned against me.

"We've been searching for my father since we regrouped and resumed operations." My attention remains locked outside. "But without success."

Raye hums her disappointment behind me.

"I don't believe he'll allow us to rebuild fully without showing his face to retake the family empire. We need to find him, Raye. And eliminate him."

"What does this have to do with the girl?"

"Warner Mead."

For several seconds, Raye holds her silence. "Wait… The asshole who works for Sabre?"

Turning around to face her, I prop my tailbone against the windowpane. "Bingo."

"You know, he's been tearing apart anything and everything he can get his hands on while searching for this crazy bitch." She smirks a little as if impressed. "That's dedication."

"It's also his weakness."

She rattles out a sigh. "Walk me through it. We don't all live on your intellectual level."

"We can find the one thing he wants." I incline my head, urging her to understand. "Now we have a starting point."

"And that's good… Why?"

"You said it yourself. He'll do anything to get his girl back. *Anything*."

Her eyes widen as she begins to catch onto my thinking. "Oh, hell."

"If we can't find my father… You can surely bet that with Sabre's help, we will hunt him down and eliminate him. If we get them off our backs in the process and clear my name, that's a win-win."

With her mouth open in astonishment, several beats of silence pass.

"Fuck me. You want to strike a deal with Sabre Security?"

"I want to throw them a bone." I shrug casually. "Then watch them come running when they want another taste of the results only we can offer them. For the right price, of course."

Her stunned expression is amusing. I don't know why she's surprised that I've concocted a scheme to save our skins. It's what I do—plot, plan then fucking attack.

All my life, I've operated from the shadows. The darkness became my home long before I could walk or talk. That's what happens when you're bred to bolster an illustrious criminal empire.

I'm going to take that empire back.

It's rightfully fucking *mine*.

Raye's laugh is stunted with surprise. "You're certifiable."

"You going soft on me now?"

"Nah. Just hope you know what you're doing. Those Sabre pricks don't mess around."

"They certainly do not."

Finishing her liquor, Raye rises to her feet. "How are you going to find 768 and free her? I told you, she's a ghost. Someone powerful is controlling her."

Grabbing my phone from the cluttered desk, I depress the power button to turn it back on. I'm usually the last to admit it, but sometimes, professional assistance is the price of doing business.

"Blaine?" Raye prompts.

After scrolling through my contacts, a name I've only called upon in times of true desperation causes goose pimples to rise on my skin.

The Hunter.

When I continue to ignore her, Raye peers over my shoulder to see what I'm doing. She lets out a low, impressed whistle.

"Are you serious?"

"Deadly," I murmur back.

"But… we can't afford his bill."

"Then we'll figure it out. He's usually willing to cut a deal, and we can't do this without him."

My calloused thumb hovers over the call button without pressing it. Pressure builds behind my eyes, adding to the rising levels of adrenaline swamping my system.

Feeling Raye's uneasy gaze on me, I turn to meet her stare. She gnaws on her bottom lip, brows curved in a frown as she appears to weigh her next words.

"You know… this genie doesn't go back in its bottle once you let it out."

Without another second of fretting, my thumb jabs the call button. Raye's stare disappears. All I can see is the mental image of that beautifully savage fighter battling for her life, splattered with blood and bruises, toned limbs contorting in blissful violence.

Fuck. Ember Lawson is just a job.

But what I wouldn't give to see those scarred curves up close. To trace my tongue along her pointed lines, ridged muscles and dark-purple bruises. To bathe in her violence. Her rage. Whatever inner beast has given her the strength to survive.

Perhaps I'll meet her yet.

No—I will. I'm fucking counting on it.

As the line rings, awaiting the demon I must be crazy to call upon to answer, I smile slyly at my loyal foot soldier. She's gaping at me like I've grown a second head.

"I know, Raye. That's exactly what I'm counting on."

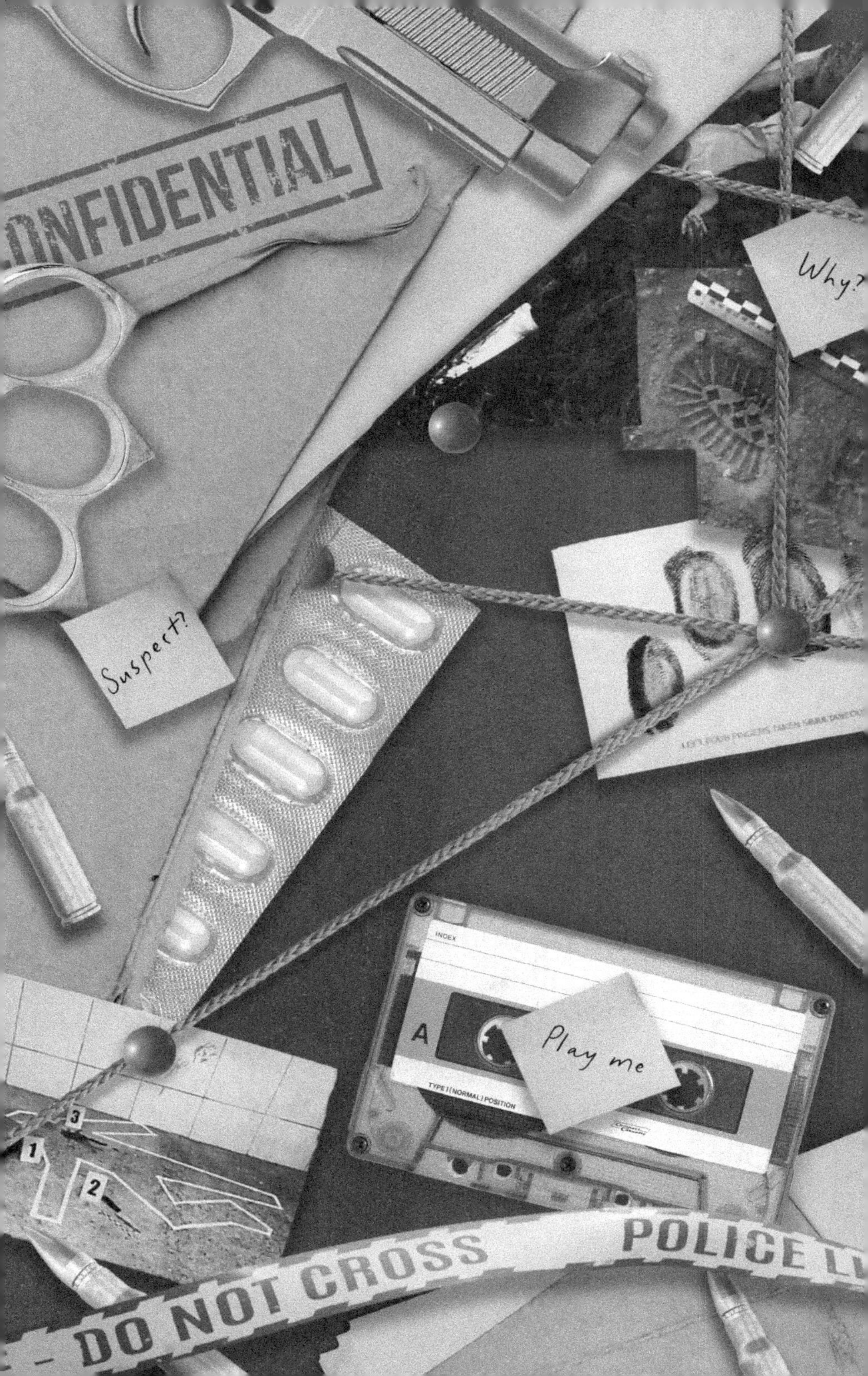
CONFIDENTIAL
Why?
Suspect?
INDEX
A
TYPE I (NORMAL) POSITION
Play me
DO NOT CROSS
POLICE LI

play
me
DO NOT CROSS
POLICE
suspect?
NOT CROSS
POLICE LI
(NORMAL) POSITION
Compact Cassette
4

1

EMBER

STARING AT THE SUN – TV ON THE RADIO

PRESENT DAY

Punch.

The boxing bag swings from the impact of my strike.

Punch.

Fire races over my bare, busted knuckles.

Punch.

My muscles clench, twitching in clear warning.

Punch.

Life was easier when I didn't care. When I didn't feel at all. When the only person's survival I had to worry about was my own. While I wasn't alive for those six long years, it was easier to struggle alone.

My sole priority was ensuring my next breath. Existing in a

constant state of fight-or-flight for so long will do that to you. All I cared about was surviving another day.

After all, I had no option for flight; all I could do to guarantee my survival was comply. In all the violence, constant fighting, injuries, training, punishments and scars… I learned to prioritise the small things.

A successful breath. My next meal. Keeping stitches dry and wounds clean. Helping Gael's other captives whenever possible. I could somewhat control those things.

But now… I can't control anything.

Least of all what happens to my brother.

It's already been one torturous week since Tom was taken, and a full twenty-four hours since Luis made contact to demand a full surrender in exchange for his life. I can still hear his smug words.

When you're ready to accept my terms, call this number. No tricks, no games. Leave Sabre Security out of this, and your brother will live.

Frankly, I was ready to hand myself over.

"Fuck Warner and his stupid fucking investigation," I hiss angrily. "Fuck Hyland. Fuck Axel. Fuck the directors. Fuck Doctor Richards. Fuck Blaine. Fuck them all!"

Every single one of them is responsible for my current predicament. Because they demanded my trust. My patience. The promise that I wouldn't do anything reckless before we locate Tom.

Delivering each blow in fast succession, thoughts of what horrors my brother could be suffering through taunt me. I know how sharp those whips bite. The way skin shreds and weeps with blood. How every strike chips away at your hope and faith.

Dark memories hit hard and fast like rapid gunfire, each bullet slashing deep into my traumatised brain tissue and disturbing ghosts I've tried to keep buried. Only now, the image of Tom locked in a cage haunts me instead of my own wails.

"Fuck!" I growl out.

Punch. Kick.

"Goddamn Luis!"

Kick. Kick. Punch.

"I'll kill you for this!"

Punch. Kick. Punch.

No matter how many times I assault the swinging bag until my knuckles split and muscles screech in warning, the fear refuses to shift. Jagged, ice-cold tendrils have already made their home, curled around my skeleton.

They asked me to trust them, but at what cost?

I'm failing again.

First Gracie. I failed her. I couldn't keep her safe. I abandoned her, despite what anyone says otherwise. And I've failed to find her in the months that I've been free from Gael. According to Luis, she's already dead.

Now… Tom.

Do I have to lose him too?

All my life, it feels like I've danced a non-consensual tango with death. First, it was our mother—the death that I don't allow myself to dwell on. But it made me who I am. At least until I was taken. Then death became a daily occurrence, and I forged myself in those icy fires.

One more day.

That's all I'm giving them. One day then I'll go. I don't care if I have to cut them all down to escape this damn building and make contact with Luis. I'll surrender. I'll be the bait. I'll do anything.

I won't lose anyone else.

At the feeling of warmth trickling from my knuckles down my jelly-like arms, I let my knees collapse. Crumpling on the hard floor of the training room, bone-deep pain and exhaustion set in fast.

I've been beating the shit out of the punching bag for almost three hours, pushing past every last physical and mental limitation I encounter. Never once acknowledging the warning signs of an attack blaring like a red flag to a bull.

Knees folding to curl up into my chest, I hug my trembling legs tight, waiting for the dizziness to subside. Despite taking my new medication, I can feel a blackout hovering on the precipice. All the signs are there.

Disgusted with myself, I unlace my arms then attempt to wrestle myself upright. The room tips and sways, eaten by spilled ink blots. Blinking rapidly does little to alleviate the intense vertigo.

I'm forced to press my forehead into the floor to halt the freefall.

My vision dips in and out as a swarm of vicious hornets drown out my hearing, filling my skull with static. The whole world is spinning out of control.

HELP.

Four letters. One word. It should be easy to ask for it. Yet if I could open my lungs long enough to scream the word, I doubt I'd have the courage to. Not when my suffering is justified. If Tom is in pain, then I should be too.

I was selfish to let Blaine free me. I was selfish to let Tom take me in. I was selfish for ever thinking that Gael would let me escape without a fight. And now I'm being selfish by denying Luis's demands and trusting the team.

The harder I fight to stand, the more my body sags. Battling scenarios worsen my steadily splitting skull, the fatigue and nausea worsening to an extreme peak. Tom dead. Tom alive. Tom imprisoned. Tom tortured. Each scene adds to my spiralling meltdown.

I'm pathetic. I can't even help myself, let alone him. How can I ever expect to save Tom's life and make Gael pay when I can't scrape myself off the fucking floor?

What feels like an agonising eternity later, doors slam open, and footsteps stomp into the large training room. The thunderclaps rouse me from a semi-conscious daze, forcing air back into my chest.

"Ember? You in here?"

The steps circle around then suddenly halt.

"Shit. Ember!"

My hand lifts to wave weakly. "I'm f-fine."

"Bloody hell."

Thick rubber soles squeak against the training room's wipe-clean floor.

"How long have you been like this?"

"I... d-don't know."

"Fuck, red."

Hyland's gravelly baritone betrays his concern. But if I didn't recognise his deep voice, then his huge legs, ever-present army boots, black cargos and bulging calf muscles would be a dead giveaway.

A calloused hand wraps around the back of my neck beneath my sweat-soaked braid, squeezing lightly. His touch is electric for all the wrong reasons, causing my skin to tighten and prickle with forbidden desire.

"Are you with me?"

"I'm not sure," I pant out.

A low huff spells out his frustration. *Well, same.* We're all frustrated.

"Deep breaths." Hyland gently massages me. "And tell me what happened."

"Dizzy… working out."

"Let me guess. You pushed yourself too hard again."

My lungs rapidly fill and empty with each heaved breath. "No."

"Sounds like bullshit to me."

"F-Fuck off." I drink in another breath.

"Otherwise you wouldn't be nearly unconscious on the floor."

"Maybe it l-looked comfortable!"

"Sure," he drawls disbelievingly.

It's not the first lecture he's given me. He was quick to shut down any plans I had to surrender. That particular argument rumbled on for several hours. Despite being the definition of protective, Hyland is a hot and cold grump with a huge chip on his shoulder.

When his hand moves from my neck to trace down my back, a shiver sweeps over my still-shaking frame. I feel Hyland move to cup both my hips as he guides me upright then backwards into his wide chest.

My spine presses against each firm, carved inch of his massive torso. He's a solid presence in every sense. Huge and intimidating but obsessively protective in all his fury.

Beneath his gruff façade and huge limbs, Hyland also harbours a gentle heart. One forged from heartbreak. He loves unbelievably hard but only shows it to those he deems worthy of his time.

"Easy," he murmurs. "Let me help. You're bleeding."

Vision swimming, I force my voice box to work. "I am?"

"Busted your knuckles. Dammit, Ember."

"Oh… Yes." I wince in realisation. "Got lost in my head. I'm alright."

"Beating a bag bloody is far from alright."

"You told me to be patient. This is how I'm doing it."

"By hurting yourself?" Judgement pours from him.

"It doesn't hurt," I try to justify. "And I don't need your help."

"Are we still having this argument?"

Letting myself slump into him, I secretly enjoy the fresh scent of a salty sea breeze that slips over me. My body works against me by relaxing into the sense of solidity his immense size provides.

Seeming to read my silent defeat, Hyland spreads his trunk-like legs on either side of me to plant his butt on the floor. Rock-hard steel cinches around me as his arms encircle my frame, holding my back to his chest.

"Fine. Just for a minute."

"Just a minute," he repeats softly. "I've got you."

Still overwhelmed by sickening vertigo, the sense of grounding that his weight provides tethers me to reality. I grab hold of the feeling, needing to find a safe landing spot before I pass out or throw up.

"Why weren't you wearing wraps?" His accusation flies like tossed acid.

"I don't know."

"Christ. What were you thinking?"

"It was just a dumb mistake."

"You can't afford to be so careless," he lectures with impassioned authority. "Not now, not ever."

Ignoring his scolding, I focus on his body heat pouring into me.

"You feel good." The traitorous admission escapes before I can swallow it.

"Me?" Hyland whispers.

"Mmm."

"Just take some breaths for me, red." Feeling his torso expand with a breath, he seems to amend his stern tone. "We need to get your heart rate down. I'll take you to the hospital if I have to."

"I'm—"

"Don't even say it," he cuts me off. "You are so incredibly *not* fine right now. Hell, none of us are."

"You're right."

"Well that's a first." Hyland snorts.

"Don't get used to it."

Head rotating, my cheek presses against the over-washed softness of his standard-issue, black t-shirt, allowing me to look up at him. His mouthwatering scent intensifies, like his wild essence is baked into the fabric.

My limbs have turned into exhausted spaghetti, but I don't want to admit that he's right. I couldn't tear myself free from his arms even if I tried. My body has turned against me.

We cling to each other for several minutes. Hyland doesn't force me to talk, holding the comfortable silence until I feel my equilibrium returning. But when he inhales, I know I'm in for a lecture.

"If you let anyone be there for you, Em, you could have this whenever you need it. We want to support you."

"Leave it," I mumble back.

"We need to talk about your behaviour."

"Hard pass."

"We're going for tough love, then?" Angry fireflies swarm his green stare. "Hiding out down here and beating a punching bag for hours on end until you collapse isn't helping anyone."

Indignation solidifies into a silver bullet, ripping through my veins. "It's helping me!"

"Helping you to do what? Avoid reality?"

"Maybe! Yes!"

Hyland pushes out a sigh, his rigid muscles moving against my frame. Softening. Embracing. Pulling me deeper into a false sense of a security that I really cannot afford.

That doesn't stop my broken body from craving it, though. Fuck, I want him. I want the comfort he relentlessly provides. Even when he's pissed, he will crack his big heart open to offer himself up. If things weren't so complicated, I'd leap at the chance to take the relief.

"I know it can't be easy to wait for results," he continues. "Lord knows, I've done it enough times on cases. But Tom is safe as long as the bounty remains on your head."

"You can't know that."

"Luis won't risk hurting him and losing his leverage against you. We have time to find a way around his ridiculous demands."

"For how long?"

Hyland winces. "I can't answer that."

"Then it doesn't make me feel better. You've asked me to trust you yet given me no time frame for when this will end. All while I could bring him home right now."

"By sacrificing yourself?" he lashes out. "Going back to Gael? To the fighting pits? Is that what you want?"

"Of course not!"

"Then trust us. Trust our team. We will find Tom."

"I'm trying!" Exasperation bleeds into my voice. "You're asking for too much."

"Is that why you're barely eating? Not sleeping? If Axel didn't make you take your meds, you wouldn't even bother. At this rate, you're going to be dead before we can bring Tom home."

His parting shot lands with the destructive impact of a megaton bomb. I feel myself recoil, dropping Hyland's gaze as tears expose my lack of control, blurring my vision.

"Oh, Em," he hushes. "Don't cry."

"Just let me go."

Pulling against his embrace, I wriggle to escape.

"No." His arms tighten. "You have to listen to me. Tom needs you alive and well."

"Tom isn't here."

My voice cracks from the weight of too much grief to name. Grinding my molars together is the only thing holding an anguished scream inside as the dam on my emotions threatens to break.

"We're going to find him," Hyland insists. "But we can't do that if we're too worried about you running off to give Luis and Gael what they want."

"You asked me to trust you. I'm doing it."

"You're free-falling," he claps back.

"I'm not!"

"What else would you call this?"

"Surviving." Exasperation gives me the courage to recapture his eyes. "The only way I know how."

"That was before." His brawny arms tighten around me. "You're not alone now."

Pulling away from him, I mash my lips shut to hold my enraged tirade inside. As much as I want to rant and rave at him… I can't. He's right. I'm falling apart at the seams, and I damn well know it.

All I can do is fight.

Fight and fucking survive.

"Ember—"

"No. I'm done talking."

"Em, please."

"Let me go! We're done."

Forcing my still-quaking limbs to steady, I pull free from him to stiffly draw to my feet. Soreness is setting in now that I've stopped to rest, sapping any remaining energy still fizzing through me.

I hear Hyland stand up with a low grunt, and when his hand clamps down on my shoulder, I know I won't get away easily. He encourages me to turn and look up at him.

"This isn't over. When your body decides it's had enough and turns against you, we'll be having a whole other conversation."

"Fantastic." I roll my eyes. "Can't wait."

"You're a sarcastic bitch, you know that?"

With a small smile pulling at my lips, I place my hand on top of his and squeeze. "I know."

His nostrils whistle with a long sigh. "Naturally, you're proud of that fact."

"Hard not to be." My knuckles twinge in pain as I lower my hand. "Why are you even down here?"

"I came to get you. Doctor Richards is waiting for your session, although I'm inclined to think I should take you home to get cleaned up and sleep."

"I just need a sec, then I'll be good."

"There isn't much about this situation that's good." Hyland's headshake disturbs his long, dirty-blonde locks. "I should be used to it by now. This is a dangerous job."

My gut twists and wrings, filling with anxiety. It takes great effort to get my tongue to form words.

"Dangerous for you, right? When it impacts your loved ones… Well, that's different."

Scanning my face, he tentatively nods.

"You're right. It is different."

"Then you should understand exactly how I'm feeling," I point out in a gentler tone. "I don't care about me right now. All I want is my brother back. Nothing else matters."

"You're wrong. You matter."

Staring up into the rugged planes of his face—soft olive-green eyes, plump lips and a strong, flat nose—I can feel my own pain looking back at me. Hyland knows better than most the crippling force of unadulterated guilt.

Hiding how twisted up all my chaotic emotions are feels like a futile endeavour. I know he can see straight through any mask I'd attempt to slide on. And honestly, I have nothing left in me to even bother.

Instead, I let it all out. Every last ugly, wretched emotion snarled up inside my nervous system, taunting me to the point of insanity. I let it all paint across my face in what is surely a vivid kaleidoscope of regret.

When his big, scarred hand reaches out to lightly brush along my jaw, heat burns behind my eyelids. Moisture swells up again before I can demand its retreat, pooling against my lower lashes.

"I understand better than anyone." Sincerity shines through his stare. "But that doesn't mean I'm going to sit back and let you kill yourself just to save him."

I hold my breath when the pad of his thumb swipes a stray tear from my skin. The vulnerability is excruciating. He can see it all. Every last conflicting urge taking me for a ride.

"Red," he rumbles deeply.

"Don't."

"It's okay to let it out. You can lean on us. Let us help you cope."

Tongue darting out, I lick my lips, but the brief pause fails to conjure a response. There are no words. None that will get him off my back. He's already peered inside my head.

Brushing aside another tear, his rough thumb moves to my bottom lip, smearing the moisture I swiped over it. I gasp when he pushes inside my mouth then withdraws.

"I need you to hear me, Ember." His authoritative tone brooks no arguments. "We're in this together. Trust us. Let us in."

"I'm trying," I whisper weakly.

"I need you to try harder."

"Why can't you just leave me alone?"

Nostrils flaring, his whole frame tenses up. "Because I care too much about you."

Caught in a vortex, I'm drawn into the mossy pools that threaten to drag me beneath their all-consuming surface. The windows to his soul are a deep cavern I'll never escape from. Not alive, at least.

Hyland doesn't just see me.

He *eviscerates* me.

Bulldozes every last defence and pointless boundary I've ever put in place to hold the world at arm's length. His need to protect doesn't obey the confines of social niceties. Nor does it respect my drive for independence.

"I care about you too," I admit thickly.

A dark twinkle flashes in his eyes, filling them with a look of determination. Fingers tightening on my face, he leans in to brush his nose against mine, our lips a single, fateful breath apart.

"You do?" he teases.

"Yes, asshole."

The hand clamping my shoulder slides lower, tracing down my arm then sneaking around my waist. I'm pulled flush against his chest, forcing my chin to tilt upward so I can see him.

Without the need for more words, Hyland's mouth meets mine. It's a gentle peck at first. Affirming. Tentative. Exploratory. Testing the waters to see if I'll punch him in the head or not.

With the pressure of his lips on mine, his declaration takes on a new dimension. This isn't the man who I taunted while we trained. Back then, he kissed me like he wanted me to feel his self-control shattering.

Now his kiss feels more like a whispered acceptance. It's the final plea of his broken resolve, begging me to carry his heart carefully because it can't handle any more loss.

Sinking into his tight embrace, I fist his t-shirt and let instinct take over. For all his lectures, I melt at the slightest brush of Hyland's lips, firm and attentive in their delivery.

His hot mouth moves on mine, lips pecking faster and faster until the assault escalates into a hard kiss that feels like it might crack my very lungs open just to steal my breath.

With every part of me screaming out for what I know I shouldn't be allowed, I kiss him back. Tongue darting out. Lips parting. Teeth clashing. Passion rolls over me in one long, intense convulsion, far stronger than any seizure.

Grasping my hip, Hyland's rough palm slides down to the back of my thigh. He lifts my leg to hook it up on his waist, sending pulses of heat down south where I can feel his muscles against my core.

The low, feral groan that pours from his throat mirrors my own hunger. My arms coil around his neck, lifting me higher so I can rock myself against his bulk, needing some relief from the building pressure.

His tongue wrestles with mine, searching out every hidden corner or part of me he's yet to claim. It's all-consuming. Overwhelming. Everywhere, Hyland stamps his touch and taste onto my mouth with utmost finality.

When we finally split apart on a mutual intake of breath, his neck cranes to rest our foreheads together for several serene seconds. All I can hear is my roaring heartbeat hammering in my ears.

"Ember?" He sounds reluctant.

"What now?"

"I think you should step back from the investigation."

Shocked, I flinch away from him. "Wait, what?"

Hyland wears a pleading mask that does little to alleviate the sting of his words.

"You need to stop. Go home and rest."

Blinking doesn't reveal a new sight. He's still staring at me with rounded eyes, making the most insane request I've ever heard. All after kissing the living daylights from my soul.

"What the fuck is wrong with you?" I blurt out.

"You're driving yourself into an early grave right now. It has to stop."

"I'm part of this team! I need to be here."

"You need to take care of yourself," Hyland refutes. "Let us do our jobs."

"It's my job too."

"It doesn't have to be. You need to slow down and take care of your health."

Even though my lips still tingle with the remains of our kiss, I wrench myself from his arms like I've been burned. Frankly, tossing a vat of acid in my face would hurt less.

"Tom is my brother," I say hotly. "I have every right to be here. You can't freeze me out."

"That isn't what I'm doing."

"You're trying to control me!"

"I want to help you."

"You have a funny way of showing it."

"Ember…"

Hyland reaches for me again, but I've already inched farther away. The sweat that's dried on my skin now feels like a tight, restrictive straitjacket, worsened by the falsehoods his tongue dares to offer.

"No one will ever control me again." I meet his eyes without a hint of fear. "Do you understand me?"

"Protecting you and controlling you are two different things!"

"Maybe to you. To me? I see another man attempting to dictate my life to me."

"You know I'd never do that. Especially not after what you've been through."

"Do I?" I snap back. "Listen to yourself. Listen to what you're asking from me, then and tell me it doesn't sound like you're making decisions for me."

He bounces from foot to foot, visibly itching to close the distance I've forced between us. "Let's back up. That isn't what I'm doing."

"You're calling me unstable! Tell me, have you said the same thing to Warner?"

Stumped, Hyland can't find the words to argue.

"Right. I didn't think so."

Turning my back on his darkening expression, I snatch my discarded water bottle and towel in my rapidly swelling hands, intent on getting the hell away from him.

My sore legs carry me towards the exit at speed, needing as much space between us as possible. I don't look back until I've reached the swinging double doors, finding him unmoved across the room.

"You are either on my side, by my side… or in my fucking way."

His eyebrows shoot up into jagged spikes, though his mouth still doesn't move.

"So choose wisely."

play
me
DO NOT CROSS
suspect?
NOT CROSS
POLICE L

2

EMBER

COLD – CHRIS STAPLETON

*O*ne day.
One more fucking day.
My inner mantra grows louder as I wave at Archer, frowning from behind the steering wheel. The leader of the Falcon Team soon drives off in his company SUV. Spending the commute home in his company was far more appealing than crawling back to Hyland to catch a ride.

Undoubtedly, I'm in for an ass kicking when my other teammates hear that I skipped my regular appointment with the flower-obsessed Doctor Richards. Seriously, that dude needs to go shopping for new shirts or find a semi-sane stylist.

With a sigh, I head up to the apartment.
One day, then I'm doing things my way.
When I signed up to join the Anaconda Team, I thought I was

getting a shot at justice. Perhaps even a way to put all the shit I've witnessed and endured to good use. I didn't sign up for a group of overbearing alpha-holes to control my life. Least of all Hyland.

"Possessive asshole," I mutter angrily.

Great. Talking to myself now too.

Freedom is going really well for me, clearly.

Our team's penthouse apartment is on the top floor of a multimillion-pound skyscraper in the illustrious Canary Wharf, deep in London's glittering financial district. It's luxurious, though I'd be lying if I said this place felt like home.

The plush carpet absorbs my furious footsteps when I escape the elevator on the top floor to head for the penthouse. Even the hallway is dripping in opulent luxury, lit by huge chandeliers and thick, tinted windows.

Warner has a vast array of security measures set up, from fingerprint recognition built into the apartment's defences to paid agents guarding the building itself. Even before Tom was kidnapped, he's always taken safety seriously.

I suppose I can't blame him for that. As team leader, it falls on his shoulders to ensure everyone's protected. That's why it cut so deep, that Luis was able to get into Tom's apartment at all. He had security measures in place, but that didn't stop him from being targeted.

Before I can scan my prints and toss the front door open with an excuse ready to roll off my tongue, the alarm disengages. Front door crashing open, a blur of purple-dyed, overactive energy escapes.

"Dimples! You're home!"

"Jesus, Ax."

Gangly limbs ensconced in ripped jeans and an oversized slogan tee almost knock me over. The impact causes me to huff as Axel envelopes me in a rib-grinding hug.

"You've been gone for seven hours!" he whines, words stretched with exaggeration. "And you didn't reply to my text messages either."

"Been… busy," I choke out.

Despite being my height, Axel is a hellhound packing the power of a violent, cocaine-fuelled army in his numerous stacked muscles. No one could ever accuse him of being downbeat or lacking enthusiasm.

In fact, he's a self-confessed whirlwind of playful energy who always craves attention. Whether he's cracking wise or cracking skulls, Axel never fails to make an impact on the world. The degree of violence that impact entails depends on his mood.

"What kept you so busy that you couldn't even reply to my messages?"

"I was working," I wheeze through constricted breaths. "Dude, let me go."

"No! You'll run off again."

"Ax—"

"Ugh. Fine."

Surrendering me, Axel plants a sloppy kiss on my cheek then takes a step back. I glance over his soft baby face, bee-stung lips and vivid-honey eyes, standing in stark contrast to the visible tattoos that reach his throat and beyond.

With his solid build being covered in more ink than skin, his amethyst faux hawk and perpetual grin create a confusing parallel. He vibrates with infectious energy, managing to look both threatening and adorable at the same time.

"I was stuck here with the convict all day, combing through CCTV feeds," he grumbles sulkily. "Alone! With that insane twat!"

"Blaine isn't that bad."

"He's lucky I haven't tossed his severed limbs off the roof yet. I'm not some psycho-sitting nanny, you know?"

"Did you find anything on the feeds?"

"Couldn't even get a couple hours of rest because I can't sleep in the same apartment as that freak show. He'll gut me the first chance he gets."

"Axel," I groan impatiently. "Focus. The CCTV feeds."

"Still nothing in Tom's building." He audibly sighs. "The footage is completely corrupted. Whoever's running Luis's tech, they're good. In and out without a single second of video evidence."

"Shit!"

"The intelligence team is working on the building opposite his to see if they can ID anyone leaving. They'll have an update for us by morning."

"We can't wait that long!"

Huffing, I stomp inside the penthouse, ditching my backpack by the entrance. After a week spent cataloguing every last bit of forensic evidence we could unearth in Tom's apartment, scouring public camera feeds and running facial recognition, we still have nothing.

Luis and his crew are skilled enough to crack a top-end security system and vanish without a trace. I have no doubt that Gael has the financial arsenal to hire the best in the business, but even if he's got a master techie working for him, this is impressive work.

"Where are the others?" Axel clicks the door shut, re-engaging the alarm with a quiet beep.

"Not a clue."

He's silent for a moment.

"You know, Hyland called me."

Whirling on Axel, I'm ready to strangle him with his insane t-shirt—the messy scrawl spelling out *Me? Sarcastic? Never!*—when he spreads his tattooed hands in surrender.

"You want to kick me off the team too?" I shout at him.

"Hey, hey. Ease up there, hot stuff. I'm not taking sides. He just told me to make sure you take your meds and rest until they're back."

"Oh, great," I reply sardonically. "I would've forgotten otherwise. How ever would I live without his wonderful interference in my life?"

Snorting, Axel folds his arms. "I told him to fuck off on your behalf."

"Thanks."

"I know what the giant oaf is like."

Toeing off my shoes, I kick them aside. "Batshit crazy?"

His full lips hook up in a grin. "That's putting it politely."

"Trust me, I have far worse I could say about him."

"I'm sure. So can I get a hug now? I've been starved of love for hours."

When his steely arms spread in invitation, I can't help but step into Axel's orbit. Enticing spice and masculine musk welcome me as he holds me against his chest.

"You've been fighting." He nestles his chin on my shoulder. "Talk to me."

"It's just… sitting in that office, hopelessly trawling through traffic cams and local canvassing reports, waiting for someone to have a breakthrough… it got too much. I needed to punch something."

"Then you should've called me."

"And say what? You'd talk me out of calling Luis and taking his dumb deal too."

Axel sucks in a breath, inhaling my scent. "Obviously I would have. Surrender is plain stupid. But we could've sparred together until that crazy brain of yours knocked itself out."

"According to Hyland, I should be lounging around the apartment having some kind of bloody siesta. Not sparring or helping with the investigation."

His purple-dyed head tilting, I feel Axel's mouth nuzzling into the side of my neck. Hot and cold prickles seep over me, entangling with my spine and electrifying each nodule.

"Hyland is complicated," he hedges.

"It's rather simple. He's an overbearing prick."

Axel's chuckle tickles my skin. "I'm not disagreeing with you."

"Then explain to me what he's thinking with this crap about freezing me out of the case."

"Um… he may have mentioned suggesting that before you left. I told him it's a bad idea."

"He's seriously out of order!"

"Not disagreeing, but he's shit scared too." Axel sighs loudly. "My guess? He's grasping at what he can control right now. That includes your proximity to this mess."

"*This mess* is my life, Ax." I force down the lump lodged in my throat. "I can't just walk away from it."

"I know, dimples. I'm sorry."

My anger drains away at the soothing croon of his voice, penetrating the fog I stormed home in.

"It's not your job to apologise for Hyland's shit."

"We're a team, right?" Axel vibrates with a snort. "That makes us a real life, fucked up family. It's my responsibility to manage Hyland's shit as much as it is yours."

"Then I want a divorce. I did not sign up for this crap."

We both laugh, wrapped up in each other's arms. For a moment, I can almost forget the looming deadline in my mind, counting down each second until I pull the plug on their little dictatorship.

"Suck it up, buttercup," he chortles. "Family is for life."

"Crap. I didn't think this deal through."

"No backsies. You're one of us now."

Kissing my braided head, Axel releases my body so he can hit me with a blazing smile. Fuck me gently, he has the most beautiful grin. Wolfish and sexy in all the best ways.

Before I can drag him back and seek out his sweet lips for myself, there's a low, whistling sound. The surrounding air displaces as something slices through the gap that's formed between us.

Barking a colourful expletive, I'm shoved backwards when Axel whirls on the spot to stare at where a small, black switchblade has embedded in the wall behind us.

"Motherfucker!"

"You're welcome," a voice drawls.

The crisp aristocratic accent reveals Blaine before I swivel to pin him with a stunned look. He casually lounges against the nearby, built-in bookcase, his slender arms and ankles crossed.

"What the hell?" I scowl at him.

"Just saving you from enduring the pup mauling you. Doing my civic duty and all."

"You're a fucking lunatic!" Axel explodes as he marches towards the stuck knife. "You could've killed me! Or Ember!"

"You think my aim is that bad?" Blaine frowns at him. "I'm offended."

"You threw a goddamn knife at us!"

"And it landed exactly where I intended it to."

"Jesus. You need your head examined, Madden."

"Don't manhandle Ember, and I won't be forced to defend her honour. Simple."

"I was not manhandling her!" Axel yanks the knife free. "Besides, who touches Ember is absolutely none of your business."

"I beg to differ."

"Meaning?" Axel's tone has reached a sub-zero deep freeze.

"Now that, dear pup, is absolutely none of *your* business."

Rolling his lip piercing as he unveils an amused smirk, Blaine scours over me, disregarding Axel's rapidly building rage. He really doesn't appreciate that particular nickname catching on so quickly.

Intense onyx eyes sear beneath a mop of untidy, raven locks, left long on top and shaved on the sides. With an old scar warping the right side of his face from his eyebrow over his exaggerated cheekbone and down to his strong jawline, Blaine's bad boy persona screams danger.

His all-black jeans, dark t-shirt and signature leather jacket only add to the image, encasing his slim but strong limbs in armour. Even if he lacks Hyland's bulk, his two long, powerful rowing oars give him height that adds to his scarily magnetic presence.

"Hello, Ember." He slowly lavishes my name like it's his favourite concoction of syllables. "You look… tired."

"No shit." I glare at him. "Having fun?"

"Living the dream."

"So I hear."

"You're back early. Trouble in paradise?"

His smirk doesn't budge, not even at my exaggerated eye roll. The scheming bastard loves to worm his way under my skin. Like his presence in our lives isn't already confusing enough.

When Sabre offered him a plea deal in exchange for his assistance, a part of me was secretly thrilled by the idea of having him close. Blaine's dark aura, his raw intelligence and silent schemes… it all exudes influence and power. We need his brand of evil right now.

It doesn't hurt that he's delicious to look at either.

A fact my ovaries have most definitely noted.

"Something like that," I dismiss quickly. "Why have you been driving Axel mad?"

Blaine flicks invisible lint off his shirt. "He's the mad one. I've been perfectly polite."

"Because throwing a knife at me is perfectly polite!" Axel

blusters.

"It's not buried in your gut, is it?" Blaine responds. "There you go. Polite."

"God, I cannot wait to demolish you with a machine gun then piss on your corpse."

"I would enjoy seeing you try. It's been a while since I practiced my skinning skills."

"Come near me with a knife again, and you won't have hands to practice anything with."

"Guys." I grapple to find some patience. "Enough."

Neither pays any attention to me. They're far too busy tossing verbal barbs in lieu of actually pulling their dicks out to measure them side by side. Fantastic. This is really productive for effective teamwork.

Escaping their pissing contest, I head straight for the kitchen to locate a cold beer from the fridge. I don't know when Warner or Hyland will make an appearance, but before they do, I need a drink.

By the time I've popped the cap with my teeth and thrown back half of the bottle, Axel and Blaine have followed me into the kitchen. Considering there are five people currently living here, the marble surfaces and array of high-end appliances are pretty spotless.

Blaine lounges on a stool at the breakfast bar, his switchblade retrieved from Axel now spinning between his fingers. Ignoring him, Axel opens the cabinet where my medication is organised and begins to dole out my evening pills.

"I can do it," I feebly protest.

"You're cute and all, dimples, but you look like a strong breeze would knock you over right about now."

He plasters on a cheerful smile while pushing the bright-coloured handful across the marble countertop towards me. Glowering at him, I ignore the way my knuckles twinge, still coated in dried blood.

"I do not."

Axel shrugs. "Just an observation."

"Then observe silently in the future."

"Is that an order or a threat?"

"Can't it be both?" I quip back.

"Well, I'd prefer a threat. That would be far hotter."

"Then it's a fucking order."

From the breakfast bar, Blaine chokes on a laugh. I ignore him and watch Axel's brows raise along with his quickly growing grin.

"That's my ball-buster."

When I move to toss the pills into my mouth, his smile falters.

"Um, probably not advisable to take those with a beer. I need to look at your injuries too. Hyland told me that he found you nearly passed out."

"That little rat," I mutter under my breath.

"Yep. He's a real snake."

Glancing at where I'm clenching the beer bottle, the damage from assaulting the boxing bag without wraps is apparent. My hands are puffy, the skin enflamed and littered with shallow lacerations.

In the moment, I felt nothing. The pain was inconsequential. It didn't matter that I blasted past every last physical limit I have, particularly since the epilepsy diagnosis. All I wanted was to get my rage out.

Setting the beer aside, I nod in defeat. Axel quickly fills a water glass then slides it over for me. The pressure of Blaine watching us both burns into my skin as I focus on swallowing my pills.

"When is your next follow-up?" Blaine asks.

"Tomorrow," I reply.

"Are the pills working?"

Axel flashes him a dark look. "Stay out of this."

"I'm not allowed to ask?"

"You're not allowed to pretend like you care or you're part of this team."

Blaine narrows his eyes on my golden psycho. "I do care."

"You're not capable of it."

"Because you are?" he combats.

"For her? Fuck yes. Ember is our family. Don't ever question what I'd do for her."

"Right," Blaine drawls. "And we all know *family* is so precious to you."

I watch Axel immediately stiffen.

"Shut it, Madden."

"After all, Sabre is all you have left now."

"Final fucking warning."

"Or what?" Blaine waggles his eyebrows.

"You do not want to find out," Axel cautions threateningly.

"I think I do."

Something festers between them—a palpable tension that raises my hackles. Studying Axel's body language, he appears to shake himself when he notices my stare, trying to relax as he looks away from Blaine.

"Bathroom." Axel points in that direction. "Let's clean those hands up."

"What's going on?" I ditch the empty water glass.

"Go on," Blaine goads, still lounging like he's on holiday. "Tell her what's crawled up your ass. I'd be happy to corroborate."

Face flushing with a red tinge, Axel ignores the shit-stirring ex-con. "It's nothing, Em."

"Sure doesn't sound like nothing."

"Well, it is. Come on, let's get you cleaned up."

Axel steers me from the kitchen without another glance in Blaine's direction. This only seems to amuse him more, Blaine winking at me as we pass him. I merely glare back.

"Maybe him working with us wasn't such a good idea."

"You think?" Axel scoffs. "That psycho's got a brain full of monkeys. Trust me, it takes one to know one. At least I'm semi-sane."

Honestly, the pair are probably far more alike than they'd ever admit. No one is happy with Blaine's presence here, but for whatever reason, Axel seems to have taken particular issue with him.

Leading me towards his bedroom, I'm offered a glimpse of Axel's private space. Unlike Hyland's blue-toned cave of dark wood and bookshelves, Axel's room is bright and lurid—just like him.

The charcoal-painted walls are plastered in movie posters, art prints, humorous postcards and more. It's a full mosaic of uncontrolled chaos that hits me with sensory overload. Every inch is covered in his madness.

The generous double bed is covered in tie-dyed blue and green sheets with a huge, fluffy blanket messily piled at the foot. While not as basic as Hyland's space nor as structured as the glimpse I've seen of Warner's militarily organised bedroom, it isn't untidy.

At the sight of a gnarly, half-destroyed blue rabbit between Axel's two pillows, I choke on a breath. It's like he tried to hide the ancient teddy but quickly gave up and nestled it on a throne of pillows.

"Oh my God."

"What?" Axel's steps falter.

"You sleep with an old rabbit?"

An adorable red flush creeps over his inked neck. "Uh, no."

"Then what's that?" I point towards the ragged stuffy.

"Ah, that's just… it's… a… um, mistake."

Hearing Axel splutter only intensifies my amusement.

"You totally do! You have a comfort bear."

"Bathroom, Ember!" he snaps, clearly flustered. "Move it."

Still snickering, I let him tug me into the en-suite. It's similar to mine—decently sized with a walk-in shower, full of sparkling off-white tiles, decadent brass accessories and scattered toiletries.

Positioning me in front of the sink basin, Axel runs the water then holds his hand underneath to test the temperature. Once it's warm, he opens the vanity to reveal more products stashed inside.

"Ah," he hums. "Gotcha."

I study the tube of antiseptic cream he pulls free. "Isn't Warner the resident first aider around here? You know, ex-field medic and all."

"If I went to Warner every time I needed patching up, he'd be sick of the sight of me. More than he already is."

Ointment placed aside, Axel beckons for my left hand first. I let him take it and run my knuckles beneath the warm water, each droplet aggravating the cuts and abrasions revealed beneath the blood.

Much like Hyland's paws, my hands are already thick with scar tissue. Six years of constant fighting and training will do that to you. This isn't the first time I've busted my own knuckles by pushing too hard.

"I can't do this," I blurt without thinking. "Wait for Tom to be found. I just can't hold on."

"You're gonna have to, Em. No one is letting you hand yourself over."

"I survived once. I'll do it again."

"Yeah, fuck that. Not a risk any of us are willing to take."

"What if it's not your decision?"

His chuckle is utterly humourless. "At the risk of sounding like Hyland, if you try to leave and take Luis's insane deal, I'll be forced to tie your sweet backside up in my bedroom until this is over."

"Like that would stop me."

"I tie excellent knots. Go ahead and test me."

Narrowing my eyes, I pin him with a look. "I could take you."

"You're welcome to try. I'd enjoy it."

Warm water stings my skin as he cleans the small cuts, letting me stew in my thoughts. I shouldn't be surprised that he's taking the same line as the others. Jokes aside, Axel is as protective as my other teammates. It just manifests differently.

"I'm following up that warehouse lead tonight," Axel reveals, causing me to jerk. "Rayna traced the unregistered license plate from the vicinity of Tom's apartment to a local delivery company."

"You know it could be anyone. Luis is too smart to be that sloppy."

"You're right. It could be." His thumb strokes over my swollen flesh, cleaning each graze. "But Warner wants us to check it out."

At the mention of our leader's name, my insides clench tight.

"He isn't okay, Ax. I've never seen him like this."

Axel halts for a moment before rising off the remaining blood. "I know."

"This morning, he just…"

Words fail me. Seeing Mr Dependable nearly broken, frantic with terror and limping around in a state of exhausted determination, is part of the reason I fled for the training room.

Warner has hardly spoken outside of yelling orders or doling out surveillance tasks. I know that he's mentally struggling just as much as I am. Tom's not just his childhood best friend. He's his brother too.

I have no idea how to help him. Fuck, I can't even take care of myself. I feel like I'm burning up, and I know Warner's following right behind me. Add in our complicated dynamic since the stolen kisses we shared, and the situation is a ticking time bomb, primed to explode.

"He can rest while we investigate those plates and the intelligence team works on getting us more video footage." Axel turns my hand, assessing his work.

"You know he won't, though."

"I'll hide his prosthetic if I have to. He will sleep."

"Not the worst idea."

"It's not the first time I've had to do it," he admits.

Probing a particularly swollen joint on my left hand, Axel glances up to measure my reaction. I wince, briefly meeting his honeyed jewels.

"Next time, wear wraps when you have a semi-suicidal boxing frenzy."

My lips roll inwards to suppress a smile. "Yes, Nurse Slaughter."

"Or at least call me so I can watch the show. You know I love seeing you in action. It's sexy as fuck."

"It wasn't a pretty sight, Ax."

"Now that I don't believe." Swapping to my other hand, he begins the same gentle process. "You're hot when you're mad. Feel free to use my face instead of a boxing bag next time."

Shaking my head, I flush cold when I hurtle back to the bottomless pit of pure rage I found myself lost in. I don't know whose face I was imagining as I went to town—Luis's evil mug or my own.

"The world went dark for a while," I admit in a tiny, fear-laced whisper. "All I could feel was hopelessness. I wanted to scream, Ax, but no words came out. Not one."

His movements still, fingertips lingering on my hand. "Sometimes I feel like that."

"You do?"

"Sure. When you feel like you're drowning, the violence and pain become the only things keeping you afloat."

My nod feels robotic. "Exactly."

"When I lost… uh, my parents… I spent a long time bouncing from one fight to another." Axel focuses intently on his task. "All I knew was anger."

Looking up at him, I study his side profile, ink-covered neck muscles visibly jolting and tightening. It's odd to see him so serious.

"The world's a scary place when you feel completely alone in it. That's what makes rage so appealing, Em. It gives us power in those powerless moments. But that's also what makes it dangerous."

He finishes cleaning my right knuckles in silence then flicks off the running water. I wait for Axel to locate a hand towel to dab my injuries dry then watch as he picks up the antiseptic cream to begin lathering it on.

"I use that anger to my advantage now," Axel explains with drawn brows. "It fuels me to hurt the motherfuckers who threaten us and our livelihoods. They get my rage instead."

Twisting my hand, I catch his calloused fingers in mine. Axel stills, his whiskey-bright orbs catching on me.

"You're a good man, Axel Slaughter."

"I highly doubt that." He flourishes a weak smile.

"Not many kids can survive being orphaned and still come out on top."

Gaze flicking away from me, he looks down at my white-slathered knuckles. Tension ripples over him, and his mouth undulates while he considers his words.

"I guess so," he finally says.

Easing my hand back, I move to slide past him. I need to collapse into bed for a few hours. My body is sagging more with each passing minute, and a worrying headache is brewing.

"Thank you for cleaning me up."

"Yeah." His tenor is thick like molasses. "Anytime."

"I'm going to lay down for a bit."

"Sure."

Before I can leave the en-suite, my name dances from Axel's parted lips. His usually-light voice is deep and stern, so far from the playful lilt I've come to know and adore.

"You're going to get through this."

I linger on the threshold. "How can you be so sure?"

"Because I have zero intention of letting all that anger tear you up."

Feet shuffling, I glance backwards to look at him. Axel's weak smile has faded, leaving a look of certainty behind. But on him, it feels more like a threat than a promise.

"Even if it's what you want," he adds.

My injured hands sting, forming fists at my sides.

"What I want is to fight. And this time, I intend to win."

Play me

POLICE LINE – DO NOT CROSS

Asset?

Incoming Call

known

20 AM

DO NOT CROSS   POLICE LI

Suspect?

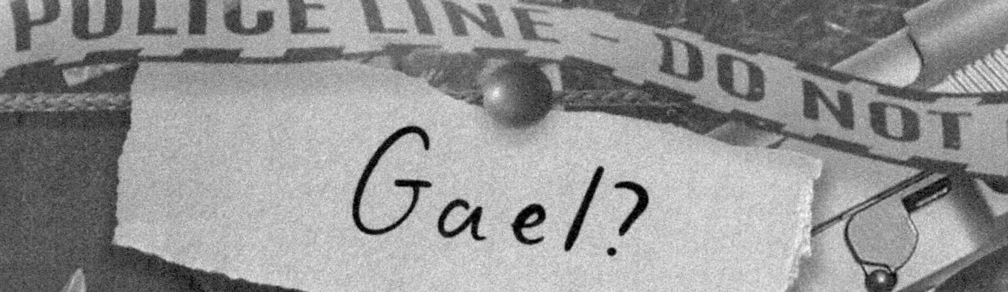

3

WARNER

FITZPLEASURE – ALT-J

The laptop screen blurs in front of me, forming drunken, wriggling lines that distort the case files I've spent all night pouring over. Perhaps searching for a breakthrough at four o'clock in the morning is a foolish quest after all.

But foolish or not, it's a lot more appealing than crawling back into that damned bed and lying there, imagining what my best friend is going through while I'm warm and comfortable.

When we got Ember back, I'd thought I'd felt this awful, gut-wrenching anxiety for the last time. I hadn't thought my terror for Ember could be matched until we got that phone call and heard Tom's agony for ourselves.

Before, the months and years without any sign of Ember allowed fear to take root in my bones. It laid down spidery vines then expanded until its poison ivy was wrapped around every last nerve cell. But I knew that no matter what happened, my girl is strong.

Hell, Ember's far stronger than any of us. She always has been, something I realised when she watched her mother being lowered into the ground and didn't even flinch while her older brother broke down. Ember refused to let him grieve alone.

I can only hope that Tom possesses a shred of her grit right now and that he'll hold onto it until I can bring him back to her. I won't watch Ember lose another family member. Not after all we've endured to get to this point. She deserves better than that.

Refocusing on the case files, I scour back over Luis's profile. We've garnered all the information we can from international law enforcement, allowing us to build a portrait of the prolific trafficker.

He's a middleman.

A cog in a bigger machine.

These people are a dime a dozen in every other country across the globe. No matter where you turn, you'll find power-hungry fools ready to sacrifice their morals to make a profit. I've arrested a thousand Luis's in my time at Sabre.

How did he get the jump on us?

I fitted Tom's place with security equipment myself, including a biometric system and a panic alarm directly keyed into Sabre's emergency line. Luis got past it all, manually disabling the power supply and its backup then cracking his apartment open like an egg.

The question is how.

He blew past our contingencies, snatched Tom then disappeared without being seen on a single CCTV feed. No system is truly unbreakable, but Tom's was damn near close. Not to mention London is one of the most surveilled cities on the planet.

Either Luis has someone incredibly skilled working for him now, or worse still, he had help from someone who knows our tech. Maybe even someone who has perfected the art of disappearing.

"Fuck." I rub my sore temples.

We're running out of time.

When Luis's offer arrived, I knew from the spark in Ember's eyes that she had every intention to blow us off to march in there and save her brother. It killed me to demand her patience. I know she's in pain.

Slamming my laptop shut, I massage my eyes with the heels of my palms. A couple hours of sleep have done little to alleviate my exhaustion. At least I've managed to rest my screaming residual limb for a bit.

"NOOOOO!"

At the sound of a wail penetrating the silent penthouse, I startle so hard that I almost fall from my desk chair. My hand seizes the grey medical crutch that I use to navigate without my limb as I manoeuvre myself up.

Hyland's bedroom door smashes open at the same time that I emerge. He squints in the low-lit hallway, chest bare and sweat shorts hanging low on his waist. We both look at Ember's door.

"No! Tom!"

"Shit," he curses roughly. "Another nightmare."

"I've got this. Go back to bed."

"Warner—"

"I've got it." I stalk past him. "Go."

Walking is awkward as fuck without my prosthetic, especially with the cuff of my sweatpants rolled up to mid-thigh on my right side. With great effort, I half-hop, half-shuffle to Ember's door then push inside.

"Em? I'm coming in."

The undrawn curtains allow lurid city light to spill into Ember's sparse bedroom, revealing her thrashing state snarled up in the bedsheets. My heart throbs hard behind my chest bone.

My little astronaut.

I've barely looked at her of late, let alone said a single word. Every time I think about taking her into my arms, I see her brother. I see the cost of my failure if I can't find him. And I see what it'll do to the girl I've secretly loved for two decades.

"Please, Tom," she screeches. "No. Stop!"

Self-loathing rattles through my shattering heart. This is so stupid. She needs me, not my selfish doubts. Stuffing them down, I hop over to the bed then discard my crutch so I can drop onto the edge.

"Ember?"

She twists in her sweaty sheets, every inch of her contorted face lit by distant skyscrapers. Ember's had punishing night terrors like this every time she's slept this week. Hyland and Axel keep me updated.

"Em," I whisper softly. "Wake up, love."

When she doesn't respond to my voice, I hesitantly rest a palm on her bare shoulder. She's sleeping in a thin tank top, leaving clammy, scar-striped skin on full display.

"Em, baby. I'm here. Open your eyes."

My fingertips begin to circle, caressing her shoulder, neck and whip-marked upper back. The old scars are rigid and gnarly underneath my fingers, my teeth locking tight to hold back my emotions.

Goddammit.

Feeling the physical remnants of all she suffered damn near breaks my self-control. The glimpses I've had of her body don't do justice to the feeling of pain immortalised in her scarred skin.

I could kill Gael with my pinkie finger right now.

We're dangerously close to losing her. Permanently. No matter what she says, I don't know if she would survive the horrors of the cartel again.

Each stroke seems to pierce her terror, so I continue, mentally boxing up my caveman urges. Eventually, her screams fade to gut-punching, little whimpers. Shuffling closer across the mattress, I prop myself against the headboard then ease her head onto my lap.

Her flame-red hair is hanging loose and soaked with sweat, but I couldn't care less as I weave my fingers through the lengthy strands. Sometimes, I braided her hair for her as a kid. She used to hate her mother brushing the snarled knots.

"I've got you," I murmur. "You're okay."

Even holding her like this feels like I'm tempting fate. She's featured in my nightly dreams ever since she laid herself out in the boxing ring like a Christmas present and thoroughly fucked herself just for me.

Chest tightening at the memory, my fingers still in her hair. I need to get a grip. She's shivering and quietly whimpering in my arms right now while I'm fantasising about how her pretty pink pussy greedily devoured her slick fingers, over and over again.

Yep, I'm headed straight for hell.

This is why I've stayed away.

Still stroking her hair, I whisper under my breath until her trembles subside, and the whimpers cease. At some point, my eyes fall shut too, lulling me into a calm bubble that holding her close provides.

At the feel of a soft hand sneaking beneath my t-shirt to rest flat against my stomach, my eyes fling open. Ember hasn't moved from my lap, but her fingers are now splayed over my abdominals and lightly stroking.

My breath hitches.

What is she...

Her hand dances over each defined plane, fingertip swirling in the dark hair that dips into my sweatpants. With each movement, the iron-clad grip around my lungs tightens beyond the point of pain.

Apparently, my body is a traitor because every nerve is firing adrenaline deeper into my limbs. Even with only one hand on me, I can feel her all over. Her touch. Her scent. Her beckoning warmth. Everything I love and want, even if it can never be mine.

"Em," I manage to rasp out.

She gives a low, sleepy whine.

"Are you awake?"

"Mmm. No."

Laughing quietly, I cease stroking her hair. "Don't play games."

"Why are you in my bed?" she whispers.

"You were having a nightmare."

"Oh. Right."

"Are you okay?"

"No. Not really."

Her hand doesn't stop, circling and teasing, undoubtedly feeling how her touch makes me tense. In the low light and peaceful silence, her proximity feels natural. Permissible. No one is here to witness my betrayal of Tom's friendship.

"I've missed you," she admits in a thick voice.

"I'm sorry, Em."

"Why are you avoiding me?"

"I have a job to do."

"But you can't even look at me?"

Guilt strangles my windpipe, leaving me no choice but to swallow hard. "You should go back to sleep. I have to get back to work."

"No," Ember grouses. "Please don't go."

"I need to check in with Axel."

Clearing the sleep from her voice, she peers up at me. "You need to rest too."

Hah. Rest. Like I'd ever be able to do that while Tom is still out there, lost and alone.

I attempt to ease her back onto the mattress so I can slide free now that she's calmed down, but she resists. I should've realised doing that would only poke the bear.

Ember sits up, rolls over then flings a temptingly bare leg over my waist. Within a second, she's crawled on top of my lap, a thigh splayed on either side of my body. Her long, tangled hair flips over her shoulder as she assumes a position of control, pinning me with her body weight.

"Em—"

"Problem?" Her shadowed face is lit by dim light.

"I shouldn't be in here."

"Why not?"

"You know why not," I reason calmly.

She stares at me through half-lids. "Then why did you come?"

"Because… you were crying out in your sleep. You needed me."

"Right." Her lips round to form the sound. "What if I still need you?"

"What you need is to go back to sleep."

"You first," she sasses back.

This is my fault. The moment I gave rise to those illegal thoughts streaming through my mind while she fought me, I opened the floodgates. I gave permission to release the intense pressure practically exploding between us.

It's only grown since then, her distant stare blazing with longing while I've avoided her. Even with Tom gone and the full weight of Sabre's power unleashed to search for him, I'm constantly aware of her. She's a huge distraction.

"You can't stop yourself." I sigh around my tight throat. "Can you?"

"I need this nightmare to end," she admits. "Even if only for a moment."

"It will end, Em. It'll end when we bring Tom home."

"And when will that be?"

My throat constricts. God, how I want to comfort her. I need to fix this. But I can't lie to Ember; she deserves far better than that. Until Tom is within my grasp, I won't risk breaking her trust.

"You can't answer because you don't know when it will end. We're up against an army, and my brother…" Her voice catches, filling me with heartache. "He's caught in the middle of the war."

"I know, love."

"Then for one solitary second… Please, Warner. Don't think. Just make it all stop. Make me forget. Take it all away from me."

Her heartfelt begging pulls at my internal organs and twists them into an excruciating knot. God, she is my fatal weakness. Everything about Ember invites me to get on my knees and give her whatever the hell she wants or needs to endure this mess.

"I have to go," I spit the awful words out.

"You're the one who told me to show you that I want this," Ember hisses. "How much I want *us*. I thought I did that in the ring."

"But that was before."

"Before what? My brother got kidnapped?"

Gut lurching, I try to avoid her attentive stare. "Yes."

"So what changed?"

"It's my job to keep a level head so I can find him."

"I'm not stopping you!" she snaps in pure aggravation.

"That's where you're wrong. I can't keep a level head when you're around. Fuck, I can't even think straight when you're in the bloody room. All I want is to grab hold of you and never let go again."

Ember braces her hands on my shoulders, frenzied eyes attacking me like she wants to rip the skin from my bones to burrow inside my carcass. Fuck, I'd let her. Anything to wipe that pained expression away.

Then the thought of what her brother would say creeps back in, and it's like being stabbed in the chest with the knife of reality all over again. The constant mental back and forth is wearing me to the bone.

"Fact is, I shouldn't be in this bed with my best friend's baby sister. It's my job to protect you. To protect everyone. And I'm failing."

"You can't shoulder the burden for everyone," she argues. "If you'd just let me in—"

"Like you do?"

She visibly winces. "That isn't fair."

"But it's true. This is my job, Em. I'm the team leader. When people get hurt on my watch, it's my responsibility to make it right. I can't be selfish."

"What if I'm giving you permission to be selfish for a second?"

It takes effort not to look at her inviting thighs, the tank top riding up to barely cover her full chest. Further evidence to my point. If only my twitching cock would get on board with my moral stance and behave.

"You're killing yourself to fulfil this duty, and I admire you for that, but this hero act is old."

"Em..."

"No. You deserve to be selfish too."

"Ember, please. I need to go."

When her hips jerk, I feel the molten heat pooling between her thighs press against my crotch. She's moved to position herself right above my rapidly swelling dick. I highly doubt that's accidental.

"Ember," I bleat again.

"I want to forget," she murmurs. "Don't you want that too? Even for a second?"

"We can't, and you know it. Stop this."

"Then make me. You could if you wanted to."

Ember shifts again, deliberately rubbing herself against me. Heat spikes deep within my cavities, creating a slow burn. The tantalisation of her body pressed on mine is too enticing to resist.

Pressure strains against my sweatpants, screaming out for relief after months of this agonising tease. Scrap that, years. It's been fucking years, and I'm still denying myself the release that I so desperately need.

How good would it feel to give in? To give Ember exactly what her filthy mouth is begging me for? I could do it. She's right—I'm the only one stopping this. If I so desired, I could have her crying my name nine ways to Sunday while my teammates listen to me take her.

My dick spasms at the thought.

Yes. I definitely desire that.

"Unless… you don't want me?" Her teeth pierce her bottom lip.

"Fucking hell, love." I pinch her pink, swollen lip between my fingers to free it. "You know I do. I think I've made that pretty bloody clear."

"Then why are you pushing me away?"

"Em… I'm trying to keep you safe."

"From whom? From you?"

Fingers tightening on my shoulders, she rotates her hips, dragging her tempting heat over my sweatpants again. My head spins from how quickly she's flipped this entire situation and brought me to my knees.

"For once, just stop thinking. Stop obsessing. Stop worrying about everyone and everything but yourself. Take what you want from me."

Heart thudding unevenly, I push out a short breath. "I don't remember the last time I did that."

"I'm guessing never."

Roughly grinding down on my dick, she studies my face in the din. An involuntary gasp breaks past my lips, rewarding her efforts. I'm harder than fucking steel at the feel of her pressed against my trapped cock.

Sure, watching Ember work herself over for me was quite literally the hottest thing I've ever seen. And sure, I came twice in the shower afterwards as I angrily fucked my hand to the memory of her coming apart. But I haven't touched her like I really want to.

I can push her aside right now. Climb out of this bed. Flee the room and lock myself away someplace where her temptation can't reach me. She's off-limits. Forbidden. And far too good for me.

But when she finds the hem of her tank top then quickly tugs it over her head, my protests die a sudden death. Distant city lights illuminate Ember's generous round tits, two rosy buds forming diamonds that beckon to be licked, bitten and sucked.

"See me." She drags a single fingertip along the canyon between her breasts. "Look how you make me feel."

My breathing has shortened to rasps, full of want and need. Nothing but cotton holds me back from feeling her skin flush on mine, and for the life of me, I'm forgetting why I fought so hard against taking her in the first place.

"Dammit, love. I can't ever have you."

"You already do," Ember whines. "However the hell you want me, I'm yours. All you have to do is take the risk."

Every single inch of her body is ethereal perfection. The years haven't dulled the beauty that first entranced me when we were little more than children dancing around the edges of something more. Now she's a temptress dipped in sin and offering her goddamn soul to me.

"Why are you doing this to me?" I growl out.

"I told you. I want more. I want to be yours. I want to be shared. I want everything and more still. So why won't you give it to me?"

With each needy whine, she grabs handfuls of her tits and squeezes. Perfect pink skin slides between her fingers, my cock stiffening further as I watch her tweak her hard nipples until she breathily moans. That small sound lands straight between my legs.

This godforsaken woman.

All the desire I've held at arm's length since she first made those declarations hits me in a tidal impact, blasting apart the walls I've tried to erect. The destruction fills my ears as I stare up at my precious astronaut, now a filthy little angel grinding on my cock like it's her personal plaything.

You know what? I'd be her plaything. Send me to hell, I'd be anything she wants me to be. If it didn't threaten my career, my focus and my entire friendship with her brother, I'd have thrown her against the wall and fucked her senseless months ago.

She has no idea how rough I can be.

Lord forgive me, I'm gonna show her.

Hands clasping her beckoning hips, I dance my fingers up her body until I can grasp her hair. Ember gasps as I use the tight grip to bend her spine, bringing her flat against my chest, parted lips within reach.

My mouth brushes along her throat, over the pounding betrayal of her pulse point to her curved, oval jawline. I deliver a series of wet kisses and tiny bites, needing to taste every inch of her.

"You're going to be the absolute death of me, Ember. I'm trying to hold it together and be a good man. But that's hard to do when you're a walking sin determined to ruin my life."

Writhing on my length, Ember lets me trail a blazing path across her skin. Her little pants hold the power to smash apart my resolve. I want to hear the sounds she'll make when I sink inside her sweet, perfect cunt.

My teeth cut into her skin, allowing me to suck the delicate flesh at her throat between my lips. Her surprised moan compels me to bite and suck harder, needing to hear more of her mewls.

Tugging on her hair, I move my lips over to her open mouth. "Is this what you want? You want me to claim you as my own?"

"Yes. I do."

"You want me to shred every last childhood memory we've shared by doing exactly what I want to your body? Even if it kills our friendship?"

Hips swirling again, she grinds harder on my cock, seeking added friction. My balls tighten and clamp, screaming out for relief. I can't stop my hips from rising to push into her, eliciting a breathy sigh.

"Yes," she moans. "Ruin it."

"You want me to show you exactly what I've dreamed of doing to you since those gorgeous curves and round tits showed up on your body?"

"Fuck, Warner. Please… anything. I want it all."

"Even though I know you're drawing my two teammates into your little web more with each passing day?" I challenge her.

"Yes!"

"You're such a greedy girl, love."

"Please kiss me. Touch me. Give me anything."

"A greedy girl who knows how to beg."

Trapping her face between my hands, I slam my lips on hers with enough force to shove every last alarm bell sounding in my mind into a quiet corner. Right now, all I want is her dirty mouth surrendering to mine.

As I furiously devour her sweetness, my tongue thrusts aggressively past her lips. I want to be gentle and enjoy each precious touch, but she's pushed me over the edge. The tension she's built has destroyed any hope I had of avoiding this huge, glaring mistake.

Ember meets me stroke for stroke, taking my anguished battering without complaint as her tongue lashes back against mine. I move one of my hands to grasp her right breast, taking the mound in my palm and squeezing like she did.

Silken skin pebbles under my touch as I roll her nipple between my fingertips. At my teasing pinch, another moan spills from her chest, making my painfully stiff dick twitch.

Teeth pressing into my lip, she nips at me in a plea for more. *Such a greedy, dirty angel.* I don't know if I can hold myself back much longer with her pulsing cunt still sliding over my shaft.

Dammit, I want to rip her panties open so I can shove myself deep inside her. But I can't rush this. Not after all this time. I want to take my time savouring her essence, taking her slowly and fully so I can finally claw her infection from my brain cells.

Maybe then I can let her go.

Right. Because that's fucking likely.

Finding her damp panties, I ease the elastic over her hips, encouraging her to strip off. Ember lifts herself off my lap to discard the soaked cotton, exposing her bare body to me. I take the opportunity to shift down the bed until I'm flat on my back.

"Bring that gorgeous pussy to me, Ember," I order curtly. "Quickly."

"Where?"

"I want you to come here and ride my face."

Eyes that shift between brilliant azure and gunmetal grey appraise me. I can't decide if she looks surprised or excited. Crooking a finger, I gesture for her to move faster.

"Bring it to me. Now."

She responds to my demands like I have direct access to her mind, and all it takes is one plucked string to bend her will. I noticed it before when I showed her my more dominant side, but as she crawls up my body now, it's clear I have to be firm with the spitfire.

"That's it, love. Sit that greedy cunt down. I'm going to feast on you."

Placing her toned thighs on the pillow either side of my head, Ember hovers above me. I'm granted the perfect view of her dripping pink heat before she sinks down, then her pleasure rushes over my face.

I flick my tongue out, dragging it over her wet folds. Salty sweetness bursts across my senses, pouring from her soaking core. She's wildly turned on. Tasting the evidence of how much she wants me only adds to the ache tearing me up inside.

"Oh," she moans languidly.

Swiping my tongue over her clit, I repeatedly lavish the tight bundle of nerves. Her hips quickly jerk, beginning to undulate above me as she rocks in time to each broad stroke of my tongue.

"Yes! Warner, fuck. More."

Grabbing the globes of her ass, I encourage her to move. She can suffocate me with her cunt for all I care. As long as I make her explode with ecstasy first. I want those juices coating my entire face.

Back and forth, her pussy thrusts against my mouth, allowing me to lick and suck her clit with each rotation. Short pants for air let me dive back in every time she sinks down on me for another hit.

"Yes… Oh God. Yes. Please, more."

Gripping an ass cheek, I guide her thrusts as I push my tongue inside her tight hole. Entering her heat feels like nirvana, but it pales in comparison to the deliciously wanton mewl she offers in response.

I could come just from the sweet, salty taste of her excitement on my tongue. The feel of her cunt sliding on my face as she uses me for her pleasure. The sexy weight of her body trapping me in utter subjugation.

Raising an arm, I reach over her thigh to locate the apex between her thighs. While I tongue-fuck her hole, my thumb quickly bears down on her nub, causing her to spasm above me.

"Yes! Warner!"

That's it. Say my name, love.

Swirling spit and come over her clit, I'm playing that fibrous bean like it's my favourite instrument and I'm a one-man band performing just for her. She's so vocal. Her cries are going to haunt me until my dying day, I swear.

Ember starts to quake above me, wavering each time I lap at her heated core. My fingers are digging so deep into her ass cheek, I'm sure she'll have a bruise to match the bite I left on her throat.

The trembling increases until I feel her walls clamp around my pulsing tongue. She's riding my face like it's nobody's business and moaning so loud, a distant part of me wonders if Hyland can hear what we're doing in here. A less distant part hopes he can.

She was mine first.

Drawing back the hand I've clamped on her ass, I smack it hard into the cheek. Ember jolts from the impact, her cries reaching a fever pitch as the pain from the spank spreads throughout her synapses. God, she's hot. So damn sexy it's killing me.

With another loud wail, Ember detonates. Her pussy tightens into a vice, and warmth gushes over my tongue, chin and face. Every part of her shakes, weight sagging as she nearly cuts off my ability to breathe.

I keep eating her out until I'm certain her orgasm has been stretched to the limit. Gently easing her hips back an inch gives me space to suck in air while watching her come down from the high.

Ember shakily braces over me, her tits shuddering with each lungful she inhales. Two blueish-grey gems watch me lick the fluids from my lips, enjoying every drop I've earned.

Her pupils are so comically wide, I can see the deep caverns even in the low, dawning light. The final flecks of my sanity are sucked into those black holes then vanish from existence.

"Don't ever doubt how much I want you," I rasp while licking up her mess. "How much I've always wanted you, Em. Why do you think I never stopped looking for you?"

"Because… saving people is what you do."

Running my hand between her breasts, down her stomach and around to clasp her waist, I pull her down so I can kiss her again.

"Not this time," I whisper into her mouth. "I've always been yours."

Seizing me in another passionate kiss, Ember steals away my confession before I dare take it back. She scurries the truth away with her lips and tongue, stealing her own essence from my mouth.

"Then take me," she demands.

Staring into her eyes, I'm ready to throw any remaining rationality aside and flip her over so I can push my cock into her when a loud bang emanates from the room next door. Cursing quickly follows.

Startling, Ember looks over her shoulder. "Is Hyland here?"

"In his room."

"Jesus. He probably heard us."

"I like to think so."

"Warner!" She gapes at me.

"What? He's had his paws on what doesn't belong to him."

The cursing grows louder along with the sound of thudding footsteps. I think I hear Hyland toss my bedroom door open across the hall before he growls, then a fist hammers on Ember's door.

"Warner! Ember!"

There's no warning before the solid wood is thrown open. Hyland's broad shoulders brush the doorframe when he storms in, hitting the light switch to illuminate the room.

"We've got an upd—"

His voice halts.

Still straddling my chest, splayed over me with her whole naked body clearly on display, Ember meets Hyland's stunned stare. His brows almost disappear into his headful of shoulder-length, dirty-blonde hair.

"An update?" Ember questions urgently.

"Uh…"

"What update, Hyland? What is it?"

I've never seen the big guy speechless before. If it wasn't because I've been caught on the verge of fucking our newest team member—an act I threatened to castrate him for if I caught him doing it—this situation would be funny.

When his initial surprise wears off, Hyland's expression grows positively stormy. He glowers so fiercely at me, I'm almost glad I have Ember still sitting on me, acting as a human shield.

"Is this why you wanted to come in here?" he rumbles.

"What update?" I ask calmly.

"You threatened me with no less than—"

"Fuck," Ember cusses in a rush. "The update, Hyland!"

"Madden," he huffs. "He's got a lead."

"Shit. Clothes. I need clothes."

Ember clambers off me, inelegantly climbing from the mattress to begin searching for clothing. Her breasts bounce with the movement, dragging Hyland's hard stare from me to her bare limbs.

With a random t-shirt clasped in hand, Ember notices him looking and freezes. "See something you like?"

"Maybe." His hungry eyes roam over her. "Just didn't know we were allowed to see it."

"We're not," I rebuke.

"Then care to explain why I had to hear our teammate screaming your fucking name while you ate her like a meal?"

Jaw clenching, I don't respond.

"Well?" he prompts.

Ember yanks the t-shirt on to cover up then approaches Hyland. His gaze leaves me to peer down at her with pinched olive eyes.

"What's the lead?"

"I don't know. He's sent us a location."

Jolting upright, I struggle to shift to the edge of the bed. "He's not at HQ?"

Hyland merely shrugs. "Evidently not."

I scrub the back of my hand over my mouth. "Shit. Give me five minutes to clean up."

Ember rushes through pulling the rest of her clothes on, Hyland never taking his eyes off her. She eventually gives him a glance while pulling a pair of socks on her feet.

"What?"

He harrumphs after a sly look shot my way. "You're riding up front with me."

play
me
DO NOT CROSS
PO
Suspect?
NOT CROSS
POLICE

4

EMBER

JOHNNY WANTS TO FIGHT – BADFLOWER

One day, I suspect historians will study how on earth someone like Blaine Madden went from evading law enforcement to summoning them like trained dogs. And to his clandestine, criminal lair, no less. The place Sabre literally tried to shut down.

That fact clearly isn't lost on Warner. He's had a face like he's chewing hornets for the entire drive. Hyland's grip on the steering wheel is white knuckled too. Neither are happy about being summoned.

"We shouldn't trust Madden," Hyland grumbles.

With a sigh, Warner checks his watch. "We've had this conversation."

"Wasn't much of a conversation. You thrust this alliance on us."

"We need his help."

"He's our enemy. We don't need shit from him!"

"You're letting the past cloud your judgement," Warner combats.

"I'm trying to protect our team. Last I checked, that's your job."

"Watch your mouth, Hy."

A snort emanates from our stone-faced driver. "Or what?"

Honestly, I should've known that insisting on riding in the back was a bad idea. These two are going to kill each other before we even arrive. Pulling out my mobile phone, I fire off a quick text message.

> Ember: You better have a good reason for this, or they'll kill you.

I'm thankful his reply comes fast.

> Blaine: You think I'm that foolish?

> Ember: I don't know.

> Blaine: A deal's a deal.

Gnawing my lip, I consider my response.

> Ember: What's in this for you?

Three dots appear then vanish. He's hesitating.

> Blaine: Besides my freedom?

> Ember: Yes.

No delay this time.

> Blaine: You.

Unsure how to process that, I tuck my phone away without responding. Blaine's motivations are muddied at best. I know why he took me, freed me, then taunted me. I was a mere pawn to him then. Now? I'm not so sure the battle lines are clear cut.

You.

I doubt my teammates would like that answer.

Steering his SUV down barely lit backstreets, Hyland ploughs deeper into the industrial landscape. It's not unlike the warehouse district that Blaine sent me to the first time we fought, though we're on the outskirts of an East London offshoot now.

Manufacturing is the backbone of the capital's wealth, and that couldn't be more apparent than out here. While the rest of the world associates this city with glittering skyscrapers and golden, royal artefacts, the beating heart lays buried beneath that faux reality in places like this.

As we pass several unlit company headquarters deep in the industrial park, Warner clicks open the centre console to access the stowed gun safe. He pulls free a black semi-automatic pistol, making short work of checking the chamber and clip.

"Blaine is investigating for us," I tell them from the back seat. "Why are we going in all guns blazing?"

Hyland laughs under his breath. *Asshole.*

"Caution is what keeps us alive, Em." Warner remains focused on the weapon.

"He signed that deal to buy his freedom."

"That doesn't mean we're trusting him."

"Then why is he living with us?" I interrogate.

"He's sleeping on the sofa where we can keep an eye on him," Warner replies. "Madden is an asset. Don't confuse that with an ally."

"Take your own advice," Hyland mutters.

"Just shut up and drive."

At the end of the block, one large warehouse glows with light in the pale rays of dawn. A cluster of different vehicles are positioned outside—two muscle cars, a familiar motorbike and one unmarked van.

Hyland parks behind Axel's baby then scans the scene. "Why are we meeting here?"

Warner frowns out the window. "Axel was due to be scouting out some false license plates we identified passing near Tom's apartment around the time he was taken."

"Sure looks like he decided to follow the convict on a wild goose chase instead," Hyland chuffs.

"You're doubting Axel now too?" I eye him.

"I'm doubting any situation that threatens to hurt our team." Hyland glares dark daggers at the scene ahead. "That's my job."

Shaking my head, I clamber out of the car before I can hear Warner argue back. I'll take a bogus trap over listening to their competing egos for a moment longer. They follow in quick succession, the sound of Warner's cursing floating over the SUV to reach me.

"What is this place?" I peer up at the warehouse.

Warner stiffly circles the car, favouring his left leg. "I did a quick search in the car. Registered to a nesting doll of shell corporations with a paper trail more complicated than a Rubik's Cube."

"Because that isn't suspicious at all."

"It's exactly how the Madden dynasty built so much infrastructure across London over the last century."

"You're saying this place is his?"

Adjusting his light jacket, Warner shifts uncomfortably. "It would appear we didn't erase his operations as effectively as we thought."

"No shit," Hyland scoffs.

Inviting his unlikely allies directly to his secret base of operations does little to explain Blaine's mind to me. He knows the guys don't trust him. Why take the risk? For all he knows, they could bring this place down on top of his head.

"How does his plea deal come into play here?"

A few steps ahead of us, Hyland checks his hip holster. "Not illegal to own a warehouse. If it's being used to manufacture and distribute narcotics... Well, then I can send a team in there to sweep the place clean."

"I'm sure he'll be happy to help us find Tom once you've done that."

"We don't need his help, red."

"You know as well as I do that Blaine has connections. He wants to take down Gael too."

"Those connections are precisely why he belongs back in

prison."

He stomps on to approach the structure, cutting off our discussion. I bite back my own laugh as we follow, sliding into professional mode. Warner has his gun drawn, covering Hyland's back, while my head rotates on a swivel.

The warehouse isn't as decrepit as the last place Blaine sent me to. With only the odd smashed window and overgrown tufts of weeds, this place seems almost functional. The bare bricks, crisscrossed windows and distant rumble of music still sets my teeth on edge.

Before we can enter, the heavy steel door at the entrance groans while opening. Two shadows emerge—both tall, darkly clothed and clutching visible handguns. My gut drops when lurid, blue hair is illuminated by the dawn.

"You've got to be kidding me," I deadpan.

Her scowl firmly fixed in place, Raye pops a hip as she stares me down. "Hello again."

"Come to slice me open? Or toss me out of a moving vehicle?"

"Calm down, princess." She sticks her weapon in the back of her waistband. "The van wasn't moving. We're not complete assholes."

"Em?" Hyland's gun is still raised.

"Right. This is Raye."

"You were there in Mexico," Warner surmises.

With a faintly bored look, Raye looks over our group. "Bingo."

"Fantastic," Hyland drawls. "You here to surrender?"

A burst of laughter spills from Raye. "Surrender. Hah. Hilarious."

The bulky shadow at her side steps into the light, revealing familiar, light hair and an acidic glare. Warner inhales when he recognises Blaine's other right hand man from the fight club. It's Spyder, though I still refuse to believe that's his real name.

"We're exposed here," he clips out. "You lot coming in or what?"

"Where is Axel?" Warner ignores him, not moving an inch.

"The purple-haired fuck?" Spyder scowls. "Inside. Giving me a damn headache, too."

Lips rolling inwards to suppress a smile, I wave a hand to indicate for them both to relax. This isn't some elaborate setup. Blaine signed that deal in good faith. Perhaps this is a test, or an extension of trust that we should honour.

"Take us to the boss."

Spyder nods at my command. "You gonna give us another show? I'll even bet on you this time."

"Yeah, not likely."

"Shame. Wouldn't mind seeing a decent fight."

I take the first step to follow, letting the other two decide whether or not to follow. Their whispers betray a rapid argument before footsteps trail behind me into the warehouse.

Spyder and Raye guide us through a warren of empty rooms and corridors. Whatever they're doing here, it isn't immediately obvious. Blaine's playing this smart, giving no clues as to what really goes on behind these walls.

After several turns and twists, I've lost track of our path deeper into the cold, echoing building. The knowledge that Hyland and Warner are armed at my back offers some assurance. The way Spyder keeps glancing over his shoulder to look at me is unnerving.

"What are we doing here?" I snap at him.

"Heard about your little problem." He eyes me knowingly. "We've been turning the city over since the boss man called to fill us in."

"You have?" Warner sounds surprised.

"He says jump, we ask how high. Just didn't expect it to take this long."

Thundering heart leaping into my mouth, I quicken my steps. Blaine's been floating around the edges of our investigation since Tom was taken yet never once mentioned that his people are out there working from the shadows.

The central hub opens to a wide, drafty space with high ceilings, exposed steel beams and rows of empty work benches. Drinking in the details, I flinch when a scream cuts the chemical-tinged air.

"What the fuck?" Hyland jerks in front of me.

"Calm down, toy soldier." Spyder snickers.

"Where is Madden?" Hyland turns to Spyder, nostrils flaring.

"You want to lower the piece?"

Jaw clenching beneath his blonde scruff, Hyland's raised gun doesn't budge. "Alternatively, I could unload it into your carcass."

"You son of a—"

"It's alright." The formal croon that seems to haunt me rings out. "No need to get all worked up, boys."

Strolling towards us like he doesn't have a care in the world, Blaine immediately catches my eye. His self-assured grin is full of smug satisfaction. Such a shit stirring drama queen.

"What is this?" Warner steps forward to meet him. "The plea deal didn't include running around the city and playing pointless games."

Blaine grants him an exaggerated eye roll. "Good morning to you too."

"Stop wasting our time. Why are we here?"

"Want me to take the trash back out?" Spyder offers.

"No, stand down." Blaine shakes his head in denial. "Our friends may be rude beyond belief, but for once, we're on the same side."

The sound of another nearby scream punctuates his words. We all collectively stiffen while Blaine's lascivious smile widens.

"Care to follow me?"

Pushing off the arm that Hyland attempts to block me with, I cut him a glower then follow behind Blaine. We're led through the empty workbenches, pockmarked with telltale scars, out towards a storeroom. Only it isn't boxes or crates being stashed inside.

"One more chance," someone yells. "Where is Luis?"

Oh, hell. Axel.

The ultimatum is levied with a firm strike, causing blood to erupt from the asshole's busted nose. Stained metal attached to Axel's knuckles glints beneath the dim-orange lighting. My lips part on a gasp when he delivers another blow.

"You won't take Antonio Gael's secrets to the grave," Axel warns in a light, teasing voice. "There's much more we can do while you're still alive."

"F-F-Fuck you!"

"I'll pass. You're not my type."

It's hard to make out the middle-aged man he's systematically beating with blood-slick knuckledusters. Nor do I recognise the three others, all cuffed and bound on their individual wooden chairs, sporting varying degrees of injuries and consciousness.

"Madden?" Warner motions to the half-dead looking men. "Explain."

"What did you call them before?" Blaine taps his chin. "Honeypots?"

Every inch of me clenches tight in anticipation. We pumped Luis's men for information after the raid, including Miguel, before tossing them into cells to await prosecution. But these guys? They're fresh meat. Brand-new players.

"How?" I rasp.

With a self-assured wink, Blaine gestures for everyone to enter the room. "I have my ways."

"Who are they?" Warner inches inside.

"Old employees of my father. Men he used behind my back to fuel his trafficking enterprise. Their allegiances soon shifted when his empire collapsed. All four of them freelance now."

"For Gael?" Hyland asks.

"Among other players." Blaine tilts his head towards the man being tortured. "I believe Sabre's been searching for this one in connection with the Sanchez case for several years now."

It's hard not to clock Hyland's visceral reaction—an almost full body recoil at that name. Then he tucks his gun into his waistband and heads to Axel's side to inspect the captive's red-stained face.

"I'll be damned." He crouches to get a closer look. "Dominic Pit. We've had a warrant for your arrest since everything went down in Briar Valley."

With a grunt, the man spits blood in our direction. "I don't know anything."

"Now, I highly doubt that. You've been at the top of our shit list for years."

"Then consider his safe delivery a peace offering from me." Blaine's tongue flicks out to nudge his lip piercing. "You're welcome."

Warner huffs. "How magnanimous of you."

"I'm a generous man. I hope this will earn me your allegiance."

"How did you even find him?" Hyland questions mistrustfully. "He's a wanted man. We thought he'd fled the country."

"I told you before." Blaine shrugs with his Cheshire Cat grin.

"You need me. I have resources that go beyond Sabre's legal scope. This is merely a demonstration."

Warner's hands fist at his sides. "So why the cloak and dagger, Madden?"

"We've been tracing shipments heading overseas for close to a year now," he reveals. "Not just heading into Mexico and South America but Europe too. It's a wide-scale market."

With each word, the nausea pulling at my innards grows exponentially. I'm no fool—I know this particular brand of evil is international. But hearing that the same mechanism I found myself trapped in facilitates trafficking on a global scale is stomach-turning.

How many more of us are there?

"I have a connection in an underground smuggling circuit. They informed me of Dominic's return to England." Blaine folds his vein-studded arms. "He's been on our watchlist for some time."

"What kind of connection?" Warner presses.

"Irrelevant."

"Nothing is irrelevant. You should've told us about this."

"Lead your investigation, and I'll lead mine. Isn't that the deal?"

"No!" Warner blusters, briefly losing his cool head. "It's not the deal. We have to communicate."

"Frankly, you won't agree with my methods. The less you know, the better."

"You're operating under our jurisdiction now," Warner snarls. "That means we don't have the luxury of secrets. You can't play these games anymore."

"My *games* yield results. You should be grateful."

"I should—"

"Why?" I butt into their debate.

Blaine's dark gaze snaps to me. "Why what?"

"Why trace those illegal shipments instead of helping the innocent people trapped inside? In fact, why do you care about this at all?"

"Because somewhere in this web of competing cartels, international crime families and trafficking rings, my father has sought refuge. He's the connecting piece to Gael and dozens like him."

Connecting piece...

Nolan Madden ran a ring of honeypots to perform paid kidnapping jobs for overseas traffickers without Blaine's knowledge. He propped up a crucial branch of Gael's business model, and likely countless others' too.

The rage churning in Blaine's black irises magnifies as the situation becomes clearer. This tangled web isn't just holding my brother hostage; for Blaine, it's his whole world on the line. His family are neck-deep in a global criminal conspiracy that he failed to prevent.

"This dickhead isn't talking." Axel flexes his arms while looking at me for the first time. "But he's here for Gael. He must have Luis's location."

Marching over to Axel, Warner grabs his shoulder. "Why the hell didn't you tell us about this? We're your team. Not Madden."

Axel shrugs him off. "I didn't know."

"Then explain this to me!"

"He got the call from whatever shady fuck he's bribing, and I offered to come help beat some sense into this lot. Don't doubt my loyalty."

"Then you should've told us about this." Warner whirls on Blaine next. "You don't have our trust in the first place, let alone the right to abuse it."

"You said it yourself," Blaine replies steadily. "I don't have your trust. Why on earth would I divulge my plans to you without it?"

The pained groan spilling from their prisoner interrupts the stare off, forcing all our attention to redirect. Dominic Pit has opened his bruised eyes. As I examine him, something tickles the back of my mind, shrouded in ancient clouds of confusion.

There's something about his eyes. The palest of greys, an odd hue visible even through the bruises and blood. Over the years, countless foot soldiers passed me, belonging to Gael and the men who would come to conduct business in his estate.

My skull throbs when I try to drag the memory to the forefront, wailing in protest. Much of that time is foggy, particularly the years around my head injury. There was no shortage of scumbags from all over the world visiting Gael in his mansion to strike deals or purchase skin.

"You." My feet carry me towards the unknown man. "Why do I know you?"

Spitting out a thick globule of blood, Dominic spares me a brief look. "Because I know you, 768. I know what you are."

His head snaps to the side, bone crunching disgustingly under the force of Axel's punch.

"Don't call her that. First and final warning."

"Ax—"

"No," he cuts me off. "It's not your name."

Barely able to open his eyes through the crimson river spilling from a forehead cut, Dominic spits a curse. My mind pulsates, trying to drag disparate puzzle pieces together.

"I do not know where Luis is," he chokes out. "And I don't work for Antonio Gael."

"You just supply him with product to sell, right?" Axel wipes blood from his knuckledusters.

"N-No!"

"Then who?"

"The European market… it's f-far more lucrative. Gael is old news to us."

"Then why are you here?"

When he doesn't respond, Axel lashes out again, cracking his fist into the bastard's cheek. His howl plunges me deeper into the shadowy past. Enough to set alight violence in my veins.

"Are you here to source new victims?" Axel shouts between punches. "Who are you selling to?"

Watching him work feels akin to chasing a tornado that's wreaking havoc on each defenceless town caught in its warpath. Axel isn't just a thug with a badge; he's a force of nature. One I'm sure Sabre is glad they have on their side.

Dominic's face resembles a meaty slab. He's puffing through each swollen, pulpy inch of battered flesh, somehow still holding onto consciousness. I step forward to rest a hand on Axel's shoulder.

"May I?" I whisper into his ear.

An enlarged pupil flicks up to me, swallowing the burnt-orange hue all around it.

"Be my guest."

Axel moves aside to let me take his place in front of Dominic's sorry state. I don't look back to see if the others are protesting his decision to let me take over.

"Come to p-pop a shot?" Dominic coughs up blood.

"Something like that. How do you know my name?"

"Everyone knows y-you, 768."

This time, I slam my fist into his jaw. "You heard him. Don't call me that."

Red spittle flies upwards from where his head is flung back, spraying all around in a crimson geyser. It doesn't elicit a speck of sympathy inside me.

"Answer the question, or I'll let my friend here continue toying with you. He has more patience for torture than I do."

"Nolan… M-Madden!" he screams when I pull back my arm.

Blaine curses nearby. "Bingo."

My fist lowers, fresh blood soaking into the scabs that have formed over my grazes. "Elaborate."

"He h-had us making connections with anyone in the market to m-make a purchase. Gael. Sanchez. All their f-friends across the globe. We worked f-for anyone."

Limbs filling with angry wasps, rage spreads like wildfire. "That's how we met."

"Barely." Dominic sucks in through a coughing fit. "Though I w-watched Gael bend your s-sweet ass over and slice your back up real n-nice with a whip."

Noxious sickness is roiling inside me when Axel shoves past me to launch a fresh attack. Any pleasure he was finding in playing with his prey evaporates as a bone-breaking beating takes centre stage.

The sound of Axel's fists hitting his flesh adds to the pain splitting my skull, a flimsy barricade barely holding back memories of the past. Worse still, it's impossible for me to say when or where I met this asshole. Gael beat me regularly enough for each occasion to blur in my memories.

Turning away from the violence, I breathe through the phantom pain of my skin being slashed all over again. I can't bear to meet anyone's gaze. Not when they're imagining what it took to scar my back.

"Sick fuck." Hyland doesn't take his eyes off the beating. "Though I'd expect nothing else from someone working for the likes of Gael, Madden or Sanchez."

"Who is this Sanchez?" I ask through gritted teeth.

Emotion contorts Warner's face as he moves closer to me, stopping short of reaching out a hand.

"An old foe."

"What happened?"

"Dimitri Sanchez was the prime target of a trafficking investigation our old team leader led years back. The victim fled to a small town called Briar Valley. She helped us bring his operation down."

So if Dominic also worked for Sanchez and that piece of shit knew Gael... it's very possible we've missed a crucial link. The messy, ever-changing spider's web shifts again, pulling us deeper into a conspiracy that, frankly, feels unsolvable.

Too many dark thoughts to sort through compete for my attention. A hatred that burns so hot explodes inside me, leaving me wondering if it will erupt from my skin and scald us all in one vicious lava spill.

Behind it all... the previously unknown figure of evil. Blaine's father. A man at the centre of a conspiracy that connects our lives. Each of us have a stake in this, from the Sanchez case to Blaine's vendetta and my own thirst for justice.

"We need his intel." I lower my hand from where I was rubbing my temples. "Dominic knows where Luis is."

"Axel," Hyland drones like it's an effort.

Smack. Crunch. Crack.

"Ax! Don't kill the bastard!"

"You heard what he said," Axel puffs in exertion.

"I did."

"This piece of shit watched her being tortured!"

"I know, but he's no use to us dead."

Looking over my shoulder, I catch the final punch to the kidneys that causes more blood to spill from Dominic's mouth. Axel begrudgingly eases off, panting hard through a mask of righteous anger.

His eyes briefly flick in my direction, and he cocks a brow. *You good?*

All I can summon is a shrug.

Warner gestures towards the restrained group. "We'll transport them back to HQ for further questioning before we hand them over for prosecution. I want an ID on Luis's location. I don't care how we get it."

"Mind if I lend a hand?" Blaine offers.

"You've earned that right. Thank you for finding them."

I'm not the only one who startles at Warner's sincere thanks. Even Blaine stares at him for a long moment like he's unsure quite how to react.

"Okay," he eventually accepts.

"Don't look so affronted, Madden."

"More like disturbed." He smirks in amusement.

When Warner catches my gaze, he offers me the first genuine smile since Tom was taken. I can't quite find the mental strength to give one back, but I respond with a semi-hopeful nod.

One step closer.

We're coming, Tom.

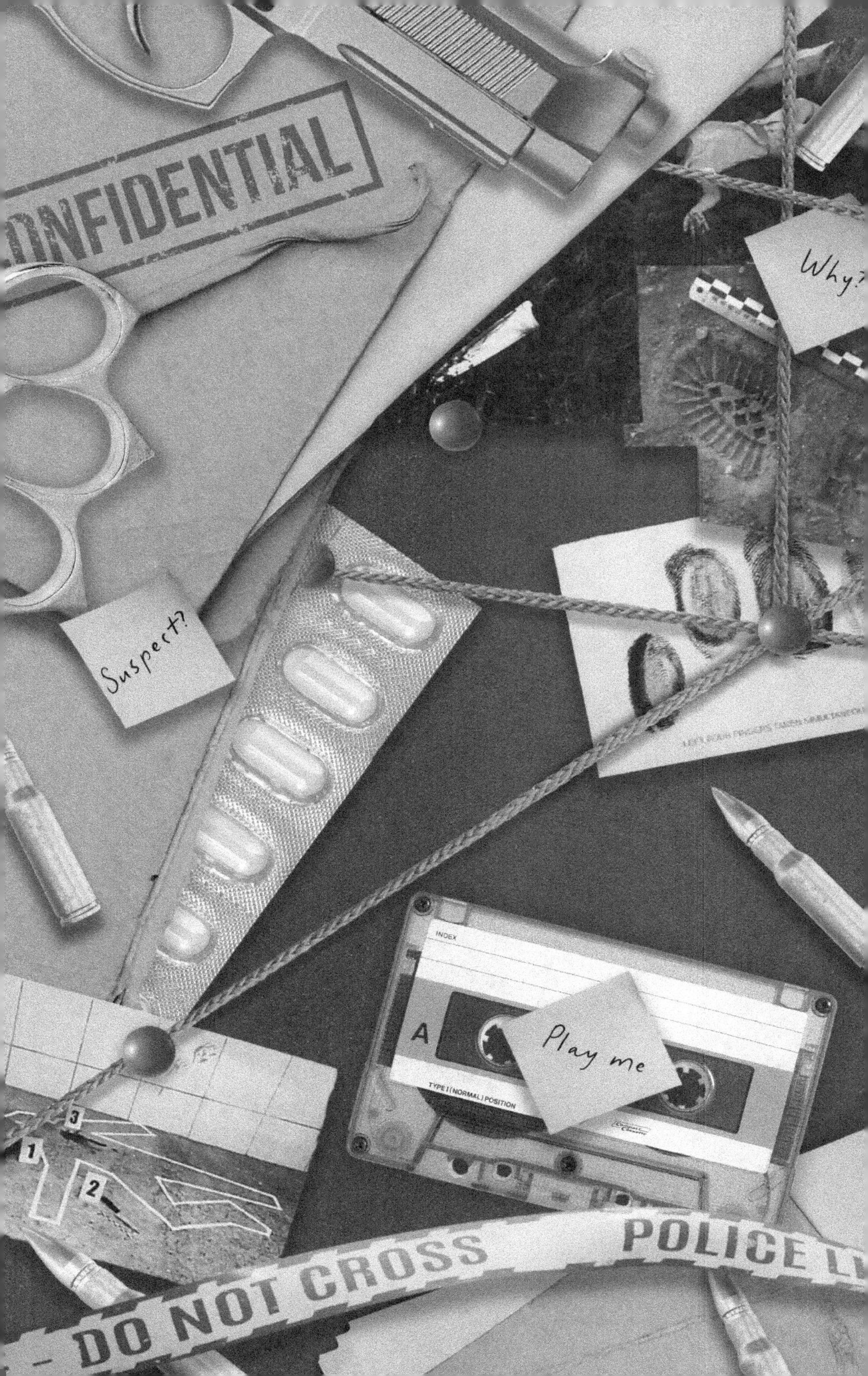

NFIDENTIAL
Why?
Suspect?
Play me
A
INDEX
TYPE I (NORMAL) POSITION
POLICE
DO NOT CROSS

play
me
DO NOT CROSS
POL
suspect?
NOT CROSS
POLICE L
4
(NORMAL) POSITION
Compact Cassette

5

EMBER

ONE LAST BREATH – CREED

Sitting stiffly in the uncomfortable examination chair, I study the medical poster on the wall directly opposite. *Your health is our priority.* The urge to snort wins out. More like the extortionate cheques that Sabre is signing off on my behalf.

The EEG itself is painless. Nothing more than a sticky sensation where the electrodes are positioned on my scalp. When the technician asked me to breathe hard and fast to simulate hyperventilation, I tried to block out the reminder of how it felt to black out with Diego straddling me.

In. Out.

In. Out.

Breathing is easy. Right? Simple. Just like existing with the constant threat of my brain attacking itself and attempting to cripple me at any moment. Only that isn't easy or simple, and

apparently, neither is breathing anymore.

"Okay, Miss Lawson." Alex, the smiley technician, directs me. "Very good. Just breathe normally for me."

Tearing my gaze from that damned poster, I focus on his name tag instead. My lungs are burning, but he wanted to measure my brain's electrical activity in a state of stimulation. Not unlike facing an arch nemesis hellbent on recapturing me.

"Any discomfort? Dizziness?"

"Some," I reply shortly.

"Okay, take a moment. Relax for me."

"What does the chart say?"

"I'll let Doctor Fawn interpret the data for you. Post-Traumatic Epilepsy is a complex condition, but he's well-versed in it."

Great. No getting away easily.

I've been dreading the thought of this follow-up since I scheduled the appointment. While I haven't had another attack yet, the other symptoms are persistent, and living with the constant threat is proving to be exhausting.

"I'm going to remove the electrodes now, Miss Lawson. You may want to wash any residual paste from your hairline."

With the examination over, I wait for Alex to finish his work then bustle from the room with a sheath of printed graphs. The hospital bay falls silent, emphasising the roar of my heartbeat in my ears.

This feels so pointless. My health isn't important right now. Not while we're still looking for Tom—AKA, beating the hell out of Blaine's captured honeypots until they give us their intel. Each hour is passing sluggishly.

When the door to the room rattles behind me, I plaster a neutral mask on in preparation to face Doctor Fawn. I'm surprised to find a set of olive eyes and a reticent smile entering in his place.

"Hey," Hyland greets.

"What are you doing here? Is there an update from Ax?"

"Not yet. He's still in questioning with Warner and Madden."

My heart sinks. "What's taking so long?"

"Those bastards are professional criminals. It isn't so easy to break their loyalty. But they will break, red. They always do."

"So why didn't you stay to watch?"

His green orbs soften, brimming with concern. "I'm here for you. This doesn't feel like the kind of thing you should be doing alone."

Gawping at him, I try to fathom his behaviour. One moment he's lecturing me about leaving the investigation, the next he's offering moral support. The whiplash is acute.

"I'm fine alone. Always am."

"You don't have to be." His canine digs into his lower lip.

"I'm aware of that fact."

"Then why ban everyone from coming with you?"

"I didn't fancy getting lectured by both my doctor and you in one day. That's why you're really here, right?"

Releasing a sigh, Hyland halts at the foot of the reclined chair. "No."

"Then what is it?"

"Believe it or not, I'm here for you."

"I do find that hard to believe," I scoff. "You've made it clear how you feel about me being on the team."

Something that looks a whole lot like regret twists his stubbled face, making the earthy hue in his eyes gleam brighter.

"If you'd just given me a chance to explain instead of avoiding me—"

"Explain what? You want me off the team."

"I was trying to protect you." Frowning, his head slowly sways from side to side. "Though I can see now that I went about it in the wrong way."

"You think?" I chortle.

"Look, Em." His huge, scar-laden hands lift in a universal plea for mercy. "It was dumb and stupid. I was lashing out."

"Great, thanks for acknowledging that. Now leave."

"For fuck's sake, will you listen for a second? Please?"

Chin jutted out, I make myself look up at him. Hyland looms over me, hands now braced on his wide hips and barrel chest heaving with each short breath. But it isn't anger on his face. Far from it.

His generous muscles, height and oversized stature would

probably be intimidating to any other woman trapped alone in a room with him, but I know Hyland would never hurt me. Not with his body, at least. His words are another matter altogether.

"You humiliated me." Pain bleeds from my flat rasp. "I felt like I wasn't wanted. Like I'll never belong with this team."

"Shit." He pinches his eyes between his long fingers.

"You alienated me, Hy."

"That wasn't my intention."

"Intention is irrelevant when your behaviour is hurtful."

"You're right." Hyland runs a hand over his low blonde ponytail. "I'm fucking scared. I want to keep you safe, and I thought that was the only way. Regardless of your feelings."

"Well, now you know what happens when you disregard my feelings." A noxious ball gathers in my throat. "I let you in. That was hard for me."

"I know, red."

"Then you threw it back in my face."

"Fuck, fuck, fuck." Cheeks staining dark, Hyland looks up to the ceiling. "I can see why it would look like that to you, even if I thought I was doing the right thing."

Wow. That may just be personal growth.

"The urge to protect and keep everyone safe..." His Adam's apple travels up and down. "It overrides everything else sometimes. Even common sense. I can't let anyone else get hurt."

The shadows that dance in his eyes fill with spiked shards of trauma. Memories I've only scratched the surface of since joining their team. I'd bet anything that he's seeing their faces right now—his ex-wife and infant son. The first people to get hurt on his watch.

"I want you on this team." His tongue darts out to wet his lips. "You're wanted. You belong with us, through thick and thin. Regardless of what I may stupidly say."

Despite his words, the pain in my chest persists.

"Ember... I was wrong," he elucidates slowly, deliberately. "I am sorry."

We hold eye contact for several loaded seconds, a host of unspoken desires filling the space that keeps us apart. It takes time for acceptance to writhe in, cracking through my emotional shields to whisper its consent directly into my mind.

Eventually, I nod once. "I suppose you can stay."

"I can?" His mouth quirks up.

"While I consider whether or not to forgive you for being an overbearing jackass, yes. You can. Just keep your bullish opinions to yourself, or you won't have a tongue left to apologise with."

"That I can do."

"Fine. Sit down."

Disregarding the blue plastic chair against the wall, Hyland leans against the wall in the corner on my left hand side. But not before pausing to brush a brief, chaste kiss on my cheek. The simple contact sends a pulse of heat swirling through my nerves.

"At the risk of pissing you off all over again…"

Seeing me tense doesn't deter Hyland's deep croon.

"…I must say, the sounds that Warner drew out of you the other morning were so hot, I wanted to interrupt to bury my tongue inside you while he was forced to listen."

A flush slinks across my face, holding my words hostage. The idea of Hyland shoving his friend aside to worship my core is far too enticing. But not more tempting than the thought of having them both touching me at the same time.

Fuck… Would they do that?

"Did you come here to tease me?"

"No," he denies. "I just wanted you to know that."

"Well, it's a little late now."

"Is it? As I recall, we all live together. Your bedroom is next to mine. I could accidentally stumble in at any time."

"What makes you think you'd be wanted?" I quip back.

A low chuckle rumbles from him. "Am I?"

To my relief, Doctor Fawn's arrival prevents me from having to form an answer. The grey-haired clinician bustles into the room with a smile that I'm convinced required its own lesson during medical school.

"Ember. How are you?"

"Good." I source a smile then plaster it on.

"Thanks for coming in today. These monthly checkups are vital as you come to grips with your new diagnosis and so we can monitor your medication regimen."

Pulling up his own chair, he takes a seat then begins to leaf through some paperwork. The wriggly black lines that indicate the results of my EEG mean nothing to me but seem to be of great interest to him.

"Tell me how your symptoms have been since we last spoke. Any episodes?"

"Not since the last seizure," I answer tightly. "Just some headaches and fatigue."

"I see. Any dizziness?"

"A little."

Nodding, he writes that down. "How is the shaking? Any involuntary movements?"

My fingers automatically curl, hiding the perpetual tremble that follows me. I can feel Hyland's attention on me like a laser beam.

"It comes and goes."

"That's to be expected. I know we discussed your career last time we spoke, and I assured you that you can continue to work. But you need to listen to your body when it asks for rest."

"I'm resting."

There's a deliberate throat clear from Hyland.

"I'm attempting to," I amend.

"Over-exerting yourself is a surefire way to trigger another episode, Ember. Ignoring warning signs won't help. Seizures are a part of your life now, but with the right self-care, we can reduce them."

I nod at his stern tone.

"What about the medication we prescribed?"

"I'm taking it every day."

"Any side effects?" He arches a grey brow.

"Not that I've noticed."

He hums a pleased response, jotting some more notes on his paperwork. I'm acutely aware of Hyland craning his neck in an attempt to interpret the doctor's handwriting from afar.

"Your EEG results indicate some evidence of epileptiform activity. This looks a bit like small spikes in your brain activity, particularly when we simulate hyperventilation to trigger a response."

"Even when she isn't having a seizure?" Hyland questions.

"Correct."

"Then what would a full seizure look like?"

"Ember's episodes would elicit a much more dramatic result—prolonged, jagged waves of abnormal activity generalised across the brain. However, this baseline does confirm her diagnosis."

"So you're just telling us what we already know," I huff.

"As I said before, finding a long-term treatment plan is a complex process." He grants me a smile. "Confirmation of our initial diagnosis is an important step."

I'm not sure how much longer I can clench my teeth to hold back my annoyance. This is such a waste of time. I've got the label. I've got the pills. I should be out there looking for Tom, not listening to this moron harp on.

"We will continue on your current regimen and proceed with regular checkups to monitor any changes to your condition. Any cause for concern or intense episodes, please contact me."

"That's it?" Hyland blusters.

Stacking the paperwork against his knee, Doctor Fawn levels him with an appraising stare. I'm sure Hyland harassed the poor man while I was stuck in here after my last attack.

"Mr Wesson, this is a long process."

"You're saying she could have an epileptic fit at any moment."

"That is the nature of Ember's diagnosis. Chronic illnesses can manifest at any time."

"How is that okay? No one can live like that."

"On the contrary, vast swathes of the population live with this condition and others like it. They live full lives, only with a few extra precautions."

"But you're seemingly okay with her walking around like a ticking time bomb?"

"That isn't language I'd choose—"

"There isn't a cure," I interrupt, fatigue weighing me down.

Pushed off from the wall, Hyland has to bend his neck to peer down at me. Aggravation is a well-versed look on him at this point.

"I found you on the floor just a couple of days ago, Em." The corners of his eyes crease into an aggrieved frown. "You were barely conscious."

"I pushed myself too hard. That's it."

"You could've triggered another seizure!"

"And it was stupid. I won't do it again. Are you done?"

"No," he replies hotly. "I'm not. You can't live like this."

"I have to!" My voice raises in volume.

Nose pinched, Doctor Fawn nods. "And we're here to help."

"Is that supposed to be comforting?" Hyland snaps.

"We're teaching Ember to manage her long-term condition, but it's enduring. She will always live with this condition because we cannot cure it. This is her new reality."

"She can't live in fear forever."

"Hy, stop," I protest.

"There must be something else… Something we can do…"

"Enough! You're not helping!"

Abruptly halting, Hyland flinches. That overprotective beast beneath his skin needs some serious training in bedside manners. It's raging out of control of late.

"This has been my life ever since I fractured my skull." I manage to spell it out in a calm voice. "It isn't anything new. I just have a fancy label now and this bundle of joy telling me what to do."

Doctor Fawn has the decency to smile.

"Point is, I'm dealing. You don't need to don some white knight armour and try to rationalise this for me. Labels aside, these episodes aren't new."

"I'm worried about you." He deflates, gaze sinking to the clean linoleum.

"If I may…" Doctor Fawn waits for me to nod. "It's perfectly normal for loved ones to struggle with a new diagnosis too. Long-term conditions affect the whole family unit."

"Ember is the one struggling." Hyland shakes his head, disturbing loose flyaways from his ponytail. "Not me."

"You're shouldering anxiety too. It's good to acknowledge that."

"But…"

"Just something to think about." Gathering his notes, the doctor stands with a final, pointed smile. "I'll give you both some privacy.

Take your time."

Once he's gone, I stare at the wheeled trolley that holds the EEG machine while Hyland pulls himself together. He circles the medical chair to squat down beside me, an oversized paw landing on my jean-covered knee, squeezing when I don't push him away.

"Em?"

All I can do is shake my head.

"I'm sure I'll apologise a million more times in the years to come, but I'm sorry… again. You know, for butting in. It's hard to hear him talk about your health like that."

"What did you think he was going to say?"

"I don't know." Hyland thrusts his free hand through his hair.

"This is a long-term condition. It's not going anywhere."

"And I knew that… I do know that." His deep baritone radiates pure sadness. "I guess a part of me hoped he'd have found some magical solution. I hate seeing you suffer."

"I'm surviving in my own way. You don't need to make it harder."

"Protecting you is making your life harder?"

"You mean when you stick your nose into my business?" I force down the growl creeping up my throat.

"I prefer to think of it as being a good co-worker."

Laughter tumbles from my throat. "Right."

"Unless you'd rather I had a different title?"

"Semantics aside, it makes it ten times harder when you resort to this crazy bull in a china shop routine. I'm coping in my own way, and I need you to respect that."

His fingers tighten over my kneecap. "I hear you."

"Good. I'm getting really tired of this conversation."

Flicking his gaze over to the sealed door, Hyland nibbles his bottom lip. "We can go back to discussing you inviting Warner into your bed rather than me. Do I have to respect that too?"

Air whistles from my nostrils. Shock is quickly followed by embarrassment, but I quickly squash it. I'm a grown woman. Who I choose to sleep with is none of his business.

"I should've known you wouldn't let that go so easily."

"Pretty hard memory to erase, Em."

"Is that so?"

His hand moves from my knee to skate upwards, rubbing my upper thigh. "The sight of you, all naked and flushed, riding Warner's face with your head thrown back and those beckoning tits thrust out..."

My quads tighten, instinctively reacting to the pressure of his touch. The path his hand travels leaves a red-hot trail of hyperactive butterflies, the tiny creatures determined to rip free from my cells and hold some kind of celebratory dance party.

"Did you like it?" he purrs.

"This isn't the time nor place to discuss it."

"Then answer the question, and we can go."

Aggravation pushes me to play along. "Did I like what?"

Hyland's head tilts, studying my reaction. "His mouth feasting on your pussy."

My legs clench, trapping his hand an inch from the apex of my thighs. The corner of Hyland's mouth twitches, the delicious darkness swirling in his green orbs intensifying his heated stare.

"Warner warned me to stay away from you," he reveals. "Threatened me even. All while he crawled between your sheets to steal you for himself. Does that seem fair?"

My head rests back on the chair. "Does it seem fair to you?"

Hand moving from between my pressed thighs, it gravitates towards my denim-covered core. I quietly gasp when Hyland cups my cunt through my blue jeans, teasing me with a squeeze.

"No, red. It sure as hell doesn't."

"Then perhaps you should even the scoreboard."

"Is that what you want?" He cocks a dirty-blonde brow.

"I'm not afraid to ask for it, but you already know exactly what I want."

"Still being so demanding." He laughs under his breath. "I admire that about you. Not many of us know what we want with such certainty."

"I've made no secret of my feelings," I squeak, feeling his fingers feather over my denim core. "You're the one who denied me for months with this *we're just colleagues* bullshit."

"Perhaps I'm done with that now."

"Since when?"

His throat undulates, betraying his anticipation. "Since I walked into your bedroom and realised that all bets are off. We're allowed to want you."

I crook my neck so I can peer down at him. Hyland may as well have his own gravity for all the power his intense presence packs. Ignoring him is near impossible. And honestly, right now, that's the last thing I want to do.

"Meaning?" I whisper throatily.

Lips parting, his tongue darts out to swipe over the pillowy swell. "Meaning I'm done playing childish games. I intend to take what I want now."

"And what would that be?"

"Allow me to demonstrate."

My lungs seize up as his big hand lifts to encircle my neck. Each individual callus grazes the sensitive slope of my throat when Hyland lightly grips it, using the leverage to haul me closer to him.

"If we were home right now, you'd already be splayed out in my bed without a scrap of clothing in my way," he growls into my lips. "I'd have your beautiful, bare body riding me while I discover how to make you cry out myself."

A fast kiss, the nip almost painful, delivers a preview of his promise. I strain against Hyland's warm hand at my throat, skin alight with tingles caused by the feel of him holding me prone. Though I never thought I'd like another man to touch me like this, he makes it feel exhilarating.

"Then I'd flip you over and bend you at the perfect angle to take you from behind." He ghosts his mouth over my lips again. "I want to fill every last part of you until I'm the only thing that exists inside your mind."

"Hy…"

"That's what you want, isn't it? You want to be fucked and shared? You want us all to own this sweet cunt, right? I understand now."

To illustrate his point, the hand that still holds me between my thighs squeezes again. A flood of heat shoots down south, flushing my system with agonising excitement.

"I can feel your heat, red. I'd bet anything that you're soaked already."

"No," I try to deny.

"Mind if I double check?"

Please, I want to pant. But I somehow hold it back.

The trill of a ringtone startles Hyland before he can touch me, dousing us both in icy water. Reality returns in a painful slap, filling me with a rush of disappointment that quickly turns into anxiety.

"Shit," he curses.

Hyland releases me then leans back to fish his mobile phone from his cargos. I take the brief pause to refill my lungs, blinking aside the lazy haze that's infected my vision.

"It's Axel."

"Answer it!"

He jabs his thumb on the screen then lifts the phone to his ear. "What?"

Ever the charmer.

My heart rate explodes into a racing staccato at the shouting I can hear down the line. When Hyland's eyes meet mine, widening emphatically, I sit upright in the chair.

"If he's just heard rumours, you need to verify the intel. He may be throwing us a bone to save his own skin now jail time is looming."

More impassioned yelling follows.

"Alright, alright. We're coming in now."

Quickly ending the call, Hyland pockets his phone then stands. He sticks out a hand in offer to me.

"We've got a location."

LINE - DO NOT CROSS
CONFIDENTIAL
Location?
Suspect?
DO NOT CROSS
POLICE L

6

AXEL

FINE AGAIN – SEETHER

On England's eastern coastline, the air is fresher beyond London's smog. Despite being a huge city within its own right, Ipswich's traffic doesn't reach the industrial landscape of the Port of Felixstowe. As far as the eye can reach, it's a lifeless sea of shipping containers and cargo.

Arms braced over my chest, I watch as Rayna navigates the complex setup for the drone's operating system on her laptop. We're flying a military grade unit over the port, scouting out which vessels are docked and searching for any signs of Luis's men concealed as dock workers.

"How loud is that thing?" I frown at the camera feed.

"Nearly silent," she mumbles back. "Drones these days are designed to be stealthy and discreet. Especially ones created by the military to be taken into enemy combat overseas."

The high-definition camera pans over the entire dockside, offering a bird's eye view of the cargo ship currently anchored. Onboard, metal cranes systematically lift containers, stacking shipments ready for departure.

"This place is vast."

"Good hiding spot, right?" Rayna hums.

"A little too good. It'll be a minefield to infiltrate."

Plonking a half-full coffee cup onto the table, Warner leans in to observe the laptop screen. "We have two teams and full surveillance from above."

"Luis could have the same numbers or more. He knows we're searching for him."

"If he's even here," he comments. "There's still a good chance Dominic gave up this location to lower his sentence. It could be a red herring."

"He held out for eighteen hours," I point out. "If your theory were true, he would've tattled much sooner to spare himself the pain. He's going to prison either way."

"I still don't trust his intel."

"You don't trust anything or anyone."

Warner casts me a glance. "That's why we're still alive."

According to Dominic Pit, Luis has criminal connections in this region. I broke his fingers individually myself. He held out well. It wasn't until I wrenched his premolar out that he finally snapped to reveal this location.

"What's our play?" I study the drone's view, high above the scene.

"We have a freight lorry prepped and ready to be driven into the port." Forehead wrinkled while squinting at the monitor, it's clear that Warner is deep in thought. "If Luis has a presence here, it'll be hidden behind legitimate operations."

"But why would he keep Tom in such an exposed location?"

"Close to the fastest exit out of the country and into Europe?" he retorts. "It's strategically placed. They can split at a moment's notice and vanish from underneath our noses."

"But these ports are heavily regulated."

"Safe to assume that local authorities are working as operatives, much like elsewhere." Warner shrugs. "It makes no difference. Once Luis's apprehended, we'll dismantle the whole thing and apprehend anyone aiding him from the inside."

"Gotcha!" We both startle at Rayna's exclamation.

Her pointer finger hovers over the laptop screen above a bright-blue lorry we clocked earlier. She's zoomed in on the European license plate.

"Fakes," she mutters in a rush. "I've run them through the freight company's online database."

"How did you access that?" Warner frowns.

"Easy. Their cybersecurity is shit."

"Damn, you're good," I whisper in awe.

"That's what you pay me for." She smiles to herself. "This right here is a Trojan horse."

"Then that's our target," Warner decides.

He turns away from us to bark orders at Josh and Oscar—the youngest members of the Falcon Team—currently helping each other pull on Kevlar vests. The others, Archer and Kyle, are in another room with Hyland and Fox.

We're camped across three rooms booked in two different hotels, housing our entire operation. After a rapid strategy meeting, each team drove here separately, setting up base a safe ten miles away from Luis's suspected bolthole.

"Move out in five. We have our target."

"Where is Ember?" I look around the room.

Pausing, Warner tilts his head towards the bathroom. "In there."

"She didn't say much at the debrief."

"I gave her the chance to stay behind before we left London." Hesitation curls around his words. "It didn't go over well."

"No shit?" I snort. "You know she wouldn't miss this for the world."

"I know. Just thinking about last time, that's all."

Unease trickles through me. "This isn't going to be like the last raid."

Warner nods silently.

"Relax, man. I'll get her."

"Thanks, Ax."

I smile at Rayna, still monitoring our suspicious cargo from afar, then approach the bathroom. Ember gives a faint response when I knock. Stepping inside, I click the door shut behind me to block out the sounds of preparation.

"You ready, dimples?"

God, she looks fucking formidable in her bulletproof vest and navy cargos. I'd spread her open on that sink top and plunge into her right now if we weren't on a time crunch. Plus, I'd have to sever our support staff's ears if they heard her gorgeous whimpers.

"Rayna's surveillance has picked up false plates on a cargo lorry. Could be something. We're leaving in five to move in."

She meets my eyes in the bathroom mirror. "Can you tighten my straps?"

"If you promise I can be the one to rip that vest off you when this raid is over."

Her mouth quirks, almost satisfying me. "If we survive."

"We've got this, babe. In a few hours' time, you'll be reunited with your brother. Luis will be dead. We can go home and celebrate… sans clothing."

"You sound confident."

"That's because I am."

Grasping the vest's thick Velcro, I work on adjusting the tightness. We're all decked out in full assault gear and will be packing significant firepower when we advance on the dock. For all we know, Luis has a small army hiding there.

"How are you feeling?" I ask more seriously.

"I feel good."

"No symptoms? Headache? Nothing we should be worried about?"

Ember shakes her head. "I'm okay, Ax."

"Better not be lying to me."

"Jesus, I'm not lying. I learned my lesson before."

"Good. Luis won't risk losing you for a second time; he'll be prepared to throw his entire arsenal back at us."

"Let him try," she growls out.

"That's the spirit."

"Once Tom's safe, I'm going to rip that son of a bitch limb from limb for what he's done to us both. I want the bounty on my head erased from existence."

"One thing at a time." I adjust the back of her vest, tugging it down to her tailbone. "First Tom. Kill Luis. Then we deal with Gael and his bounty. No one else is going to come looking."

"That easy?" She tsks.

"Not exactly, but we'll get it done."

When I move to step away from her, Ember's hand catches mine. Her lip is trapped between her teeth, forming a bright-red petal against her pearly white.

"What is it?" I step back up to her.

"Just… tell me he'll be alive." Her croak betrays a glimpse of her inner vulnerability. "Tell me we made it in time."

"You know Luis wouldn't risk killing Tom."

"We don't know that for sure."

"Your brother is tough. You should've heard him calling Warner every week on the dot to demand updates when we were searching for you. Give him some credit. He's a survivor."

"That's different. You don't know Gael and his… *methods.*"

"You think he's my first monster?" I laugh without humour. "Think again. I've seen plenty of his kind even before I joined Sabre. I know what he's capable of."

Fear inches over her delicate oval features to warp her face into a twisted caricature. I wince at my own idiocy. Right… Not the correct thing to say when she's secretly terrified for her only sibling.

Wonder what that's like.

I prefer to pretend mine doesn't exist.

Dropping my chin to her shoulder, I circle my arms around her cargo-clad figure from behind. Ember is stiff but slowly relaxes into my hold as I maintain eye contact in the mirror.

"My point is, Tom has waited all these years to get you back. I know for a fact that he would endure just about anything to have the time with you that he prayed for."

"But if they've hurt him—"

"Then we will deal with it," I say with certainty. "They'll pay in blood, and we'll ship their carcasses back to the monster who sent them to find you."

"Gael will only send more in their place." Her expression is bleak.

"Then I'll kill each and every one of them too. When we track down Gael, he'll receive the same treatment. No one is going to hurt you or this team again."

Pulling at my arms, Ember turns to face me. She lifts a hand to cup my jaw, her fingertips skating along my cheekbone and beneath my eye. A slow, luxuriating shiver rolls down my spine at the feel of her fingers on my skin.

"You'd risk so much for me."

"Are you only just realising that?" I study her reaction.

"I'm understanding the reality of it. You had to spend all those months in Mexico. It was your job. But everything you've done for me since… I guess I still don't understand why."

Disbelief tugs at my quivering heartstrings.

"How could you not understand?"

"Because I was just a job," she replies like it's obvious. "Perhaps I still am."

"You're a member of our team, Em."

Her mouth turns down at the corners. "Right."

"Stop that. I know Hyland said some stupid shit, but none of it is true. You belong with us."

"It's not that. He did apologise. It's just… Well, maybe I want to be more than that."

Regardless of the urgent preparations taking place all around us, I refuse to leave this bathroom until I've erased that damn look from her face. Ember lets me spin us around and walk backwards until she's pressed up against the bathroom door.

I quickly flip the lock to seal us inside then pin her against the thick wood with my hips, feeling every hard line and tempting curve locked against me. Shit, it's been too long since I felt her. All of her. I need to remedy that.

"I'm only going to say this once, Em, so listen well. Don't for a second think that you're just a job to any of us. That ship sailed a very long time ago. Hell, I never boarded it to begin with."

"Sure doesn't feel that way when you're counting pills for me while Warner and Hyland seem determined to dictate my every move."

"You mean caring for you?" My eyes widen of their own volition.

Her nostrils flare with a sharp inhale. "Babying me."

"There's a big difference."

"I'm not sure I agree with that."

"I know you're used to being all independent and shit, but you need to get it into your brain that we're all obsessed with you. That's *why* we're tripping over our feet to help. It isn't babying, it's love."

She pushes against my hips, attempting to wriggle free, but I keep her pinned against the door. Fuck it. Let them all talk. I'll lock her inside this room until she relents and cries out my name. Then let her tell me we're just fucking colleagues.

"Listen to me," I urge, clenching her biceps.

"Axel, we need to go—"

"No. Not until you understand. I'd worship the literal ground you walk on if it meant I could be in your presence for a single second. That's how I feel about you. I'd bet my left foot it's how Warner and Hyland feel too."

"We don't need to talk about this right now."

"Yes, we do. This insecurity you have is based on a lie." I search her cringing face. "You're our family, Ember. The minute you signed on the dotted line, that's what you became."

"I just find it hard to believe." Her eyes drop down to the floor. "That anyone cares, you know? I had to survive alone for so long. Accepting help now... it's difficult for me."

Sliding a finger beneath her chin, I tilt her gaze back up to meet mine. "I get that, babe. It's all the more reason for me to pin you down and remind you how much we care. Even when you make it harder than it needs to be."

"That's me," Ember jokes.

My forehead presses against hers, bringing our noses flush. The sounds of conversation and barked orders on the other side of the door melt away, leaving me to tune into Ember's strained breaths. She's on edge. I can almost imagine the violent thrashing of her heart muscle.

"When this is all over, I intend to lock you in my bedroom and prove to you that I mean it," I whisper over her mouth. "I'm sure the others would join me in that mission too."

"You'd want that?" Her lips flutter against mine.

"I'd like nothing less. You know I'm down for whatever you want. As long as I get to watch, that is."

"Be serious, Ax."

"I am. If it's what you want, then you're ours. Whether those idiots realise yet or not. You belong to us, and I'm done skirting around it. Life is too short."

She melds her lips to mine, stealing a passionate kiss. "I do want this."

"Then let's make it work. After we survive this."

"Right." She laughs.

When a loud bang raps on the door, we both sigh. This isn't the right time to be discussing our relationship—or rather, what it could be—but I wasn't about to let her doubt my intentions.

"It's go time!" Warner hollers through the door. "Out. Now."

Smirking, Ember's mouth briefly touches mine for a final kiss. "You heard the boss."

"Fuck the boss."

"Believe me, I'm trying to."

Laughter tumbles out of me. "No dice, hmm?"

"I'm playing a long game. Now, come do some heroic shit with me?"

I plant a heavier kiss on her lips, pushing my tongue inside her mouth to ensure my essence is imprinted on her taste buds. She better feel me all over her body when we march into this fight. And on the other side of it, I'm finally gonna make her mine.

We separate when Warner yells our names again, causing Ember to jerk. With a final peck, I release her to reach for the door's lock.

"Let's bring your brother home."

She unveils a full, excited smile.

"I'm ready."

ONFIDENTIAL
Why?
Suspect?
INDEX
A
TYPE 1 (NORMAL) POSITION
Play me
DO NOT CROSS
POLICE LI

Compact Cassette
I (NORMAL) POSITION
play
me
DO NOT CROSS
POLICE
Suspect?
NOT CROSS
POLICE LI
4

7

EMBER

SOUTHBOUND – ARTEMAS

Fragments of images from the last time I found myself in a dockyard creep into my mind like stealthy attackers, determined to imprison me in the past. The flashes are muddied and intense, despite my attempts to focus on the vehicle we're riding in.

Bound wrists. Drugged grogginess.

Screaming women. The yells of our captors.

Blood. Terror. Darkness.

It's near impossible not to think about the poor, terrified girl I was tossed into that black container with. Gracie's never far from my thoughts. When I'm not thinking about Tom, I'm tormented by what Luis threw in my face.

You should be glad that she's dead. Her fate could've been far worse.

If it's the last thing that I do, I'll ensure that he pays for the

suffering she endured. Gracie deserves justice. They all do. That's my purpose now—to dismantle this sick, twisted machine and protect all the would-be victims out there.

"Are you in position?" Hyland asks into his comms.

The sound of Kyle's gruff voice filters through our earpieces.

"Affirmative. I've got eyes on the vehicle. It hasn't moved."

"Watch our backs. Only fire if necessary."

"You mean I don't have permission to put a bullet in your back?" The pout is evident in Axel's voice.

"Knock it off," Warner scolds from beside me. "You're covering the Falcon Team, Ax. Behave."

"When has he ever been able to do that?" Hyland grumbles.

"Fuck you, Hy," Axel whines unhappily.

"Not with a thousand condoms, pup. Do your job."

Nothing but silence follows. I catch Blaine's eye roll from across the debris-littered lorry bed. He looks good, decked out like a real Sabre agent. Warner even permitted Blaine to carry a weapon. We must be in serious shit if he's breaking his own dumb rules.

The four of us are crouched at the rear behind two pallets laden with shipments. Kyle, our resident sniper, is with Archer on a rooftop outside the docks, while Axel assists them.

Oscar complained when Warner ordered him to remain behind with the intelligence team to maintain contact with HQ. The directors rarely engage in active ops these days, but they'll be waiting for mission updates back in London.

The sound of Josh greeting someone from the driver's cab floats to us. Warner tenses beside me, his semi-automatic pistol clasped tight in his hands while Hyland is crouched to leap into action at a moment's notice.

When Blaine's booted foot nudges mine, I look up at his silent, moving lips. *Breathe.* Yeah, helpful. Still, I make a show of sucking in a lungful as Josh's fake documents are checked by port security. Blaine smirks at my antics.

It would have been so much easier to call the authorities, clear the port then storm it with nothing but brute force. Problem is, we have no idea who is on Luis's payroll. It's clear he's greased palms to embed himself in local infrastructure like the other honeypots.

We can't trust them to lead us to him.

Just when panic has bloomed inside me, I feel the engine rumble to life. Josh distantly barks a *thank you* to whoever has waved him inside the port. Meanwhile, I'm silently thanking Rayna. Her forgery skills are impeccable and fast.

My leg bumps into Warner's prosthetic as we drive through enemy territory, prompting him to flash me a tight smile. He's trying to hide it, but I can feel his body shaking beside mine, and he keeps tugging at his trimmed salt-and-pepper locks.

"Warner," I murmur. "Hey, what's going on?"

"I'm fine, Em."

"You're vibrating. Talk to me."

"We can't let him slip through our fingers." He wears a fretful mask.

"I know." I nudge my shoulder into his. "We won't let that happen."

"There's a decent chance he isn't here."

"Someone knows where Tom's being held. If Luis has people based here, we'll make them talk. We're getting closer."

It feels alien to comfort him when I hardly believe a word I'm saying, but I hate seeing steady, dependable Warner more uncertain than ever.

"Stick close to me." His hard stare pins me in place. "I'm not losing you too."

"You're not going to lose me."

"Just be careful, love. They're here for you. I'm not willing to save Tom by giving you to them."

Regardless of our two bystanders and all the potential ramifications, I shift closer to press my mouth to his. Warner accepts the soft kiss after a second's hesitation, replying in kind with a sensual plea straight from his soul.

When we break apart, I feel Blaine's heated stare searing through my skin cells from across the lorry bed. A peek reveals the mystified expression on his face, caught somewhere between intrigue and annoyance. Pretty much sums up how I feel about him too.

Warner leans back with a wan smile and mutters, "Let them

look."

"You've changed your tune."

"No. Just re-evaluating my priorities."

"Took you long enough."

"Better late than never?" He smiles faintly.

At the feel of the lorry parking, Blaine abruptly tears his gaze from us to stand up. We all follow suit, straightening Kevlar and smoothing cargos, checking that our weapons are all in place. The engine cuts out, marking our cue to prepare.

After an elongated pause, we hear two short raps on the sheet metal that separates us from the driver's cab. Coast is clear. No one has leapt out to intercept Josh, believing him to be making a regular delivery.

Hyland takes the lead, grasping the rolling door and yanking it up after unlatching the industrial clasps. Warner covers him with his gun raised in caution in case our surroundings change, and I swallow a barb when Blaine moves to my side.

Three... two... one...

Nothing. The dockyard is deserted.

With the door fully rolled up, we're free to peer around at the drizzly landscape. Greyscale buildings labelled with directions towards the docks proper, the odd discarded pallet, an array of ancient-looking CCTV cameras that I highly doubt still function.

No assailants.

"Stay alert," Warner orders curtly.

"You're all clear," Kyle informs via the comms. "No movement."

"This doesn't feel right," I mumble.

"They're running a clandestine trafficking operation from a legal port," Blaine replies quietly. "Hardly going to roll out the welcome mat and have flashing signs."

Checking my hip holster for the fifteenth time, I glare at the know-it-all dickhead then follow Warner and Hyland out of the vehicle. We have to jump down onto the rough tarmac, in sight of a nearby building equipped with professional signage.

INTERNATIONAL FREIGHT TERMINAL.

Everyone tenses at the approach of footsteps, the muscles in my shoulders unclenching when Josh greets us with a grin.

"Those were some decent forged documents. They didn't even blink."

Holding a finger to his lips, Hyland shushes the excited recruit. We gather at the rear of the vehicle, naturally falling into a tight formation to protect one another in case we've been spotted.

"Dominic's intel placed Luis's operations in this quadrant." Hyland nods towards a nearby lorry. "There are your fake plates."

Sure enough, Rayna's observation checks out. Only one of the rear doors is now gaping open to reveal an abandoned interior. Completely empty. The sense of unease pooling in my stomach grows, twisting into a knot.

Blaine tentatively circles the empty lorry, crouching to check beneath it before completing a full circuit. He returns, seemingly satisfied it isn't going to explode.

"We still need to check that building," Hyland suggests.

Blaine rolls his lip ring between his teeth. "We don't have the numbers for a fight. Now, if you'd allowed me to involve my people…"

"A bunch of untrained criminals infiltrating an active crime scene? Excellent idea."

"Just a suggestion," he clips out. "No need to use that tone."

"Rayna, can we get a heat scan?" Warner trains his sight on the building. "I want to know what we're sneaking into."

After a couple tense minutes, Rayna's voice crackles down the line.

"Nothing detected, but those concrete walls have to be three feet thick. The drone's infrared camera can't capture accurate readings through that."

"Copy. Thanks."

My head tilts upwards so I can locate the faint black dot of her drone in the air. "We'll have to do this the old-fashioned way. If anyone's left inside, we'll deal with it."

"Quietly," Warner adds.

"Still could be a trap," Josh mutters.

Blaine provides a derisive snort. "Likely."

Cursing, Warner scans over the multiple-story structure. "We move fast and silent. Clear each floor, watch each other's backs and look for any signs of Luis's operation."

"Backup?" Hyland suggests.

Warner adjusts the piece tucked into his ear. "Kyle, I want you to remain above. Stay sharp in case anyone is watching. I need Axel and Archer to come down to follow us."

"Copy that," Archer acknowledges.

"It's going to take us a bit to reach you," Axel advises, rustling with movement. "We're fifteen floors above the dockyard."

"Then you'll just have to catch up. Oscar, update HQ. Have backup on standby in case we need it. Medical evac too."

"Medical?" I gasp.

"There's still a chance Luis may have other victims held here to be exported. Even if he's decided to cut his losses and relocate already."

Fiery strands of anger strengthen my spine, allowing all distractions to fall away. I roll my shoulders back as we approach the set of double doors, marked with workplace warning signs.

Stepping through the entrance, a rudimentary reception area with badly poured concrete floors houses a sole security guard. The pudgy-faced man immediately stands when he sees us barging in, his eyes bulging at our guns.

"What the...?"

"Easy." Warner quickly trains his gun on him. "We have a warrant."

"Who are you people?"

"Sabre Security. Put your hands up."

"You can't just barge in here!"

"Sir, I need you to stand down. This is now an active crime scene."

"I'm calling—"

At the sight of him reaching for the walkie-talkie on his cluttered desk, Blaine erupts into movement. He disregards Warner's yell, launching across the room to elegantly vault the man's desk.

Shouting emanates from the fast-moving tangle of limbs as the two men grapple. Hyland grabs the walkie-talkie when we close the distance, peering down at the floor where Blaine has the poor sod restrained with an arm pinned behind his back.

"Madden." Warner sighs.

"Do you want anyone to know we're here?"

"Get off me!" the man screeches. "I'll call the police!"

Blaine yanks his arm higher, slapping a hand over the man's mouth to silence his scream. "We are the fucking police."

Damn. I do not find this hot.

If I repeat it enough, I may believe it.

When Blaine looks up at me and winks, I nearly lose my panties. My eye roll earns me a dirty grin next. He knows exactly what he's doing, and the asshole is proud of it.

Taking the handcuffs that Hyland tosses at him, I watch Blaine trap the guard in place. His proficiency at securing handcuffs with only one hand is far too intriguing.

"Where should we put him?" Warner muses aloud as his eyes scan our surroundings.

Josh turns to study the barebones space. "Perhaps…"

CRACK.

With little ceremony, Blaine smashes the guard's skull against the concrete, turning his limbs to jelly. Blood trickles down his unconscious face, causing a stream of choice words to spill from Warner.

"We're operating within the confines of the law, Madden!"

"You are," he agrees. "I'm here to get the job done."

"He's a bystander!"

"That's your problem to worry about. Not mine."

Pushing the guard's limp form aside, Blaine deftly rises to his feet. Naturally, he stops to brush the odd speckles of concrete dust from his t-shirt and leather jacket like the mere sight offends him.

"Onwards? He won't be out for long."

When he steps past us all to lead the way, Hyland makes no attempt to block his path. "Fucking lunatic."

"You just realising that?" Warner spits in frustration.

"Hey, you pardoned the psycho."

"Don't remind me."

We catch up to Blaine then inch deeper into the terminal, passing empty offices filled with filing cabinets and dark desktop computers, boards plastered in shipping manifestos and half-empty vending machines.

The farther we traverse without seeing another soul, the deeper my anxiety sinks its claws in. Everything about this place seems normal. There's nothing to suggest it's a front for something far darker and illegal.

"There's nothing here," I whisper.

Warner walks beside me, his gun still raised. "If Luis was here, he's long gone."

"Did they know we were coming?"

"I don't see how."

"So what do we do now?"

"Keep moving," he replies in a low tenor. "We need to check for any evidence."

Beyond the offices and storage rooms, a vast loading bay is cluttered with neat rows of packed pallets. Each row is organised alphabetically, labelled with plastic-wrapped customs documents and shipping manifestos.

We carefully search every inch of the massive storage room, hackles raised and guns at the ready, but not a single threat presents itself. The place is empty. Not so much as an unlabelled box or splatter of blood to suggest anything illegal passed through here.

With each corner of the main floor assessed, we converge in the centre of the cardboard box city to debrief. Our infiltration was silent, invisible. Nothing to tip off anyone inside. Yet Luis isn't here, and we're empty-handed.

"Anything?" Axel whispers into our ears.

"Beyond the security guard Madden knocked out?" Warner grunts. "Not a damn soul."

"Well, fuck. That's disappointing."

"We'll sweep the place in case Luis has anything stowed away. Looks like it may be a false lead, though. The vehicle was abandoned, and if he was here, he's already cleared out."

"Bollocks," Axel hisses. "I'll pluck the rest of that asshole's teeth out for wasting our time."

"Why play this game?" I frown at our surroundings.

"Dominic Pit is a snake," Hyland seethes from behind me. "He's going down for a long time and he'd do anything to disrupt our investigation. This is him fucking with us."

"No."

"No?" Warner echoes.

"We have to be missing something." I scan up and down the rows of boxes. "Dominic held out for hours before giving us this information. What was he protecting if Luis is already gone?"

Silence falls. Palpable. Tension-riddled. Half-formed thoughts fill the still air all around us, the echoing emptiness holding secrets we can't seem to grasp hold of.

"He wanted us to come," Josh eventually breaks the quiet.

"Why?" Warner flaps his empty hand. "If no one is here, then this isn't a trap."

A living darkness falls over Blaine's face, capturing my gaze. "A trap is only a trap if you don't know about it. If you do know about it… then it's a challenge."

"And what better way to lure us in than by giving us exactly what we asked for?" The words make my throat spasm.

A distant-sounding crackle causes us to collectively flinch, all searching around for the source of the odd sound. When a voice trickles from the PA system tucked into the corner of the lofty building, fear chews away at the lining of my stomach.

"Close." A voice cackles. "But not everyone left."

"Motherfucker," Hyland blasts. "Get down!"

The first red beam of light appears from high above us. In those precious few seconds, my brain is too slow. It slices through the dust too fast for any of us to comprehend, landing on my immediate left.

Josh.

The scream that rips out of me feels deafening in the silence of the sniper shot. One moment, we're standing in a close circle. The next, Josh smashes to his knees with violent force, a burst of red exploding from his unprotected throat.

"GET DOWN!"

My eardrums protest the volume of Warner's shout. I'm barely able to process the blur from Blaine throwing himself in my direction. Watching Josh grapple at his spewing throat is sending me into a spiral.

Another sniper shot streaks above us, slashing straight through where Blaine had been standing. His body crashes into mine, bones smacking together, sending us both plummeting to the concrete floor.

Deep pain bites into me as we twist and roll, grinding to a halt behind a fully-loaded pallet. The feeble protection allows me a moment to look up, frantically searching the space where we'd stood.

"Josh!" I scream.

Around his curled-up body, deep crimson splatters coalesce to create an oceanic wave of red. Josh gargles and jerks like a fish on a hook as blood pours from his neck, forming a geyser-like spray.

"No!" Hyland howls.

He and Warner have taken cover behind a pallet of wrapped boxes, watching Josh choke on his own blood. None of us can move an inch to step in or help him. Not without meeting the same fate.

"Shooter," Warner pants into his comms.

"Incoming!" Archer booms back. "Location?"

"Main floor. We… have a casualty."

"Who?" Axel's voice wails into my ear canal.

Their urgent yelling fades into the background as Blaine shifts his weight on top of me, using two hands to tightly cup my face. His long, lithe body presses me into the floor, ensuring I'm fully covered.

"These boxes won't protect us from a bullet," Blaine rushes out. "We need to move now before they take another shot. Get ready."

"Josh… Shooter… The…"

"Ember? Snap out of it." Fingers dig deep into my skin, pinching my jaw in a tight grip. "I'm going to get us both out of here, but I need you to focus."

After a second, I summon a numb nod.

"Good girl. Let's move."

Blaine rolls sideways to free me. I scrabble up to press my back into the stack of boxes, spotting the others crouched in preparation to move. We all take one last look at Josh, his gargling becoming quieter as the pool of blood grows around him.

Survival mode feels like slipping back into comfortable clothing. I let the cold detachment sink into me, wrapping me in a chill that crystallises the world into one simple task. Outlive my opponent.

We're still in the centre of the building, far from the entrance we slipped in through. Backup won't reach us yet. Blaine's right—this room is a shooting gallery. We wandered straight into the lion's den.

"We have to move." I shift in anticipation.

Warner raises a fist, clenched in a clear sign to hold. "Steady."

"What about Josh?" Hyland's growl is thick.

"Too late. He's gone."

The fury spreading on Hyland's face is fucking apocalyptic. He spares Josh's now-still body a long look, face warping and eyes darkening with threatening storm clouds. My heart shatters for him. For Warner. For another loss this represents.

"Hy?" Warner clasps his shoulder. "You need to hold it together."

"Yeah." He visibly swallows.

"Ready?"

"Affirmative."

"Then let's go."

Hyland pulls the gun from his side-holster, checking the clip and tensing in preparation to flee. When the speaker high above us crackles again, we all freeze, going stock-still.

"No one else has to get hurt. We only want you, 768."

Icy prickles nudge the back of my mind.

That voice...

"Shooter is positioned at approximately two o'clock from me based on the direction of the shot," Blaine murmurs into his earpiece. "Fire three shots, then bail left, ducking behind that pallet there."

"You're assuming there's only one gunman," Warner rasps.

"Praying."

"We'll be shot either way," Hyland utters grimly.

"Then there's no other option," Blaine asserts.

"Agreed."

Warner shakes his head in consternation. "On my count."

All hunched in anticipation, we wait for Warner's cue. He jabs a hand to the left, fingers outstretched, then he rises to fire off three successive shots high into the terminal. Hyland takes the opportunity to dive after us towards the next pallet.

"Go, go, go!"

More shots. A whoosh of displaced air. Boxes exploding behind us as we duck and dive, treating each flimsy stack as an armoured fortress rather than cardboard and shrink-wrap. Between popping off shots, Warner sticks close on our tail.

"There!" Blaine points towards a fire escape.

"Move," Hyland barks. "Faster!"

I'm half-shoved through the heavy metal door, a shower of dust raining down on us when a shot embeds itself in the wall mere inches above our heads. We tumble outside, emerging into a litter-strewn back alley. Cloying salt in the air tells me the water is close.

"Keep moving!" Warner bellows.

Blaine urges me forwards, a hand at my back. "Go, Ember!"

Somehow, I end up at the front of the convoy, leading us towards the light spilling into the alleyway. Tall cinder block walls guide us to the pier where a built-in loading dock stretches before us, directly attached to the open sea.

But we aren't alone.

A welcoming committee awaits.

My feet skate to an abrupt halt, almost causing Blaine to slam into me before he pivots. Directly ahead, a semi-circle of armed assailants train multiple guns on our group. One by one, each masked figure slams the lid down on Luis's intricate trap.

No... wait. It can't be.

That isn't Luis.

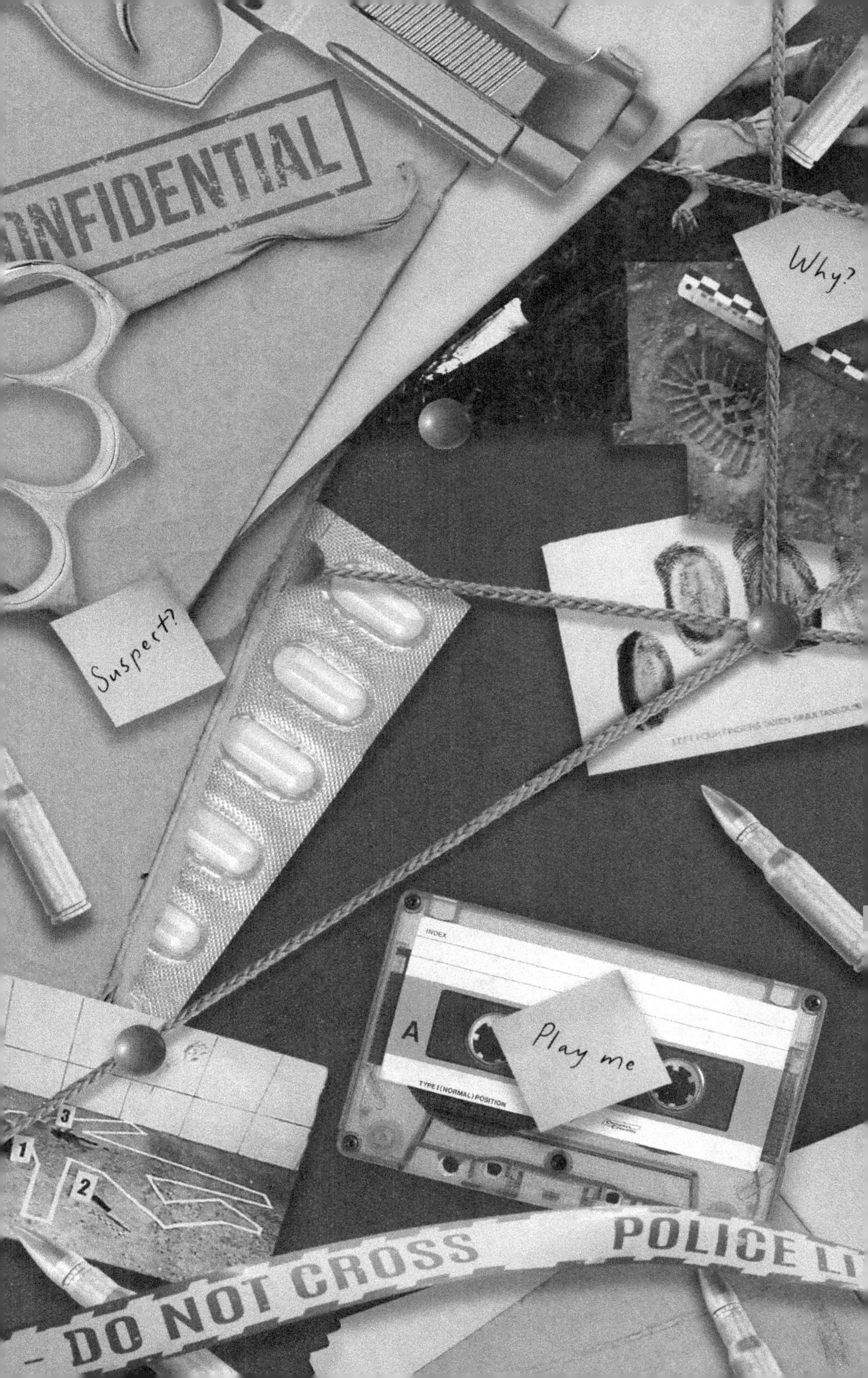

CONFIDENTIAL
Why?
Suspect?
A
Play me
INDEX
TYPE I (NORMAL) POSITION
DO NOT CROSS
POLICE LINE

play
me
DO NOT CROSS
Suspect?
NOT CROSS
POLICE L

8

EMBER

GODDESS – XANA

Past and present collide somewhere in the battleground that separates our two groups, carving deep fissures in my mind that unravel my sanity. It's familiar territory after spending six years existing in those crevasses to survive the trauma of captivity.

Each iteration of those horrific years lives in the face grinning at me. The torturous training sessions where survival was hammered into my broken skeleton. Fight after fight, proving my worth to the masters who held me hostage. Shedding blood to guarantee my next breath.

Carlos Morello.

Unspeakable, twisted memories form an onslaught, pouring from his painfully cold stare. At his amused chortling, my state of shock shatters, allowing rage to infest the skin stretched tight over

my bones.

"You," I spit out.

"Took you long enough, 768."

Flashing pincer-like teeth, emphasised by his wrinkled olive skin and piercing eyes that gleam with victory, Carlos looks perfectly at home in the breezy dockyard. He's unchanged. Stocky. Corded with muscle. Shoulders slightly hunched. Fists curled.

"*Mierda,* it's been a long time." Carlos smiles slyly. "Thanks for joining us."

"Where's Luis?"

"Indisposed. You'll be dealing with me now."

"Meaning what?"

"Meaning he has outlived his usefulness. Even Señor Gael's patience is limited."

The others hover around me, creating a circle of protection. All my focus remains on Carlos. My ex-trainer. Gael's right-hand brute. The monster who helped to break me. And he's standing literal metres from us.

"Weapons down," Carlos commands.

"Like hell!" Hyland yells back.

"You're outnumbered."

Multiple red target dots appear on the three men surrounding me. It doesn't take long for terror to take flight inside me.

"Do as he says," I plead urgently.

"Ember." Hyland starts to move, freezing when the dot follows. "Shit!"

"He won't hesitate to shoot every one of you and drag me away from your dead bodies, kicking and screaming. Trust me. Just drop the guns."

"I'd listen to her, boys." Carlos chuckles.

Blaine releases a snarled curse. "We have no choice."

"I'd rather die," Hyland lashes out.

At his grumbling, Carlos's calm façade shatters. "Now! Do it!"

"Weapons down," Warner concedes defeat in a huff. "Now, Hy."

Metallic clanks signal the discarding of multiple guns, tossed aside and out of reach. I tug mine from my holster then lob it into the mix. If I surrender my gun, Carlos may wait to search me. I can use that to my advantage.

Hyland is the last to surrender his pistol, lip curling in revulsion. Still, Carlos refuses to lift the cavalcade of scopes trained on us, a hair's breadth from sending every single one of us into an early grave.

"Why are you here?" I silently count the men circling my nemesis. "You're a long way from home."

"For you."

"Then it was a wasted trip."

"That remains to be seen." Carlos's laugh is downright sinister. "This all could've been avoided if you'd simply obeyed. No one had to get hurt."

Venom turns my mouth sour. "You killed Josh."

"Señor Gael is most concerned by your continued refusal to return home," Carlos explains pointedly. "This bloodshed is all your fault."

Casting a critical eye over my entourage, Carlos pauses at Blaine's presence. The sneer he unveils is sickeningly smug.

"Blaine Madden."

"You're looking better than the last time we met." Blaine smirks in cold, calculated rage. "I'll take great pleasure in amending that."

"I believe you're standing on the wrong side of this dispute. Your interests would be better served over here."

"I'm fine where I am."

"Your father will be disappointed to hear that."

I don't need to look at Blaine to feel the impact of Carlos's cheap shot. Armed or not, I'm certain that Blaine wants to tear his head clean off with little more than a huff for the inconvenience.

"Where is dear old dad?"

"Give me the girl, and I'll be happy to share," Carlos offers.

Blaine's mouth slams shut, his expression stormy.

"Pity. You're all fools."

"We're here for Thomas Lawson." Warner clutches to a facsimile of control. "This doesn't have to end in a fight. Surrender him to us."

"Ah, the infamous Anaconda Team, I presume." Carlos rolls his neck from side-to-side. "You just couldn't give up on the bitch or her pathetic brother. Could you?"

"Coming here was a mistake, Mr Morello. You're in our jurisdiction now."

"How has that worked for you so far? We've been operating in this country for two decades, *pendejo*. It's never stopped us before."

"You know what happened to Dimitri Sanchez," Hyland interjects from my right side. "Would your employer care to follow in his footsteps?"

"Dimitri was eliminated by his own foolishness," Carlos dismisses. "He had grown reckless, obsessed. We don't mourn his loss."

"Then what happens when you meet the same fate? Who will Gael have left then?"

"We have plenty of allies. This isn't a fight you can win."

Tension creates an unbearable pressure in the sea air, encasing us all in a suffocating bubble that only bloodshed can penetrate. The same fortitude that entered me when I tackled each fight Carlos arranged allows me to step forward now.

Every last gun pointed at us remains locked in place. That's when I realise they aren't aiming at me. Not a single one of Carlos's thugs. All of them remain focused on the men spread out behind me, holding them hostage.

"Em," Warner warns.

I hold up a hand. "Don't move. He only wants me."

"Quite right." Carlos beams at me.

"Where is my brother?"

"Do you want to see him again?"

"Where is he?" I repeat.

"Come with us and find out."

I take another step forward, despite more protests coming from behind me. I have no idea how Hyland is holding himself back from charging after me—bullet or not. My next words won't help his turmoil.

"I'm tired of running. We can discuss a mutually beneficial surrender… once I have proof of life. I want to see Tom."

"Surrender?" Hyland hisses. "Fuck no!"

A scuffle from behind causes all of Carlos's backup to tense, fingers dancing on triggers. I glance back to see Warner and Blaine restraining Hyland's arms, barely stopping him from chasing after me and killing himself.

Returning my gaze to Carlos, he stares at me, and I stare right fucking back. Both assessing. Weighing up our opponent. Backup aside, I think I could take him, though we'd both emerge bloodied. But if that's the way it has to be, then so be it.

"Caged rats always sing for their supper in the end." His smile drips revolting satisfaction. "Very well, 768. Have it your way."

Carlos nods to one of his men. My heart rate ratchets up several notches when two foot soldiers disappear down the steps at the back of the dockyard towards where the cargo ship is moored for its resupply.

"You know, helping these fools is a waste of your talent," he adds in distaste. "All that time spent training you… and this is what you choose to do with your gifts."

"Gifts?" I laugh flatly.

"We created you."

"You beat me! Tortured me! Broke me!"

"I created the perfect weapon." He gestures towards the men at my back. "Not a whore to be kept on display in Sabre Security's hall of fame."

The wind blowing off the North Sea cuts into me, adding to my shaking. My nails slice into my palms where I'm clenching my fists tight enough to hold my rage back. By a fucking shoestring.

The two goons quickly return, ascending the dock's steps with a sagging heap of skin and bone between them. My entire line of sight narrows to that barely recognisable ghost as bloodthirst rages through me.

Ghostly pale. Limp. Unconscious.

Misshapen from bruises and swelling.

My big brother.

Heartbreak is such a weak term. Frail. Pathetic. As if a human heart could quietly break like a cracked eggshell. The sight of my brother doesn't break my heart—it smashes, pulverises and sweeps it away without any care for the remaining dust.

"Tom…"

"Here you are." Carlos waves grandly towards his captive. "Proof of life."

"What the hell did Luis do to him?"

"It's safe to say that disobedience runs in the family," he chortles. "You weren't just being a brat all those years to make my job difficult."

Tom's level of disobedience is spelled across every inch of visible skin beneath the ripped, bloodstained shirt and trousers hanging from his starved body. Another chunk of my shattered heart splats against the floor of my stomach.

The single dependable constant in my life despite our ups and downs... is now almost unrecognisable beneath mottled bruises. Purple, angry blotches that tarnish his pasty-white face, neck and arms.

The crusted lacerations that slash each bruise appear to be oozing. He's being dragged, his legs buckled and unresponsive, head swaying like a loose bag of change attached to his shoulders. A terrified part of me worries he's already lost to us.

Pure hatred turns my words to icy daggers. "For every mark on him, I'm going to tear a chunk of flesh from your body with my bare fucking teeth."

"Ah, the fighting spirit. Nice to see you haven't lost it in retirement."

Fuck this. I'll go with Carlos just for the privilege of killing him myself. He's taunted me for the very last time.

"What will it be, 768?" Carlos watches his men drop Tom's lifeless carcass at their feet. "Perhaps I'm open to a trade after all."

"Tom walks free. My team too."

"Ember—"

"Shut up," I cut Warner off.

"We don't trade lives."

With great restraint, I don't scream at him.

"Em!" he urges. "Listen to me!"

Carlos studies the scene with visible exasperation. It's the same glare that still features in my nightly torment. He spent hours watching me get beaten to a pulp just to criticise me afterwards.

"What makes you think we'd accept those terms?" he challenges.

My eyes narrow to slits. "Because you want me."

"I personally couldn't care less about you." He flicks his wrist dismissively. "But what Señor Gael wants, he gets. My job is rather simple in that respect."

"Then let's keep this simple. Hand over Tom, and let's go."

"Just like that?"

"Just like that."

"Compliant isn't a word I'd use to describe you." Carlos looks down at Tom's still body. "However, the sooner I'm out of this cesspit, the better."

"Then give me what I want."

"Ember!" Hyland calls my name.

Biting my tongue, I glance over my shoulder at their frozen statures. Only Blaine wears an unreadable expression while the others boast matching masks of conflict and terror. None of them have dared to move an inch.

My lips mouth a single command.

Be ready.

Hyland angrily shakes his head from side to side.

Trust me, I mouth.

As defeat sinks into Warner's baby blues, I don't give them the opportunity to protest. Carlos is muttering to his men when I turn back around. To hold my nerve, I refuse to look at Tom on the ground. I'll only want to collapse beside him.

"Are we doing this or what?"

"Very well." Carlos straightens to attention.

"Then let my team have Tom, and we can be on our way."

"One move otherwise, and I'll send them all to an early grave. Is that understood?"

"Loud and clear."

Two of Carlos's men hoist Tom up, dragging him into the no man's land between our two factions. I ignore Hyland, shouting like a madman and move to meet them. A single look warns the approaching assailant to keep his hands off me.

"If you want to keep those attached, I wouldn't do that. I'll walk alone."

"Suit yourself." He shows me his palms.

The idiot rightfully backs off, indicating for me to follow them into enemy territory. I keep my chin held high, shoulders back and muscles tensed while walking straight into Carlos's orbit. Each step closer feels like battering another nail into my coffin.

"Hello, 768."

"You got what you wanted after all."

"Wasn't that easy?" he preens, eyeing my approach. "Good choice."

I halt in front of him. "Lower the guns on my friends."

"Why would I do that?"

"Tom needs medical attention. Let them go."

"Do you think I'm that foolish, *puta*?"

"You already have me," I snarl. "They're unarmed. We're still outnumbered. Lower the guns, and let them see to my brother."

"You'd do well to remember that tone never worked on me."

When Carlos darts forward, the heavy strike shouldn't be a surprise. He always did teach with his fists. I don't move to dodge the blow, allowing it to smash into my cheek so hard, I know his knuckles will be imprinted on my skin.

Blood seeps across my tongue as my teeth clack down, and the punch's force sends me crashing to my knees. My neck wrenches to the side, eyes streaming and skin burning from blood rising to form a bruise.

"Ember! Em!"

Hyland's yelling reaches a fever pitch, cutting into the ringing that fills my ears. The full force of Carlos's strength is enough to shake loose bones and teeth. And I haven't taken it without a fight for so long, I almost forgot what it's like to absorb his anger.

"Don't touch her!" Hyland's yelling is anguished. "Fuck! Ember!"

"You've cast a spell on them." Carlos tsks above the enraged yelling. "That one would risk a bullet just to keep you from me. Shall I put one in him?"

I blink through the hazy fog infecting my sight. "Of course, you don't understand the concept of loyalty."

"I understand it perfectly well. You ran from us. How is that loyal?"

Carlos's leg extends to deliver a hard kick to my chest. Pain cracks across my breastbone, sinking into my muscles. The momentum pushes me backwards onto my spine where I let myself crumple.

A kick to the ribcage follows, causing my bones to creak and groan. The flaring of painful heat in my torso is acute, and the blood that's gathered in my throat erupts, spraying across the ground. Carlos seems to relish in the shouts his beating is creating.

It's like he wants to provoke them. He wants an excuse to tell his men to fire. For each kick and stomp he lays out on my defenceless body, I can imagine Hyland battling to escape his teammates' restraints. One step and those red dots will seal their fate.

"What? No fighting back?" Carlos goads me.

All I offer is a grunt as he takes his pound of flesh. Not the first time he's beaten me stupid.

"You disappoint me. I thought you were better than this."

Let him think that he's winning.

Each time his limbs slam into me, my determination solidifies into an invisible dagger. One I'll soon slip between his fucking ribs. I want him to relish in beating me down one last time before I show him that now… he isn't the one in control.

I am.

Staring up at the greyscale sky allows my vision to settle, the fuzz at the edges receding after a few short breaths. I don't make a sound when Carlos hauls my floppy body up, wrapping his big, hairy hand around my throat.

I'm pinned like dangling prey, blood seeping from my nose and mouth. My throbbing body is already going numb. In the aftermath of a fight, I learned to tune everything out. The injuries were the price of success.

"That's better. You need to relearn your place."

A whimper sneaks through my blood-stained lips.

"If you survive Señor Gael's punishment, perhaps you'll be allowed to live and fight again. But you have to prove your worth to our operation, 768. Earn back his trust."

I'd rather die.

Right here, right now.

"You may approach now," Carlos calls to my team. "Take your prize and go."

One by one, the guns are lowered. Targets disappear. Relief burgeons in me at the sight of Warner releasing Hyland, but not before whispering in his ear. I can see Hyland's reaction from here—throat bobbing, jaw clenched, nostrils flaring.

As a silent unit, they approach Tom's lifeless form. Each movement is jerky and tentative, prepared for the scene to ignite at a single move in the wrong direction.

"Watch them abandon you." Hot breath tickles my ear, driving the torment home. "Now that they've got their boy back."

Kneeling beside Tom, Warner clasps his slack face between his hands, murmuring his name but getting no response. Hyland stands over them in a protective stance, his dark gaze locked on me. Then I find Blaine's stare.

He nods once. Subtly. Commanding. Full of trust and encouragement. Wiggling my fingers loosens the cuff of the tight black jacket hiding the sheath strapped to my forearm. The same blade he insisted that I wear today.

Cool steel kisses my wrist, sliding free from its hiding spot to nudge my palm. The blade gives me the courage to strain against Carlos's grip. He peers down at me with a leer.

"Time to go. We have a long journey ahead."

Lips puckering, I gather saliva on my tongue. *Splat*. The blood-tinged globule lands in his eye, causing his hand to slacken long enough for me to twist. It's all I need. The blade is already nestled in my cupped hand.

"I'm going nowhere with you!"

"You little..." Spittle flies from Carlos's mouth.

Necks are delicate things. Fleshy. Vulnerable. I suppose that's why they aimed for Josh's. It's precisely why I aim the curved switchblade upwards, ramming it into his throat at a perfect right angle.

Soft squelching rewards my efforts as his skin parts like warm butter. Muscles slice without protest. Blood erupts from the wound, granting me immediate gratification as I let the warm moisture spatter on my face like hot oil.

Sticky. Fresh. Sweet.

An unspoiled reward for enduring his punishment.

His arm slides away, body shuddering and lids blown wide open to show the veiny whites of his eyes. I watch every detail. Each second of deathly agony played out in real time. Lips flapping. Saliva bubbling. Muscles slackening.

"You killed the person I was," I murmur to him. "Now I get to take your life from you too."

Sliding the blade from his throat, my fingers slip on warm copper. Carlos collapses against me, his nearly-dead weight dragging me to the ground. It's a welcome defeat. Triumphant. He spasms and gurgles, holding me in an involuntary embrace.

Still, I hold his dying body closer than a lover. I want to feel the moment his heart ceases to beat. When the life drains from his veins, he'll be in my arms. The woman he tried to break. The fighter he forged in fire.

With palms sliding in the crimson stickiness flooding around us, it takes all my strength to shove Carlos to the side when his jerking ceases. My battered body screams for relief, a familiar form of fierce agony.

When I look at Carlos, glassy vacantness stares back. Two empty pits that once held malice are little more than soulless oblivion now. The confirmation slices invisible strings that have held me hostage since the day I fled, puppeteering my every move.

Carlos is dead.

I killed him.

I fucking won.

Lost in those void chasms, I fail to mount a defence against the heavy weight that cuts short my triumph with a tackle. One of Carlos's men locks me in a grappling match, two steel-hands attempting to cinch around my neck to choke the life from me.

"Stupid bitch," he spits in accented English. "You will die for that!"

The instincts I honed across hundreds of battles snap into place. *Play dead. Reposition. Attack.* My fingers clench around the sticky blade, waiting for Carlos's brute to roll and flip me onto my back.

His ragged nails bury deep in my throat, miniature razors piercing my oesophagus. Fire fills me from head to toe as oxygen becomes a rare commodity.

"Señor Gael can have your rotting bones!"

The moment I slip the blade into his exposed midriff, I see it in his gaze. His pupils blast open, and his mouth flops with a shocked gasp. I pull back the blade, sinking it into his stomach. Then his side. His torso. Over and over until organs pierce and skin rips open.

I can hardly feel the movement of pushing him aside and wrenching myself up to advance on the next target. Fists flying. Limbs wrestling to gain the upper hand. My blade sinking deep into soft tissue and between bones.

Slash. Stab. Slash.

Blood replaces skin, forming a tight curtain across my whole existence. I'm drenched in it. The warmth. The triumph of unshackling a part of myself I've only ever accessed in the ring then buried the day that jet landed back in England.

Slash. Stab. Slash.

Human life shouldn't be so easy to take. Little more than the snuffing out of a candle. Inconsequential. In seconds, families are destroyed, lives changed, lines crossed. Yet that doesn't halt me from mowing down each obstacle in my path.

Slash. Stab. Slash.

None of it matters. Not even those watching the return of 768. Her inevitable comeback. The moment she overpowers my body to find a permanent home—one that won't allow her to be buried again. She's back and here to stay.

When my knees buckle, carrying me to the hard ground, the blade clatters at my side. Liquid death drips from my face, hands, torso. Coating rapidly forming bruises and mangled flesh. Evidencing the severing of mortal coils without so much as a single regret.

The world flashes in and out. Red-soaked carnage becomes bright strobe flashes, cutting reality into bite-sized trauma. Voices nearing. Footsteps. The blast of gunfire. Strong hands on my shoulders, fingers pressing into my wet cheeks.

"Em?"

I blink. Breathe. Shudder.

"Come back, dimples."

Amber-orange eyes beg me for recognition.

"Let 768 go now. She did a good job, but I need you to come back to us. Come back to me, babe."

"A-Ax?"

"Yeah. I'm here now. Sorry I'm late to the party."

Clenching my eyes shut, it takes monumental effort to fight off the red lens across my vision. All I can see is blood. Everywhere, covering everything. Shredding my morals to the bare bone. Unleashing a monstrous, mind-numbing thirst to rain hellfire on every last threat we face.

The feel of Axel's hands on my face cuts through years' worth of conditioning, giving me the chance to claw my way back. Piece by piece. Cell by cell. Retaking control of my brain is a monumental effort, muddled by pain and trauma.

"It's okay, Em. Tom is safe. Everyone's alive."

When I peek at Axel, he's crouched in front of me, blurred movement zipping all around us. All I can see is his wide ember-like eyes, lashes thick against fear-filled honey.

"Still want to save me?" I whisper brokenly.

"No need. I was wrong. Sometimes… rage does have its place."

POLICE LINE
POLICE LINE — DO NOT CROSS
Weapon?
CONFIDENTIAL

9

HYLAND

WILL YOU LOVE ME WHEN I'M DEAD – AMIRA ELFEKY

My grip on the phone tightens, aggravation pouring from every part of me. Why does co-parenting have to be so goddamn complicated? I'm putting the past aside. I just wish Jayce would do the same.

> Hyland: I'm not cancelling Luke's visit for the hell of it. There's no need to create an argument.

> Jayce: An argument? The news is reporting every hour on Sabre Security's latest cock up. A fatality! Luke clearly isn't safe with you.

Frustration blows from my nostrils.

Hyland: It was an active operation. Everything is under control. Bring Luke over next week.

Silence. She's ignoring me now.

Hyland: Please.

My short nails drum against the phone case as I wait.

Jayce: I'll think about it.

Fine. I'll take that over a straight-up denial.

At the sound of the nearby door opening, I tuck my phone away to greet Doctor Richards. He emerges from the ICU's quiet room with a frown, wrinkled beneath his coif of silvery hair. I swear, the old dinosaur is fucking immortal.

Arms folded, I tap my foot impatiently. "Well?"

"Good afternoon, Hyland. Pleased to see you too."

"Give it up, Richards. Did she talk to you?"

Positioning his leather satchel on his shoulder, Richards skates a hand down his floral shirt. It's another particularly ugly number, the lurid-yellow flowers stark against sky-blue fabric. I'm convinced he dresses in a dark room each morning.

"No." He sighs.

"Shit. This isn't good."

"Ember wants to be here with Tom right now. I'd suggest you appease her."

I move farther down the wipe-clean linoleum that lines the corridor in case Ember's listening from behind the closed door. Richards follows with another world-weary sigh. I don't know why he's so tired; it's not like he's been awake for over thirty hours straight like we have.

"She tore through five men using nothing but a foldable switchblade to gut them," I hiss out. "It's a miracle she wasn't more badly injured."

"I'm aware of the situation."

"And?"

"While Ember's actions are troubling, I cannot force therapy on someone who is refusing to talk. Her brother's on a ventilator. Allow her some grace."

"She needs our help!"

"Then listen to me." He raises an expectant brow. "What happened was extreme, to say the least, but you can't force her to open up. She needs time, compassion. Patience."

While his advice makes total sense, I'm struggling to have an ounce of patience right now. Not while Ember's clammed up like she's forgotten how to speak and simply stares ahead with dead eyes. She saved our skins, but killing those men did something to her.

Something cataclysmic.

And I'm afraid it's irreversible.

"You're sure this isn't tied to her epilepsy?" I worry my bottom lip. "Like an absence seizure or something?"

"I'd advise a follow-up with her specialist, but it's clear to me this is a trauma response. Ember spent a long time in survival mode. It's bound to kick in when she's triggered."

My head bobs in a loose nod. Survival mode. Right. Like a crashed computer booting back up in safe mode. The idea of the girl I'm falling for needing to be in that mode at all makes me want to punch the fucking wall.

"Speaking of…" He pins me with an assessing stare. "How are you handling the events?"

"Me? What? Fine. I'm fine."

"You watched a colleague lose his life," Richards elucidates.

"Trust me, I know."

"It isn't the first time this has happened either."

His words cause long-gone faces to flash through my mind's eye. The women and men we've lost along the way. Lives sacrificed in the pursuit of justice and a few taken as penance too. Grief is an unfortunate side effect of our work.

Doesn't make it any easier, though.

"You need to take some time to process your own thoughts and feelings, Hyland. It's understandable for this to bring up bad memories."

"No." I wave him off. "Go give Warner the annoying therapy talk. He's lost far more people than I have, and I don't care what he says. He's not okay."

"I'll be having the same conversation with him, but right now, I'm concerned about you."

"I don't need your concern."

"You're not in shock?"

"No! I'm not!"

My deep yell bounces off the walls, echoing down the corridor to reach nearby hospital bays. Immediately, I recoil and clamp my mouth shut. The acknowledgement in Richards's gaze only intensifies my humiliation.

"Debrief." Richards's tone brooks no argument. "Monday morning, 8am sharp. I want you in my clinical room at HQ, or I'll be driving back here."

Gritting my teeth, I nod once.

"Warner, Axel and the Falcon Team will be receiving the same instruction. I want you to keep a close eye on Ember's behaviour too and call me immediately should further violence ensue."

"Further... violence?"

"She isn't herself right now," he says ominously.

With a light squeeze on my shoulder, Richards trundles off towards the elevator. I watch the doddery old man leave, my gut burning. Why is he making this about me? I can handle loss.

Like he said, it isn't the first time.

But... fuck. Josh.

I experienced this god-awful feeling during our last large-scale trafficking investigation. That saga was equally as messy. Violence, betrayal and bloodshed defined the Briar Valley case, and now we're back in the trenches of the same damn fight.

And Josh is dead.

On my fucking watch.

Pulling my phone back out, my thumb hovers over Willow's missed calls from the last few hours. She must've seen the news. I bet she's pacing up and down in her cabin. I'm about to return her calls when there's a crash from inside the quiet room.

When I barge inside, the scene pulls me up short. Ember stands in the middle of the small space, blandly decorated in neutral, inoffensive colours. Her shoulders heave as she stares at the smashed vase in front of her, broken glass and shredded flowers littering the floor.

I gently click the door shut. "Ember?"

She doesn't react.

"Hey, red."

Nothing.

"Ember. It's Hyland."

Tentatively, I inch closer to crowd her shaking back. She doesn't react when I rest a hand on her hip, thumb skating over the sliver of badly bruised skin that her cropped t-shirt reveals above comfortably loose, grey sweats.

Oscar volunteered to source everyone a change of clothes when we followed medical evac—with Tom in tow—to the local hospital. None of us have been home. Not to rest or debrief. Though we did convince Ember to shower the blood off after her examination.

"I need you to talk to me right now."

It takes a couple of seconds for her to come alive.

"He's on a ventilator because of me."

The hit of relief her broken voice provides is intense but fleeting. Her words are flat, matter of fact. Even I can sense the abject pain underscoring them.

"What happened to Tom isn't your fault."

"He was taken to get to me. That's as close to the definition of *my fault* as humanly possible."

"Tom consults for Sabre. He knows the risks."

"He didn't sign up to be beaten, starved and locked in a freezing shipping container." Heartache drips from her tone. "You heard the doctors. Severe pneumonia."

"I heard."

"He can't even breathe for himself right now, and his lungs may never recover. All of his wounds are infected. He's malnourished, dehydrated. The lot."

"How exactly is any of this your fault?"

"If I weren't here, he would be safe!" she explodes, high-pitched and furious. "How the fuck do I live with that? He almost died!"

With gentle hands, I slowly steer Ember to turn around. The sight of her barely open, swollen eyes makes my insides twist. There's a white strip across her nose, stark against the purple and green bruises that match her arms, chest and ribs.

She's technicoloured and barely able to move without wincing, but this formidable warrior still finds a way to turn the blame inwards. I don't know if it's selflessness or bone-headed stubbornness, but she can cut it out. I'm not listening to this self-deprecating shit.

"You didn't just save his life, Em. You saved all of us. As much as I fucking hated it, your actions got us out of there. You took down Carlos and his men."

"I allowed Tom to get hurt."

"You allowed nothing." I grip her hip tighter, pinching her chin with my other hand. "Matter of fact, you saved his life. You're the reason he's still breathing at all."

"Fixing my mistakes doesn't deserve praise, Hy."

"But bravery and skill does."

Letting my thumb graze over her lips, they part on a ragged breath that matches the sorrow rioting in her blue-grey flecks. She's exhausted, hardly able to stand straight from fatigue. But still, Ember doesn't move to accept my comfort.

"Next time you sacrifice yourself, I'm going to tie you to my bed and spank your ass until it's fucking raw," I say gruffly.

Her brow raises. "Is that so?"

"We make decisions as a team. Not alone."

"I did it for the team," she replies. "To save it."

"You infuriating woman. Don't you get it yet?"

Nestling my forehead against hers, I breathe in the scent of hospital soap. Cheap shampoo. And beneath it, the dark, tantalising essence of our girl. The victim who refused to take that title laying down.

"There is no team without you, red. Not anymore. Sacrificing yourself will never save us. It will be the absolute death of this team… and our family."

The impenetrable lake that's frozen over her irises cracks enough for hope to light a dull spark. I latch onto that flash of light and capture it before she can extinguish the flame with her own self-doubt.

Her lips part like they were sculpted for me to capture. My touch is featherlight, careful. The last thing I want to do is hurt her. The world has done that plenty enough, and right now, I want to fucking *cherish* her. The way she deserves to be.

Fingers gliding through her slightly damp hair, I cradle her head as my tongue slides into her mouth. Her warmth is all the reassurance I need. Ember's still in there. She's still the woman I've spent months watching, assessing, training. The woman we need.

If she needs my touch to come back to herself, I'll give it to her. Fuck everything else. I've wasted enough time dancing around my feelings for this beautiful creature, and I'll be damned if I'm going to waste another second holding her at arm's length.

"Hy." She sighs into my mouth. "What are we doing here?"

"I thought that was rather obvious."

"You just saw me with your team leader. And Axel's… well, Axel. But he's involved. I know I said that I wanted this, but not if it hurts you. I won't risk that happening."

My thumb traces painfully swollen flesh around her right eye socket, studying the striations of purple lightning that intermingle with the black and green bruises.

"We're big boys, Ember. Trust us to choose what we're comfortable with. What we're willing to share. And how we navigate the fact that we're all falling in love with you."

She unsteadily drags in air.

"You hadn't figured that out yet?" I tease.

"Well…"

I peck her soft lips again. "I'm not going to pretend this isn't complicated as fuck or will be easy to manage, but I'm also done denying the way I feel. Professional or not, I want this. Us."

She rests her head against my chest. "Complicated as fuck seems like an understatement."

"I'm feeling optimistic." A chuckle cascades from me.

"Someone has to, I suppose."

Two quick knocks on the door announce the shattering of our peaceful bubble. I know it's Axel by the light, fast footsteps moving inside. The pup bounces around like he's perpetually high on life.

"Sorry to interrupt, but Warner asked me to track you down."

Reluctantly, I release Ember. "What does he want?"

"Tom's still sedated, but the doctors have said he's stable enough to be airlifted to London. A bed's opened up in St Thomas's ICU."

Tucking hair behind Ember's ear, I press a kiss to the corner of her mouth. "You hear that? We can go home. Tom's good to be moved."

More vulnerability than I've ever seen from her before stares back at me. Beneath all her invisible, protective armour and sassy responses, Ember's just like the rest of us. All too human. All too breakable. I'd do well to remember that.

"Why didn't I get the invite to cuddle time?" Axel whines.

"Fuck off, pup. We're having a private moment."

"Since when are those allowed? Learn to share, big guy."

Stomping over, Axel makes himself at home behind Ember. His chin lands on her shoulder as he traps her between us without sparing me a glance. Instead, he leans close to bite down on her earlobe.

"Having all the fun without me, dimples?"

"Hardly," she mumbles. "I was ignoring Richards until he admitted defeat and fucked off. Then Hyland decided to declare his undying love for me."

"Brat." I narrow my gaze on her.

The smile it earns me is worth any amount of heartache. I'll disregard the fact that she's ignoring the trained mental health professional… *for now.* At least until I know our Ember's back.

"Well…" Axel grins conspiratorially. "I know circumstances didn't allow for me to rip that Kevlar vest off as promised, but don't forget who was first in line with their undying love."

I glower at the little asshole. "There isn't a fucking queuing system."

"Why not? Gotta be fair, Hy. If we're sharing Ember's affections, I want an even slice."

"I'm not a cake." Her hands push against my chest to wriggle free. "Take me to see Tom. We can discuss this massive clusterfuck later."

Before she can escape, Axel grabs her wrist to pull her towards him. Spinning Ember between us, he backs her up into my chest, his body covering hers so she's well and truly sandwiched. My hands fly down to her waist.

"Going somewhere, babe?"

"Ax, we're in a hospital—"

"Frankly, I don't give a damn. We're discussing this now."

His mouth descends on hers, far more hungrily than the way I gently kissed her. I can feel Ember tense against me, her spine stiffening and ass pushing backwards into my crotch. To my surprise, my cock stirs in response to Axel's meddling.

Each time he kisses her lips, she rocks back and forth, pushing back against his domination. Her fighting spirit is still there, bubbling beneath the surface. It adds unbearable pressure to my growing erection.

Fuck, I'd half made my peace with this whole sharing deal. But I had no intention of getting into this situation. I don't want to watch Axel devouring my girl. Yet seeing her arousal is so fucking hot, I find myself relaxing into it and… hell, craving more.

I wanna know how far he can push her. How she'll react to his touch, his tongue. The way only he can make her feel. My cock grinding into her ass seeks its own satisfaction. Shit, she feels so hot imprisoned between us. All squirmy and flustered.

"Can you feel how hard you're making him?" Axel moans into her mouth. "I'd bet my last paycheck that Hyland's ready to slide between your legs right now."

"God… Ax. Fuck."

"That's my intention, dimples. Not here. But soon—very fucking soon. I need to feel you wrapped around me."

"You've got her all worked up now," I grunt.

Axel flicks me a look. "Well, we can't have that."

"No."

"You good with this?"

"With what?" Ember asks.

I hold Axel's challenging stare. "I am."

"Good," he hums.

Lifting a hand from Ember's waist, I push it underneath the

hem of her cropped t-shirt. She's only wearing a soft, stretchy sports bra to avoid putting pressure on her sore ribs. I can easily inch my fingers past the fabric to cup her breast.

"Hy," she moans.

"Shh, red. Let us make you feel better."

"Both of you?"

Finding her firm nipple, I pinch the bud. "Yes."

As I roll her stiff peak back and forth, eliciting carnal moans from her lips, Axel works on undoing her drawstring. Ember grinds into me, sending another jolt straight to my rock-hard dick.

"Hold her still," Axel instructs.

Pushing her sweats down, he exposes the plain, cotton panties she was given to wear. Ember whines when I grab a handful of her tit and squeeze, my mouth descending on her neck from behind. The little sound is exquisite.

"You heard him." I suck her skin between my teeth, laying down a light bite. "Still, baby. Or I won't be held responsible for bending you over and fucking you against that door."

Her breasts thrust out, filling my palms. Axel snickers from where he's stroking her bare thighs, tracing a single fingertip along her panties' elastic waist.

"Think she likes that idea. I can smell how wet she is."

"Damn you." Ember's curse is guttural.

"Just an observation," he teases. "You've soaked through your panties, Em. Is it the idea of us sharing you that makes you drip like a hungry little slut?"

Hips bucking, she's pushed back against me by Axel's grip on her thighs. I grunt and suck her neck harder, the jolt causing my cock to strain against my cargos for attention. God, I'm fit to burst. But this isn't about me. We're bringing Ember back to herself.

"I said still," Axel chastises.

"Please," she gasps.

He leans in to plant a kiss on her covered mound. "I do love it when you beg. It's so out of character."

"Ax," I warn.

"Alright, alright."

His fingers hook into her panties, drawing them down to pool at her ankles. Ember whimpers, head thrown back against my shoulder. I laugh sinisterly in her ear.

"You'd think I wouldn't be into this, but the idea of Axel eating that wet pussy while I hold you still has me harder than fucking steel, red. How's that for a surprise?"

Axel glances up at me. "I'm surprised."

"Shut up and do your job, pup. The lady's waiting."

He smirks a little. "Then open her legs for me."

Goddamn. That shouldn't be so filthy hot.

"Oh," Ember moans louder.

She's loving this too.

Turned on by her pleasure, I reach down to hook a hand beneath Ember's left leg. She lets me guide it up and open, the stretch exposing her centre to Axel's hungry stare. I hold her there, spreading her cunt wide for his viewing pleasure.

"How's that?" My growl is thick with lust.

"Perfect." He licks his lips. "Look at that pretty pink pussy, all laid out for me."

Lowering his head full of amethyst hair, Axel buries his face between Ember's splayed legs. She shivers against me, her leg jerking in my hand at the feel of his mouth on her cunt. I feel her suck in a stuttered breath and smile.

"Tell me how it feels, red."

"Hy…"

"Do it now."

Axel's head shifts, allowing him a breath before he dives back in. Ember shudders again, gasping lightly. My hips rock forward to push my hard rod into her backside again, showing her how affected I am.

"It feels… good. Fuck! Yes, Ax. P-Please."

"Beg him, Em. Beg for his tongue to make you come."

One hand flicks back to fist my trouser leg. "Touch me too."

"So greedy." I tut under my breath.

Manoeuvring her leg to hook over Axel's shoulder, I bring my hand up to Ember's mouth. She seems to understand without asking, parting her lips to accept two fingers. I swirl them on her tongue, gathering saliva, then lower them to her clit.

"Yes," she whispers.

"Be quiet. I don't want anyone walking in."

With Axel slicking his tongue around Ember's entrance and making a meal from her heat, I take charge of strumming the throbbing bead that makes her squirm. Light shivers are wracking over her.

She's lit up like a live wire, undulating against me with each flick. Seeing how wild and free she is while stripped bare is second only to watching her come back to herself. With our hands on her, Ember's responsive again. *Alive.*

"Do you like that, babe?" Axel peers up with moisture scored across his lips. "When we both play with you like the dirty girl you are?"

"Yes," she mewls.

"You're close, aren't you?"

I feel the moment that he pumps a finger inside her below where I'm rubbing small circles over her clit. Ember bleats in surprise, her head bouncing on my shoulder and legs trembling. My thumb bears down on her clit, making her squeak.

"You're going to come for us," I breathe into her ear. "I want you to soak Axel's hand then watch him clean your mess up so no one knows what we've been doing."

"Yes…" She shudders against me. "Please don't stop."

"Then show me how well you fall apart."

Axel eases my hand from her clit so he can suck the bud into his mouth while finger-fucking her. I return my hand to Ember's breast, tweaking and rolling her stiff nipple. I want her to feel us everywhere.

To think I wasted so much time worrying about some pointless professional boundaries. Like this little vixen didn't barge into my head the minute I laid eyes on her in that crop field, terrified but alert, ready to fight for her life.

I don't deserve another chance at happiness. Not after what happened to my family. But fuck if I don't want one, even if that means sharing Ember's soul with the men I call my brothers. I'll take whatever portion of her heart she wants to give me.

"That's it," Axel praises. "Let go."

Ember's muscular frame tenses as her orgasm hits. The hand fisting my trouser leg flies back to Axel's head to grip his hair. She drags in a breath, rasping our names in blissful agony. I kiss behind her ear, murmuring encouragement as her release races through her.

Axel's head draws back, lifting to watch each iteration of her climax play out. We're both enraptured. Fascinated by the sight of Ember unravelling, allowing her shields to slip and reveal a state of purely physical instinct.

Damn, is it a sight to behold.

I'll do anything for the privilege to make her surrender.

"Incredible." Axel sighs contentedly.

"Isn't she just?"

"Perfect too. And all ours."

"Seems so."

Balancing Ember's weight, I tug her t-shirt back down to hide her breasts. With Axel still kneeling below us, I nudge Ember, encouraging her to watch him licking the release that shines on his lips, pupils blown wide as he stares up at the goddess we've captured.

"Next time you're going to be covering my cock in your juices," he vows confidently. "Hyland can watch, if you'd like, or he can have a turn too."

"Maybe I'll take her mouth while you fill her up." I push my still-aching cock into Ember's ass.

"You guys," she grouses.

"Problem?" I nuzzle into her hair.

"This is what you wanted." Axel arches a brow.

Lifting her head from my shoulder, Ember pulls her leg down to hide her bareness. She turns to glance at my face, her lips puckered from biting down to quiet her moans.

"You want this too?" She inclines her head.

Neck curving, I seal my mouth on hers.

"All I want is you."

play
me
DO NOT CROSS
POL
Suspect?
NOT CROSS
POLICE LI

10

EMBER

HOSTAGE – BILLIE EILISH

When I was a kid, it was normal to watch Mum endure her own personal hell. Doctors. Needles. Prognoses. Countless packets of pills, endless prescriptions, CT scans, bleak news delivered in softly painted rooms. After a while, the terror of losing my only parent became workaday.

Then she died.

In that final act, my entire world came collapsing down. Tom was inconsolable. Despite being the younger sibling, I had to care for my big brother rather than mourn. It was easier to stuff that pain down. Lock it away. Silence the grief.

But I can feel it now.

I feel it fucking *everywhere*.

Grief and regret too overwhelming to successfully bury grip me

as I stare at my brother's pale face. I can't lose him too. He's all I've got left. My last family member.

I'd give anything to see his smile again. Hear his voice. Feel his hand squeezing mine back. It's been three days of excruciating waiting, and there's no end in sight. The fact that Carlos is dead provides little comfort.

Tom is stable for now, but while he's on the mechanical ventilator, the ICU doctors are keeping him sedated. As far as we can tell, Luis locked him in a freezing shipping container, buried in the bowels of the cargo ship, after beating him stupid.

I'm thankful Luis is dead.

But I wish I'd been the one to kill him.

Between the severe pneumonia and numerous infected wounds, Tom's recovery promises to be slow. I understand the ordeal he's been through since he was kidnapped. But I still long for a single sign that he knows he's safe and no one is going to hurt him again.

"I'm sorry," I whisper through held-back tears. "If I'd known this would happen, I never would've come home. I hate that you're hurt because of me."

Nothing but mechanical whirring answers.

"I'll make it right, Tom. I'm going to find Gael and all the others like him. I don't care how long it takes or where I have to search... I'll end this."

My fingers clench over his. He's cold to the touch. Still. So far from the warmth and unconditional love that I associate with my better half. Tom shouldn't be here. He's fighting for his life, and it's so fucking unfair.

Gaze straying to Warner, I watch his chest slowly rise and fall. He's finally dropped off, limbs awkwardly curled up. That visitor's chair can't be comfortable, but he's strung-out and dead on his feet like the rest of us.

The solitude allows my tears to flow without fear of being seen. Warm dribbles trail my cheeks, stinging like the lash of a whip carving deep into my back. Even in the safety of St Thomas's ICU, I hear the monster who's done this to us.

I don't have room for disobedient products in my business.

Gael sure bit off more than he could chew with the pair of

us. Against the odds, we're alive. Scarred and beaten but not yet broken. Not quite. I have enough left to seek vengeance for the suffering my big brother has endured.

Tears bite into my cheeks as I turn my back on Tom and Warner to stalk from the room, skin rippling with a fire-like itch to tear into the next person I lay eyes on. The Sabre agents assigned to Tom's security instantly avert their gazes at my glare.

"Do not leave him unattended," I snap.

The bald-headed agent dips his head. "Yes ma'am."

"I'll be back."

"Do you need security?" his colleague asks.

"No I fucking do not."

A ball of heartache too large to talk around lodges in my throat, causing my steps to speed up. I flee the ICU, white hallways and beeping heart monitor machines forming a blur around me. All I can feel is that damn lump.

My mind splits then reforms, swallowing the time it takes to break outside into the cool air. The strobe lights floating across my vision are back, growing brighter each time my skull pulses with pain.

"Move!" I growl at bystanders.

When a pregnant woman and her partner accidentally bump into me, I break away from the hospital's main entrance to escape the hustle and bustle. It's quieter down the side street where flagrant staff members smoke out of sight.

"He isn't answering his phone. We should leave. Warner will call when he can."

"I'm not going anywhere until I see him, Xan."

"If he were hurt, we'd know about it."

"You saw the news. There was a fatality!"

A nearby couple argues, leaning against the hospital wall. I spare them a glance through tear-clogged eyes, assessing their lack of uniform and plastic shoes. Not gossiping staff, then.

"Hudson already told you he's here," the white-haired man reasons calmly.

"As a patient or what?" His companion—a pacing, tattooed woman—snarls at him. "That son of a bitch didn't tell me anything."

"And you're surprised by that?"

"I have a right to know!"

"Who are you?" I blurt.

Both gazes shift in my direction. Recognition fills the woman's round hazel eyes, validating my suspicions. I tense upright, pulling out my phone in preparation to call for backup.

"You're Ember."

My trembling hand pauses. "You know me?"

"Warner talked about little else for the last six years." She shrugs with a wry smile. "I heard you're home."

"Look, it's been a long week, so excuse me for not feeling chatty. Tell me who you are, or I'll have a squad of agents on your asses in seven seconds flat."

"Seven?" Her friend frowns, appearing confused. "Bit slow. I could do all kinds of things to you in seven seconds."

"Xander!" she hisses.

"What?" He seems utterly nonchalant. "It only takes two seconds to slit a human throat. Her backup would be useless in that situation, unless she decides to kill me first."

I feel my brows climb to my hairline. "You think it would take me two seconds?"

"Maybe three."

"Wow. Now I definitely want to slit your throat."

"I'm being conservative. You appear injured."

"Thanks for the vote of confidence or there lack of," I drawl sarcastically. "Seriously, who the fuck are you people?"

The tall, white-haired smart ass with slender limbs and frost-bitten eyes seems to catalogue every detail available to him as he spares me a bland smile.

"It's encouraging that you don't recognise us. At least there are some people left who haven't seen the damn documentary."

"I'm Ripley." The girl steps forward, hands spread. "We're here to see Warner. Hudson told me he's here, but that prickly bastard slammed a classified lid down on my questions. I'm worried."

Surprise punctures my chest. "You're Ripley Bennet."

"Shit." Xander clasps the back of his neck. "She does recognise us."

"Not you, dick." I glower at him. "Your girlfriend."

Ripley looks different than the vague image I remember from old news reports during Warner's investigation. Harrowdean Manor was his defining case ten years ago. He helped dismantle a vast criminal conspiracy wrapped up in multiple psych wards across the UK, including Blackwood Institute.

"Is he okay?" Ripley wrings her hands.

"He's fine." I blink through another wave of dizziness. "The casualty was another agent on our secondary team. Warner's upstairs with my brother in the ICU."

Cursing, she tilts her gaze up to the sky for a pause. She's relieved, I think. Warner's relationship with Ripley has always been a bit of a mystery. He's protective of his friend and her place in his life, rarely discussing the case once it was resolved.

"I'll tell him to call you back," I offer.

Xander nods, resting a hand on his girl's shoulder. "Thanks."

"Thank you for the throat-slicing debate. If I get it down to one second, I'll give you a call."

"It's all in the wrist action." He winks at me.

"Speaking from personal experience?"

"Are you?" Xander challenges.

Mouth closing, I shakily smile back at him. *Yep. I see how they survived.* The motley, fucked up family that Sabre Security seems to attract certainly doesn't disappoint.

"I'd offer to take you upstairs, but Sabre's got the ward locked down tight, and Warner's asleep." I hook a thumb over my shoulder. "I can pass the message along, though."

"Thanks." Ripley nods. "And I'm really sorry about your brother."

"Yeah. Me too."

Turning away from them to head back inside, I halt at the sound of my name being called. Ripley has stepped forward to follow me, but she stops to rattle off some kind of address.

"What's that?" I stare at her.

"My home studio. In case you want coffee or something stronger."

It takes a second for me to find an adequate reply in my state of surprise.

"A coffee?"

"Or something stronger." She hikes up a shoulder. "Looks like you could use it."

"Right. Uh, thank you."

She tucks a chunk of curls behind her ear. "I'm an okay listener, though I tend to zone out when I'm painting. Feel free to come talk to me though if the team drives you insane."

"Maybe I'll take you up on that."

"I hope so." A grin stretches her lips.

With another nod, Ripley turns to snag Xander's slender arm. My gaze catches on the rows of silvery, symmetrical scars that mark his visible skin. When I look up, he's staring at me. Without an ounce of embarrassment. I try for another smile, and the corner of his mouth hooks up.

"See you around." He loops an arm around Ripley's neck and kisses her cheek. "Let's go. Raine and Lennox are waiting for us."

The pair walk off down the busy street towards the distant underground station. I watch Xander's head turn on a swivel, always alert, monitoring their surroundings for any threats. He keeps a tight, protective hold of Ripley the whole time.

Huh.

Taking a few more minutes to calm down, I wait for my still-pounding heartbeat to settle a little before considering going back inside. My vision is wavering, the headache refusing to let up. Inside the hospital, I locate the shop, in search of coffee and painkillers.

"Were you making friends?"

The gruff rumble of Hyland's voice startles me. "Jesus. Where did you come from?"

Towering over a magazine stand, he appraises me with a quirked brow. There's a duffel bag over his shoulder and a grease-stained paper bag of food clasped in his hand. He looks showered and rested.

"Saw you outside."

"And you just kept walking?" I narrow my eyes.

"Neither Ripley nor Xander will hurt you. Not if they value their lives. Though I am surprised to see them out and about in public."

Locating the in-store coffee machine, I jab the buttons to fill a Styrofoam cup with black nectar. Hyland grunts in affirmation when I wave a hand towards the cups before filling one for him.

"What's this about a documentary?"

He moodily eyes the rows of magazines. "Ripley talked to the press about the Harrowdean Manor case. She's being featured in an anniversary documentary. It's caused a bit of a fall out."

Grabbing three sachets of sugar, I dump them into my cup. Hyland abandons the rack to come stand next to me, his mouth wrinkling.

"You don't take sugar."

"Today I do." I sigh tiredly.

"Go home and rest, red. I can stay with Tom."

"I want to be here when they ease the sedation. He shouldn't be alone."

"We don't know when that'll be."

"I don't care. I'm staying."

Taking both coffee cups, Hyland fits plastic lids to the steaming receptacles. I try to reach for mine, but he clasps my wrist in a loose hold, urging me to look up at him.

"You know what Doctor Fawn said. Pushing yourself to your limit will only trigger your seizures more. Are you having symptoms?"

"No."

"You're a good liar, but I can see through your shit. It's my job."

"Unfair," I complain. "Don't use your secret agent crap on me."

"Secret agent crap?" He barks out a laugh.

"You know what I mean."

"What other tactic would you prefer I use?"

Thoughts of being caught between him and Axel while they played my body like their favourite line of music flash through my mind. The grin on Hyland's face tells me he knows exactly what I'm thinking about.

"Well?" he urges.

Snatching the coffee back, I ignore his taunt and head for the pharmaceuticals. Hyland grunts under his breath when I locate a box of painkillers, adding them to my stash with some snacks.

"You need to rest," he insists.

"Tell me something I don't know."

"We can handle the incoming evidence from the docks. Until we get some new leads, you need to get your strength back. It's been an intense couple of weeks."

"This isn't the time to take our foot off the gas." I cut him a stony glare. "We just struck a decisive blow. Now we need to put the pressure on and find Gael while his operations are wounded."

"You're in no state to be finding anyone."

"Do I need to remind you who saved our asses in that dockyard?"

"No." Hyland shakes his head. "The bodies in our morgue do that well enough."

"Then get off my case. I don't need to rest."

"Look at yourself, Em. You're black and blue, barely able to walk. Stuffing yourself with painkillers and shit coffee instead of getting a few hours' sleep. This isn't sustainable."

"Living our lives in fear isn't sustainable!"

Heading for the cashier, I'm sidestepped before I can pay. Hyland draws out his wallet then tosses two crumpled notes down. I'm on the verge of yelling when both of our phones chirp simultaneously.

I pull mine out, glancing over the message. Axel's in HQ this morning, meeting with the directors and the Falcon Team. He's sent a group text to all three of us—wait, four. Blaine's number is included.

Well, this is new.

"What is it?" Hyland grabs my elbow to steer me into a quiet corner.

"Axel's made a new group chat. With Blaine."

"You're fucking kidding me."

"Nope. He's sent an update in it."

Flipping the screen, I let him read the text.

Axel: A package has arrived.

Warner: What kind of package?

His nap clearly didn't last long.

Axel: Addressed to Ember and covered
in international postmarks. It's been
bounced around. Can't track where it
originated from beyond Europe.

Warner: You scan it?

Axel: Fox did an X-Ray. It's non-
explosive. Can't tell much else.

"Fucking hell," Hyland mutters.
"Gael?"
"Could be. He knows by now that Carlos and his men are dead."
"But what on earth could he possibly be sending me?"
At Hyland's shrug, I tap back a quick response.

Ember: We're still at the hospital. Hold tight.

Blaine: I'll open it for you.

Ember: What if it's some kind of trap?

Blaine: Then I'll take Sabre to court for a
workplace injury when my arm's blown off.

Warner: Don't let him open it, Ax.

It feels strange to laugh after recent events, but it bubbles out
of me anyway.

Axel: Let the criminal take the risk. I'd pay to
see his face get melted off by whatever's inside.

Blaine: If Ember will kiss my face better, I'll do it regardless.

Warner: DEFINITELY don't let him open it.

Axel: Why's babysitting my responsibility?

The phone is plucked from my hands and replaced by a coffee cup. I have to bite back another laugh at the thunderous look on Hyland's face. Someone doesn't approve of Blaine's desire for me to kiss his boo-boo better.

"Come on," he growls.

"Are you done being an overbearing prick?"

"For now. Let's check on Tom then head to HQ. If the criminal bastard gets his face melted off, I wanna be the first to see it and make sure he doesn't get medical help."

"Hy…"

"Take your pills and drink the coffee, red. Though we will be continuing this conversation later."

"You know, barking orders isn't making you a more appealing choice."

"Do you think I'm trying to be appealing?" he huffs.

"Evidently not. But your jealousy is showing, big man."

Coffee in hand, Hyland towers over me. It's almost intimidating. He's a solid wall of muscle, standing between me and the world's dangers, but sometimes, I wonder if the biggest threat lies within him.

"I'm only going to say this once, Ember. You're *ours*. And we are not in competition with Blaine fucking Madden."

Delicious treacle pulsates through me at his possessive words. Fuck, I want to be theirs. It's all I've wanted for a long time. But frankly, we do not need any distractions or in-fighting right now.

"Isn't our current predicament a little bigger than your ridiculous rivalry with Blaine? He's part of this investigation. You need to put everything else aside."

Hyland slurps his coffee with a heavy grimace. "People like Madden are the reason why we have to investigate. Just because he sold drugs and not people doesn't make him any different."

"He's atoning for his father's sins."

"He's cashing in on an opportunity to clear his name and remove a threat to his enterprise," Hyland corrects haughtily.

"Do you really believe that's all he's here for?"

For a millisecond, I can see conflict flash in his olive spheres. "Yes."

"Now who's the shit liar?"

Grimacing at me, Hyland stomps off towards the elevators, leaving me to catch up to him while swallowing a handful of painkillers. He holds his silence for the journey back to the ICU, a stormy frown fixed in place.

While I don't understand Blaine or his motives at the best of times, he isn't like the monsters we're chasing. Not by a long shot. If Hyland could stop seeing threats all around him, he wouldn't spend his life perpetually afraid of the past repeating itself.

Back in Tom's hospital room, Warner is pacing up and down in front of the windows with his phone pressed to his ear. I'm checking on Tom as Hyland sets down the bags when Warner's curse draws me to his worried stare.

"How many photographs? Are they dated?"

The colour drains from his face, blue eyes darkening with a look of rage.

"Can the techs confirm that?"

I place my coffee down on the bedside table to cross my arms over my lurching stomach.

"Alright, I'll tell her. Start analysing the images for any locations or spatial context. We'll be there soon."

With the phone call finished, Warner drags a hand down his weary face. His short, silver-streaked hair is as rumpled as his dark clothing, far from the pristine professionalism he usually exudes.

"What is it?" I almost don't want to ask.

"Madden opened the package."

Hyland spits a cuss. "Of course he did."

"It appears to be some kind of taunt," Warner continues grimly.

"The parcel's full of polaroid photos. All recently dated."

"Photos… of who?"

His hesitation unfurls a dread-filled infestation inside me. The blood-sucking creatures take flight in my veins and almost knock me off-kilter after days of emotional exhaustion.

"Warner?"

"I'm sorry, Em." He scratches at his stubble-covered jaw.

"Who is in the photos?"

Wincing, he looks outside then back to me.

"Gracie. She's alive."

ONFIDENTIAL

Why?

Suspect?

INDEX
A
Play me
TYPE I (NORMAL) POSITION

POLICE L
DO NOT CROSS

play
me
DO NOT CROSS
Suspect?
NOT CROSS
POLICE L
POLICE

11

EMBER

ZOMBIE – YUNGBLUD

I abandoned her to die.

Bickering voices wash over me, converging into a senseless wave that fails to drown out my own hate-filled chant. The pins and needles burrowing into my tight, hot skin drive the torture home.

I left Gracie behind.

Between Warner and Hyland trading information with the intelligence department and Axel talking non-stop to ease the tension screaming off the Falcon Team, the debrief room is riotous. It almost rivals the chaos ripping me apart on the inside.

If I had to explain what living with a chronic illness is like, I'd struggle to describe the sense of wrongness. Like your body isn't your own. Organs feel alien. Limbs disobedient. The anxiety of waiting for an attack to take hold feels like balancing on a knife's

edge.

My palms sear where I'm digging my nails in to conceal the shaking, worsening by the hour. I haven't slept more than a few hours since we got Tom back. The constant fear, exhaustion and adrenaline are taking their toll.

"He's toying with us!" Hyland booms across the room.

"Gael's intentions are irrelevant," Warner argues.

"Dangling Gracie Livingstone in our faces is a distraction technique. Gael lost his leverage, so he found more. He wants us to look for her."

With a wince, I rub my temples. Hyland's deep voice is slicing into my fucking brain, and I can't see straight as it is.

"We don't even have a location yet." The strain in Warner's words tells me he's struggling to keep his cool. "There's no need to jump to conclusions."

"You're playing into his hands."

"We're following up a lead on a missing person relevant to our case. That's it."

"Rayna," Axel chimes in, bizarrely acting as the peacekeeper. "What do we know?"

"From what we can tell so far, the package passed through three European countries." She clicks her laptop, deep in concentration. "Awaiting further analysis on two of the images."

"Can we tell where Gracie is being held from them?"

"Hard copies lack the metadata of digital photographs, but we're looking into the spatial clues we identified. We may be able to deduce a rough location. A country, at least."

"Then what?" Hyland throws his big hands. "We're going to waltz into another trap?"

"No." Warner gnaws his bottom lip.

"You were all ready to go in guns blazing a moment ago."

"Will you just sit down and take a breath?"

"No! We've already lost someone, and we're no closer to tracing Gael or his estate overseas. Carlos is dead. Dominic and his honeypots are headed for prison. We should be focusing on bringing Gael to us next, not taking his bait."

The loud screeching of a chair being shoved back precedes

Archer abruptly stalking from the debrief room. He doesn't look at anyone—not even his remaining teammates—as he leaves.

Oscar and Kyle stare down at their note-cluttered paperwork. Neither offers a word nor dares to lift their heads. To their credit, the team hasn't missed a day since Josh's death. They've picked up the slack while we've been with Tom.

Warner dons a mask of pure frustration. "We're here to discuss our next steps, Hy. I know you're hurting, but be professional or leave. That's an order."

"How dare you make this about me?"

"We lost a man on our watch."

"If you have something to say, just spit it out."

"Trust me, I know how it feels to lose a colleague in the line of fire. But right now, we need to focus. Go make this right, then come back with a level head."

Hyland's bulky shoulders deflate as the weight of the world settles onto them. "I'll get Archer."

"Good."

With Hyland gone, conversation returns to the images that have been dated, printed and shipped to us like a fucking Christmas present. I struggle to see the floor-to-ceiling case board that holds every scrap of evidence we have, years' worth of investigative work laid out in an elaborate display of failure.

Countless surveillance ops, interrogations, arrests and dead ends. Long-range shots of potential locations for Gael's estate. Washed up trafficking victims. DNA profiles. Shipping manifestos. Now Gracie—older, visibly beaten and posed in all manner of sickening ways.

I wish it wasn't her, but it is. Each shot captures her in high-definition horror. Her devastating blue eyes, swimming with numb detachment, offer a dead stare beneath matted, dark hair. She's gaunt, her cheekbones pronounced, skin smeared with vivid bruises.

"Gracie…" I trace my finger over the pallid features in the photos.

She's grown up so much. It's not the first time I've seen her naked since our time in the cage, but the terror in her eyes as her abuser snapped each photo is unbearable. Pain and dizziness muddy the proof of my failure to keep her safe.

I did this. I left her there.

"While authorities are continuing to search for Gael's estate with our intel, we're going to focus on Gracie." Warner looks around the room. "I want to know where she's being held. Her captors may lead us to Gael."

"We know he has connections to illegal operations across Europe." Axel cracks his knuckles. "That asshole Dominic confirmed as much. So it's feasible that she could be there."

"Let's reach out to our international partners and update them. Circulate these new images of her face. We'll have to bring her next of kin in first; we don't want her parents finding out about this online."

There's a chorus of agreeing sounds. Just the mention of her parents makes my gut roil with nausea. I haven't met them yet, but I know they're keen to speak to me about Gracie.

"Why send the photos at all?" Fox asks, huddled with his fellow techies.

"Ember killed his guy." Kyle speaks for the first time, staring at his clenched fists. "Gael's been wounded. He's scrambling to source new leverage because he still wants Ember to break."

"Well, if Gael wants a final showdown, then that's what he's going to get," Warner states flatly. "We'll locate Gracie and take the fight to her."

"Excellent," Axel grumbles. "We're all going to die."

"Don't you start with me too."

"I'm just saying."

"Ax," Warner cautions.

"Every time we get close to a breakthrough, the cartel dances back out of reach. Not even Madden can find where Gael or his father are hiding out. We're constantly on the back foot."

"We found Tom," Warner argues. "And we have eliminated Gael's right-hand man. I understand tensions are high, but we need to remain positive."

"Positive?" Kyle repeats.

Warner's mouth flaps open before closing.

"Our teammate is waiting to be buried, and you're asking us to be positive?"

"Kyle—"

"No! You can't expect us to risk our lives for *her* personal vendetta!"

Kyle spits the single syllable with venom. I recoil at his outburst. He's never had a problem with me before. Not until the rescue op that killed his fellow agent, that is. Now he's looking at me like I'm an armed nuclear warhead, and he's caught in the blast radius.

"This is the job." Warner's neck muscles clench as he battles to remain calm. "It isn't personal. There are no vendettas. We're here to serve justice, plain and simple."

"What's impersonal about having your lead witness working for you?"

"Ember is a Sabre agent. She's part of this investigation."

"She's a walking liability!" Kyle snarls with genuine contempt. "Just look at the mess left behind in Felixstowe."

"Watch your tone."

"Or what?"

"Go cool off!" Warner erupts, his temper finally shattering. "Now."

Pressure burns into the side of my splitting head. When I glance to the right, I find Blaine staring at me instead of the arguing men. He too lingers at the edge of the room, a silent sentry primed to intervene but remaining stoic.

Since Carlos's death, Blaine's the only one who hasn't treated me like I'm made of glass. If anything, he seems quieter. Observant. Like he's seeing me in a new light, and he's processing what he saw, strategising how to use it to his advantage.

With a furiously spat curse word, Kyle departs the room, leaving Oscar to chase after him. He has the decency to look embarrassed. Honestly, it's unnecessary. Kyle has every right to be mad. He's right—I left a hell of a mess behind.

"Fantastic." Axel drops his purple head into his hands, yanking his hair in aggravation. "Our entire secondary team is in timeout."

"They'll come back." Warner dips his chin in consternation.

"They aren't cut out for this job. Let them go."

"Nobody is cut out for this shit."

"You're telling me!" Axel rebuffs. "We're falling apart!"

"What the hell do you want me to do? Give up?"

"No, of course not."

"Then get on side and help." Warner shifts his weight onto his good leg. "I can't focus on finding Gael if I'm fighting fires on the home front."

"Alright, alright." Releasing his hair, Axel appears to gather himself. "What evidence do we have from the port?"

As Warner settles into a seat to pour over the evidence log from Felixstowe, I find myself tuning out. My jaw aches from the force of gritting my teeth, and my bleary vision is worsening with the stabbing needles making my fingers twitch.

Not now. Not now.

I can feel my racing heart behind my eyes, each muscle in my body throbbing. The symptoms have been intensifying for days, growing fiercer by the hour. Nights spent camped out in Tom's ICU room anxiously watching a machine breathe for him haven't helped.

"B-Bathroom," I announce.

Multiple gazes snap to me.

"Em?" Warner starts to rise from his seat. "You good?"

"Yes. Carry on without me."

"You look pale."

"I'm f-fine. Back soon."

Waving him off, I find the sense to nod reassuringly then leave the room. Our team is stretched to a breaking point right now. Warner said it himself—he can't simultaneously fight fires and find Gracie. I need to deal with this alone.

To my relief, Hyland and the others aren't in sight. A heavy exhale pours from my lungs upon finding nothing but an empty corridor that resembles a ship adrift in tumultuous waters. Even my feet feel too heavy to lift as my legs and arms shudder involuntarily.

I stumble to the second floor bathroom to avoid being tracked. The guys won't check here first. My knees soon give out, and I land in the middle of the bathroom, jolting the still-healing bruises and scrapes that cover my body.

Hopelessness isn't all that familiar. Sure, there were plenty of times in captivity when my situation felt bleak. Inescapable. But if I'd allowed myself to wallow in the defeat, I never would've survived. I had to shut that voice out to keep going.

Disassociate. Bury. *Survive.*

Now there isn't an ounce of strength left inside me to hold the floodgates at bay as the bathroom dips in and out. Defeat infiltrates my last conscious seconds, bringing that soul-crushing despair into sharp focus.

I can't fight this any longer. Not as my whole body tenses and spasms, a thick layer of sweat soaking into my spasming limbs. The bathroom ceiling flashes bright-white then fuzzy darkness invades, but in the involuntary surrender comes silence.

At least I'm out of sight.

No one can see my weakness.

The vast, empty expanse of nothingness is a welcome break. Pops of colour shift. Shadows morph before the black cloak returns. Pain ceases. The shaking stops. I don't have limbs, fingers or even toes to feel the discomfort caused by the seizure taking hold.

I'm floating, untethered and numb, while time ceases. Free at last. An untethered balloon testing how high it can climb before the atmosphere causes its exoskeleton to rupture. Only I can't break when I'm already shattered beyond repair.

"Easy, sweetheart."

Who…

"Come back when you're ready. It's okay. You're safe."

No.

Voices don't belong in this floating nothingness. Not even that ridiculous, aristocratic drawl. This is wrong. I don't know why… or where I am… But no one is allowed to be here. It isn't safe. I can't let them see me like this or they'll surely leave me.

"I'm here with you."

Through the mental blackout, a flicker unveils glistening emerald eyes. The scent of peppermint cuts through my confusion, wrapping me in an embrace.

"You're not alone, Ember."

So many times, I wished for my brother to hold me tight.

During countless, terrifying attacks. Sprawled out on bloodstained concrete. Petrified and utterly alone. I longed for him to appear like a guardian angel hovering just out of reach.

But he never did.

And now... he's unable to.

Something soft penetrates my mental fog. A feather-like brush against my skin allows sensation to sluggishly return. With it comes blistering pain that's too much for the darkness to contain. Lightning splits the blackness behind my eyelids, the strobes scalding my retinas.

Cold sweat suspends me in a frozen prison, each limb still locked tight in total paralysis. A pained keening fills my ears. It sounds so broken. So afraid. Like a wounded animal caught in a trap and forced to gnaw its own leg off.

"Sweetheart... Fuck, I'm shit at this. Just breathe. You're going to be okay."

The sobs rattle my bones and bring my awareness back to the burning that slices through the core of my being. The sound isn't distant after all; it's echoing inside my skull, bouncing from throbbing bone to bone.

Wait... I'm the one crying. It's my dry throat smarting. My lungs gasping for air. My arm being rhythmically stroked. This is my failing body, wracked by fiery needles penetrating my skin to drag me back down to Earth.

"Breathe," the voice croons. "Come on. You can do this."

"T-Tom," I whimper.

"No, Ember. I'm sorry... It's only me."

"Who..."

When my vision clears, the emerald eyes that shine with love and care inside my head are replaced by midnight-flecked obsidians. Pitch-black hair that looks like it has been urgently shoved from his forehead unveils worried grooves in his skin.

Tom isn't here. I'm squinting up at a familiar, cocky criminal with the kind of smile that causes wars to break out. And he's touching me. *A lot.* Calloused fingers smooth over my skin with a welcome coolness.

"We need to stop meeting like this," Blaine jokes.

My tongue darts out to wet my lips. "Where?"

"Bathroom. You didn't hide well enough."

When I attempt to move, nothing responds to me. Not even my fingers will twitch. Blaine kneels at my side, stroking my arms and bruised face. From the scent of leather, I think his jacket is cradling my head like a pillow.

"Take it easy." He continues caressing me. "That was an intense one."

"How… l-long?"

Blaine glances at the silver Rolex on his wrist. "About three minutes. I read somewhere that you're supposed to time it. You took a bit to come around after."

My eyes squeeze shut as tears pool in the cavities, threatening to break cover. The cold hand running up and down my arms stills.

"Hey, I can go get someone. If you'll just let me—"

"No," I bleat.

"You don't have to hide this from them, Ember."

"N-No."

"Alright, then. You're stuck with me."

"Go a-away."

He scoffs under his breath. "Unlikely."

I'm unable to move or shove him aside. Frankly, his chilled fingertips feel great on my clammy skin. Blaine pushes hair from my face, adjusts his jacket to support my neck better then resumes rubbing comforting circles on my arm. It's soothing.

"F-Feels… nice."

He smiles faintly. "I've got you. Just focus on breathing."

We fall into an easy silence until the excruciating needle-tingle phase has come and gone. Relieved that my body is my own again, I let my lungs expand on a deep inhale. I'm exhausted and aching like I've been hit by a loaded truck.

"Water… p-please." My voice is wispy as it pulls from my dry throat.

"Hang on." He climbs to his feet. "There's a vending machine outside."

When Blaine returns, I've managed to wrestle my trembling body up and weakly shuffled to rest against the stall door. My hand wavers as I wipe tears from my face, avoiding the cuts and scrapes from Carlos's beating.

"Here." Blaine sits next to me, extending a water bottle. "Drink up."

Once he's popped the cap, I take several long gulps, ignoring the trickles running down my chin because I can't hold the plastic steady. Embarrassment forces me to look ahead, avoiding his stare.

"What else do you need?" he asks.

"Just rest."

"I've come to realise you're pretty terrible at that. I have half a mind to kidnap you and not return you to those assholes until after you've had some real rest."

"Doubt Sabre would agree to that." I laugh hollowly.

"I'm excellent at making people disappear. They wouldn't find you."

His long leg brushes mine where he sits next to me on the floor. Too tired to fight, I let my head slump to the side, resting it on Blaine's shoulder. After a pause, his head leans against mine almost tenderly.

Around the others, I want to be tough. Unbreakable. The powerful warrior they all seem to think I am. With Blaine, it's different. He saw me in the cage, made to fight and save my own skin. He already knows the worst parts of me, and still, he chose to save my life.

There's comfort in that. An acceptance.

I can't scare him into leaving me.

"Want to talk about it?" Blaine offers.

"You can't help."

"Try me, sweetheart."

Taking another gulp of water, I attempt to moisten my parched mouth, hoping it will allow my voice to come out more steadily.

"I don't know if I can do this."

"We can go back to the hospital, see if a different doctor—"

"No, the case. The constant fight. We're getting nowhere."

"Right, I see." Peppercorns and citrus-spiked bergamot seep from Blaine's presence beside me. "Some fights feel insurmountable."

"Then what's the point?"

"Because if we don't fight, then nobody will. I've been trying to find my father for years, and he feels further away than ever. That doesn't mean I'm going to give up."

"Don't you get tired?"

Briefly, I think he won't open up. Then his posture softens.

"Sometimes," Blaine admits in a gruff tone. "But in my world, weakness isn't tolerated. Whether I'm tired of this or not, I have to find and eliminate Nolan Madden."

"But what if you gave up?"

"Impossible. My father used us all to inflict suffering behind my back. I intend to right that wrong even if it's the last thing I do. He has to pay."

Blaine is usually too cool and aloof to reveal anything that could amount to true emotion. Unless it's confidence or swagger. Which he has in spades. But at his harsh tenor, I can't hold in my curiosity.

"Will you tell me why you hate trafficking so much?"

"What?" He laughs bitterly. "Because criminals aren't allowed morals? Perhaps I despise the exploitation of innocent lives."

"Perhaps. But I think you have a personal stake in it."

Rather than refute my statement, Blaine's laughter trails off.

"Why?" I press again, desperate for him to reveal more about himself. "You can trust me. I'd never judge you, if that's what you're worried about."

"And why not?"

"Look at the state of me, Blaine. Yet you've never judged me."

He contemplates that. "I would never."

"Then trust me to do the same for you."

In the bathroom's solitude, sprawled out on the floor, Blaine's scar-warped face cracks. Just a fissure. A tremor in his usually unshakeable surface. But it's enough to glimpse the abused kid who lives behind his smirking mask. The same kid who earned that scar.

"I was raised motherless," he whispers like the words might just hurt him. "But I idolised my father, so I didn't care. The great Nolan Madden… I wanted to be just like him for the longest time."

Placing the water bottle down, I command my fingers to obey as they wrap around his. Blaine hesitates for a second then squeezes my hand in gratitude.

"When I was a teenager, the punishments began. Light beatings at first before he graduated to knives and cigarettes, using my body as a blank canvas for his violence. That idolisation turned to terror, then later… hatred."

My molars grind together. "You were just a kid."

"But old enough to understand real evil."

Bitterness spreads in his voice like a viral contagion. I hold my tongue, giving him time to choose how much to share.

"I started searching for the woman who birthed me." His words are barely audible. "I don't know what I was looking for. A better parent, perhaps. One who didn't hurt me quite as much."

"Did you find her?"

"No." The denial is strained, hesitant. "Just whispers of a young girl he purchased then left pregnant. Once she birthed his heir, he sent her back to her masters. I don't know if she survived."

Horror holds me hostage. For all those years he spent under his father's thumb, Blaine refused to dabble in the skin trade. Little did anyone know, it was because his own mother was a victim.

"I know what you're thinking." He looks down at our entwined hands. "Why stay after that?"

The memory of his marked body flashes through my mind. Years' worth of abuse and torture. There's no way I'm questioning his choices. He's a survivor too.

"If I left the family business, no one would've stopped my father. I had to work from the inside to keep trafficking off our books… Though I failed at that too."

"It wasn't your fault, Blaine."

"Tell that to all the women and girls he's hurt on my watch."

"He was hurting you too," I say gently.

"I was weak. I failed to stop him."

"You did the best you could."

"It wasn't good enough," he snaps.

"You're talking to someone who willingly fought for her captors pretty much on a daily basis for six years. Did that make me weak or a failure?"

"No!" Blaine turns to hit me with a glare. "Of course not."

"Then extend yourself the same grace. You survived hell."

"You don't understand. It's different."

"How?" I take in a deep breath, hoping it will ease the pain drilling into my skull.

"I wasn't a prisoner."

"He beat you? Tortured you? Made you do things against your will?"

Blaine doesn't immediately reply, uncertainty dancing in the sapphire flecks deepening the cavernous fissures in his eyes. I'm going to split them wide fucking open. Enough is enough. Now that I've glimpsed the real Blaine Madden, I want to pull that broken child into the light.

"Whatever you're getting at…"

"He carved you up like meat and burned your skin when you disappointed him. Do you hear how that sounds? And you want to tell me you weren't a prisoner too?"

"I had the chance to leave." His tongue flicks out to nudge his lip piercing.

"So do plenty of victims."

"Not like this. I lived a comfortable lifestyle."

"Control isn't always cages and shackles. It can be silent. Sometimes near invisible. No one sees it or hears it, but the hand on your neck is still there."

"I helped him!" Blaine raises his voice. "I didn't know about it, but I still helped. I protected him. The *family business*. He hurt people just like he hurt my mother… all while I kept his assets safe."

Twisting on the floor is difficult, but I wrangle my exhausted limbs enough to face him. Blaine's eyes dart away until I catch his stubble-smattered cheeks in my hands, forcing him to look at me.

"It isn't your fault, Blaine Madden. You're a crook, a criminal, and quite frankly, a psychopath at the best of times, but you are not a bad person. I won't hear it."

"Sweetheart—"

"No. If you want to help us catch these monsters, then do it for the right reasons. Not to punish yourself for the sins of your father."

"I need to make it right," he insists.

"Why?" I stare deep into his irises.

"Because... Fuck, Ember." He halts to drag in a breath. "I want forgiveness, alright?"

Behind bruised skin and battered ribs, my aching heart cracks clean down the middle. A sheer fracture that sweeps me into an avalanche. This is the person no one else sees. The human behind the criminal mastermind.

He's punishing himself.

Blaine just wants the world's forgiveness.

"Then I'll help you find it, but not because you need it." I rest my forehead on his, needing to feel him close. "Please hear me, Blaine. You're already forgiven."

Darkness swirls in his gaze. Powerful. Intense. A violent promise tainted by the most innocent and childlike of needs. We all want to cleanse ourselves of our parents' sins one way or another. Despite how destructive that quest might be.

No matter what Hyland says, I refuse to believe that Blaine is all bad. He may disregard the law like it only applies to mere mortals and won't ever touch him, but I don't care. I don't want or need a law-abiding wallflower.

I want a monster.

A powerful force of nature.

The mutual understanding that passes between us feels electric. A magnetic force lassoing us both in the same knot, drawing our bodies together. Common sense nor reason can stop me from leaning into his orbit.

Heat pulses between my legs when his tongue darts out to wet his bottom lip. The air grows thin as Blaine wraps me in a fragrant bergamot haze, and one hand lowers to clasp my thigh.

"What are you doing to me?" he murmurs throatily.

"Nothing."

"Don't play dumb. Three men are vying for your affections. Is that not enough for you?"

Lie. Run. Do anything.

"No," I confess instead.

"Good. Then I don't need to apologise for this."

His mouth ensnares mine, hot and heady. Lips smack, and his

piercing adds to the overwhelming sensations the kiss unravels. Blaine's other hand cups the back of my head, tilting my neck so he can ravage my mouth with the ferocity of his hard kiss.

He swallows my gasp, tongue sliding past my lips to launch an invasion. The faint taste of coffee mixes with a fresh spearmint hit, drugging my senses. I place a hand on his bicep, fingers curling around soft cotton, needing something to hold me steady.

Blaine Madden, notorious mobster and heir to a prolific criminal dynasty, is kissing the motherfucking life out of me. And hell if it doesn't feel good to surrender what's left of my soul to this monster.

Fingertips move against my skull, easing knots and aches from the attack that drew him to me like a moth to a flame. The feel of his attacking lips shoves out any remaining doubt or fear. All that matters is every last place his skin touches mine.

My thighs push together, seeking relief from the tendrils of arousal that ignite my core. His fingers grip me tightly, delivering a bolt of pain that I'll happily accept.

I want him like I want all of them. Regardless of greed or consequence, our paths are intertwined, and Blaine's brand of broken belongs with us. He needs us. And I think I may just need him too.

Gripping his firm bicep, I deepen the kiss. Taking control of the frenzied tempo only drives me to demand more. He groans into my mouth, letting me take what I want, allowing me the control I crave to hold over this formidable man.

Not even the sound of thudding steps can pull my mouth from his. I'm lost in the sensation of teeth nipping my lips, his hot tongue winding with mine, the hand skating down my spine… until it's all ripped away.

"Motherfucker!"

Blaine's body is wrenched from mine, half-tossed across the bathroom by an angry blur. I blink past the lusty haze that's descended over me, gawping at Warner holding his newest teammate by the throat.

"You *dare* touch her!"

"Warner!" I yell, attempting to stand and failing. "Stop!"

"Stay out of this, Ember!"

"She wanted me to," Blaine wheezes.

"I'm going to kill you, Madden. Ember is off-limits. You've crossed a line."

"Hey!" I try again to pull myself up.

Tearing his gaze from Blaine's flushed face, Warner grimaces at me. "I said stay out of it!"

"Put him down. He wasn't doing anything I didn't want him to."

Warner recoils like he's been slapped. "You kissed him?"

"I kissed her," Blaine corrects unhelpfully.

"We kissed each other," I supply.

"Enough!" Warner has turned an alarming shade of pink. "You were warned. Ember isn't yours to touch and still you decided that rule doesn't apply to you."

"I can make my own decisions!" I jab an angry finger at him.

"You want to kiss this son of a bitch?"

"Maybe I do!"

Wrong answer.

Not even my startled shout can stop Warner's fist from sailing directly into Blaine's face, causing bone to crack and sending blood everywhere. Over and over. All while I'm powerless to intervene, held hostage by warring loyalties.

They tear into each other.

Viciously. Violently.

And it's all because of me.

CONFIDENTIAL
Why?
Suspect?
A
Play me
INDEX
TYPE I (NORMAL) POSITION
DO NOT CROSS
POLICE LI

Play me

POLICE LINE – DO NOT CROSS

Asset?

Incoming Call

known

DO NOT CROSS   POLICE L

Suspect?

12

WARNER

DOCTOR DOCTOR – LOWBORN

I've never considered myself to be an angry person. Not like some of the hotheads working for Sabre Security. With authority comes an innate need to remain cool-headed and fair, attributes I've worked hard to embody across my years of service.

Then Ember came crashing back into my life, far more confusing and bewitching than the sharp-tongued slip of a girl I once trailed behind like a lovesick puppy. Years spent being beaten and tortured didn't soften her.

Instead, her hard edges were filed into razor-like points that seem determined to cut me wide open at any given opportunity. Every time she speaks, I feel myself bleeding out at her feet, frantic for a second of her attention. All those childhood feelings are full-blown, obsessive earworms now.

My busted knuckles ache, the scabbed lacerations smarting each time I turn the car's steering wheel. There's not much dignified about being the team's medic when you have to patch up the very man you beat bloody.

"Dickhead." I slam my fist on the dashboard, mentally berating myself for the pain that rushes through my hand.

Dickhead is a polite word for that snake. I should've known offering Blaine Madden a plea deal would bite me in the backside. Though it never occurred to me that he'd even think about looking Ember's way, let alone kissing her while vulnerable.

Car horns blare when I accidentally swerve, almost crossing lanes in my rage. Blinking hard, I focus on the busy road into Hackney. Even as the sound of fists hitting flesh still vibrates in my ear canals.

Fuck it!

Blaine deserved a broken nose. He also deserved to leave that bathroom in a body bag instead of slumped between two agents, but I held back for Ember's sake. She doesn't know what she wants. Hell, she thought it was a bright idea to hide a seizure from us.

Every time my phone rings via the handsfree, I decline the incoming call. Hyland and Axel will have to do without me running their disastrous asses for a few hours. I needed to get away—I can't think straight in the penthouse with Ember there.

My tyres skid against the curb as I pull up outside the block of artsy apartments. I texted ahead, so I'm unsurprised to see Lennox lounging against the gate, the tip of his cigarette glowing in the evening din.

For an ex-patient of Harrowdean Manor, Lennox Nash has made a hell of a life for himself. From his newly opened gym to somehow successfully navigating a poly relationship with the inmates he escaped with, not many can say they rebuilt as well as he has.

The last decade hasn't done much to soften his imposing presence. Like Hyland, Lennox packs a punch in pure aura alone. His broad, muscular shoulders, dark-chocolate hair and gym-honed bulk all scream intimidation, but I know him for the good soul he is beneath his damage.

"Fantastic parking," he mocks.

"Fuck off, Nox. Not in the mood." I slam the car door shut.

"So you decided to come spread your joy to us?"

"I need to speak to Ripley."

With a final drag, he flicks his cigarette aside. "She's coming down from a three-week manic episode. Don't go in if you're here with bad news. She can't take it right now."

"Ease off, I'm just looking for some advice."

"You are?" He frowns at me.

"Don't look so surprised. We all need a friend sometimes."

"Jesus. You must be in trouble if you're here looking for help."

"Hilarious. Didn't you quit smoking?"

"Hence why I'm hiding outside." He smiles wolfishly. "Good to see you alive, by the way."

Lennox accepts the hand I outstretch to shake his with. Old fighting scars pull taut over his knuckles as our palms grasp.

"Sorry about the scare. This case is getting out of control."

"It's Ripley you need to apologise to." He nails me with a stern look. "She was worried sick when you didn't call back."

"Yeah, I will."

"Good. Come in then. Raine's cooking tonight, so I hope you already ate."

The thought of Raine, their visually impaired fourth house member, navigating any kind of meal prep is slightly amusing. He may be an aficionado with his violin, but the kitchen isn't his strong suit.

"When's he back on tour?" I ask as we ascend.

"Couple weeks. We're all flying out to Stockholm."

"Who's covering for you at the gym?"

Lennox waves a hand dismissively. "Lincoln has it under control. We're planning to expand next year by opening another two branches across the city."

"Shit, Nox. That's awesome."

He shrugs, stopping to key in the code for their Sabre-provided security system. I updated it myself when Ripley sat down with reporters for a tell-all interview about their case. They've been harassed by the media ever since.

"I can't complain. The place is full every day."

"You should be damn proud." My shoulder nudges his. "I know we all are."

"Thanks, man."

Their loft apartment is a modern, open-plan layout that benefits from vaulted ceilings and huge steel beams. Ripley has the space divided by rows of drying racks and a massive bookshelf, all draped with art paraphernalia and damp canvases.

The kitchen faces their living room, cluttered with mismatched, antique furniture. Raine is stirring something in a saucepan behind the stove, his glasses-covered eyes fixed ahead as he cocks his blonde head.

"Hey, Raine."

"You should take a shower," he says by way of greeting. "I can smell you from here. Old coffee and three-day sweat aren't attractive if you're searching for a girl to turn that frown upside down."

"How do you know I'm frowning?" I rebuke.

He gestures in my vague direction with a sauce-slicked spoon. "You're here on a weeknight, and I know for sure it isn't because you want my spaghetti carbonara. Something's up."

My whole body deflates with a loud sigh. "Missed you too."

"There's beer in the fridge. Xan's finishing up a phone call."

"I'm here for Ripley."

"Then… you're in luck." He stops to listen then resumes stirring the pasta sauce. "She's just washing up in the studio."

"Do his freaky Batman senses ever get old?" I head for their fridge.

Lennox leans against the kitchen island, watching Raine cook. "After about three seconds, yeah. There's no such thing as privacy in this flat."

"Just because I make being blind look cool." Raine chortles. "No need to hate."

"You wouldn't know cool if it smacked you around the face," Lennox supplies.

"One more word and you get to go to bed hungry."

Lennox's grin twinkles with mischief. "Why wasn't I told that was an option earlier?"

"That's it. No dinner."

"Thank fuck."

Swallowing half the beer in three long pulls, I ignore the way Lennox studies me and Raine falls silent to decipher what I'm doing. When Xander strolls in and pulls a face at my presence, I decide Ripley's had long enough to clean up.

"Next time you almost die on an active raid, have the decency to call us back," Xander deadpans. "She's your fucking friend."

"Yeah, yeah." I rub my tired eyes.

"Make it right with her."

"On it, Xan."

His cool stare follows me across the room and into Ripley's art studio. It's a bright, airy space, despite being cluttered with used palettes, half-finished canvases and more splattered oil paint than clean surfaces.

Ripley's up to her elbows in soapy water, rinsing off a stack of different-sized brushes. She offers me a look when I walk in with a sheepish smile. Her curls are pinned back from her face today by two charcoal pencils tucked into the updo.

"Hey, Rip."

"You're alive. That's fortunate."

"I called you back," I try to justify. "Left a voicemail."

"Days later, sure. I had to hear from Ember that you weren't blown to pieces or shot by a rogue sniper. You're an asshole."

Nearing her, I risk laying a palm on her shoulder. "I'm really sorry."

She shakes me off. "We were all terrified when we heard the news."

"It's been an intense few weeks. The team's running on empty, Ember's brother is still sedated, and we lost someone in the crossfire during the raid. It's no excuse, but I didn't ignore you on purpose."

"I guess I know that." Ripley heaves an exasperated breath.

"Thanks for coming to the hospital."

"Ember's cute, by the way. A bit standoffish, but who isn't?"

"She's kinda the reason I'm here. I know I don't have much of a right to ask you for anything right now, but…"

Pulling the plug free, Ripley drains the sink then stacks up her clean brushes. I watch her dry off before she turns to face me fully with a cocked brow, her septum piercing askew from where her nose wrinkles.

"Did you come here for a girl talk, Warner?"

"Maybe?" I wince.

"Kill me softly."

"I just need some advice."

"Alright, fine. But I need a drink for this."

Ripley shouts at the guys to make themselves scarce then breaks open her emergency 'inspiration' juice. Namely, a half-empty bottle of dark rum. We set ourselves up in two armchairs, tucked into the corner of her cosy studio.

She curls her legs beneath her, tugging her long sleeve down to cover the tattoo botched by old scar tissue. Years later, she hasn't bothered to fix the mess made during her time in Harrowdean.

"Let me guess. She doesn't love you back?"

I choke on a mouthful of rum. "You could beat around the bush a little."

"Not my style. Spill the beans."

"I don't think… uh, loving me is the problem." My stare fixes on the glass. "It's her feelings for my teammates and our criminal stowaway that's causing the issue."

She snorts into her drink. "So that's why you came to me."

"Rip," I groan.

"Come on. You've watched us navigate a shared relationship for a decade, and your bloody directors are married to the same woman. What's the issue?"

"Ember is vulnerable. I'm trying to protect her."

"Protect her or protect yourself?"

"Rip…"

"She's far from vulnerable," Ripley points out. "If Ember knows her own mind, you damn well better respect that. She's an adult."

"An adult embroiled in an international criminal investigation with stakes higher than any of us signed up for!"

"Yeah, whatever. What's really the problem?"

"We're all falling apart, Rip," I admit after a beat. "It's my job to keep our team safe."

"Safe or controlled?"

"Stop with the closed questions already. I know you learned that shit from me."

"You always asked open-ended questions, actually." She grins while sipping her drink.

"Bloody smartass."

"Cut the shit. Why are you here?"

My aching fist balls, thudding on the hollow expanse of my prosthetic. "Because I just beat the shit out of the criminal my girl was tongue-fucking, and now she won't speak to me."

The quiet thud draws Ripley's eyes down to the carbon fibre limb I keep covered. As shadows dance over her face, I know she's remembering the accident that took my leg from me. She was there too. It's one of many shitty memories we share.

"I don't know what to do." I sigh.

"Was it consensual?" She looks up at me. "The kiss."

"Apparently."

"And are you exclusive with this girl?"

Unease churns through me. "Not exactly. It's complicated."

"Then she's done nothing wrong, and you need to check your jealousy before you lose her for good. Ember spent years being held against her will. She's allowed to explore."

"Not if it risks her safety!"

"We're all vulnerable," Ripley argues. "We all get hurt. Nothing you or anyone can do will ever stop that from happening."

"So what the hell am I supposed to do?"

"Get in the boat, or let it sail away without you."

Not fucking happening.

"And if I don't want it to sail away?" Frustration thickens my voice.

"Then you best be good at grovelling to barter your way onboard. If one of my guys tried that shit, I'd break their fucking kneecaps for presuming to tell me what I can do with my own body."

"Well, shit." I slurp another mouthful of liquor. "You got all grown up and smart. When did that happen?"

"Shut up, Langley."

"Whatever."

With years' worth of emotional baggage between us, she matches my smile. The shared trauma of that case bonded me to Ripley and her men for life but also earned me their friendship. I should never take it for granted.

"I'll talk to her," I decide with a nod.

"And apologise."

"Yeah, I heard you. I'll fix this."

"While you're fixing things… Next time you almost die chasing bad guys, give us a head's up so I don't have to leave my apartment to track you down."

"What have you got against getting some fresh air?"

Ripley rolls her eyes. "It's way too people-y out there."

"You'll get bored of the quiet life one day, Rip."

"Nah. I fought hard for my peace after Harrowdean. You can be sure I have no intention of jeopardising it."

With our drinks finished, I stand up to envelope Ripley in a bear hug. Her head tucks beneath my chin, the scent of paint and varnish clinging to her oversized tee. Still, the embrace soothes something wild inside me.

"Stay for dinner?" She squeezes me once more and steps back.

"I'm not sure that I fancy getting food poisoning."

"Raine's cooking isn't that bad. Ignore those idiots."

"I should get back to the team. The case is getting to us all." My head shakes. "It feels like we're constantly three steps behind, and there's no end in sight."

"Sounds familiar." Ripley's lips twist into a grimace.

"Doesn't it just?"

She clasps my shoulder, smiling sadly. "We won against all the odds before. That investigation nearly killed us too, but we still made it."

"And it cost us everything."

"Not everything," Ripley challenges. "Not us, and not this family. Don't lose hope yet."

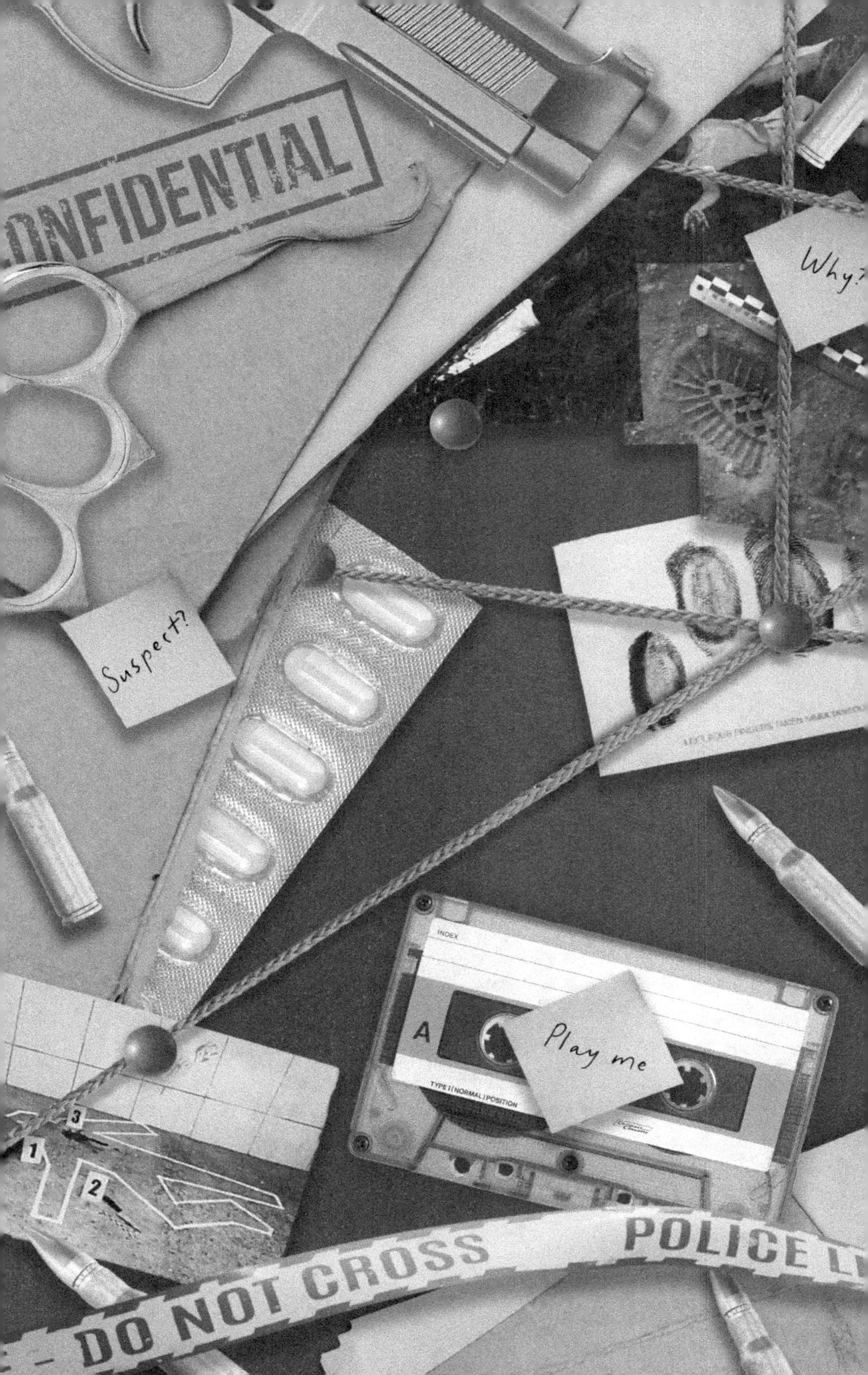

CONFIDENTIAL
Why?
Suspect?
Play me
A
INDEX
TYPE I (NORMAL) POSITION
DO NOT CROSS
POLICE
1
2
3

(NORMAL) POSITION
play
me
DO NOT CROSS
POL
Suspect?
NOT CROSS
POLICE LI

13

EMBER

WHICH WITCH – FLORENCE + THE MACHINE

"**A**xel Slaughter, get back here this instant, and unlock me!"

No matter how loudly I scream, the purple-haired fuck fails to make an appearance. I suppose he thinks this is funny. All I said was that I planned to go into work today after being bedridden post-seizure. I can't just lay here.

Now I'm pinned to my bed frame by a silver handcuff closed around my left wrist, keeping me trapped like a fucking prisoner in my own home. That wanker is on 'watch Ember duty' and took it to mean he could restrain me.

"You asshole!" I holler.

Worst part is, I doubt anyone else would free me even if they were here. Warner's off on some *Eat, Pray, Love* soul-searching mission, refusing to look at me after the fight. Hyland's cataloguing

evidence from the docks. Plus, I haven't seen Blaine since Warner broke his nose.

Leaving me with the psycho.

And his fucking handcuffs.

"I'm perfectly capable of looking after myself!" I screech loudly. "I cannot lay in this bed for another day when we have an investigation to run. Let me out!"

This is exactly why I hid the attack in the first place. Their worried fussing is unbearable. Between Hyland hovering like a goddamn mother hen, Warner stomping around in a cloud of jealous rage and Axel wanting to spoon-feed me medication, I'm going insane. We don't have time for this.

"Axel! You controlling dick!"

"Did someone call my name?" His head pops into the room.

The evil glint in his whiskey-orange eyes is making me want to do some nose breaking of my own. Axel leans against the door, thumbs hooked in the waistband of his sweats, his bare, tattooed torso on full display.

I don't know if showing off his stacked abdominals, muscle-carved chest or beautifully defined pectorals is some kind of tactic, but I'm not falling for it. Even if my mouth grows dry at the delicious sight.

"You look suitably rested," he teases.

"Unlock the cuffs."

"And let you kick my ass? I'll pass. You're on bed rest."

"I'm not a fucking child!"

"Then don't act like one." He winks at me. "You need to learn to trust us with your condition, once and for all. If that involves forcing you to get some rest, then I'll take one for the team."

"How often does handcuffing a girl result in trust for you?" I sass back.

Axel runs a hand over his faux hawk, smoothing the flyaways. "All the time."

"Bullshit."

"Surrender can be quite fulfilling. Care to try it?"

"Fuck you!"

"Me? Or Blaine Madden?"

Straining against the cuff, I long to wrap my hands around his throat. This is such a mess. And honestly, an unwelcome distraction. We don't need to be fighting over this right now, and I definitely don't need to be confined to this bed.

"I have a job to do." I glower at him.

Axel shrugs. "You can go back to work once you've seen the specialist next week. Warner's orders. Until then, get used to me waiting on you hand and foot."

"Next week? No chance!"

"Then the cuffs will stay. To be honest, it's fun to watch you wriggling around like a fish on a hook. I don't mind if you continue to struggle."

"Argh!"

Flopping back, I slump against the pillows. I'm still recovering from the intense seizure and don't have the energy to play his stupid game all day. Especially not if he's enjoying it.

Axel pouts then vanishes, his footsteps padding away from my bedroom. I stare up at the ceiling, attempting to breathe through my indignation until I hear him returning. The dick hums under his breath all day long.

"You want peanut butter or cheese?"

My head lifts. "Huh?"

Axel waves two plates, approaching the bed where I'm still restrained. "Ladies' choice. Gotta keep my caged bird fed."

"I'm not a pet."

"No, a pet would take the sandwich without being difficult."

"Peanut butter." I stick out my one free hand.

"Good girl. Now, promise you're not going to throw it at me or slit my throat with the shattered plate?"

"Now that you mention it..."

Axel rolls his eyes at my evil grin. "Give it your best shot."

Setting his plate down, Axel dips a hand into his pocket to pull out several brightly-coloured pills. He deposits them on the side of my plate then scoots it closer to me, moving the bottle of water from my bedside table so it's within reach.

"You're drugging me now?" I lift a brow.

"It's your medication, genius. Evening dose."

Looking down at the sandwich, I make a point of analysing it like he might've spiked the bread or something. Axel huffs at my attitude, sitting down to jam a cheese-filled triangle into his mouth.

"Just checking you haven't sedated it or some shit to keep me compliant."

"Damn," he says through his mouthful. "I missed a trick there."

"Ha fucking ha."

"Eat. Please."

Pushing the plate aside after a few bites, I take my meds then return my focus to escaping the cuffs. Even with one spare hand, I can't find a weakness in the mechanism or work my wrist free. I'll have to break the bed at this rate.

Axel leans back on his elbows, legs outstretched and empty plate set aside. He watches me with an amused smile.

"Some people try to dislocate their thumb." He flicks crumbs from his chest.

"Stupid. Doesn't actually work."

"Does too."

"How many action movies have you watched?"

"All experience, babe."

"You're not a secret agent, Ax. You're just a fucking idiot."

"Ouch." He rubs between his pecs. "You wound me."

"Get over it."

"Learn to rest, and take care of your body without being restrained," he hits back.

"I'll rest when I've seen my brother and found Gracie. Killed Gael. Dismantled an international trafficking ring. Located Blaine, wherever he's sulking. Oh, and kicked Warner's ass for being a jealous prick."

"That all?" He chuckles.

"It's a working itinerary."

"Then I best carve out my place in it." Axel eyes me lasciviously. "With all these men lining up to stake their place, I can't have you forgetting me now."

"It isn't like that, and you know it."

"Do I?" he challenges. "Madden's a freak show, Em. You have no idea what he's capable of. But apparently, that's reason enough to stick your tongue down his neck."

"Careful. Your jealousy's showing."

His leg loops over mine, tangling together. "Is that such a bad thing? Just shows how serious I am about us. I'll cut off Madden's head and deliver it to your doorstep to prove my point."

"We literally live in the same apartment."

"Irrelevant. I'm making a grand, romantic gesture."

My wrist burns and chafes where the metal bites into it each time I try to break free. Axel narrows his eyes but doesn't move to stop me from hurting myself.

"What's romantic about first-degree murder and a beheading?"

"Clearly, we are not the same person." He sighs in mock-disappointment. "How else am I going to make you behave?"

"Learn to accept defeat," I answer snarkily.

"Hm, not my style."

Shifting onto his haunches, Axel knee-walks up the mattress. He easily pushes my legs apart to settle between them, looming above my prone state. His eyes greedily drink in my bare thighs and hips where my t-shirt has ridden up.

"Nice t-shirt. Looks a lot like Warner's to me."

"It's not."

"You're mad at him but still wearing his shit." He observes intently.

My teeth grind together. "This isn't Warner's t-shirt."

"Keep telling yourself that. How'd you steal it?"

I'm definitely not going to admit that I snuck into his empty bedroom and pilfered it from his wardrobe while he's been avoiding me like the plague. I wanted to feel close to him. Even though he, apparently, hates my guts right now.

Axel circles my kneecap, fingertips dancing upward to tease my thigh. Each playful stroke causes my hair to stand on end, every nerve straining for the relief his touch brings, though I won't allow myself to have it.

His callouses move over my skin, thumbs circling the sensitive inner slopes that lead to the molten heat gathering inside me. My body doesn't care how mad I am. In fact, that seems to be making it all the more responsive to Axel's mind games.

When the tip of his index finger traces over my black panties, right where my pussy lips are encased in rapidly dampening cotton, I feel my spine arch.

"Don't t-touch me!"

"What was that?" He watches my face.

"Stop… ah, fuck."

Dragging his nails over my mound again, I try to bite back my enjoyment. It's impossible. The slightest pressure and I can already feel my clit pulsating. I'm too frustrated and wound up to pretend I don't need his touch.

"Is this how I have to make you obey?" Axel wonders aloud. "Fuck you into submission?"

"I'm going to break every last one of your fingers."

"Then I wouldn't be able to do this."

He pushes my panties to one side, easily sliding beneath the elastic to glide two fingers straight through my heat. I gasp at the intrusion, my legs widening reflexively, allowing him to access my core.

Axel teases my slick folds, orbiting my clit then moving his finger lower to breach my entrance. When he pushes it inside me, rotating softly before adding a second finger, I whine his name.

"That's a yes." A sadistic grin quirks his lips.

"What?" I moan.

"I do have to fuck you into submission. You can't run around disobeying orders if you're pinned to this bed by my cock, right?"

"Jesus, Ax."

He drives the threat home with a fast pump, drawing his fingers fully out then shoving them back inside my weeping cunt. I cry out in pleasure, fisting the bedsheets with my unrestrained hand.

"So angry and yet so wet for me." Axel continues working me over with fast thrusts. "You're desperate to be touched, babe. Touched and thoroughly fucked."

"I… am… not!"

At my protest, he withdraws his hand. I can't help calling out in shock, mourning the loss. My legs are shaking as warmth gathers between my legs, begging for his attention.

"What was that?" He scowls down at me.

"Goddamn you."

"I've got all night, Em. Keep fighting me if you so wish."

"Let me go! Now!"

"I'm not quite done with this disobedient little pussy yet."

He bends down, pushing my legs wider apart as he peels my panties down. I'm exposed to his stare, a shiver wracking over me at the pure, animalistic lust that fills his uncut ambers.

"You're going to learn, dimples. Good girls who do as they're told are rewarded."

"I'm not good at following orders," I whimper in need.

"By the time I'm done here, you will be."

Axel pauses to take a deep sniff of my underwear, his eyes refusing to leave mine. Desire unfurls inside me as he tosses the scrap aside then retakes his position. All I can see is his tousled, purple locks when I feel his tongue glide over my sensitive skin.

Lips secure themselves to my clit, sucking and rolling the bud until I can't hold in another cry. Axel's tongue laps at me like I'm his favourite flavour of ice cream, never once letting up.

When his digits return to my slit, the combined effect has me thrashing against the damn handcuff. I don't know if I want to punch his smug face or bury my fingers in his hair while he eats me alive.

"Ax!" I whine frantically.

His fingers curl inside me, brushing the sweet spot of pure ecstasy. With his thumb bearing down on my clit and tongue greedily devouring my essence, it's too much. He's chasing my traitorous body down a path I can't stop it from taking.

"Please." My protests turn to pathetic gasps. "Oh, God. More... Ax!"

One more swipe of his tongue and I feel myself detonate. He's pumping into me relentlessly, drawing the orgasm from my depths at a furious pace. My walls clench, muscles tense then my mind explodes with all-consuming bliss.

Still, Axel doesn't let up, pulling his hand free to make room for his mouth. He drinks in every lick of moisture, teasing my release to its maximum. I writhe and shudder underneath him, the evening-lit room turning hazy all around me.

When I come back down to earth, the playful rogue who's spent months taunting me is nowhere to be found. A dark, determined angel stares down at me with a raw look of hunger that makes my spine tingle.

"They all think you're theirs." He wipes moisture from his mouth. "And I don't mind sharing you, but I'm going to be the one to fuck this sweet cunt first."

God, I should say no. Kick him in the face. Tell him and his overbearing, alpha-hole teammates to fuck off to high heaven. Anything but moan at the spasms his words evoke inside me.

I mewl like a needy animal when Axel dips out of the room, leaving me soaked and spreadeagled. He returns with a foil packet clasped between his fingers, already shoving his sweats off at the foot of the bed.

A hedonistic thrill barrels through me at the sizable swell stretching his boxers. I can already imagine the burn of his huge dick stretching me open. God, he's big. All the reasons I'm mad at him suddenly seem unimportant as he shoves off his boxers.

"Touch yourself," Axel orders. "Now."

His stare devours my movements, watching me tug on the restraint with one hand while I play with my juices. I'm already slick and tingling from the orgasm he plucked out of me.

"Perfect," he hums, his pupils blown.

"Please. I need… I want…"

"What, babe? What do you want from me?"

"Fuck me."

"So demanding for such a stubborn girl, don't you think?"

He fists his hard cock, stroking the vein-studded length. Axel's generous and thick, his rosy head glistening with pre-come. My pussy tightens as I imagine exactly what he'll feel like.

I'm on the verge of begging when he tears the condom then slowly rolls it onto his steel while stalking back over to the bed. The mattress shifts as Axel settles onto it, braced between my trembling legs.

He smiles to himself while rolling my shirt up, taking the sports bra I'm wearing with it. The fabric bunches around my trapped wrist, leaving my chest bare for his perusal.

"Are you going to release me?"

His fingers trail over my breasts, thumb circling one hard nipple. "Nope."

The head of his cock rounds my wet heat, sluicing back and forth without entering me. After all this time, he still feels the need to tease. I curse him out as Axel rolls my nipple, lightly pinching it.

"Tell me you're going to listen from now on." He runs his length over my clit and down. "You're going to take care of yourself."

"Ax…"

"You're going to trust this team. Let us in. Cooperate."

"Please. Ax, please—"

"Submit, Em. Let us love you."

Each time he nudges my entrance, the pressure vanishes before I can find relief. He won't slam into me. Not like I want him to. I throw my head back and scream out his name in frustration.

"In return, I'll never deny you." Axel's jaw clenches from the effort of holding himself back.

"Wha… What does that mean?" I pant.

"It means if you give yourself to us fully, you can have whatever you want. I'll make sure of it. But I'm not watching you swan around, worrying about everyone but yourself any longer."

When I don't agree, Axel presses inside me just the barest amount. Enough for me to hug his cock in gratification then ache from loss when he snatches it back.

"No!" I shrill.

"It can all be yours, Ember. Just say the word."

When he inches in again, my mind splits apart. All the anger and suffocating loneliness that's driven me to keep these toxic secrets… The fear of abandonment… The need to protect myself because no one else ever will. It all boils over, causing a monumental system failure.

"Say it," he commands.

"Ax… please…"

"I want to hear it!"

"Yes! Fuck!"

Axel pistons into me hard enough for a guttural roar to spill from my lips. His girth stretches me wide, filling every last microscopic speck of space I have to give. We smack together, hips aligned and bodies attached, leaving nothing between us.

He draws out only to slam back home, the momentum causing the handcuff to clatter loudly. I'm still half-pinned, one hand above my head and the other seizing Axel's shoulder. If I don't hold onto him, I think he'll break me in half.

Our breath exchanges in a stuttered conversation of mindless, pent-up lust. I can hardly think past the place where our bodies join, shattering the sexual tension of countless shared looks since the night he entered my motel room.

"You take me so well." Axel's tone is guttural and rough. "So fucking well."

I melt under him, lavishing his praise. "More."

"Yes, babe. Take it."

Each thrust hits deep, battering his ownership into me. Over and over. A brutal, bruising collision that shatters any meagre hint of professionalism between us. Axel takes a fucking sledgehammer to that lie, and for once, it feels good to surrender to another person.

When Axel halts, sliding himself free, my mewling sounds frantic even to my own ears. He reaches above me to unlatch the handcuff cutting into my wrist, letting my arm flop and clothing scatter. I don't have a second to recover before he's seizing my waist to flip me over.

Fingers bite into my hips as Axel lifts my rear end high. I'm bent over like a dog, ass up and spine bent, head buried in my warm pillow. His tip strokes over my pussy then pushes back inside from a new angle.

I shout into the pillow, feeling fuller than ever. From this position, Axel is seated deep inside me. His hand runs down my spine, then fire races over my ass cheek where it smacks into me.

"You wanted more," he grunts.

"Yes! Please!"

"Christ, Em. You're so goddamn tight."

I'm fucked rough and hard. Tits bouncing. Leg muscles burning. Walls squeezing tight around Axel's cock, repeatedly bulldozing into me with enough force to ignite another meltdown. I'm seconds from exploding around him.

Another firm spank and I spiral, quickly falling apart. Every last internal boundary collapses into spectacular pieces, letting Axel barge his way into my whole being. Every nerve. Every sense. I'm lost to his touch, the strength of his thrusts, the way my limbs turn to blissful jelly.

Still, he won't let up. Not as my system sprints into overdrive or my brain feels like it's going to fracture from the drawn-out orgasm. Axel grips my hips hard enough to ache and rides me like he's spent months fantasising about this exact moment.

"You're mine." He puffs for air. "So fucking perfect for me."

"Yours," I moan in a daze.

"That's right. I want everyone to know it."

My head pulls upright when his hand takes hold of my loose red hair, forming a leash. Axel grips my locks, using the leverage while he fucks me like a vengeful god out to prove a point.

Every doubt flies from my mind, ejected by brute force alone. No amount of turmoil for crossing this line could stop us now. Axel leaves no room to question exactly what he wants from me as he batters an imprint into my very soul.

After he dips a finger through the wetness leaking from where we're joined, Axel finds my backside. I jerk on the bed, pushing back into his crotch, the sensation startling me.

"Easy, babe."

Pressure builds at my rear where his finger is slowly penetrating me. It's an odd intrusion, half-pain and half-pleasure that has me squirming for something I can't quite name.

"I'm going to take this hole soon." Nerve endings I didn't know I had spark to life as he eases his digit inside me. "Maybe I'll let one of the others fuck your pussy while I do it."

"Oh God," I mewl.

"You like the idea of that, don't you?"

While he worships my core, his finger swirls inside me from behind, unlocking a new thrill. The punishing cinch on my hair grows tighter, adding to my sensory overload. All I can do is rock back and forth into each ragged slam.

"Take my cock," he grunts, driving deep into me.

"Ax! Can't… take more…"

"Yes, babe. You can. Come all over me, cover me in your juices. Give me everything."

Another digit breaches my asshole, and I see stars. The stretch is too much. I'm overwhelmed by Axel, drowning in every place he's claiming my body, and it's too late to stop the inevitable meltdown.

His fingers scissor in time to his undulating hips, wringing every last drop of desire from my veins. Before exhaustion can creep in, I sense the edges of another release creeping over me. He's determined to find my breaking point.

"I'm close," Axel huffs.

Nails dig into my hips, the zaps of pain hitting like sparks from a flame. It's nothing compared to the inferno that's been stoked within me, reaching every corner of my mind. All my boundaries, secrets and bullshit excuses crisp in the flames.

The final pump sends me catapulting off the precipice, straight into the arms of another eruption. My body is wrung out, tingling with stimulation, barely able to hold itself up.

Axel roars my name, his grip on my hair slackening, hips stilling as he finds his release. Despite the condom, heat spreads through me, warming my inner walls. The feeling only intensifies the orgasm charging through me at breakneck speed.

Each internal tremor saps the last of my energy, roughly depositing me in the blissful oblivion of aftershocks. We collapse simultaneously, slippery limbs entwining to form a sweaty heap on the bed.

I twist to land cradled between Axel's arm and his heaving chest, dotted with beads of moisture. He's limp too, flopped on his back with his eyelids hanging at half-mast.

"Did you die?" I taunt between pants.

"Yes. Went to heaven."

Smiling, I hook my leg over his, uncaring of the sticky warmth covering my thighs from multiple orgasms. Axel tugs off the condom then ties it off and sets it aside.

"You okay?"

"Mm." Dazed, I moan in reply. "Think I quite like being fucked into behaving."

"Then you should be a stubborn pain in the ass more often."

"Perhaps I will."

"Preferably without causing a fight or fitting in secret somewhere," he clarifies, two narrowed eyes turning on me. "Warner's heart can't take it."

"His heart needs a damn good talking to."

"I'll leave that pleasure for you."

"Gee, thanks."

We curl into each other, basking in the post-sex glow. I'm in no rush to leave his arms; I need a minute until I have to face the music. We're alone here, but that doesn't mean things haven't changed. I know where Axel stands. Hyland? Blaine? Warner? Complete unknowns.

I'm not stupid enough to think that what I'm asking for isn't too much. By any normal standard, what I want with all of my teammates is wrong. Greedy. Immoral. But I know what I want and who I'm willing to share my life with. After years of powerlessness, this is my decision.

I want Axel. Hyland.

Warner.

Blaine too.

I want us to find the love and security we've never had before in each other. To endure this storm as a team, a unit… a family. After so much heartache, it's clear to me now. The only way we end this is if we work together.

The soft vibrating of my phone eventually breaks our peace. I disentangle myself from Axel to check, finding two missed calls and a text message from Hyland in the group chat.

"Shit."

"What is it?" Axel props his head up.

"Tom's doctor tried to call me. He's waking up."

Compact Cassette
I (NORMAL) POSITION
play
me
DO NOT CROSS
POLIC
Suspect?
4
NOT CROSS
POLICE L

14

EMBER

WHAT I NEED – HIGH JUNE

Impatience forms an electrified cattle prod, jabbing into my soft tissue as I watch the doctor talk to Tom through the pane of glass in his door. He's disorientated, still confined to the hospital bed, his heavy eyes forming slits that seem reluctant to open at all.

I doubt he even knows where he is after being sedated while the antibiotics did their work. As much as I want to race in there and throw my arms around him, I'm holding back until the doctor's done his job.

But Tom's awake. Safe. Alive.

That's a small *fuck you* to Gael and his men.

The off-beat thud of approaching footsteps warns me that Warner is near. His gait is entirely unique. I avoided his gaze when I arrived with Axel, leaving them in the ICU's waiting area.

"Ember?"

Turning to face him, I reluctantly move away from Tom's hospital room to meet Warner in the middle of the long corridor. He tentatively scans over me, blue gaze brimming with a confusing blend of concern and reluctance.

"Hi."

"Hey," he returns.

An awkward silence pulses between us.

"They let you in yet?"

"No." I shake my head, teeth gritted tight. "Could be a while."

"I see."

His clipped tone causes the hair on my arms to spike. God, I fucking hate it when he talks to me like I'm a client. Still I bite my tongue and study his stoic mask, lined with exhausted grooves beneath a crop of mussed, silver-flecked hair.

Even his form-fitting black t-shirt and cargos are rumpled, body weight visibly lurching to one side as he leans on his good left leg. My heart wrings, aching with the need to inch closer.

"I have someone for you to meet in the waiting area."

"Who is it?" Confusion causes my brows to dip.

"Jamie. Tom's boyfriend."

"Oh, crap!"

I'm officially the worst person ever for not even considering him in all this chaos. Warner must read the panic on my expression, his features softening with understanding.

"It's okay. I've been keeping him up to speed for the past couple of weeks. We've met a few times over the years. He wasn't kept in the dark."

"You did that for me?"

"Tom isn't just your responsibility," Warner deflects like it's nothing. "I took care of it."

Appreciation warms my cold shell. "Thanks."

"Don't mention it."

"I can't believe I forgot him." I cringe at my own selfishness.

"You've had a lot on your mind," he empathises. "Don't beat yourself up about it."

"Too much to make a quick phone call?"

"Relax, Em. He's fine."

Scrubbing a hand down my face, I wince when I hit one of the yellowing bruises. Warner watches me warily, his hand outstretched like he wants to touch me but can't find the bravery to do it.

"You always think of everything."

He rolls his lips, seemingly weighing a response. "I told you that you don't have to do this alone."

"I'm starting to understand that."

"This is what teams do. We support each other. Share the load. We keep each other afloat when the world comes crashing down around us."

"Do teams attack each other too?"

As soon as the question slips out, I internally curse myself. *Wrong time, wrong place.* But I hate this weird tension between us, the physical distance that feels like a whole fucking country.

Warner sighs, the sad sound laden with bone-deep fatigue. "Jamie can wait. Let's talk somewhere more private, Tom doesn't need to hear this."

"Probably for the best."

I gingerly take the arm he extends to guide me into a vacant examination room, flipping the door sign to 'occupied' on his way past. When he closes us in, the balloon in my chest threatens to rupture.

"You've been avoiding me."

"I have." He glances around the white room. "I needed some time to think."

My lips seal shut as I lean against the wall. "Is that all?"

"Yes."

"Just admit that you didn't want to see me."

"That's not true." Warner folds his arms, biceps bulging against his cotton tee. "I need space sometimes too."

"From me?"

"Maybe. Yes."

More pain lances across my chest, causing the backs of my eyes to burn. I stare down at the floor until the sensation passes. His silence feels deafening in the small space we share, temporarily tucked away from the world.

"Em…"

"I was worried about you." My voice comes out croaky, borderline ashamed. "That's all."

"Look, I regret what happened with Madden." His taut posture reveals the reluctance of his confession. "But seeing his hands on you was more than I could handle. You need to understand how I feel."

"I'm trying to, but you're not making it any easier. You don't open up. You run away and hide when things get tough. You beat the shit out of Blaine rather than taking a moment to actually think."

Warner's stubbled face cringes like he's tasted something unpleasant.

"What did you expect me to do? Shake his hand?"

"How about behave like an adult?" I suggest.

"I'm the only one acting like an adult by considering the consequences of my actions. I'd recommend trying it."

"What consideration?" I laugh in his face. "You broke his nose!"

His head throws back so he can stare at the ceiling. "That asshole had his hands where they don't belong. He's lucky I didn't hack them off along with his wandering tongue."

"Jesus. You know what? Forget it."

Pushing off from the wall, I move to escape the small room. What I don't expect is for Warner to barge in front of me, literally blocking the exit.

"Move!"

"No." He braces his hands in the doorframe. "I want to talk to you."

"I'm done talking about this."

"How I reacted was wrong, but I'm not going to apologise for how I feel. He had no right."

"That isn't your decision to make! You don't control me."

Anger churns in his baby blues, roiling like the open ocean. "Is that what you think I'm doing?"

"That or throwing your toys out of the pram. You assaulted him, Warner! You told him to leave, and no one has seen him since!"

The vein in his forehead throbs. "He deserved more than a broken nose."

"Do you hear yourself?" I hiss furiously.

"Do you understand how I feel about you?" he fires back.

"No! Fucking enlighten me!"

"Fine!" Warner thunders. "Let's put all our cards on the table."

Releasing the doorframe, he marches right up into my face. We end up nose-to-nose, almost touching, our breath exchanging in an angry debate as his stare sears me down to the bare bone.

When he clasps my chin between his thumb and forefinger, I don't have to resist the urge to flinch away. I'm trapped. Enraptured. Held hostage by a force far greater than I can resist. He holds me prisoner in the heavy weight of his passionate glare.

"You want the real, honest to God truth?" Warner appeals.

He's so loud, I'm surprised nobody has come in yet.

"Yes!"

"Ember, I have loved you since we were children." He lashes the words like an invisible whip. "I grew up watching you become a gorgeous, strong, selfless woman who took on the world each bloody day without a word of complaint."

My tongue glues to the roof of my mouth, all moisture vaporising.

"Even in the years I spent fighting overseas, I thought of nothing but when I'd see you again. I dreamt of you at night. I hoped and prayed that you were happy. I fantasised about a life where I could come home and finally call you mine."

His forehead teases mine, mouth a mere brush from my open lips. My rioting heart rate seems to beg for him to close that minuscule gap and end this torture.

"No matter how many times I told myself that it's wrong to want the girl I grew up with, my best friend's baby sister, and that I'd lose him by loving you… it changed absolutely nothing. I don't care anymore."

"Why?" I summon the courage to ask.

"Because I have loved you for two agonising fucking decades," he whispers breathlessly. "And I'll love you for the rest of my life and further still. You're the beginning and the end for me."

Realisation is a seismic force that levels my anger in the blink of an eye. It isn't indignation churning in his vivid irises. No, I was wrong. Warner looks at me with bottomless adoration.

It's the same way he's looked at me since I was young and stupid. The same way he's always looked at me. Even when I refused to look back. It's plain as day as he struggles to catch his breath now that the truth is out there.

"Say it again." I grip the fabric of his shirt, wanting to pull his lips to mine.

"I love you," he repeats.

My tongue darts out to wet my lips. "You love me."

"Yes."

"All this time?"

"Yes," Warner affirms.

"You're really in love with me."

"How many other ways are there to say it?" His mouth twitches.

"But all this time… you… you said this was wrong. That we could never be together. You held back."

"That doesn't change the truth, nor does it stop me from wanting you now. After everything that's happened, I'm ready for us to take a bit of happiness for ourselves. No matter the consequences."

Inevitably, doubt resurfaces faster than I can revel in my victory. "What about Tom?"

He sighs heavily through his nostrils. "No matter the consequences, Em. I'm not losing you. I don't know how yet, but I'll make this work."

Shock churns through me, our chests brushing together when I waver on my feet. Warner's pine and patchouli scent is hardwired into my dopamine receptors, and I can't stop myself from pressing into his hard chest.

He loves me.

After all this time… I have the truth.

Warner fucking loves me.

His thumb smooths over my bruises, eyes bouncing from side-to-side as he weighs my reaction. Hope and terror form a perplexing concoction in his heated stare, undoubtedly mirroring my own confusion.

"I'm falling for you," I admit hoarsely. "I have been for a while now. You're not the boy I grew up with anymore, and I don't want us to go back to just being just friends."

He rests one hand on my hip while the other cups my jawline, holding me in a loose grasp. Each brush of his hardened fingertips sends electric zaps into my out-of-control heart.

"What do you want?" he murmurs.

My throat thickens. "To belong."

"You'll always belong when you're with me, love. I've carried a piece of you in my soul since the day we met, and I brushed the knots from your wet hair when you refused to let your mum do it."

Grief blazes across my breastbone, tempered by the sweetness of the old memory. "She tugged too hard with the brush. You were gentler."

"I used to love being the only one who could make you stop crying."

"Because I felt safe with you."

He pushes hair behind my ear so tenderly it hurts my heart. "You're always safe with me. No matter what happens between us, Em. You're safe by my side, and I will always protect you with my life."

We rest our foreheads together, exchanging a silent vow. One riddled with all the words we don't need to say. For a second, I can just be a girl, letting the boy she liked as a kid hold her tight.

But this isn't a child-like world of fantasy, and nothing comes quite so easily in reality. It doesn't take long for every last complication that's kept us apart to barge into the forefront and reclaim my thoughts.

"Why the change of heart?"

Warner inhales sharply, his eyes ducking. "I went to see an old friend."

"Oh. I see."

Leaning back in to catch my gaze, he offers a tentative smile. "You can wipe that hurt look off your face. Ripley put me in my place over a few drinks then sent me back here to make things right with you."

I fight off a grin. Sounds about right.

"I know this is all messy as hell and far too complicated to figure out right now, but I now realise I have no right to dictate your sex life. Even if I don't like who you choose to be with."

"Blaine just happened," I admit. "I didn't plan it."

"I'm not judging you, Em."

"Maybe you should be."

"Well I'm not," he rasps. "All I want is for you to be safe and happy. If you need my brothers for that… then I can think of worse people to share you with. I've made my peace with it."

"Does that include Blaine Madden?"

The nerve in his neck tics. "Em…"

"He isn't a bad person, and he's trying to prove his worth to the team. Without his help, we never would've found Tom."

"I see that. But you don't know him like I do."

"That's the point. I see what you don't, and I know he's a good person. Imperfect, sure, but he's determined to do the right thing. He belongs here with our team."

The thumb stroking over my cheek shifts lower, tracing the outline of my mouth. My head tilts up, letting me melt into his touch, seeking whatever validation I can find in his gentle caress.

"Blaine Madden is an asset." He pushes out a breath. "I told you that I'd share your heart with my brothers if I had to, but he is not part of this family. Madden can't be trusted."

"He's helped us."

"And I'm grateful for that, but he's an outsider. Just remember that."

"What are you saying?" I swallow hard.

"I'm not saying anything. This is your life and your decision. I was an idiot for thinking I had any right to shame you. All I want is for you to be happy… But please be careful who you trust."

Lips sealed tight, I nod. Warner tugs my bottom lip, still drinking in every last detail like I'm an unknown entity that threatens his entire existence.

"If anyone one hurts you—even Hyland or Axel—I'll fucking kill them, Em. Without hesitation or regret. You just say the word."

"They're your family," I point out.

"So are you."

He's deadly serious, and I can't help but grin.

"You're insane."

"I refuse to lose this chance with you. I'm willing to try this your way, but don't think for a second that I'll let those men break your heart without paying a steep price."

At my own peril, I brush my mouth over his. "Yes, boss."

"Hell," he groans. "Call me that again."

"Boss?" I chortle.

"Shit. Never let Hyland hear you say that. The oaf's jealous enough."

"Yes, boss."

"You're fucking trouble, Em. Then again, you always were."

Before I can pull away, Warner's mouth crash lands on mine with an audible smack. His lips take me prisoner, gliding over mine in a messy tangle of rampant desire. I let him devour me—mind, body and soul. Whatever he wants.

A slow fizzle becomes a raging fire deep inside me with each stroke of his lips on mine. When the warm swipe of his tongue glides in, I can't suppress a moan. Every place he touches breaks out into scorching tingles.

The cold wall of the clinical room presses into my back when Warner slams me up against it, his knee shifting between my legs. I'm pinned in place by his hips, mouth still ravaging mine as his hardening crotch pushes into me.

Every moment I've dreamed of this condenses into a rush of unfiltered satisfaction, eliminating the agony that's kept us apart. The boy who once made me smile and laugh as a sad kid is the man laying claim to my body now.

And it feels oh-so fucking right.

He was always meant to be mine.

We don't even break apart at the light tap on the door, signalling an interruption. To his credit, Warner nuzzles into my neck when the door clicks open, allowing me to blink through my haze-covered vision.

"Apologies," Hyland rumbles from the doorway. "But Tom's ready for you, and I can't keep Jamie back much longer if you want to go in first."

"For fuck's sake." Warner shoots him a displeased look.

I squeeze his bicep before lightly pushing him back. "It's okay."

"No, it's not. I can't go in there like this."

"Why not?"

Gaze averted, Warner shifts to adjust himself. A flush creeps over my cheeks at the knowing look on Hyland's face, watching us de-tangle from each other as his team leader deals with his now-obvious arousal.

"All good?" Hyland asks slyly.

"Mind your own business." Warner glares at him.

"Ember is my business. Upset her again and my fist will be having words with your face, chain of command be damned."

"Well, likewise."

"Guys," I protest weakly.

Hyland leisurely winks at me. "What?

"We've had enough fighting."

"Relax, Em. I won't break his pretty little nose just for your benefit. And he won't get close enough to break mine without losing another limb."

"Dickhead," Warner chunters.

"Nah. That would be Madden."

"On this we agree."

At the reminder of the spiralling disaster that is our honorary fifth team member, I can't help but groan. Both men sober, exchanging a long look.

"I'll go find him." Hyland visibly deflates after their silent debate.

"You will?" I blink up at him.

"Sure, why not? He's probably just off licking his wounds somewhere. It won't be hard to track the idiot down and drag him back here to do his fucking job."

"Thank you." My smile feels forced, painful.

"For the record, if I'd been the one to walk into that bathroom… he'd have a lot more than a broken nose to worry about. So be thankful that it was Warner and not me."

With that ominous threat, Hyland departs the room. I watch him go with a sinking feeling in the pit of my stomach. Perhaps it's best if Blaine decides not to come back. I can't exactly blame him for making himself scarce.

"This is a disaster." I rub the tight knot forming between my brows. "It was simpler when I was held captive and didn't have a choice about anything."

"Not funny, Em." Warner cringes.

"It's a little bit funny."

"Agree to disagree. Come on, let's go see Tom."

"Together?" I flash him a look.

"Probably best that we don't give him a heart attack when he's just woken up. But we will figure this out, I promise. I meant every word that I said."

"I'll hold you to it, Mr Mead."

"Please do."

His hand snags mine then clenches tight. I squeeze back, ignoring the tumult raging inside me. It takes great effort to force a few deep breaths in preparation to face my brother.

Back outside his room, we take a moment to collect ourselves before knocking and entering the hospital room. My anxiety soars to the forefront as I sidle in behind Warner, palms slick with sweat.

"Tom?" Warner sounds tentative. "Hey, bud."

As he steps aside to let me in, trepidation shatters into a million shards, leaving me awash with so much relief I can hardly form a coherent thought. Tom sits upright in bed, tangled in wires and IV lines, but his emerald stare is locked on me.

"E-Em," he croaks.

"Oh my God."

My feet carry me over to his hospital bed almost too fast for my shaking body to follow. I hover over the layers of IVs to bury my face in Tom's neck, sucking in his clinical, antiseptic scent. Unexpected tears burst free in huge, back-heaving sobs.

"You're okay," I weep loudly.

"Hi, trouble." His hand cups the back of my head. "Long time, no see."

"I... I thought I'd lost you."

"Never, Em."

We both bawl in sync, hiccupping and laughing through shared hysteria. His voice is weak and broken, but I don't care. Nothing can spoil this. My big brother is back, alive and safe.

We fucking did it.

My throat closes up, the entire hospital fading into the background as I run my hands over Tom's stubbled cheeks, forehead and oil-slick hair. He's gaunt as anything, paler than snow and visibly shaken, but those love-filled green orbs haven't changed.

Somewhere behind me, Warner rests a reassuring hand on my shoulder. A quick glance reveals tears in his eyes as he watches us reunite, the first genuine smile in what feels like weeks stretched across his face.

"Hey," Tom greets in a hush.

"You back with us now?" Warner teases.

"I think so." He winces in pain.

"Take it slow. You've been out of it for a while."

"So I h-hear." Tom's raw voice trembles from the strain of speaking. "Thanks for coming for me."

"Like we'd ever stop searching for you." I sob listlessly, unable to halt the tears. "I'm so sorry, Tom. So sorry. I had no idea... I never meant..."

"Hey." Tom sniffs through his own tears. "I'm okay, Em."

"You got hurt because of me! They kidnapped you!"

"It was not your fault. Don't even think that for a second, okay?"

He attempts to sit upright, huffing when he can't move more than an inch or so. I lean into Warner's strong arm, his fingers still gripping my shoulder, as my built-up sobs refuse to ease up now that they've found an escape route.

Tom stares at me with bloodshot eyes, appearing bewildered by my unexpected breakdown. I've never been the one to sit and fall apart. Not even when our mother died. I can't decide if he looks happy or disturbed by this new me.

"Breathe." Warner attempts to soothe me, gently holding me through the painful sobs. "Tom's here now. He's home, and everything is going to be okay. You can let it all out."

"It's all my fault..."

"None of this is your fault," Tom wheezes out. "Christ, Em. How can I fix this?"

"No!" I erupt through my tears. "You almost died! I d-did this.

I'm the reason you're here."

"I'm back now. You can't get rid of me that easily."

Taking his papery hand in mine, I hold it tight while leaning back into Warner's chest. Emotion like I've never experienced before overwhelms me as the sheer exhaustion of the past few weeks takes over, leaving me exposed and defenceless.

All the times I've swallowed my terror and plastered on a faux mask leave me sitting in the rubble of the person I once was. I'm not the numb, embattled girl who picked her brother up off the floor or strolled into the fighting ring despite her terror. Not anymore.

Is that a good thing?

I have absolutely no idea.

With my brother's fingers curled around mine and Warner's unshakeable strength keeping me upright, I can let those ashes scatter. The sensation of being stripped bare is acute. All the armour that's kept me alive can't hold up against my turmoil.

"She'll be okay." I hear Warner whisper over my lowered head. "A lot has happened recently."

"I hardly remember anything after they broke into my apartment." Tom's audible uncertainty breaks my heart. "It's all a blur."

"Luis called Ember while he… he was beating you." Warner sounds distinctly uncomfortable, barely holding in his contempt. "He threatened Ember with your death if she didn't surrender."

"Shit! That evil bastard."

"When we tracked you down, Carlos Morello was waiting. Ember pretended to surrender to him long enough to secure your freedom. She got us all out of there, Tom. But it was a bloodbath."

Tom spits out another shocked curse.

"Ember saved our lives." Warner pecks the top of my head. "She's incredible."

Sucking in air, I look up to find Tom eyeing me like I'm an exotic creature he's never seen before. The fading bruises across my face twinge when I scrub tears aside to regain some composure.

"Sorry," I choke out. "It's been a long few weeks."

"Are you okay?"

Tom's concern for me is a living, breathing entity, filling up the room.

"Shouldn't I be asking you that? You're the one who got kidnapped."

"I'm asking you," he says sternly. "You're the one he was trying to break. So are you okay?"

"Honestly, not even remotely. I don't think any of us are. But that's a problem for tomorrow."

After Tom adjusts the nozzles slotted into his nostrils, hooked up to the still-flowing oxygen machine, I reach for the water on his bedside table. He takes a sip when I fill the plastic cup and hold it to his lips. My hand quivers while returning it to the table.

"How'd you find me?" Tom's gaze flits between us.

"Blaine Madden tracked down an old suspect from the Briar Valley case," Warner explains. "He gave us intel. It seems our past is a lot more connected to this mess than we thought."

Tom licks his cracked lips. "Carlos… He… He was talking to Gael on the phone. I watched them drag Luis away unconscious before I was locked up again."

"Apparently, he's dead now." I watch Warner carefully weighing how much to reveal. "So is Carlos Morello and all of Gael's men."

"All of them?" His red eyes widen.

"It's a long story."

"Bloody hell. Who was hurt?"

"You don't need to worry about any of this right now." Warner releases me to stand and lightly clasp Tom's shoulder. "The case is under control."

"Gael won't ever stop." Tom winces against his white pillows. "Not until he has Ember back under his thumb. If Carlos is dead… then someone else will take his place."

"We know." Warner nods. "Gael has already made contact to continue taunting us. We're putting pressure on the feds to locate his estate while we chase new leads."

"What new leads?"

"No." I hold up a hand. "Warner's right, that's enough. You need to focus on healing, Tom. Not me and not the case."

"Em—"

"No! Enough! I won't lose you too."

Making eye contact with Warner, I jerk my head towards the door, indicating for him to go get Jamie. He nods then quickly slips out, giving us a moment of privacy.

"I need to get out of here." Tom tugs on the wire taped inside his elbow. "With Carlos dead, he's going to come at us hard. Gael's obsessed. He's fanatical. He won't rest until—"

"Stop right there."

"You don't understand! You're in danger!"

I carefully pin his arm to the bed, easing his fingers from the IV line. "You're going to lay here, let the doctors take care of you and heal. That's it."

"London isn't safe. I need to protect you!"

"I have the entire weight of Sabre Security behind me," I reason calmly. "While I may be a bit of a mess right now, I'm okay. You're safe. Carlos is dead. We're making progress."

"It's my job to protect you," he wheezes through agonised gasps. "Look at you, Em! You're covered in bruises. You've lost weight, and I… I have to…"

"Stop worrying about me. I need you to get better. Warner and the rest of the team have got me. Trust them, okay?"

The fight seems to drain out of him as his meagre energy depletes. Tom slumps, his near-translucent skin seeming even paler. I fuss over him, straightening wires and bedsheets, until Warner's lopsided steps return.

"Look who's here," he chirps.

Staring off behind me, Tom's eyes fill with tears again. "Oh, Jamie."

"Tom! You're awake!"

I move aside to let the couple reunite, sharing a happy smile with my brother's boyfriend. He's still drop-dead gorgeous, elegantly dressed in his pressed polo shirt and glittering watch that's undoubtedly worth a small fortune. That much hasn't changed.

Jamie's at the bed in a flash, pulling Tom into a tentative hug to avoid his injuries. Both of them crying, I take my cue to give them a moment, catching Warner's hand and leaving the hospital room.

Axel jerks upright where he's leaning against the wall in the corridor. He watches me collapse into Warner's arms, unable to hold it together for a moment longer. I nestle my chin on his shoulder and stare into Axel's whiskey-orange orbs.

"Okay?" he mouths.

All I can give is a wordless, watery smile.

"Yep. Stupid question, right?"

Axel moves to my back, easily snuggling into me to cradle my body close. Warner doesn't utter a complaint as his chin rests atop my head, pressing a soft kiss into my hair while his teammate makes my bones creak.

"That was more intense than I was prepared for."

"Tom's going to be fine," Warner assures me.

"And so are you," Axel adds. "We're here, dimples."

Melting between their stacked muscles, I take the free comfort. Every last ounce of it. The reassurance that old Ember never would've allowed herself. She falls to her knees in the shadowy crevices of my mind, relegated to the sidelines after years of taking centre stage.

Without her stubbornness holding me back, I can allow the safety of my men to hold me firm instead. They're driving me forward now. Giving me love, safety and acceptance. They're my home.

With that, I let myself break.

Safe in the knowledge that they'll put me back together again.

CONFIDENTIAL
Why?
Suspect?
A
Play me
INDEX
TYPE I (NORMAL) POSITION
3
1
2
DO NOT CROSS
POLICE LI

A
TYPE I (NORMAL) POSITION
INDEX
Play
me
CONFIDENTIAL

15

BLAINE

2005 – SOUTH ARCADE

Spyder dances out of reach before I can slam my fist into his ugly mug. Growling in frustration, I amble forward into his space then duck the blow he attempts to land, using momentum to strike him in the gut.

At his grunt, my foot sweeps out to catch his ankles. The giant bastard lands with a thud that seems to shake the factory floor and every last empty workbench scattered around us.

"Motherfucker!" he roars.

Raye snickers from her nearby perch, watching us fight with a beer in hand. "You suck, Spyder."

"Fuck off." He glowers up at the ceiling. "Shit, that hurt."

"He's half your size!"

"And twice as fast," I reply coolly.

Spyder takes the hand that I outstretch to heave him up. We clap each other's backs, breaking apart to take swigs from our beers. I can feel them both eyeing me, but I don't react. I'm a breath from snapping, and they don't deserve to bear the brunt of it.

Instead, I'll continue systematically beating the shit out of my crew until I can think logically again. Something tells me I'll run out of volunteers before I can screw my head back on straight, but I'm still willing to try anything.

"Again?" Spyder invites.

"Nah." The beer moistens my dry throat. "Raye's right; you suck."

"I wasn't trying to hurt you!"

"Then you're a fool."

Smirking, I polish off my beer then turn to face Raye. I'm not afraid to hit her. Raye's gender has no bearing on me. I think she'd give me a run for my money, even though I really hate to lose. And right now, I need a challenge.

"Now you want to play in the big leagues?" She grins at me.

"Come give it your best shot."

"Not sure hitting my employer is the best career move, but you're the one offering." She cackles. "Frankly, I'd love to punch your stupid face to stop you from moping around here like a lost puppy."

"I am not moping." I roll my tense shoulders.

"Could've fooled me."

"Warner Mead told me to leave, so I left. That's all."

"You got caught with your pants down," Raye lectures. "Big deal. Ice your fucking face, strap on a pair, and get back out there. We made this deal for a reason, or have you forgotten?"

"I've forgotten nothing."

"Then step up. We have to find Nolan."

"Agreed," Spyder chimes in. "Before he decides to wipe out the last of his abandoned operation and kill us all while he's at it."

"You included." Raye motions to me.

"I know what's at stake!" I shout in exasperation.

"Then what are we doing here, wasting time?"

Without an answer to give, I resist the urge to scream at my two foot soldiers. Lord knows that loyalty is hard to come by these days. Instead, the beer bottle sails from my hand, smashing against the warehouse wall and scattering across the stained concrete.

Neither speaks when I stalk off to ascend the rattly staircase leading to my mezzanine office. Once safely inside, I let my frustration boil over to escape in a violent expulsion. Better this than actually killing one of my people.

The threadbare armchairs crash onto the floor where I tip them over. Paperwork scatters as I toss boxes across the room in a fit of rage. Screwed up shipping documents and receipts are upended from overflowing bins. Nothing escapes my furious whirlwind.

"Goddammit!" I scream. "Fuck!"

What an utter disaster.

This was not the plan.

Find the girl, rescue her, drop our prized bargaining chip into Sabre's lap. Reap the fucking rewards. Simple, right? Calculated. This was supposed to be our road to eliminating my father for good and clearing my name along the way.

Now we're almost a year into this disaster, no closer to mounting my father's head on a stake, and I'm standing here obsessing about what that slip of a woman is doing right now without my lips on hers.

Thanks to Warner fuckin' Mead, I'm here.

Losing my goddamn mind.

If that straight-laced piece of shit thinks he can toss me out like I didn't just deliver their best lead to them, he's got another thing coming. Ember is entitled to be with whomever she likes. Warner's lucky I didn't put a bullet between his eyes.

Chest heaving, I dig around in my desk drawer until I locate a rolled joint from the wooden box I keep stashed. A woodsy fragrance curls from the tip when I spark up, taking the smoke deep into my lungs.

If I were a smarter man, I'd cut my losses. Pack up shop. We have connections across the UK and beyond. It would be easy enough to relocate our operations, leave this sordid city and all its bad memories behind for the wolves to tear apart.

Yet the idea of never again looking into Ember's fierce, blue-grey eyes fills me with dread. Never seeing her carved, scar-stippled muscles. Each luscious curve and tempting angle. The way her gaze narrows in anger when she unveils the beast writhing beneath her skin.

She deserves justice.

I want to be the one to give it to her.

It has to be me.

Smoke pours from my nostrils as my head bows, the suffocating weight of an entire dynasty crushing my bones into worthless dust. Everything I've done has been for the family business. Now it feels like I'm salvaging the remains of a corpse.

"Food for thought?"

My spine lengthens, steeling with tension. "You're not welcome here."

Heavy thuds mark the big bastard's entrance into my office. I don't startle or even turn to face Hyland Wesson. My people wouldn't have allowed him up here if he were armed.

"Why give us this location if you didn't want us to find you?"

"Poor decision making." I suck in another drag.

"I doubt the infamous Phantom does anything without a good reason. You're incapable of poor decision making."

"At any other time, I'd quite enjoy receiving a compliment from the likes of you. However, I'm fresh out of fucks today, Mr Wesson, so I would advise you to piss off before I have you thrown out."

"Come on, Madden. No need to be so prickly."

"Right. Because you've been the epitome of welcoming to me so far."

Bracing the still-smouldering joint between my thumb and forefinger, I turn to face the surly agent. Hyland cocks a blonde brow as he studies my face. The two black eyes are an unfortunate side effect of my newly-broken nose.

"Damn," he remarks. "Warner really kicked your ass."

"Your team leader should consider himself lucky that I haven't ordered a hit on him for this." I gesture towards my face.

"Pretty sure that would violate the terms of your plea deal."

"Do I seem overly concerned with your pathetic paperwork right now?"

"If you wish to continue consulting with our team on this

investigation, perhaps you should be. This case is far from over."

Bitter laughter breaks out of me. "As I recall, Mr Mead instructed me to leave and never return. I'm merely following his command."

"Warner… reacted emotionally," Hyland grits out. "He's sorry."

"Espionage isn't your strong suit. Leave the lying to the other one."

"The other one… Axel?" His brows knit in perplexion.

"Bingo."

I take another drag then stub out the joint in my ashtray. Yet another sting in the tale. Perhaps it would provide some satisfaction to blow their lives to high heaven before I leave the city by revealing Axel Slaughter's not so little secret.

"Regardless, I don't intend to trouble you with my presence any longer." I level him with an assessing stare. "Tell your precious team leader that. You never have to see me or my people again."

"That isn't in the terms of your pardon, Madden."

"Politely, fuck your deal."

"What, you can't take a bit of competition?" He chuckles mirthlessly.

"Ember isn't some kind of contest to me," I bite back.

"Why is that?"

"Because she matters to me. I want her to get the peace she deserves and to choose her own future without the cartel breathing down her neck. I want to watch her walk free for the first time."

"Good." He cocks his head, seeming to internally catalogue something. "Then I don't have to kill you where you stand. Yet."

When he grins, I realise that I've tripped into some kind of loyalty test. Of course, they'd send their resident guard dog to get the lay of the land. The team enforcer gets to do all the dirty work.

"Cut to the chase. All I care about is seeing Ember."

"Meaning?" Hyland challenges.

"You know precisely what that means."

"Humour me with the specifics."

"This investigation has moved beyond a business transaction. If remaining at a distance is what she wants, then I'll do it. But don't think for a second that I'm staying here because I want to."

A myriad of expressions crosses his face, ranging from primitive jealousy to something almost resembling thoughtfulness. To be honest, I didn't know the caveman was capable of such emotional range.

"I'd be very interested to know what you do want." He folds his arms, jaw set tight. "The whole team would be."

I stand tall, unflinching and unafraid, while delivering my answer. "Her."

Hyland curses under his breath, glancing up at the vaulted ceiling like it will provide him with an alternative response. It's almost amusing. If I weren't knee-deep in this fiasco, I'd laugh.

"She wants you to return," he reveals unhappily. "I've been sent to bring you home."

"Is that so?"

"You're part of this team, however temporarily. Warner's actions were a one-off. Return with me, and help us track down Gracie Livingstone."

"Last we spoke, you had no desire to find the girl and risk your team."

"That isn't true." He rapidly shakes his head. "I just don't want us waltzing into another one of Gael's elaborate traps. We almost didn't escape the last one."

"I doubt Ember sees your reluctance that way. You know what that girl means to her."

"I know," he snarls.

"Yet I'm the problem?" I smirk good-humouredly. "You treat Ember like she's made of glass. She's far from that, and it's high time the lot of you realised her strength and value to your operation."

"Are you seriously lecturing me? You of all people?"

"Somebody has to."

"How gracious of you," he huffs. "Anything else to say?"

"As a matter of fact, I do."

Hyland warily watches me saunter up to him, ensuring there's no mistaking my words and every speck of humiliating derision I want him to feel.

"If Warner is insistent on keeping me from Ember, that's his prerogative. Let him try. But don't for a second think that you're good enough for her either. She deserves far better than any of you will ever be able to give her, and I hope you beg on your knees for her attention every single day because she owes you nothing."

His face flushes red, staining a delightful shade of downright humiliated. How wonderful. These Sabre assholes needed taking down a peg or two.

I clap the dick's broad shoulder and unveil a grin. "Now that we've got that cleared up, let's go. I'm not giving Warner a chance to change his mind about my expulsion."

Hyland splutters for a comeback while I gather my valuables and shrug on my leather jacket. Truthfully, I had intended to break into their apartment to check on Ember sooner rather than later anyway. I'm ready to go.

"Coming?" I gesture for him to go ahead.

Hyland turns a dark glower on me. "I don't like you, Blaine Madden."

"Fantastic. The feeling's mutual."

"The minute you step out of line, I'll be right here to toss your worthless hide back in prison where you belong. Whether it breaks Ember's heart or not."

"Then you won't mind me saying that the minute she changes her mind about you, I'll take great pleasure in placing a bounty on your head and denying all knowledge when you're shot between the eyes."

His smile is all teeth and lethal threat.

"It seems we're on the same page."

I nod for him to exit. "After you."

With a final wary look, Hyland descends the staircase back to the factory floor. I exchange a quick whisper with Raye, ensuring she doesn't follow, then trail behind him as we exit the warehouse. Spyder watches us leave with narrowed slits.

Climbing into Hyland's blacked-out, company SUV feels somewhat like climbing into the jaws of a great white, but I hold back my reservations. He throws the vehicle into gear then pulls out with a squeal of tyres, setting his sat-nav for their penthouse.

The ride is fraught with uncomfortable silence. His total ignorance of my existence allows me the opportunity to think. We may have eliminated several of Gael's operatives, but his location still remains elusive.

Dangling the Livingstone girl under our noses screams of desperation. He wants us to acquiesce to his demands. But luckily, there are ways of finding people without relying on the whims of madmen. Methods I happen to be well-versed in.

By the time we reach their fancy high-rise building buried deep in Canary Wharf, I have the formations of a plan. A risky, dangerous plan that would involve calling on someone bound to destroy the precious Anaconda Team.

Even better.

As Hyland manoeuvres into his assigned parking spot, I pull out my phone to fire off a message. Our last conversation was nine months ago, but for my liking, it's still too soon to ask for help again.

> Blaine: Got another job for you.

At any given time, my dark web contact can be located on any continent. Meaningless things like borders or lines on a globe mean little to him. Once a mark has been ordered, results are guaranteed. That's the service you pay a small fortune for.

"Move it," Hyland grumbles, clambering out of the car. "Before I change my mind."

I don't deign to respond, tucking away my phone and following him out in silence. The atmosphere remains frosty until he lets me into their apartment, illuminated by London's eternal nighttime glow.

"I need a drink," he announces.

"Where is everyone?"

"Warner's at the hospital with Tom. He was eased off sedation earlier. Ember agreed to come home to rest before we talk about pulling Gracie's parents in for an update."

I nod and move to escape the awkwardness, heading down the corridor towards Ember's room. I'm half-expecting Hyland to follow and crack my skull when I lightly tap on her door, but he remains out of sight in the kitchen.

When she doesn't answer, I click the door open to peer inside.

Her bedside lamp is on, bathing the sparse room in low light. There are two figures tangled up in the bed—the purple haired liar himself is wrapped around my girl like a python.

Sprawled out on her back, Ember looks peaceful. Her lips are parted as she lightly snores, completely oblivious to my presence. Neither stirs when I sneak in on light feet to sit down in the chair tucked into the corner.

Watching her brings me a sense of peace that I have never experienced before. Not even in the time since I retook the family business and enacted my plan to clean it up. With her, the bleeding wound still leaking inside my chest feels closer than ever to sealing shut.

She doesn't just see The Phantom. Nor the caricature of a person I've built over the years. The almighty Blaine Madden. Ember couldn't care less for the pomp and circumstance that my family's generational power has gifted me.

No.

She sees the real me.

The person I didn't even realise existed until her little smiles and cutting remarks pulled him out from the deep grave I'd constructed in my psyche. No one has ever looked at me like I'm little more than another fallible human… and I fucking love it.

I don't have to be invincible.

Or anything but… me.

Watching her quietly rest, even in the arms of another man, settles my still-racing heartbeat. I get comfortable in the chair, content to observe. I'm almost falling asleep when my phone vibrates in my pocket, prompting me to move.

The Hunter: You still owe me for the last job. What's in it for me?

A smile tugs at my mouth as my gaze lifts to the shock of purple hair splayed across Ember's pillow.

Blaine: The man who erased your existence.

It doesn't take long to get an answer.

The Hunter: When do I start?

CONFIDENTIAL
Why?
Suspect?
Play me
A
INDEX
TYPE I (NORMAL) POSITION
DO NOT CROSS
POLICE LI

play
me
DO NOT CROSS
Suspect?
NOT CROSS
POLICE L
PO
(NORMAL) POSITION
Compact Cassette

16

EMBER

BE GOOD – ROSEBURG

The shower's warm spray beats down on me as I stare at the draining water. Despite standing here for an eternity, I've yet to find a speck of courage to face what lies ahead. After my meeting with Richards in a few hours, I have to face Gracie's parents.

It's a heartbreaking, full circle moment I've avoided since I returned to England. No amount of mental pep talks will make this any easier. If Gracie's alive and we're going after her, they deserve to know, regardless of the outcome.

"Em? You nearly done?"

Through the steamy glass, I can make out a purple-hued blur. "Not even remotely."

"I've got your meds and coffee waiting. Hyland's on breakfast duty."

"The others?"

"Madden stepped out a while ago to make a phone call, I think. And Warner's in his office, checking in with Tom's medical team."

My forehead rests against the tiled wall, already throbbing with a headache. It's been a permanent feature behind my eyes ever since my recent seizure.

"Dimples?"

After a beat, the shower door creaks. A stray tear leaks from my eye as Axel appraises me—naked, dripping with rose-scented shower gel and boasting yellow splotches where my body is still healing.

"Hey." Axel forces a bright smile. "Talk to me?"

"I don't know what to say."

"Just tell me how you're feeling."

"I'm not ready for today," I confess after a beat. "I can't face Gracie's mum and dad after leaving her there all alone."

"We've been over this. You didn't leave her anywhere."

"Do you think they'll see it that way?"

"They're fucking idiots if they don't see it that way."

Head lowered, I run my fingertips over the wet, gnarly skin that brands the crease of my elbow. *768.* I know Axel's right. Deep down, I didn't have a choice. That doesn't lessen the guilt that's been eating me alive for months, though.

I'm determined to hold it together after one too many meltdowns of late. That mental promise splinters apart when Axel steps into the shower, uncaring about his low-slung pyjama bottoms.

He tugs me into his bare chest, banding two heavily inked arms tight around my shivering torso. I snuggle into his tattooed skin, letting the soothing water cascade over us.

"Gael thinks he can break our team with these mind games." He kisses the side of my head. "It's your job not to let him. We'll find Gracie on our own terms and end this for good."

"What if it's too late?"

"If he's sending us those photos, then she's still alive. Wherever she is, we'll find her. You get to bring her home to her family."

"Don't do that." I peer at him.

"Do what?" He drags the back of his knuckles down my cheek.

"Don't give me hope."

"Hope is what sustains us, babe. Hope keeps us alive when everything seems so fucking bleak, it feels like there's no way out. Without hope, we're all just waiting for fate to arrive and praying it's kind."

Looking up, I peer into his uncut, honey jewels. It's rare to see Axel serious. Solemn, even. But when he reveals the poet's heart he keeps hidden behind layers of hyperactive energy, it reminds me how hard he performs for the world.

"Damn. Sometimes you're too smart for your own good, Ax."

"Don't tell anyone. I have a reputation to maintain."

"Your secret's safe with me."

Axel swipes amethyst hair from his eyes, left long to maintain his faux hawk. His smile fades when he sees the moisture that's burning my eyes.

"What is it?"

"Gracie's parents… What if they hate me?" I manage to whisper the question that's been eating me up inside.

He shakes his head with a patient smile. "You did the best you could to keep their baby alive. How could they ever hate you?"

"I still failed her."

"No." He nudges my nose with his. "The world failed you both."

"They may not see it that way."

Fingers comb through my hair, pushing snarled strands back from my face so he can search every inch. I lose myself in the roiling, golden expanse of his expressive orbs, full of determination.

"You don't have to face them today. No one is going to force you, but if I'm being honest, I think it's time. You need to forgive yourself for what happened to Gracie."

When I try to push him away, Axel tightly cups my face between his hands. Water sluices between us, sealing his inked chest to my naked breasts.

"What if I can't do that?" My voice trembles.

"Then I'll be right here every single day to remind you that you deserve to be forgiven until you believe it too."

"You can't do that."

"Just fucking watch me."

His mouth brushes over mine, sealing the declaration with a light, almost innocent kiss. Our lips linger, trading gentle pecks in the tiled oasis. His touch is a balm to the ball of dread growing inside me with each second.

When Axel's hand dips to smooth down my spine, curling around my hip, a faint tingle flickers over me. His lips slant on mine, firm and attentive, ensuring I can't spiral any deeper into my thoughts.

I take the lifeline he's offering with open arms, deepening the kiss by sliding my tongue into his mouth. He happily accepts, filling my senses with the taste of freshly brewed morning coffee as our tongues dance a slow waltz.

Then the fear creeps back in.

The dread. The guilt.

No. I want to forget.

Reaching behind me, I flick the shower off then place my hands on Axel's bare shoulders to walk him backwards. He grunts faintly, letting me steer him from the walk-in shower and back out into the steamy bathroom.

The tingle under my skin has grown into a sizzling spark that consumes every thought. I hungrily peck his lips, needing more reassurance to stop myself from falling back into the bottomless pit I'm rapidly drowning in.

He breaks the kiss to clasp my chin. "I didn't come in here for this."

"That's too bad."

"Em—"

"I need to feel you, Ax. Please."

"Shit, babe. You know I can't take your begging."

"Then stop arguing, and give me what I need."

"I don't want to take advantage," he mutters.

"I'm giving you full permission to distract me from the hellish day ahead."

Knocking his hand aside, I stroke the dark stubble that's formed on his baby face, ensuring he can see my certainty. Axel visibly swallows, his bee-stung lips clamping shut on any more protests.

He huffs in surprise as I drop to my knees on the floor, ignoring the way they twinge on the hard bathroom tiles. Water chills on my skin while I tug down the waistband of his soaked pyjamas.

Axel watches me intently, a fascinating eagerness swirling in his bright gaze. He lets me strip the dripping cotton from his legs, unveiling powerful calves and bulging, muscular thighs that make my pulse thrum.

"You don't sleep in boxers?" I gulp.

"No," he replies gruffly.

His long, thick cock is eye-level with me. Already firm and deliciously twitching, the red tip drips with a beckoning droplet of pre-come that's begging to be licked up.

"I want you to fuck my mouth." I stare up at him through my lashes. "And I'm going to let you ride it until I can't think of anything but your cock filling me up."

"Jesus Christ, Em."

Axel's head is thrown back when I press a teasing, open-mouthed kiss to the side of his velvet shaft. He curses gutturally, a hand sliding into my wet hair, loosely holding me in place.

I glide my tongue along his steel, tasting each inch of promising heaven. His skin is hot and veiny, moisture spilling from the round tip as I swirl my thumb over the slit.

Taking him farther into my mouth, I love the uncontrolled sound he growls out. It's all hedonistic pleasure and animal lust. His cock fills me up, already nudging the back of my throat.

"Fuck, Em. Fuck, fuck, fuck. That goddamn mouth of yours."

My hand curls around the base, eagerly pumping in time to each deep suck. He tenses and jerks under my touch, his fingers tightening around my locks with each pull.

Even on my knees, letting him take my mouth with increasing roughness, the power is heady. I could demand anything. Axel's putty in my hands and beholden to my mouth on him.

"Perfect, babe. You look so incredible right now."

Slick heat gathers between my thighs from the thrill of working him over. Every gasp increases my satisfaction, causing my clit to pulsate between my clenched thighs. I'm wet. Needy. Aching to be touched.

Hips grinding in time to my movements, Axel pushes into my

mouth at a steady pace, head tilted back and breath short. I keep my jaw slack so he can find his own rhythm, content to give him an illusion of control.

"That's it. Take my cock, babe. Take every inch of me."

My thighs push together again, core burning with the need to be relieved. I release his shaft then cup a handful of his soft balls instead, giving them the lightest of squeezes. He judders against me as a result.

"Shit! Yes!"

His thrusts change pace, growing longer and more frantic. Each time he pushes past my lips, I hold back a gag response. His cock is plunging deep into my mouth, teasing my throat with each hard pump.

My other hand lowers between my folded legs, easily locating my screaming bundle of nerves. I circle my clit while Axel uses my mouth, pushing down on the sensitive bud to find my own bliss.

Between his tight grip on my hair and the pressure on my tingling clit, I can feel myself growing wetter. I don't just want to forget; I want him to take every last haunting thought from my mind and replace it with nothing but us. Right here, right now, in this room.

Twisting my head, I pop off his dick then lick around the tip, lavishing the butter-soft skin. Axel moans loudly, slackening his grip on my hair for a second before clenching it tight enough to make my eyes water.

I suck him back into my mouth, greedily inhaling every rock-hard inch. This time, I'm setting the pace. Fast. Punishingly determined. I want him to fall apart. To surrender for the pleasure only I can give him. I need to feel this control, this sense of immense power.

Axel moans my name under his breath while shallowly fucking my mouth, leaving me to decide when to suck deeply. His fingers press into my skull, keeping my head still while his hips rock back and forth.

Sticky warmth slicks over my fingertips where I'm strumming my clit, teasing each prickle of desire to its maximum peak in-between sucks. The empty ache is growing fierce, urging me onwards.

God, I'd happily let him bend me over the bathroom sink and plough into me. He can take me as roughly as he so desires. For all the pain tearing me up inside, I want to feel something good. Something pure. I want to feel him.

"Babe, stop. I'm going to…"

Lips tightening, I hold his length in my mouth. It jerks against my tongue, his grip on my hair creating a sharp burn. Just as I flick my tingling bud, Axel loudly barks my name for the whole apartment to hear.

"Fuck yes! Ember!"

Hot seed spills from his cock, hitting my throat and filling my mouth with salt. I keep sucking, pulling every last drop of pleasure from him. I want it all. Axel doesn't disappoint as he pours himself into me like he's never been given a blowjob before.

As I sit back on my haunches, he pulls from my mouth. Strings of come stretch between us, his eyes widening at the sight. I make a show of licking my sticky lips and swallowing every drop he spilled into me.

"You make me fucking breathless," he pants with wide-blown pupils. "Fuck me, dimples. I did not expect you to drop to your knees like a goddess and do that."

"Why not?" I grin cheekily.

"I just came in here to check on you."

"And I wanted to do this."

He bends at the waist, fighting to catch his breath. "You should've stopped. I still need to…"

As an idea dawns, Axel extends a single finger to me and grabs a spare towel to tuck around his hips. Then he vanishes. Huh. Great. I stiffly uncurl my legs, walking over to the sink on shaking legs. I've barely rinsed my mouth when he returns.

"What the hell, Ax? You can't just barge into Ember's bathroom."

"You'll be thanking me soon, big guy."

Tantalising need bolts through me at the sound of Hyland's grumbling, all rough and grumpy. I look over my shoulder in time to see him entering the bathroom, stopping short when he sees me naked and trembling.

For once, Hyland doesn't have a remark. Not one. His olive eyes flit over me, lingering on the way my breasts shudder with each short breath. He gasps when I grab a handful and tweak my nipple, never once looking away from him.

"I told you to fetch her for breakfast."

"I heard *have her for breakfast*." Axel grins, hands braced on his hips. "But Ember had other plans. Now you get to finish our girl off for me."

If I could quake any harder, I'd be in a puddle on the floor. More warmth floods my core at the filth that Axel's suggesting. Based on Hyland's primal expression, his thoughts mirror mine.

"Please," I whine, sliding my hand over my belly to glide between my thighs. "I'm so wet, Hy. I need it badly."

"Bloody hell." He reaches down to adjust his cock.

Grinning to myself, I push a finger through my folds. Yep. Soaked. His gaze doesn't stray from my swollen cunt as I slide a digit inside myself and moan. It doesn't take much more to break him.

Hyland moves in a flash across the bathroom, sweeping me into his huge arms and securing his mouth to mine. I squeak at the rough handling, his lips beating mine with pent-up ferocity that promises to leave a bruise.

The edge of the bathroom counter cuts into my back where I'm shoved backwards, allowing him to spread my legs with a thigh and push his swelling erection into me. The friction of his cargos feels exquisite against my exposed centre.

"Don't tease her," Axel scolds from nearby. "She's ready for you."

Pulling our lips apart, I lick across the seam of Hyland's mouth. "Please fuck me. Please… fill me up. Make this ache go away."

"This isn't what I had on our agenda this morning."

"But I want you. I need you."

"You're dangerous when you act all innocent," he growls.

My arm curls around his neck, allowing Hyland to lift me onto the bathroom counter. I spread my legs wide to let him step between them, his mouth lowering to my neck. Teeth nip and lips attack as he wrestles to undo his cargos and shove them down.

I help him yank the thick material over his ass, taking his boxers with it. When his cock springs free, my throat spasms at the sight of his girth. He's not quite as long as Axel but much thicker and more intimidating. It's quite the sight to behold.

"Well, shit."

"Don't worry, baby." He simpers at my expression. "You can take me."

"Are you sure?"

"I have no intention of breaking you yet. Not when the fun's just getting started."

"Condom," Axel interjects. "Top drawer, right of the sink."

"You put condoms in my bathroom?" I gape at him.

He merely shrugs. "You're welcome."

Axel seems to enjoy my look of astonishment while Hyland searches the bathroom drawers to locate protection. With the rubber slid on, he retakes his position between my splayed legs.

"The pup's prepared." He grins smugly.

"A little too prepared."

"Stop complaining, and give us a show." Axel pouts like a child.

"Who said you were invited?" I challenge.

"Well, I'm not leaving. I wanna see this."

Ignoring his antics, Hyland slides a hand around the back of my neck, holding me and biting down on my throat. "Focus on me. Nothing else."

I feel him suck my skin between his teeth, leaving a mark that he can boast to the rest of the team about later. As he suckles above my pulse point, he drags me forward to the edge of the counter, letting his hardness tease my swollen pussy.

The feel of his soft, round head sliding through my lips makes me mewl in abject desperation. Desire has crystallised into a white-hot need that feels strong enough to burn me alive if I don't have him inside me immediately.

I don't need to be kissed and teased. We've circled one another for long enough without giving in. The countless months of whispered desire and impromptu kisses pale in comparison to the feel of his weight pressing into me now, a second from taking the final leap.

I'm free to reach down and wrap a hand around his dick, quickly working him over with a few fast pumps until he's pressed up against my entrance. The anticipation nearly splits me apart when he pauses on the precipice.

His forehead meets mine, gazes locking and rapid breathing mirroring each other. Neither of us cares that Axel lingers nearby, watching us. Every agonising second since Hyland first kissed me boils down to this.

"Take me," I plead.

"Right here? In front of him?"

"Yes. Please. I want to feel you inside me."

Hyland grabs hold of my ass cheeks, squeezing hard enough to sear. "God, I'm going to fuck you so hard, you won't walk straight for a week. Hold on, baby."

When he slams into me, the bathroom whites out. The intensity is too much for my skeleton to hold. I cry out, slicing my nails into his shoulders. My moans become pathetic little whimpers as I adjust to the burn of his cock stretching me.

"Ember!" he thunders.

Drawing back, his hips piston forwards to surge back into me. It isn't gentle or tender. The teasing playfulness in his and Axel's combined touches feel like a distant memory as he ruts into me like a man possessed.

I eagerly take each ruthless pump, legs hitched around his waist and back tilting so I'm poised on the very edge of the counter. At this height, he only has to duck a little, creating the perfect angle to worship my core.

His head dips to locate my right breast, lips clamping around the peak that hardens at his attention. Hyland bites down on my nipple long enough to provoke a moan then sucks it deep into his mouth.

With his tongue slithering over my skin and fingers digging into my ass, all I can do is let him roughly pummel me into a lovesick oblivion. He relentlessly drives into me like he's chasing some kind of sexual achievement.

"Yes!" I scream out, feeling blood beneath my fingers. "More, Hy! Yes!"

"That's it, baby. Say my fucking name."

Toiletries rattle and fall over all around us, rocked by the momentum of his passionate thrusts. My bones feel close to collapsing into dust every time he grinds into me, teeth gritted and face red.

An orgasm strikes out of nowhere, quickly rushing up to overwhelm me in a mere instant. My body tenses, nerves strung out and brain misfiring. Everything grows hazy with the speed of my impending release.

"I can feel you clenching around me." His voice is rougher than gravel. "Let go. Cover my cock in your sweet juices."

"Yes… Hy. God, yes."

"Now, baby."

When Hyland tweaks my already-sensitive nipple, the sharp burst of pain sends me spiralling. It's a sudden meltdown. Beautifully destructive. Neck muscles ache as I toss my head back to cry out in ecstasy.

I'm not granted a second to recover as Hyland pulls out of me, planting a heavy kiss on my lips. He lifts my boneless limbs from the bathroom counter then drops me back onto my feet long enough to tear his t-shirt from over his head.

Spun around, I'm now roughly bent over the counter at an almost perfect right angle. The marble surface is cold against my cut-glass nipples, making them twinge deliciously.

"Your cunt looks so perfect, all laid out for me," Hyland rumbles from behind. "Even if another man did get you all wet and ready for me to fuck."

"You're welcome," Axel quips.

"Shut it, pup."

"Hey, I invited you in here. Show some gratitude."

"Ember's benefiting from all my gratitude right now."

Hyland surges back inside me without warning, using his bare foot to nudge my legs open. My vocal cords strain from moaning, too overwhelmed by the sensation of being filled to the absolute max.

Bent over at his complete and utter mercy, there isn't a part of me our team enforcer can't reach. His thick cock fills every available space, driving deep inside my slit. Each time he spears into me, my chest shifts on the counter, barely able to drag in a breath.

"Hy… please. Fuck, don't stop."

"I've got you, Em. Give it all to me. I want all your pleasure, all your pain. Let me take it all, baby."

My hands hold onto the edge of the counter for dear life, offering me a counterbalance for his onslaught. One orgasm isn't enough. Already, I can feel my body stiffening up, the knot of tension inside me forming a taut coil.

When I twist my head to the side, two golden flames lock on me. Axel is lazily lounging against the wall, quite happily watching us fuck like wild animals in heat. That lunatic looks far too satisfied for a bystander.

"She likes her ass being played with." He directs the advice to Hyland without looking away from me. "We need to get her ready to be filled there next."

"Is that so?" Hyland grunts.

"Oh yeah. Goes crazy for it."

"Hm. Good to know."

Unbidden moisture sears my eyes, gathering on the rims and begging to spill over. I don't know if I'm relieved or just over-stimulated. Perhaps just so wildly turned on, I can't figure out how to feel.

Between Axel watching us and Hyland bracing to break me in half, it's all too much. The end result of all our back and forth leaves me carved out and exposed like an open cavity, ready to be filled with their possessive ownership.

"I'd happily fuck this hole too." Hyland drags a rough digit between my cheeks, teasing my ring of muscle.

"We could take turns," Axel suggests.

"Or fill her sweet cunt and tight little asshole together. I bet our girl would take us both."

"Oh fuck," I bleat.

"Sounds like a yes to me." Honey irises slice into me, twinkling with amusement.

"We know Ember's greedy, after all." Hyland circles my backside with what feels like his thumb. "The least she can do is let us both own this tight body."

Axel nods in agreement, watching me unravel as his teammate works a finger into my asshole. My high-pitched whines sound frenzied even to my own ears. The extra stretch intensifies the force of his huge cock buried inside me.

Hyland's finger swirls, pushing against the resistance until it's fully seated in my rear. With the repeated slam of his length filling me up and the invasion into my backside, I doubt I'd be upright if he wasn't keeping me still.

"She does love it," he observes in a deep, pleased grumble. "You're full of dirty little secrets, Ember Lawson. I'm going to uncover all of them."

A wanton part of me loves that Axel is drinking in every last detail while Hyland taunts me. He watches us without a hint of embarrassment or shame, lounging like the fucking king in his castle being gifted a live show.

"Imagine how wet she'll be when we fuck her in front of her *friend.*" Axel's grin is viciously wide. "Let Warner give me some bullshit about honour and ethics then."

My walls clamp tight around Hyland, reacting to the thought of being shared between all the men I'm falling so fucking hard for, it borders on insanity. He growls in response, pressing his finger in and out of my ass fast enough to bring me to the edge.

"She likes that idea," Hyland moans.

"I bet she does. Ember wants to be passed between all of us like some kind of bitch in heat. Don't you, babe?"

"F-Fuck you," I groan out.

"There's no shame in it." Axel winks at me. "I'll happily pass your ass back and forth as long as I can sink my mouth between your thighs once in a while too."

Pain crackles across my butt when Hyland delivers a fast spank, jolting his finger still fucking me from behind. With all the places his body is touching mine, I can't think clearly enough to argue.

Axel saunters closer as Hyland's movements grow ragged. He stops at my side, lowering enough to fasten his mouth on mine, swallowing my desperate gasping. His lips massage mine in a dominant tangle, reclaiming his place in our messy moment.

As his tongue battles with mine, Hyland smacks my rear again.

Hard. The pain quickly melts into blissful pleasure, and I moan into Axel's mouth. There's no escaping either of them.

I feel the moment Hyland reaches his limit, his pumps growing unstable as he rides me from behind. The finger in my ass scissors, causing stars to burst behind my eyes. I cry out against Axel's lips at the myriad of overwhelming sensations.

He breaks the kiss to lean back long enough to watch me fall apart again. Right on time, Hyland drops me over the edge of a steep cliff then dives headfirst after me. With two more long, driving pushes of his hips, he roars my name.

Heat fills the rubber barrier covering his sheath inside me before the weight on my back multiples, countless stacked, sweat-slick muscles pressing into my spine when his knees grow weak.

I screech through my own orgasm, eyes closing to manage the impact of each invisible explosion that detonates deep within my core. Knowing Axel is watching Hyland finish me off only makes it hotter.

When the world settles back down around me, my face rests against the cool marble, drinking in big gulps of oxygen. Every nerve feels strung out and exhausted, like I just sprinted a marathon.

Legs jostling, I lean into the thick arm that Hyland braces around my stomach to stop me from collapsing in a heap on the floor. He's sweaty and shaking, but he still manages to keep me upright.

"I've got you," he whispers in my ear. "Shit, baby. That was intense."

"I don't think I can move right now."

"Please don't bolster his ego too much, Em." Axel flicks the tap on to wet a washcloth then hands it over to Hyland. "He already thinks he's better than me."

"That's because I am."

"And what gave you the authority to decide that?"

"The multiple orgasms I just got out of our girl," Hyland grunts back. "Top that, motherfucker."

To my chagrin, Axel puffs up his chest.

"Game on."

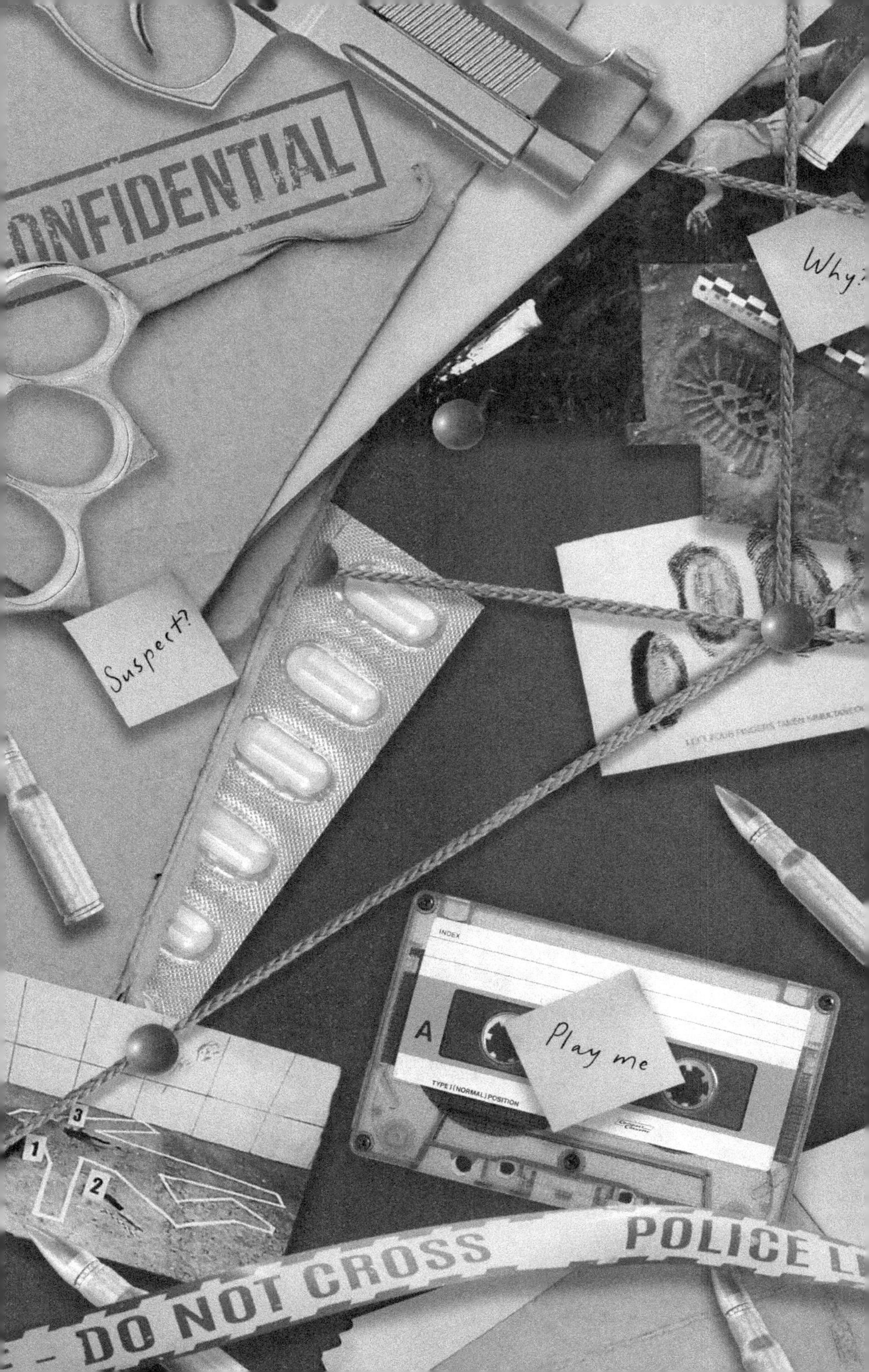
CONFIDENTIAL
Why?
Suspect?
A
Play me
INDEX
TYPE I (NORMAL) POSITION
1
2
3
DO NOT CROSS
POLICE

(NORMAL) POSITION
play
me
DO NOT CROSS
POL
Suspect?
POLICE LI
NOT CROSS
4

17

EMBER

OIL AND WATER – INCUBUS

"**I** can't let you in that room until I know you're of sound mind. Work with me, Ember."

The silver-haired shrink is going to earn himself a black eye if he doesn't get off my case. That'll clash with the ridiculous, canary-yellow shirt he's wearing today. Another colour-blind classic.

"I'm fine," I repeat for the fifth time. "Just here to debrief Gracie's parents and get on with my job. What happened with Carlos and his men was self-defence. I've moved on."

"So you've said every time we've spoken since." He pushes his sliding spectacles higher on the bridge of his nose. "Trouble is, I'm not buying it."

While everything about his open body language and affable smile scream well-honed reassurance, I'm not buying *that*. Richards is on Sabre's payroll. He can play friend all he wants. This entire set-up is a pantomime designed to catch me out.

"Isn't it your job to believe your patients?"

"You're not my patient." Richards produces a thin smile. "I'm simply here to ensure that the stressors of this role don't impact public safety. Namely, are you fit for active duty?"

"I'm working to ensure public safety by bringing down the threat that Gael and the cartel pose."

"Is that how you see what happened at the docks?"

Standing up, I resume pacing my least favourite room in HQ. I've got the bland canvas prints memorised by now. I stare at them enough during our pointless, weekly sessions where Richards prods my mind in every way possible.

I'd thought that I'd gotten away with flying under his radar in our debrief sessions since I killed Carlos. Richards loathes the silent treatment. Yet he hasn't given up and refuses to budge on pumping me for whatever information he thinks he'll find.

"I saved the lives of my team members and our hostage." My response is flat.

"You also used lethal force. Multiple times."

"Would you prefer I let them all die?"

"I'd prefer if you could talk to me about how it made you feel. What it triggered for you. How you've been managing the difficult emotions since. You're allowed to slow down and reflect."

"No!" I glare at him.

Richards halts spinning the fountain pen between his wizened fingers. "No?"

"I said no."

"Tell me why you're afraid to confront these feelings. Give me something."

The incessant pain pounding behind my eyeballs reaches a cutting peak. It feels like something is attempting to escape. Some confession or emotion that I can't bear to consider revealing. No one can know how it made me feel.

Because I *liked it.*

And I'd do it all over again.

"Ember..." Richards's cool gaze locks on me. "There's

no judgement in this room. Whatever you say will remain confidential."

"Until you write a report that has me booted off the Anaconda Team."

"I'm on your side, no one else's. For the record, I think you're doing a fine job as an agent, and I do not wish to have you removed from duty. But I will if you continue to fight me in these sessions."

His firm words startle me. "You will?"

"Yes," he confirms with a tense smile.

"So much for being on my side."

"Debriefing is an important part of keeping you healthy. So talk to me if you wish to avoid the consequences. Tell me why you're so afraid to talk about what happened."

My hands curl into fists, nails forming grooves on the insides of my palms, gnarly tissue pulling taut over my knuckles. The bruises across my body have healed, leaving nothing but invisible scars that match the ones I still wear on the outside.

Taking a human life should leave a more permanent mark. I've beaten enough poor souls over my years in the ring—some that I'm sure never got up again after sparring with me—but this was the first time I did it of my own free will.

Nobody forced me.

Nobody held me under threat of death.

I chose to kill those men, evil or not.

"I can't do it." My words come out in a heavy breath.

"Tell me why."

"I don't want to think and regret. If I do, I'll never dig myself out of that hole. This is how I survived, doc. I just kept on pushing forward, even when they made me do awful things."

"You didn't have a choice then," he points out. "You do now."

"What choice? This case is my life. If I'm taken off it… what would I do?"

Richards gestures for me to retake my seat. I eye him suspiciously but eventually acquiesce, putting us back at eye-level.

"You can't live for this work, Ember. Your dedication to seeking justice is admirable, but you're still a human being with needs and desires beyond this building. That is crucial."

"I can't have any of that until I've brought down the men who hurt me." I shake my head in protest. "And until I know that no one else is going to suffer what I did. I can't rest until then."

"There will always be another dragon to slay," Richards replies softly.

"What are you saying?"

"I'm saying… if this job is your life, then it's better not to have it. You were held prisoner for so long. Don't you want to live a little now?"

My nails dig deeper, forming painful slashes. "You are trying to have me fired."

"I'm looking out for your best interests."

"By telling me to let go?"

"By encouraging you to look beyond your anger and hatred," he corrects curtly. "You can't save everyone. Not even from this case. It isn't your responsibility to capture those who trafficked you."

Gracie's sweet, badly bruised face flashes through my mind. Her skin mottled purple and stained with blood from fresh wounds. Hair matted. Bones protruding. Not a single hint of hope or life left in her big, beautiful eyes.

"Yes." My jaw aches from grinding my molars. "It is."

"Why?"

"Because I left her behind!"

The words ricochet between us like a fired bullet. It's too late to shove them back in. No matter how much I want to keep the truth locked behind steely mental bars.

"I shouldn't have been rescued first." My heart pounds against my breastbone, lurching with noxious regret. "I don't deserve to be free, but Gracie does. I have to find her if I have any hope of a future."

As soon as I've said it, the honesty guts me. It opens a floodgate I didn't realise was bricked up around the weeping wound carved inside me years prior, allowing self-loathing to fester.

Instead of letting tears boil over, rage stretches my already-fragile nerves into breakable violin strings that wind tightly around my bleeding heart.

"Why don't you deserve to be free?" he asks, pen and paper now discarded.

"You know what I did in Mexico. The people I hurt. The pain I inflicted. I didn't want to fight anyone, doc. I hated it. But I still did it to spare my own pathetic life. How selfish is that?"

Richards pauses, licking his lips. "Survival is never selfish."

"It's the most selfish act there is," I clap back.

"Would you be saying the same thing to Gracie if she were here? If she'd been forced to fight for her life? Would you tell her that she's selfish for putting her own survival first?"

Each question tears into my carcass and disturbs the carefully ordered understanding I've formed about what happened to me. I hadn't realised that I'd painted myself a spiteful little picture of my own existence.

Her face returns, growing clearer with each of his challenges. I try to imagine what I'd say to Gracie if she were sitting here, wrestling with huge, existential guilt. Or how I'd approach her after a fight, bloodied and wounded, telling her that she should just let them kill her instead.

It's unthinkable.

"No," I choke out. "I wouldn't."

"Then Ember… Please, for your own sake, treat yourself just like you'd treat that poor, innocent girl. Give yourself the same grace you'd offer to any other victim. You are no less worthy than them."

That's when the tears spill over. I should be used to the sensation, considering how regularly they make an appearance after years of being stifled. The hot dribbles make my cheeks ache as they pour free, carrying my grief and pain with them.

Richards reaches over to the tissue box on the small console that holds his tea, passing me a handful. I avoid looking at him while drying my face. No doubt he's proud of getting me to crack.

"Processing what you've been through is scary." He picks his pen back up to jot something down. "But it can also be a relief if you let it. Confront the past. Allow the pain to flow. Let it roam free."

"This doesn't feel good," I hiccup.

"But it will," he attempts to assure. "One day, the world won't feel so heavy. You'll have the desire to consider a life beyond these walls because it's what you want. Not what I've ordered you to do."

The tissue is soft and soothing on my face, allowing me to hide for a moment. When I regain control of my emotions, Richards is focused on his paperwork, allowing me the pretence of privacy.

"Thank you."

He glances up to smile. "Therapy isn't so bad after all, huh?"

"I thought this wasn't therapy." My own smile is strained.

"Right you are."

A quick look at the clock reveals our sessions is almost up. Gracie's parents will be being escorted into HQ as we speak. Balling the wet tissues up, I bite down on my lip.

"I'm going to meet Gracie's parents."

"I heard." Richards nods. "Meeting her family after all that's happened is a huge emotional milestone. You need to be prepared for what it'll bring up."

"All I want is to get it over with so I can find their daughter and bring her home."

"Responsibility, Ember." He caps his pen, setting our session notes aside. "Consider what you're taking on and whether it's reasonable or fair to you. That's all I ask."

Taking the cue, I stand to ditch my used tissues in the wastepaper basket. Richards meets me at the door. Usually, I flee this room like it's on fire. But today I stop to offer him a long, searching look.

"You're right; it isn't fair," I reply solemnly. "I didn't want to leave her behind, but I had no choice. Saving her isn't my job. But it is my road back to being someone I recognise when I look in the mirror."

Richards contemplates me. "Perhaps you need a different mirror."

I break out in a snort. "Do you ever let anything slide?"

"Infamously no." He smiles, nudging his sliding specs back into place. "Same time next week. You have my emergency line if the meeting proves challenging."

The door clicks shut behind me when I escape with a final nod. Rather than my usual deflating routine after escaping one of Richards's sessions, I stand still. Breathing. Blinking. Adjusting to the new, strange lightness inside my chest.

"Did you finally snap and kill him?"

My head turns, finding Blaine lingering nearby on my immediate right. We haven't been alone together since he returned in the dead of night, but I was relieved by his arrival.

"Not quite," I hedge.

"Pity." He lazily eyes me up. "Want me to do it for you?"

"Pretty sure that would get you permanently booted off the team."

"Perhaps." His usual smirk is especially shark-like today. "But it would appear I'm more vital than your team leader previously thought."

Looking over his battered face, the discoloured skin stark against his short, jet-black locks and obsidian stare, I can't help but wince. I've watched him fight before, but he took no prisoners. Seeing Blaine injured is wholly unfamiliar.

"That looks painful."

"I've had worse." Blaine pushes off from the wall to inch closer. "Worth it too."

"Blaine–"

"Whatever speech you have lined up, don't bother."

"Who said I have a speech prepared?" I snipe at him.

"You've had enough time to think and doubt," he responds like it's obvious. "But it will hold no bearing on my intentions. I'm here because you want me to be, and little else matters now."

"I wasn't sure if you'd come back."

"Here I am. Satisfied?"

He halts in front of me, chin tucked to peer down at my expression. His tongue flicks out to roll over the silver lip piercing that takes the brunt of his frustration while thinking. It's a tic that I often find myself observing.

The scent of bergamot mingles with his leather jacket, forming an addictive concoction that hooks me in. I find myself edging closer. Blaine's dark, understated aura of raw power never fails to intrigue.

"What do you want from me?" I whisper thickly.

"Your soul, if it's available."

"That's a little bit complicated right now. But... I don't regret our kiss."

He preens like a deadly jungle cat eyeing up its next meal. The glimmering, midnight-blue flecks that pepper his irises seem to glow, deepening the velvety depths.

"Then I'll take whatever you're willing to give, sweetheart." Blaine's lip curls in a cocky grin.

"You understand what that means? There are others involved here."

"Believe me, I'm aware of exactly who else is involved." He captures the end of my braid, fingertips stroking the dyed-blonde tip. "It doesn't scare me in the slightest."

"Because you trust them, or because you intend to eliminate them?"

"Ah, Ember." Blaine tuts. "Still so impatient. No more spoilers."

Tugging on my braid, he guides me forward to ever so lightly brush his mouth on mine. Not a kiss. Not even a tease. It's a mere whisper that absolves the insecurity his disappearance built inside me.

Surging desire and unmet need make me dizzy. Despite everything, I want something from each of them. Blaine included. The heart-pounding danger he incites inside me can't be fulfilled by anyone else.

He's a beguiling but deadly force that may just topple the fragile house of cards I've managed to stack. Our team doesn't trust him. Most of the time, it seems like Axel actively wants to kill him. Yet here I am, dragging Blaine into this tangle regardless.

I must be crazy.

Or simply tired of being told *no.*

"They're all waiting for you," he murmurs in that spine-tinglingly crisp voice. "Else I'd take you into a quiet corner and demonstrate my commitment to you this very second."

"Right." I clear my throat.

"Next time one of those fools interrupts us, I won't hesitate to remove their head with my bare fucking hands. Consider that before taking this any further."

Gawping at him, it's clear that Blaine's serious. Not a hint of humour to be seen. I'm not sure if I find his unhinged brand of attraction terrifyingly insane or downright hot. Maybe even both.

"It's considered," I croak out.

"Excellent."

Before I can step away from his enticing body heat, Blaine curls a hand around the back of my neck. I meet his stare, teeth sinking into my bottom lip.

"Now that I'm a free man, relatively speaking, I'd like to be a little more formal. Permit me to take you out sometime without your bodyguards."

Copper slicks over my tongue before I find the sense to release my bottom lip.

"I'm sorry... Is the infamous criminal leader and prolific mobster, the actual Phantom himself, asking me on some kind of date?"

Blaine's sore-looking nose wrinkles at my description. "I suppose so."

"What does an average date even look like for you?"

"Say yes, and you'll soon find out."

My lips curve upwards. "Now I'm intrigued. Yes."

"There's a good girl."

His mouth secures on mine once more, this time harder. I relax into the kiss, my fingers finding his tee and curling into the worn fabric. His lips are firm and confident, applying just the right amount of pressure to scramble my inner monologue.

Everything about him is intoxicating. Least of all the way he languidly nudges his tongue past my lips, testing the boundaries of what I'll accept. The hand fisting my neck tightens, applying a light pressure that holds me in place.

All too quickly, Blaine releases my neck. He gives my braid one last tug and steps back while I blink rapidly to regather my thoughts. He looks far too smug at the stupefying power of his lips.

"Come along before those boys start searching for us."

"Boys." I tut under my breath.

"Don't tell them I said that. I'm on thin ice already."

His hand finds mine, our fingers hesitant then curling together. With Blaine anchoring me, I leave Richards's manipulations behind, creating space between me and his room full of exposed secrets. We ascend to the upstairs conference room in loaded silence.

Two figures stand outside, trading whispers. Warner straightens when he sees us coming, immediately locking onto where Blaine's fingers grasp mine. It takes great effort not to tug my hand from his.

Looking over his shoulder, Sabre's most fearsome director, Hudson Knight, nods at me. It's been a while since our paths last crossed. His icy demeanour, layers of tattoos and multiple piercings fail to intimidate me despite his reputation around the office.

"Finally decided to do some work?" I call out.

His crystal-clear blue eyes roll. "Look who's talking."

"I was with that nutcase, Richards."

"So I hear." He casts a hand over his ever-messy, raven hair. "Done pandering to the shrink now?"

"Remove the requirement to sit with that weirdo every week, and I'll be at your beck and call, Director Knight. Until then, I just go where I'm told."

Blaine surrenders me so I can shake Hudson's big, scarred hand, though he grips it a little harder than necessary. The way he assesses me is far from cold and professional. He appears concerned.

"You good?"

"Peachy." I shrug off his worry. "How's the wife?"

Hudson grimaces. "She's at the stage of pregnancy where she can't stand the sight of us. We're safer hiding here until she decides that she's ready to see our faces again."

"So… never, right?"

"Right." He chuckles.

Looking over to Warner, I find him glaring at Blaine like he can scare him off with a mere frown alone. Clearly, the invitation to return hasn't resolved their issues.

"Are they here?" I glance back at Hudson.

"Yeah, inside." He hooks a thumb over his broad shoulder. "Are you ready for this?"

"As I'll ever be."

"We'll cover the updates, but I understand they have some questions for you too. Keep your answers short and brief. Anything you're uncomfortable with, you can leave."

"Have they seen the photos?"

Lips pursed, Hudson nods.

"Fuck." I attempt to roll my tense shoulders back. "Okay."

"We've put out an international BOLO for Gracie Livingstone with updated images and information. The intelligence team places her somewhere in Eastern Europe, though we can't be sure it isn't a red herring."

"How the hell did she end up there?"

"When she was purchased from Luis's trafficking operation six years ago, she could've been sent anywhere across the globe. But Rayna and Fox are confident in their assessment of the evidence."

Finding Warner's worried eyes on me, I swallow roughly. He tries for a smile, but I can read him like a book. He's tense too. We have no idea who purchased Gracie or what she's been through since then.

Hudson looks over my shoulder to where Blaine lingers. "Madden."

"Yeah?" He arches an ebony brow.

"Do you still have underground criminal contacts in Europe?"

"Are you asking me as a suspect or as a member of this team?" Blaine counters.

"The latter."

"Then my answer would be yes. Though none involved in the human trafficking trade. That was my father's forte, not mine."

"Any help is better than nothing," Hudson says dismissively.

Warner harrumphs at that. "Not his kind of help."

"Put the word out." Hudson ignores Warner to continue giving commands. "Spread Gracie's name and face among them with a reward for any information leading to her location."

"I can ask my crew to make contact." Blaine's tone is noticeably hesitant. "But it may not go down well with some of the families. Our reputation was damaged after Sabre's investigation. They don't trust us."

"Try regardless."

"You want to offer a reward?" Warner reiterates.

"I'm willing to move beyond the playbook." Hudson splays his palms. "I want results, and I want them fast. Time is running out for us all. Josh's death was our last failure, understood?"

Mouth snapping shut, Warner reluctantly nods. "Yes, sir."

"Very well. Let's get this meeting done."

Hudson turns around to take the lead into the conference room. I exchange a look with Warner before we enter, grateful for his arm squeeze, while Blaine follows behind us. His thumbs are already flying across his phone screen.

"Just say the word, Em," Warner whispers to me. "You can leave the meeting."

"I know. Thanks."

"Deep breaths. You've got this."

The conference room is relatively empty compared to recent large-scale team meetings. Hyland and Axel wait inside, both standing as silent sentries in each corner, stoically watching us enter.

Hudson's blonde-haired brother, Kade, sits with a stack of paperwork opposite a couple. They're huddled together with an untouched carafe of water between them, both quickly looking up at the sound of our arrival.

The fear-filled, blue gaze of a middle-aged man almost knocks me off my feet. He's the spitting image of Gracie. In comparison, his wife's bloodshot stare is flat and dull, though she does share the same dark hair as her daughter.

Warner pulls out a chair and gestures for me to sit. There's a decent distance between me and the Livingstone's. I'm grateful for it. I slide into the chair, thankful for the two men who position themselves behind me, one on each shoulder.

"Mr and Mrs Livingstone." Hudson takes the seat beside his brother. "Thank you for coming in today."

"Mr Knight." Gracie's father's voice shakes. "Please call me Geoff."

"And Sabrina," his wife croaks.

Kade wears his best, PR-perfect smile as he stacks his paperwork. "As discussed on the phone, we've had an update in Gracie's missing person's case. We're now in a position to confirm that our search will be focusing on Europe at this time."

"You think she's that close to home?" Sabrina squeaks.

"Perhaps. We intend to find out."

"Has there been further contact?" Geoff gulps.

"No." Kade shakes his head. "Our forensic intelligence team has analysed the images we received, and we feel confident to focus our efforts based on their observations."

Geoff deflates like he had hoped for more. I try not to focus on the wave of guilt his reaction creates. We're trying our best. But like him, I know how it feels to be desperate.

"We intend to use the full force of international law enforcement to distribute the new images of Gracie across multiple countries," Hudson adds, mirroring his brother's calm professionalism.

"You're going to share those photos?" Gracie's mum whimpers.

"Only the non-explicit ones, Mrs Livingstone," Kade clarifies. "I appreciate this is difficult, but being able to provide an updated likeness of your daughter will help us to confirm any recent sightings."

Both parents appear numb, wearing matching dazed expressions. After all these years, this development must be a lot to process. Particularly given the graphic nature of the images.

"This will reignite significant media attention on her case." Kade looks between them. "Especially given Ember's recent return. You can expect the national press to take an interest."

"We handled their intrusion before." Geoff clenches his wife's hand hard enough to turn his knuckles white. "If it brings our daughter home, we will endure any amount of harassment. Do what needs to be done."

"Please…" Sabrina's sorrowful eyes are like an ice pick to my heart when she briefly meets my gaze. "Bring her home."

"We will try our best, ma'am." Kade nods respectfully.

"Do you need anything else from us?" Geoff asks.

"Not at this time," Kade replies. "Just your continued patience and cooperation. We will be in touch as soon as we have news."

When the room falls into a hush, the eyes of all the men at the table slide over to me. Sabrina is openly crying, but it's Geoff who stares at me so fiercely, I worry he's seeing more than he should ever know about what we endured.

"You have questions for me," I say simply.

"We do, Ember." He attempts a crooked smile. "If that's okay with you."

"I'll do my best to answer."

"We're so glad you were found safe. How have you settled back in?"

Rather than traumatise the poor man with an hour-long recap of seizures, deadly raids, exhausting training and a pile of medication larger than the leaning tower of Pisa, I settle on a neutral response.

"As well as can be expected."

"We were surprised to hear you'd joined the investigation. Thank you for fighting for our daughter." He wells up, brushing beneath his eyes. "It means a lot to us."

I don't trust myself to speak, so I merely shrug.

"Please." At the sound of Sabrina's voice, I shift my attention to her. "I just... I need to know how she was the last time you saw her. Tell me what happened to my little girl."

"Mrs Livingstone, I begin.

"I miss her so much." She buries her face in her hands.

A searing ball swirls in my oesophagus. "Gracie missed you too. Her sisters as well."

Sabrina hiccups then breaks down into uncontrolled sobs. Her husband reaches over to wrap an arm around his wife's shoulders, tugging her into his side so she can cry.

"Um... Gracie talked about her sisters." I blink several times, trying to hold my own tears at bay. "Annie and Gabby."

"That's right." Geoff drags in a breath.

"She missed her mum's homemade baking. I remember her talking about cookies... Oatmeal ones, I think. Gracie just wanted to be home with her family again."

His lip trembles. "She did?"

"She loved you so much."

His features promptly crumble, joining his wife in crying for their lost little girl. I stare down at the table, too emotionally wrung out to feel much at all. Not after pouring my soul out for Doctor Richards.

"I promised her that she'd taste your cookies again and hug her sisters tight." The table swims in front of me. "We held each other between our cages. Gracie kept me strong. She made me smile and laugh when I thought we were already dead."

"That's our girl," Geoff cries.

"She's amazing, sir."

"She is. Our sweet baby girl."

"Remember her like that. That's all you need to know."

"Thank y-you, Ember. I'm glad she wasn't alone."

Their raw grief is agonising to observe. What hurts more is the look on Hyland's face as he watches them break apart in each other's arms. His own loss is splattered across his expression, dripping pain too vast to ever overcome.

Geoff kisses the side of his wife's head, cradling her close. There's nothing else I can offer them now. Looking at the directors, I catch Kade's sympathetic stare first.

"May I be excused?"

"Yes." His hazel eyes crease at the edges. "You may go."

With Richards's warning still ringing in my ears, I stuff any doubts I have down and flee the room alone. This barely controlled calm won't last long, and I have no desire for Gracie's folks to witness its departure.

Never let your guard down, Carlos used to preach. He trained me not to think. Feel. Dream. Hope. He taught me how to put those pointless feelings in a box then shove them into the back of my brain.

Now I'm dragging it all back out and blowing off the cobwebs... Because Richards is right. Ember Lawson does want a life beyond this building. She wants to hope and dream. Just not yet.

I need 768 to win this.

Then she can finally rest.

POLICE LINE
DO NOT CROSS
POLICE LINE – DU NOT CROSS
Weapon?
CONFIDENTIAL
DO NO

18

HYLAND

BLACK CHANDELIER – BIFFY CLYRO

Luke bounces from foot-to-foot as I wrangle with our newly updated security system. Didn't think it was possible to make our penthouse even more secure, but here we are.

Warner's turned the entire floor into Fort Knox. With the manhunt for Gracie ramping up, we're all on edge. We'd be fools to think that removing Carlos has mortally wounded the cartel's operation. If anything, we've just kicked the hornets' nest.

They will retaliate.

It's a matter of when, not if.

"I'm so excited!" Luke's chirp drags me back to the present. "Let me in!"

"Easy, kid. Uncle Ax is working today."

"No." He pouts up at me. "I want to see Ember."

I snort at his little face. "Right."

Of course he does. The kid's as besotted with Ember as I find myself being these days. He's only met her once, and she's already won his heart with her mindless superhero chatter.

"Hurry up! Let me in!"

"Be gentle with Em." I pinch his cheek. "She's in a bit of pain today."

"Oh no!" His forehead crinkles. "We should've brought her ice cream."

"We have ice cream, bud. But that doesn't fix everything, you know."

"Yes it does," Luke replies defiantly.

"Okay. Sure."

"Or flowers! Mummy likes when Owen buys her flowers. She always smiles. I don't like it when they kiss, though. That's gross."

My fingers slip while disabling the alarm. "Owen?"

"Yes," Luke chatters without a care in the world. "He's her friend."

"I see. How many times have you met Owen?"

"Oh… loads! He comes around all the time."

"How often, Luke?"

"Every day!"

Huh. Interesting.

Schooling my face into a neutral mask, I work on opening the apartment door, making a mental note to run a full, thorough background check on this *Owen* bloke. If Jayce's going to have someone around my son, I reserve the right to ensure that his record is clean.

I don't hold any romantic feelings for my ex-wife. Not after all that's happened. But I still respect her greatly, and she is the mother of my child. Her safety is of interest, but more importantly, the type of people Luke is exposed to at home.

Just one little search. That's all.

And maybe a quick, tiny stakeout.

That's really it.

"In you go, bud." I swing open the door for him to enter. "I think Ember's on the sofa."

"Yay!" he squeals.

"Volume, Luke! She isn't feeling so good."

"Okay, okay." He bounds off inside the penthouse.

Following after him, I juggle the bag of supplies that I picked up enroute to meet Jayce for Luke's handover. He's with us for the weekend after some careful negotiating. Not ideal timing after what happened last night, but I wasn't about to cancel on my boy.

I'm hesitant, walking into the open-plan living area. Ember insisted on getting out of bed, despite being found seizing on her bedroom floor twelve hours ago. Axel screamed his head off so loud, I thought someone had died.

My heart did damn near stop.

Since she was responsive once the seizure had passed and was able to answer our questions, we agreed to keep her out of the hospital. But Warner was ready to shove her in an ambulance against her will for a while.

Now I'm armed with her refilled prescription, cold compresses for her residual headache and all manner of snacks. While the team prepares the press release relaunching the investigation into Gracie's disappearance, I'm watching Ember like a hawk.

"Did you hurt your head?" I can hear Luke asking.

"No. I'm just tired."

"My daddy said ice cream doesn't fix everything, but I know it does. Do you want some?"

Ember's laugh tinkles through the apartment. "Will you have some with me?"

"Oh yes!"

"Then how could I refuse?" she retorts.

"Great! I'll get it!"

Luke races past for the kitchen, sticking his tongue out at me as he passes. I roll my eyes, walking over to the huge, L-shaped sectional where Ember's still tucked up under a fluffy blanket.

She laughs at the sight of the bulging bag in my hands, despite looking pale and exhausted. I laid next to her last night, terrified to take my eyes off her while she fitfully slept. Neither of us got much rest.

"Did you buy the entire grocery store?"

"Just the entire chocolate aisle." I raise one of the bags.

"My hero. What's up for grabs?"

"Literally every chocolate bar I could lay my hands on. I also refilled your meds and got some headache stuff. The pharmacist said these cold eye patches are great. Give 'em a shot."

"The pharmacist or your little self-help book?" Ember teases.

"The pharmacist, but the book did actually say that sugar overload is bad post-episode," I correct her. "So you can choose one chocolate bar to eat while I make us all a real meal, but that's it."

"I'm going to burn that thing," she groans. "Ruining all my fun."

"Finding you passed out and convulsing on the floor is no one's idea of fun, Em. Protein, medication and rest. That's all the fun you're allowed today."

"Harsh terms." She pouts at me.

"And maybe some ice cream, if you're good."

"I'm always a good girl... *sir.*"

Fuck, if my kid wasn't rootling around in our kitchen, I'd show her exactly what I think of that playful taunt. Maybe I can fuck her brain into functioning properly for once.

"What about the BOLO?" Ember winces as she sits up. "Is it live?"

"That's all!" I call while walking to the kitchen.

"Fuck you, Hy."

"Anytime, baby."

"I'll just call Warner if you don't keep me updated!"

"Try it!" I shout back.

Locating Luke with his nose buried in our freezer, I yank him out then set the kid up chopping veggies to earn his dessert. None of us are particularly good cooks, but I can rustle up a decent enough meal. Fajitas are pretty hard to ruin.

We're talking about school and his favourite classes when Ember pads into the kitchen on bare feet, still in pyjama shorts and an oversized tee. She sits at the breakfast bar and watches us work, seemingly content to listen.

"I don't like peppers." Luke scrunches up his little nose.

"Gotta eat your greens." I chuff the back of his head. "Then you can have ice cream."

"With a superhero movie?"

"Only if I get to pick which one," Ember chimes in.

Bottom lip jutted out, Luke considers her for a moment. "Fine. But only because you're sick."

"Thanks, little man."

He leans closer to whisper to me. "I told you girls have germs. I don't want to get sick too."

"That's why you have to eat your veggies. Then you don't need to worry about anyone's germs, not just girls."

Ember covers her mouth with her hand to conceal a laugh. I wink at her, loving the way her smile chases the fatigue from her eyes, even briefly. She hasn't had enough reasons to laugh recently.

We work messily, systematically destroying Warner's kitchen organisation by the time the chicken has finished sizzling. I study the disaster before declaring it his problem to fix. I'll only clean it all wrong.

Ember smashes avocados with the back of a fork, whipping up some guacamole, while Luke moans the entire time about green slime. The way she ribs him like they're old pals warms my heart as I dish up the food into sharing bowls.

"You hear from Tom today?" I ask her quietly.

Adding seasoning to the guac, she slowly mixes it in. "Yeah, Jamie's with him. I explained what happened before Warner could rat me out. Couldn't get him off the phone for forty-five minutes."

"He's worried about you."

"Tom should be worrying about himself. Just because he's been moved out of the ICU doesn't mean he's in the clear yet."

Laying out three plates, I dump cutlery and napkins on the side then declare it done. Luke immediately dives in to begin rolling three over-stuffed tortillas as I circle the counter to approach Ember.

Her head lowers when I rest my chin on top of it, arms loosely curled around her still-trembling body. Luke bounds out of the kitchen to begin munching on the sofa, granting us a private second.

"Tom is going to be fine. The BOLO will go out to our international partners without a hitch. Gracie's parents got what they wanted. There isn't anything else for you to do right now but heal."

"I'm doing everything I should be." Her flat words sound so despondent. "My body just keeps failing me."

"It's been through a lot, Em. Cut yourself some slack."

"You were the one yelling at my specialist not so long ago."

"I'm allowed to be frustrated on your behalf." I peck her loosely braided hair. "You need to be focused on looking after yourself and getting the seizures under control."

"They'll never be under control, Hy. This is it for me."

I fucking hate the note of defeat in her voice. It rams a sharp, determined dagger into my gut, slashing me wide open. If it's the only thing I can do, I'll make this easier for her. She doesn't have to manage her diagnosis alone.

"Then we focus on getting you into the best shape possible," I say decisively. "We could even get a second opinion or try alternative medicine. You don't have to live in fear of the next attack."

Slipping a finger beneath her pointed pixie chin, I tilt her sad face upwards to drop a kiss along her temple. Ember shivers in my arms, looking younger and more afraid than I've ever seen her.

She's changing. Softening. Gradually letting us see the hidden sides of herself that weren't permitted to exist for the last six years. The fact that she feels safe enough to be herself now means the world to me.

"Go choose your movie. I'll bring the food over."

"I need to take my medication." She sighs.

"I've got it. Sit down, Em. My boy came to see you more than me."

"Well, I am the most awesome out of the both of us."

"Yeah, yeah. Shift your ass, baby."

Ember strains to peck my cheek then gingerly hops down from the breakfast bar to join Luke. I watch her go, for once not studying the delectable curves of her tight body but worrying about the weight she's lost and the pallor of her skin.

She needs to eat more.

I'll pin her down and force-feed her if needed.

With a generous heap of fajitas wrapped, I deposit the huge

plateful on Ember's lap. She's curled up back in her original spot but with Luke snuggled next to her now. The pair are animatedly debating three different movie choices.

I fill my own plate then take the other end of the sectional, sliding my feet beneath Ember's blanket. She smiles when I tangle them with hers, needing to feel her touch. To my pride, she's nibbling one giant fajita while Luke's devoured his already.

"What are we watching?" I take a big bite.

"Still debating." Ember shrugs.

"She likes the villains." Luke wipes his mouth with the back of his hand. "I thought girls were supposed to like the good guys."

"They're boring," Ember argues.

"But the baddies are bad for a reason!" he exclaims.

"It isn't always that simple." Ember pokes him in the side. "Villains have an origin story for a reason. Most are just misunderstood and deserve a bit of forgiveness."

He frowns at the TV, visibly confused. "Then why does everyone hate them?"

"Because it's easier to hate someone than consider that we all make mistakes," she tells him. "Life isn't that simple, Luke. Not even when it comes to the good guys and the bad ones."

Letting them continue debating, I stuff down mouthfuls of jam-packed tortilla. Moral debates are not my thing. But I can hazard a guess at what's on Ember's mind.

It doesn't take a genius.

She's wrestling with her own conscience.

We all know that she blames herself, not only for Gracie's current predicament, but for all that she was forced to do while being held captive. Not to mention Ember's refusal to discuss what happened at the docks. She's been emotionally fragile ever since.

I have a lot of experience with guilt. It's hard to avoid in this line of work—casualties and failure go hand-in-hand with criminal investigations. We toe the line between life and death on a daily basis, and unfortunately, that means losing people along the way.

It also means taking lives.

No matter the damage that leaves behind.

My phone pings in my pocket, capturing my focus. I pull it out with one hand while wolfing down the last of my food, clicking on our team's encrypted group chat.

> Warner: Press release has been issued. Prepare for the onslaught.

> Blaine: Raye made contact with a few of our sources this afternoon too.

I tap out a quick reply.

> Hyland: Any joy?

> Blaine: Not yet. May take some time. These people don't like to rat even for a reward.

> Warner: Then we'll double it every week until someone talks. Management's orders. I want to know who purchased the girl ASAP.

Shit, Hudson and Kade are not fucking around. Our contact with the Falcon Team has been extremely limited since the blowout, but it seems Josh's death is having far-reaching repercussions.

"Hy?" Ember watches me type.

"Nothing important. All went according to plan."

She visibly deflates, nodding to herself.

"The others will be back later. Warner will check on Tom then come home."

"That's good. He shouldn't be alone."

"Just watch the movie, Em. Everything is under control."

She half-heartedly blows a raspberry at me before focusing on whatever crap Luke's settled on. I watch her over the top of my phone in between checking the building's security feeds and backup systems programmed into my phone.

It's not often that I pay attention to my gut feelings. After all the shit we've survived in years of investigations, I doubt my gut thinks rationally anymore. But this sinking feeling has been screaming at me for days, and I can't ignore it any longer.

We took down a trafficking ring once before at great cost. Briar Valley is one of our biggest success stories. A big enough victory that our ex-team leader, Ethan, felt ready to retire and move across the country to live there.

I don't know if we can do it a second time.

This monster is already far larger than we realised.

All the signs point back to our past—to the evil we thought we'd vanquished when we served justice to Willow and her family. The connections are glaring. Dimitri Sanchez may be rotting in the ground, but his ilk is still wreaking havoc on us.

Rolling my lips together, I draw up my most recent conversation with Willow. She keeps in touch, especially after all we went through together. More so recently as she understands exactly what we're facing now.

> Hyland: Case is spiralling. Think we're
> getting closer, but it's complex. Keep your
> family close - everything is connected.

To my surprise, she replies relatively quickly. Willow isn't usually super responsive. Running their sprawling refuge deep in the Welsh mountains while raising children keeps her hands full.

> Willow: We watched the press release
> on the news. Ethan's been on the phone
> with Warner for an hour. You alright?

I chew on the inside of my cheek, weighing how honest to be.

> Hyland: No. Don't know how this will all end.

> Willow: If you need a place to
> escape, you know there's always a
> home for you here. All of you.

I lower my phone to study Ember and Luke when they both burst out in giggles at something on the screen. Luke's now laying half-sprawled over her while Ember absently fiddles with his golden hair.

In less than a year, she's barged into our lives and made herself the fucking centre of our entire universe. Even if it wasn't deliberate. As long as Ember's threatened, none of us are safe. Nor is our family unit.

Gael isn't above dangling a young, innocent girl in front of us to get what he wants. There isn't a level he won't stoop to. With our focus shifting to Europe, the threats will only multiply, and there's Madden's deranged father to consider too.

We're surrounded by enemies.

It feels like they're inching ever closer.

I want peace and justice, not just for Ember, but for all the victims still out there. Of course, I want to give her closure too. She deserves it more than anyone. Perhaps more than she even realises. But I will not jeopardise what we've found in each other to do so.

Malignant wasps swarm inside my skeleton with each letter that I type, allowing me to consider the possibility of failure. Up until now, I've refused to give power to the notion.

Hyland: If things go south, I'll take you up on that.

Willow: Good. We always keep each other safe.

My mouth dries up as unsettling fear takes root.

Hyland: Always.

CONFIDENTIAL
Why?
Suspect?
A
INDEX
Play me
TYPE I (NORMAL) POSITION
DO NOT CROSS
POLICE LI
3
1
2

TYPE I (NORMAL) POSITION
play
me
DO NOT CROSS
PO
Suspect?
NOT CROSS
POLICE L
4

19

EMBER

REDEMPTION – JEVON

Smack. Smack. Smack.

My feet beat a rhythmic pattern on London's cracked concrete. Even in our illustrious neighbourhood, weeds and potholes run riot. It's the one recognisable feature you'll find across the entirety of the UK.

It took a lot of convincing to get Hyland to loosely follow my jog in his company car. The overbearing grump didn't want to let me out to exercise, let alone in peace. But after a few days' rest, I've gotten my strength back.

Smack. Smack. Smack.

During that time, the news coverage in response to Sabre's press release has been relentless. After six years with no results, many had labelled Gracie's disappearance as a cold case. Now that it's been reignited, the criticism is flooding in fast.

Autumn leaves paint the road as I dodge past distracted commuters drinking in the crisp November air. In all this unruly chaos, it dawns on me that next month will be my first Christmas at home. The first time I've celebrated the holidays in years, in fact.

Nobody knows what will happen between now and then. From the meagre information that Blaine has received from his contacts so far, we have a vast search radius spanning from Estonia to Belarus. Gracie could be anywhere.

Smack. Smack. Smack.

Gael got those images from somewhere. He paid off whatever person or criminal organisation purchased Gracie years ago. All to taunt me, to unhinge me, to reassert his power. The message is simple and unchanged.

Return or pay the price.

Like we haven't already paid dearly.

Plunging into the hubbub of Mile End, I push past the weakness in my legs. When the time comes to face Gael, I need to be ready. My body can't fail me then. No one else gets the honour of taking him down.

Hyland doesn't disturb my thinking time when I pause to stretch and swig water. The SUV idles at a distance, granting me some semblance of normalcy. I blow him a kiss then take off again to keep working out.

At the end of my sixth mile, I feel my energy fading. The greyscale streets are growing hazy, indicating the end of my tolerance. I begin to slow, letting my muscles cool down after such a gruelling pace.

I've got a couple of hours until visiting time with Tom. Long enough to head back to get cleaned up. Perhaps I could even take Blaine up on that date offer later. He's been patiently waiting since he extended the invite, letting me rest post-seizure.

"Excuse me, miss? You seem to have dropped something."

I'm bent over with my hands braced on my knees, but I quickly straighten at the approaching voice. A man is crossing the road to reach me, young and attractive in his form-fitting, athletic clothing. Another jogger.

"Are you talking to me?" I pant.

"Yes." He stops a metre or so away. "You dropped this."

My hair stands on end when he outstretches a phone, still wearing a friendly smile that's meant to set me at ease. But I know for a fact that I left mine safely in the car with Hyland. I take a big step backwards, my hackles rising.

"You've got the wrong person."

"It's definitely yours."

"No. What do you want?"

His smile drops, a dangerous edge taking over his features. "Take it, Ember."

"Who are you?" My stomach twists then plummets.

"Just a concerned party here to take you home."

In a rush of panic, I leap into action to bolt past him. "I'll pass!"

The SUV is idling just down the street. Hyland must know that something's up with this freak approaching me. The tyres soon speed up as he careens towards my position, bringing help within reach.

"For his sake, don't move a muscle!" The man barks after me. "Final warning!"

Racing away from the stranger shouldn't be so easy. He doesn't even attempt to block my path or trip my feet when I dodge him to flee. It's a faint realisation that doesn't quite sink in as I focus on reaching my getaway car.

We're on a quieter street, more residential than commercial. With little more than a couple of corner shops and a closed restaurant nearby, there aren't any witnesses around. No bystanders. No collateral damage.

Only Hyland.

A single target.

He squeals to a halt, almost bumping the curb in his haste to brake. I launch myself towards him, watching Hyland climb from the car with his gun half-drawn. His mouth opens to shout my name.

An engine roars, and brakes scream. The once-calm air fills with the sound of a howling approach. Tyres protesting. Music raging. Hyland yells in my direction as he fully draws his service weapon.

"EM! MOVE!"

Behind me, a large transit van rapidly gains on us. It's racing at breakneck speed down the street, chasing after me. Before I'm run down in the middle of the road, I hurtle to the side, hitting the pavement in a fast roll.

Bones howl in protest at the hard impact with solid ground. I swallow a cry, focused on slowing my momentum across the filthy concrete. The street distorts all around me, adrenaline crackling through my veins while a rush of air fills my ears.

THUD.

My hands and arms flail until I crash into a nearby building. Smashing into the solid brick creates a sickening, bone-grinding crack that cuts off my panting. Air shoots from my lungs as bruising whiplash consumes my entire world.

I whimper in shock, blinking through my wavering vision, waiting for the heavy, storm-carrying clouds to settle above me. I'm inelegantly sprawled out on my back in an aching heap.

"EMBER!"

I can't decide if I've blacked out or lost the ability to understand what pain is supposed to feel like. Confusion lays me out, forming a numb haze until sensation sluggishly returns. With it, Hyland's shouting finally registers.

"Em! Ember!"

My whole body feels like one massive bruise, battered pain receptors wailing louder than I can comprehend. It's like torture to roll onto my side, giving me a horrifically perfect view of the van speeding past.

Not towards me.

It's headed straight for Hyland's position.

"Hy," I wheeze.

Not even the round of gunfire he unloads into the quickly shattering front window halts the van's advance. Glass flies, and exhaust fumes billow as reality slows to a petrifying crawl.

"Hyland!"

He tries to jump aside, but the collision hits faster than Hyland can react. I scream like a banshee when the van's bonnet smashes into him. He flies over the windscreen, toppling down the other side of the vehicle and out of sight.

"HY!"

Metal twists and screeches where it crashes into the abandoned SUV, warping the beast into a tangle of battered machinery. Thick, black smoke spurts from the wreckage, an ear-shattering bang accompanying the destruction.

Flames lick at the misshapen wreckage, hiding Hyland from sight. I bite down hard on the inside of my cheek to hold in a cry, commanding my body to obey. It takes great effort to draw myself back up.

My feet can barely hold my body weight, vibrating violently as I stagger towards the car wreck. I've stumbled a few feet when a solid weight smashes into me, the freight truck of muscle and bone sending me straight back down to the ground.

"Should've taken it," the weight crushing into me spits.

"Get the fuck off!"

"You're coming with me, 768. I want that bounty."

Mr Friendly himself straddles my waist, attempting to pin my wrists above my head so he can subjugate me. I buck and struggle, pushing against his attack. He's toned but nowhere near as strong as he seems to think he is.

Wrestling on the hard ground, we both vie to control the other. He wrenches my arms upwards as I use my knee to slam him in the back, attempting to shake the asshole off.

We're a seething, grappling tangle in the midst of billowing black smoke. Neither comes out on top. It's an even match. While he's taller, our muscle tone matches, preventing him from overpowering me.

"Fucking bitch!" His spittle coats my heated face.

"I'm not going anywhere with you," I shriek back. "Let me go, and I'll think about sparing your pathetic, cowardly life."

As he crumples to one side, groaning in pain from my hard kicking, I take the chance to roll us over. Mr Friendly hits the ground, allowing me the chance to boot him right between the legs. Seeing his eyes bulge is a sweet reward.

The victory doesn't slow me down. My straining muscles lament but comply, letting me manhandle myself on top of him this time. I wrap my hands around his throat then start wringing.

"Who do you work for? Where is Gael?"

His skin mottles and grows even more purple with each second that I control his oxygen. When I briefly release his throat to bark the same questions, there's no answer so I resume choking the bastard out.

"How did you find me?" I yell in his face.

Still he refuses to cave. Not even when I grant him a breath. My fingers clench and tighten, contorting his windpipe with nothing but barbaric determination. It doesn't take long for Mr Friendly to pass the fuck out.

Climbing off his limp form awakens the injuries my fall has earned me, but I stuff it all down while staggering over to the car wreck. Behind the wheel of the transit van, a male driver is slumped over, unconscious or dead. I don't care to check.

Flames lick at the twisted vehicles, the acrid smoke charring my lungs. I cough and splutter, eyes streaming liquid acid. The route around the wreckage blurs, making it nearly impossible to search.

"Hyland!"

There's not a single shout or cry for help in response to my howl. Putting one foot in front of the other, I circle the back of the crashed van, crunching through smashed glass. My wobbling vision sharpens into clear focus when I spot a sprawled-out body.

"Hy!"

Several feet from the two burning vehicles, a colossal lump of muscle lies discarded in the street. The puddle of rapidly spreading blood around his still limbs spikes the adrenaline flooding my body.

I've crash-landed on my knees next to Hyland before I can process what's happening. He's collapsed on his side, unresponsive and quickly paling. Blood pours from a deep gash in the back of his head, turning his dirty-blonde hair crimson red.

"Hey, big man." I cup his gravel-scraped cheeks. "Wake up. Open your eyes."

He doesn't respond to my shaking. A petrified sob tears at my chest as I shrug off my workout jacket to quickly ball up then press to the back of his head. Hot, slippery blood covers my hands, adding to the pool all around us.

"Hyland," I whimper, applying as much pressure as I can.

With no signs of life, I'm forced to fumble at his neck, searching for a pulse. The low, thready beat grants me some relief. It's short-lived as I search for the phone in his pocket, quickly dialling emergency services.

My voice doesn't sound like my own while I rattle off a frantic plea for an ambulance. The call handler's questions hardly compute. All I can see is Hyland's slack face, lips turning bluer while blood quickly soaks through my jacket.

"Please hurry," I cry uncontrollably.

"Is there anyone around, ma'am? Are you alone?"

"I can't s—"

The phone flies from my hand, cutting off my reply. A heavy blow strikes the side of my head, knocking me off-kilter. I'm shoved away from Hyland's body and grabbed hard, tossed several metres to the side.

Fresh pain ignites with the force of smacking into the ground. A still-purple face looms over me, one hand clutching his throat, the other forming a bloody fist. Mr Friendly is back with us.

"Last chance to surrender." He coughs in pain.

"No! You did this!" I screech at him.

"You're the one with the bounty on their head, bitch."

The punch sails towards me, attempting to make impact. I throw myself flat against the road then roll, catching the asshole's ankles. He yelps and topples, landing hard on his backside beside me.

Clambering onto my knees, I levy the first blow. It's a decent punch across the face, rendering my attacker momentarily stupefied. Blood drips from his nostrils, one eye rapidly swelling.

When he moves to strike me back, I'm too slow to react. The slap creates a fiery lash down the left side of my face, wrenching my neck. Thankfully, I'm long past caring and don't hesitate to launch a fresh assault.

He topples backwards, taking the brunt of my weight. We're propelled onto the ground together, fists trading strikes, spit and blood catapulting from our raging bodies. Indignation and terror fuel my bloodthirsty rage.

"The only bounty you'll be getting is a one-way ticket to oblivion," I hiss between punches.

He visibly seethes, his forehead surging into mine, smacking our skulls together. Dizzy stars explode over my vision, sending me toppling backwards once more. My skull feels like the bone is being chipped away by a drill.

"I don't think so, 768. You're as feisty as they say, but I need that money."

Metal glints in his hand, prompting a sizzle of terror to sharpen my focus. My attacker struggles to rise long enough to wield the knife he's pulled. I try to haul myself upright, folding inwards. Witnessing my struggle only widens his unhinged grin.

"You can't kill me. Gael won't pay."

"He'll still pay for your butchered corpse." Crimson trails spill from his mouth. "That's good enough for me."

A search around reveals no weapons. Hyland's body is too far out of reach, his gun lost in the melee. I've got nothing on me, not even a switchblade. And there's a fucking knife pointed towards me.

"Gael wants me alive," I pant frantically.

"Too bad. You should've come easily."

"Just stop! Think!"

My feet scratch against the ground, failing to push me far enough backwards. Mr Friendly grabs hold of my ankles and yanks, moving to sit on my legs so I'm pinned. His blade is thick, at least two inches long and glinting with lethal threat.

The smoke-laced world narrows to that steel implement. Its proximity to carving my chest wide open. The way my attacker's leer borders on psychotic. If I can get close enough to claw his eyes without taking a hit, then I'll fight to the death.

When the blade curves through the air in preparation to land a fatal strike, a million moments flash before my eyes. Every time I faced mortality head-on in a filthy fighting ring. The times I wished it would be my end.

But I don't want to die now.

I writhe and scratch, attempting to wrangle the knife from his hands, earning myself another blinding punch to the cheek. Cold gravel cuts into my back where I land spreadeagled, drained and defenceless.

Encroaching sirens clamour.

Glass shatters and explodes.

Smoke pours, thick and heady.

Fatigue sets in fast, slowing my efforts to escape. With the blade slamming down, I scream through the final few inches it has to travel into my body. Only the glinting metal never quite makes it.

BANG.

My attacker freezes, spasming on top of me as globules of red blood spurt from a jagged, smoking hole that appears in his shoulder. The sticky liquid hits my face then spreads in a fine mist.

BANG. BANG.

More scarlet balloons spill from multiple gunshot wounds, tearing through his chest and stomach. The knife slips from his fingers and clatters to the ground beside me. His eyes blow wide, more blood spilling past parted lips.

BANG.

When the bullet tears through his skull, the dead weight of his lifeless body traps me on the ground. I'm covered in warm moisture, compressed beneath his still twitching corpse. Not even the blustering sirens can match my shouts.

"Help! Please!"

Powerful, authoritative footsteps. Crunching glass. A huff strained by exertion. The body on top of me is heaved to the side and dumped like trash, giving me a perfect view of two glassy, empty eyes that were so certain I'd be beaten.

Looming over me, it takes a second for my saviour's appearance to register. His vibrant, purple faux hawk. Fury rioting in honey-dipped eyes. Bee-stung lips and a perfectly boyish baby face.

"Ax," I sob.

He flinches, glancing away from me without a word.

"Oh, A-Axel… Thank God."

"Stop calling me that."

A cold chill flushes over me. "Ax…?"

His rasping voice is so unlike the playful baritone I love. "It's not my name."

"Who... Who are you?"

The man's shoulders sinking with some unidentifiable emotion is the last thing I see before he braces over me. A fist quickly lashes out in my direction. It connects with my solar plexus, then in a fateful instant, unconsciousness takes hold.

CONFIDENTIAL
Why?
Suspect?
Play me
A
INDEX
TYPE I (NORMAL) POSITION
DO NOT CROSS
POLICE LI

LINE - DO NOT CROSS
CONFIDENTIAL
Location?
Suspect?
DO NOT CROSS   POLICE

20

AXEL

CHALK OUTLINES – REN & CHINCHILLA

Not a single traffic law can stop me from laying a lead foot on the accelerator, blasting us past countless pedestrians and red lights. Blaring horns don't penetrate my terror. Nor does the madness we're causing across Central London.

Screw them all.

My knuckles are stark-white on the steering wheel, making my ink stand out even more than it usually does. I'm surprised that I have the focus to drive at all. Warner certainly doesn't as he actively works on tearing his fucking hair out.

"Who's securing the crime scene?" he bellows into his phone.

Muffled voices respond, causing him to curse.

"Sabre Security is taking jurisdiction. We'll have the Falcon Team on-site in eight minutes."

More audible protests follow.

"Tell the superintendent to fuck himself for all I care. This was an attack on our people! Seal off the scene, or I'll have you fired."

When he hangs up, Warner smashes his clenched fist down on the dashboard and lets out an eye-watering string of expletives. Somehow, his phone doesn't break as he slams the offending article into the centre console.

"Those idiots couldn't investigate an RTC if their lives depended on it. Let alone an outright hit on two members of our goddamn team!"

"Hospital is four minutes out," I mutter back.

"Shit." He looks over his shoulder into the backseat. "Madden, call the directors. Get the Falcon Team sent to Mile End immediately. I'm not having some junkyard police recruits messing this up."

"Me?" Blaine squarks.

"Yes, you! I can't think straight right now."

"I don't exactly have their contact numbers," he replies.

"Then use my damn phone! Fuck!"

Warner tosses it over his shoulder, barely able to retrieve the discarded device without losing his shit. If I wasn't responsible for getting us all to the emergency department, I'd be shaking like a leaf too.

"Broad daylight." I spit the words in disbelief. "Gael attacked them in broad fucking daylight! And in public, no less. He's unhinged."

"He's desperate and out of cards to play." Warner strains against his seatbelt, jittering from head to toe. "The medic said they were both found alive. Ember's conscious too."

"Thank fuck." Blaine releases a loud exhale.

"They got lucky. Sounds like the crime scene is a disaster."

Alive can mean all number of things. The information we received wasn't exactly reassuring, coming from some hospital worker who called Warner as their emergency contact. But at least Ember was coherent enough to confirm her identity.

All our phones are Sabre-issued and equipped with tracking software, but we had no reason to be following Hyland and Ember this morning. While trawling through classified MI-5 files covering known European criminal rings in HQ, their location was far from our minds.

Last I heard, Ember and Hyland were getting some air after being cooped up in the penthouse for several days. Now we're violating every traffic regulation known to man to find out exactly how hurt our teammates are and whose head is going to roll for it.

"There are bodies at the crash site." Warner leans forward, elbows on his knees as he digs his palms into his eyes.

"Says who?" I flinch.

"The DCI in charge of the crime scene. Two, apparently."

"Motherfucker. What has Gael done?"

"There's still a bounty on Ember's head. We never should've allowed her out in public. Even with backup and protection."

"She isn't our prisoner." I turn hard, sending us almost sailing on two wheels. "And we both know Ember wouldn't listen to any of us if we told her she can't do something."

In the backseat, Madden mutters an affirmative into Warner's mobile phone then flings it back up front.

"The terrible twosome are going down there themselves," he announces.

"Lord help the Metropolitan Police," Warner mumbles.

"Hudson said they'll take control and update us later."

"Fine. Let's focus on finding Em and Hy."

East London's closest hospital comes into view, denoted by glaring emergency department signs. I park up directly outside the Accident and Emergency, my Sabre ID badge at the ready to ward off the security posted outside.

They chunter in disapproval before waving for us to head inside. I follow Warner's heavy steps, letting Madden bring up the rear. Warner bellows at the receptionist so loud that her cheeks turn pink as she waves us through to the ward.

"Ember Lawson and Hyland Wesson!" Warner doesn't wait for the two nurses behind the counter to look up at us before he's shouting at them.

One of them checks the stacks of patient rosters behind the desk, asking a bunch of stupid questions rather than giving us what we want. Patience expired, I rip the clipboard from her hand, causing her to yelp in shock.

"Excuse me! Sir!"

"You're too slow," I growl.

"This is highly inappropriate—"

"Then sue me."

She huffs, ranting about calling security while I scan the list of occupied bays. Bingo. Twelve and Eighteen. Ignoring the nurses' chorus of rants, Warner storms inside when I point straight ahead.

The hospital curtain is practically torn off its metal rings, ripped open to reveal the occupied clinical space inside. Perched on the edge of a white bed, Ember stares at the doctor in front of her, holding up several fingers for her to count.

"Em!" Warner lumbers towards her.

She blinks slowly like we're little more than a mirage. When her muddied gaze lands on me, Ember frowns, the motion pulling the butterfly stitches across a big, swollen cut along her forehead, visible despite a misting of blood.

"Ember." I stumble in my rush to approach the bed. "Fuck, babe. You scared us to death."

"You came back." She slurs a little. "Where did you go?"

"I'm right here, Em. All of us are."

Warner hovers his hands over her face, pulling short of yanking her into him. I tangle my fingers with hers while Madden loosely clutches her scrape-littered shoulder, exposed by her torn workout tank.

"I'm never letting you out of my sight again." Warner drops a kiss on the top of her head. "You terrified us for a second there."

"A-Accident." Her stilted words tumble out. "Crash."

"We know, Em. It's okay."

"H-Hyland?"

"He's okay," Warner tries to calm her. "You're both alive."

"Bleeding… H-He wasn't waking up."

All over her arms, shallow grazes and lacerations mark her skin along with a severe case of road rash. She's already bruised up, her lip fat and head sliced, though it could be a lot worse if the wreckage they left behind is to be believed.

"You." She gawps at me strangely. "You were there."

"I'm right here." I clench her quaking fingers.

"You saved me… then everything went dark."

Unease settles over me. "Is she okay?"

"And who might you be?" The female doctor demands.

"I'm her emergency contact." Warner cuts the medic a harsh look. "Your team called us in."

"Not to barge in here all at once, I'm sure."

"You know who we are, so spare us the lecture. An update will do."

The doctor sighs tiredly. "Ember's taken a bit of a beating, but nothing too serious. She was struck in the head and rendered unconscious. It's created some lingering confusion."

"A concussion?" Madden asks.

"Mild, thankfully. I'm sure her regular physician will want to do some scans, given her pre-existing condition to ensure there's no exacerbation of her symptoms."

We exchange worried looks. Ember's in no state to be managing a head injury. Not when she's already adjusting to life with a long-term condition and trying to find a treatment plan that works for her PTE.

"What about Hyland Wesson?" Warner straightens up.

"Mr Wesson was taken for a CT scan after his head wound was stitched. He briefly regained consciousness upon arrival, but we're concerned about swelling."

Shit, he's lucky to even be alive. From the little information we have, Hyland was the one driving Sabre's SUV. The same one now burnt to a husk in some East London suburb after being rammed.

"What happened?" I mostly ask myself.

"Bounty," Ember gasps, her gaze still clouded. "Someone wanted to collect."

"Not Gael?" Warner questions.

She licks her split lip then cringes. "No. Hit and run. He tried to k-kill me, but… Axel…"

"Yeah, babe?" I perk up.

Staring at her, Ember continues to frown right back at me. If anyone's left alive after that wreck, I'll kill them myself. I hate seeing her all muddled like this.

"Axel saved me," she finishes hoarsely.

Warner crouches to meet her eyes. "Axel was with us at HQ when we got the call. You went jogging with Hyland this morning."

Blood-caked eyebrows furrowed in a perplexed look, she doesn't seem to comprehend Warner's words. Her groggy attention remains fixed on me.

"What h-happened to your tattoos?" she croaks.

"What do you mean?" I suck in a breath.

"Your hair... the same... the tattoos. They vanished. Where were you?"

"She isn't making any sense." Warner drags a hand over his paling face. "We need to call her specialist in ASAP. Get his medical opinion."

"I can make the call," the doctor offers.

"Please. It's Doctor Fawn at St Thomas's in Westminster."

"You hit me," Ember mumbles in a rush.

"Em?" I ask nervously.

"You... Why? Why did you do that?"

The strange sensation crawling all over me could be confusion. It could be fear. Or simply emotional exhaustion at the sudden loss of adrenaline now that we know they're both relatively intact.

I'd be lying to myself if I believed any of that crap, though. Ember may be concussed, but even injured, she's always known her own mind. The alarm bells firing inside my skull point in one very real direction.

"No," she moans. "You have tattoos now. D-Different."

"My... tattoos?" I repeat.

Ember blinks again, blue-grey irises swimming with moisture. "They were gone. B-But you looked the same."

"Where, Em? Where did you see me?"

"No... no. Not right... Something... Something else. Different name."

Her rambles descend into unintelligible noises, but I've picked up enough to feel sick.

"Axel." Madden grabs my attention. "Don't push her."

With a sinking weight filling my gut, I turn away from Ember and Warner. Madden backs up a step at the arctic glower that I train in his direction. My words are laced with such intense malice,

I almost don't recognise my own voice.

"What did you do?"

"Ax? What is it?"

I ignore Warner, focusing on the criminal thug. "Answer the question."

Madden rolls his neck, mouth opening and closing several times. "She's concussed. Confused. Ember knows you weren't really there."

"Then why is she so damn sure?"

"How should I know?" Madden's shoulders jump.

The worthless motherfucker actually thinks he's a better deceiver than I am. Like I can't see through his bullshit. I've lived a lie my entire life.

"He saved me." Ember's voice sounds like it's getting stronger. "Then… he hit me. Knocked m-me out. Axel, you hit me! But… it wasn't you. Was it?"

"What the hell is this?" Warner thunders.

Madden exhales, still acting evasive. "Beats me."

"Tell me what the fuck you've done, Blaine Madden. Before this hospital has to make a space in its morgue for a fresh fucking body."

"Someone explain," Warner demands. "Right now."

"Nothing." Madden smiles wide, the smarmy fuck. "I've done nothing. Ask your teammate."

"Don't lay this at my door," I seethe.

"Your business, your door," he snarks back.

"Until you decided it would be fun to meddle, and now Ember is hurt! I warned you. I damn well warned you to leave this be. Are you happy now?"

I've stepped closer, fists balled at my sides and itching with the desire to pummel Madden's face into a meaty, unrecognisable pulp. He squares his shoulders in preparation, eyeing my body language.

The female doctor inches between us, hands outstretched in a plea for calm. "Do I need to call security and have you both removed?"

"No." Madden shakes his head. "We're fine. All calm. Right, Axel?"

"Just admit it."

"You first, *pup.* This is your secret."

"One you had no right to unleash! Do you have any idea what you've done?"

"Someone explain what the hell is going on before I toss you both out." Warner wraps a protective arm around Ember, like he can shield her from us. "Axel?"

Fucking Madden.

On a good day, I tell myself I've made peace with the fiction that became my life story. The horrific lies I've told. The even more terrifying truth that I erased. Especially from the men I now consider my brothers.

The possibility that they'd ever know otherwise isn't something I've dared to entertain. Not once. This isn't a single white lie. It's a monumental, life-changing, trust-shattering lie of epic proportions that will devastate my entire existence.

Worse still, I can see the goddamn amusement twinkling in Madden's stare. He knows exactly what he's done. All I want is for the motherfucker to admit it before I end his pitiful life.

"Fuck this," Warner grumbles. "We have more important things to be worrying about than your ego contest. Shelve it, and we'll have a very thorough conversation later on."

"Sure, team leader." Madden winks.

"Get out!" I howl at him.

"Come along now, Ax. You heard the man."

"I'll shelve it, but not while looking at your smug face. Get out."

"I stay where Ember is."

"Then I'll get her as far away from you as possible!" I recoil at the feeling of my erratic heartbeat.

With a small, amused smirk, he throws up his hands then departs the clinical bay to wait outside. Not without taking a long, hard look at my girl first. Yep, walking corpse. He has a death wish that I'm happy to endorse.

Warner finishes chatting with the doctor then orders me to watch Ember while he's taken to Hyland's booth next. I nod curtly, looming over her bed as the pair depart to find our missing enforcer.

"Ax?"

Her pained whisper rips me wide open, letting anger and fear melt into plain old relief. I slump next to her on the bed, allowing Ember to cuddle into my side. She smells like blood and smoke, but I still hold her close.

"Sorry," I offer against her dirty braid. "I never meant for any of this to happen. Sometimes the right decisions aren't the easiest or even the moral ones."

"My head hurts," she murmurs.

Yeah. Mine too.

"Lay down, dimples. The others will be back."

"Will you hold me?"

"Yeah. Always."

Ember curls up in my arms, the hospital gown bunching around her scraped, bruise-smattered legs. She tucks her head beneath my chin, fingers winding in my t-shirt, forming a strangling grip.

I don't know what pain killers they've given her, but she's already softening against me. Her breathing grows longer as exhaustion takes hold.

"I'm so sorry." I moisten my mouth, trying to find the right words. "I've got secrets, Em. Big ones. Stuff that I should've told you all long ago but never could."

"We all have secrets," she replies sleepily.

"Not ones like this. I thought I could protect you from my past, but it's arrived, and I can't stop this disaster. Not if he's here."

She heaves out a tired sigh. "Who's here?"

"Madden isn't our only ghost. This one's just been buried for a long time."

Between the head injury, exhaustion and drugs, I know she isn't grasping what I'm saying. Perhaps that's giving me the courage to say it aloud. Soon enough, I'll have to explain properly. Then Ember will never want to look at me again, let alone allow me to hold her close like this.

None of them will forgive me.

And I'll lose everything.

All around, the constant hum of hospital life fails to overcome the pounding that fills my ears. Relentless. Terrifying. A countdown clock that leads to one place—the destruction of the fantasy I created. The tale that I was told to weave.

With Ember passed out, I manoeuvre my arm free then pull my phone from my pocket. It isn't often that I call home. A life sentence is more than a signed piece of paper. It's also a death warrant. The part about being an orphan is true in that respect.

"HMP Wakefield."

"Phone call for inmate Meredith Slaughter, prison ID 6243. It's urgent."

"This is out of hours," the bored voice drones.

"Family emergency, I'm her son. Locate her please."

"Damn family members… Hold the line."

The miserable operator vanishes with a click. I adjust Ember's position on my chest, ensuring my sprinting heart rate doesn't wake her up. She's still breathing steadily in her medicated stupor.

After what feels like an eternal wait, the line rings out then connects with a low muffle. I hold my breath, waiting for the rattly voice that I only converse with once or twice a year. If that.

"Axel? Is that you?"

"Hi, Mum." I gulp hard. "I don't have much time."

"What is it, boy?"

My eyeballs sear, a childish part of me rearing its head. Traumatised by what he'd seen then twisted into a lie that he never wanted to tell. But life doesn't give us fair choices. Not even when you're young and afraid.

If I'd had the option, I wouldn't have erased my twin brother. Nor would I have covered up what he did back then. Mum did the best she could. She protected her baby. All while I bore the brunt of her carefully woven lie.

"Ax?" she prompts.

"Gunnar's back."

She wheezes, adding to my building terror. "Not possible."

"It's true."

"You're sure?"

"Positive. He's in London."

For an awful, stomach-clenching pause, there's no advice. Not even a word of motherly comfort. Then the inevitable nail in my coffin comes in the form of a stark warning.

"Axel…" She sniffs back tears. "Run."

play
me
DO NOT CROSS
PO
Suspect?
NOT CROSS
POLICE

21

EMBER

WHO ARE YOU – MEHRO

My fingertips slide back and forth over the gauze on my forehead, absently fiddling with the adhesive edges. Prescription painkillers aside, I'm nursing a straight whiskey while contemplating the late night skyline.

Behind me, the sound of ice clinking on glass breaks the awkward silence. Warner retrieved the unopened bottle of single malt from his desk for our sombre mood. Though he outright refuses to pour Hyland a measure.

"Can I get a refill?" I raise my glass hopefully.

"No." Liquid splashes into his. "You shouldn't be drinking at all."

"Be glad that you got one," Hyland groans nearby.

"Some of us got discharged." I whirl to glower at him.

He's sprawled out on our sofa, chest bare and covered in blackish-purple clouds. Every inch of him bears the evidence of

our near death experience. Hyland can barely move, but he still insisted on coming home to recover.

"I'm not spending another second in a hospital bed," he grumbles.

"You're the first to lecture me about my health, but you flee in the face of medical advice when the doctors want to keep you in for another night. Swelling or not, you should've stayed there."

"My CT scan was all clear."

"I don't care!"

He adjusts the pillow tucked behind his neck, keeping pressure off his bandaged head wound. "I didn't need to hear anything else. Got a clean bill of health and a lovely stack of pills. Job done."

"You were hit by a van!"

"Don't waste your breath, Em." Warner is clearly exhausted and limping with each stunted step. "He's as stubborn as a mule."

"Why did you agree to pick him up?"

"Because if I didn't, he would've walked instead, and I was already dealing with keeping Tom at bay. He was ready to hightail over here himself to check on you."

Shit, I need to call my brother back. My phone was inside Hyland's SUV while I ran. I didn't need it with him following hot on my heels. Unfortunately, that also means it's now a puddle of melted glass and plastic.

Hyland chuckles weakly. "Not quite. But I would've gotten a cab."

"When someone tried to kill you twenty-four hours ago?" I jab a finger at him.

"They were obviously just eliminating your protection," he refutes. "Look how that turned out for them."

"I'm looking, Hy. We're a mess."

For once, Hyland's smart mouth clicks shut. He's in no position to argue. By all accounts, it's miraculous that neither of us were more seriously injured.

Behind the breakfast bar, Warner knocks back an amber shot then pours another. It doesn't escape my attention that he doesn't offer one to the dark shadow in the corner, silent and contemplative.

Axel hasn't uttered a word since we got home. Not even when

Warner requested that Blaine give us some time to talk. The Phantom didn't say much, all too happy to depart this boiling pan of tension to take a stroll.

"Do we have an update?" I finish my final mouthful.

"Kade called." Warner refills his glass again, barely landing the whiskey inside without spilling. "Bodies have been ID'd as two thugs, known to police."

"Motive?" Hyland grunts.

"Unclear, but it's likely they saw Gael's dark web ad. Fancied themselves a payday."

"Any signs of other players?" I ask carefully.

His baby blues flick to mine. "Only empty bullets."

This news causes our silent shadow to shift, arms protectively bracing over his chest. I couldn't quite string together what happened until I came around for a second time, feeling a lot more lucid.

It's all painfully clear now. Hyland's unconscious body. The knife attempting to slice me up. Gunshots. A dead body nearly crushing me to death. Purple hair and honey eyes... but no tattoos.

That's not my name.

It was Axel. But... not.

A stranger wearing Axel's face. Axel's hair. Axel's features. Yet not a hint of the man I care so deeply about. The one I thought I knew. This person was a carbon copy that my imagination definitely didn't conjure.

"There's no ID on the bullets found at the scene," Warner continues. "So the gun is unlicensed and unregistered. We've got a ghost out there, assassinating in broad daylight."

"He did save my life." I run a fingertip around the rim of my empty glass.

"We don't know who *he* is, so I'll hold my thanks in reserve."

With that, Warner turns to face our lovable goof. No hint of playful, jaunty Axel resides in his stone-carved posture. He's been wordless since I got discharged after a full eval with Doctor Fawn. The displeased specialist gave me a list of warning signs longer than my left arm to look out for.

"That's not my name." The repetition tastes like ash on my

tongue. "He said that to me. I thought it was you, Ax. But... it wasn't you. He told me so himself."

"You're right," Axel finally speaks. "It wasn't me."

"Then who?"

"Madden did this, he should be here."

"I don't care what bullshit Blaine wants to spew right now." Warner slams his glass down. "Start talking and make it good. Tell us what the fuck is happening."

Staring at him now, it's hard to discern this Axel from the man who rescued me. They're virtually identical. Honestly, part of me worries it was him. That I'm falling into some kind of trap. There isn't another explanation for it.

"It wasn't me. I didn't save Ember, nor did I knock her out."

"Then who did?" I gawp at him.

He races a shaking hand over his hair. "It's a long, complicated story."

"Then uncomplicate it," Hyland entreats.

We all watch Axel stare down at the floor, his usual oversized slogan tee failing to penetrate his misery. It's a classic. *I'm not angry, this is just my face.* Yet none of us are laughing. Not even him.

"I lied to you." Axel shamefully glances at me then the other two. "I've lied since the day we met. In fact, I've lied to every person I've ever met since I was thirteen years old."

"Who is he?" Warner lashes out.

Distant neon lights cast strobes across Axel's devastated expression as he steps into the centre of the room. Nowhere to hide. No armour or protective humour to keep him safe. His bare, broken parts stripped bare for the world to see.

"My twin."

To my shock, Warner erupts into disbelieving laughter. "Is this a joke?"

Axel shifts on his feet, visibly antsy. "I wish it was."

"You know that I combed through your background the day you were recruited. I'm sure MI-5 did the same thing. There was absolutely nothing about a sibling of any sort."

"And you told me that you're an only child," I add.

"Officially, I am." Axel shudders at the way his voice cracks.

"Can I please get a drink?"

Warner huffs. "Fine."

"Come sit, Em." Hyland pats the spot next to him. "You're making me nervous."

"I'm fine here."

"You're clearly not. Sit down before you fall over."

While Warner pours Axel a drink, I reluctantly plop myself down. The pair join us in the living room, taking opposite sides of the sofa. For all the tension lingering between us, there might as well be a whole ocean separating them.

"His name is Gunnar." Axel takes a large mouthful. "He doesn't exist on any public record. Not under that name, at least. I think he had another once… Before he found his way back to us."

"What does that mean?" Warner massages his right knee between winces.

"I didn't know that I was a twin until he came home. My mum kept his birth a secret. He was relinquished as a baby and never legally tied to her… so I had no idea."

"Why would she do that?" Hyland questions.

"Because I'm not my father's son." Axel stares down into his glass. "He was infertile. Mum had an affair and fell pregnant, but he agreed to raise me. Just not a set of twins. Gunnar had to go."

"She gave him up," I state the obvious.

"It was a little more than that." He smiles brokenly. "My father forced her to get rid of Gunnar unless she wanted to be a homeless, single mother. She was literally bullied into it."

Warner scrubs his face. "I don't understand."

"She was young and terrified. My father could be coercive, even abusive. Having me around kept Mum vulnerable and under his thumb, but he didn't want the hassle of two mouths to feed."

"Evil bastard," I snarl.

"Yeah." Axels snorts. "None of us knew what happened to Gunnar after that. I grew up with an asshole who couldn't stand the sight of me and a mother who was too emotionally fragile to be a real parent. When Gunnar returned, I don't think she was surprised that her past had found her."

Attempting to wrap my head around Axel's tale only worsens

the throbbing from my head injury. I can't imagine how Hyland's coping with the information in his state.

"How did he find you?" I ask more gently.

"Not a clue. Gunnar learned the art of disappearing a long time ago, but he also learned how to hunt along the way. You can ask Madden all about that."

After a long pause, Warner clears his throat. "Your mother is serving a life sentence for first-degree murder. According to public record, she killed your father."

"Convenient, right?" Axel laughs without humour.

"Tell us the real story."

"It's irrelevant now."

"If this man is coming after us, then it's all relevant. We need to know what we're dealing with."

"It's me he wants." Axel swirls whiskey around his glass. "I helped our mother cover it all up. I lied for her. I erased Gunnar's existence from our lives."

"Why?" Hyland prompts.

"Because Mum isn't a killer. All these years she's served… it's a lie. She took the wrap to cover up the fact that Gunnar stabbed my deadbeat dad forty-three times when he returned and learned the truth behind his abandonment."

Howling wind whips outside the floor-to-ceiling windows, the gusts almost drowning out Axel's dejected whispers. Hyland stares at Axel without a single word to offer. He's doing better than Warner—head bowed and face buried in his hands.

"I don't know what happened to Gunnar after he was sent away." Axel wipes beneath his leaking eyes. "But whatever it was… he was desperate when he came looking for a home. Instead he got the truth, and it broke him."

"He killed your father?" I whisper.

"Nearly tore the man apart."

"Jesus, Ax."

His shoulder lifts in a half-hearted shrug. "I'm not saying he didn't deserve it, but what Gunnar did was inhuman. A thirteen-year-old child. He didn't even know the man."

"Then why cover it up?" Hyland shakes his head.

"Mum blamed herself for the state Gunnar was in. We don't know what happened to him, but he was close to starving, all beaten and bruised. Could barely talk. She never got over abandoning him and refused to watch his life be taken away by a prison sentence too."

"So you wove a lie." I nod in sick understanding.

"Not me," he corrects. "It was all her. Gunnar didn't exist to us. Not outside of her memories. She ordered him to disappear and never return. In exchange, she'd make it all go away."

The realisation that Axel had no choice but to conceal a brutal crime as a young kid leaves me cold. Not only did he lose his family, but he also had to rewrite his own family history. All to protect a child forged into a monster.

"I don't know what kind of life he thinks I had after losing everything." His shoulders shake, voice trembling hard. "But Gunnar believes that I took his future from him. Now he wants it back."

"You were just a child," I reason.

"The one child who didn't get sent away. Who wasn't abandoned and left to survive all alone. In his mind, I got everything that he never had, no matter how false that really is."

"So that's why he's back," Warner muses.

After knocking back the last of his whiskey, Axel places the glass down. He takes a pause to wipe his face, still not looking at any of us.

"I don't know much about my brother, but Gunnar is tangled up in Madden's world. *He's* the reason this is happening. I told you that criminal can't be trusted."

"Can you be trusted?" Warner's jaw tics.

"Yes. I'm your teammate."

"You fucking lied to us, Axel! You've been lying to us for two years!"

Honey-hued sadness begs for forgiveness, bouncing between the two men Axel calls his brothers. A part of me aches for him. Whatever evil he's hiding, I can see the toll it's taken. Nobody lives a lie for no good reason.

Another part of me remembers all the strained looks between

him and Blaine. The tension so thick, no blade could hope to cut it. Their constant sniping. It has been going on for months, and still, Axel didn't think to trust us.

He kept lying.

On and on and on.

It's far worse for Warner and Hyland. The Anaconda Team is built on trust. That was made clear to me on my very first day. This secret isn't just Axel's cross to bear—it shakes the very core of their foundation.

"Why did Gunnar save me from those jackasses just to knock me out?" I ask the room.

"He clearly didn't want to chat." Axel stares down at his hands.

"But why intervene at all?"

"Truthfully, I don't know what he hopes to achieve."

"Then let's ask someone who does." Warner pulls out his phone, angrily jabbing the screen.

We all watch him make the phone call that will bring our fractured team back together. I doubt Blaine's gone far. Whatever game he's playing, he did remain in the hospital while I was checked over and declared fit to leave.

Fraught silence reins until the penthouse's doorbell rings. The fact that Warner hasn't clued Blaine in on our security system yet speaks volumes. At this rate, our enemies could pull our team apart like wet tissue paper.

Warner hobbles on his prosthetic while escorting the obsidian-eyed troublemaker into the room. Blaine shoots me a searching look, parking himself in the corner against the built-in TV unit where Axel can't launch a surprise attack.

"How do you know Gunnar Slaughter?" Warner doesn't beat around the bush.

Seeing Blaine's surprise is a novelty. He clearly didn't expect Axel to come clean. The fact that he knew about the deceit all along only adds to the burn of betrayal I'm sure we all feel.

"Professionally," Blaine responds.

"Meaning?"

"He's known to the criminal underworld."

I watch Warner pinch the bridge of his nose. "Be more specific."

"Gunnar provides services to the international community. We met years ago while I was running a drug operation in Argentina. He's done a few jobs for me over the years."

"What kind of services?" Axel gets hold of his emotions long enough to ask.

"Your research didn't turn that information up?"

"Fuck you, Madden. You're playing with forces that you don't understand."

"I think I understand a lot more than you do, pup. This is above your pay grade."

"Don't antagonise him," Warner barks, halting their heated stare off. "Just answer the question."

Blaine tears his dark gaze away, delaying an all-out war. I have a feeling that Axel would be happy to get his favourite knives out to play for Blaine's execution right about now.

"Gunnar Slaughter is what we would call a bounty hunter." Blaine shrugs. "Codename, The Hunter. He only takes the most complex cases and charges fees higher than the GDP of most European nations."

"How do you know this?" Warner presses.

"Because I used him to track down your precious little jailbird almost a year ago." His black stare strays to me. "The Hunter found Ember for us."

No one speaks for a second. Then the whole room erupts with shouts and questions. Only I don't have a single word to offer. Not yet. All I can do is stare back at Blaine, attempting to fathom his mind.

Regardless of his motivations, he rescued me. It sounds like that cost him a pretty penny too. I was a bargaining chip then. A tasty morsel to be dangled in front of his prey. What I need to know now is whether or not that's really changed.

"Enough!" Warner shouts over the barrage of voices. "This doesn't explain what on earth this man is doing in London, butting into our criminal case."

"He's supposed to be on a job for me." Blaine rolls his lip piercing.

"What job?" Hyland booms.

When Blaine drops his stare from mine, I know we're in for a treat.

"I hired him to locate Gracie Livingstone."

"You did what?" I blurt out.

"It's the fastest way to locate the girl." He smooths a hand down his clean t-shirt. "You wanted her found, right?"

"Well… yes. Obviously."

"So I called Gunnar. He agreed to take the hit."

"The hit?" Axel splutters.

"The case, the target, whatever." Blaine waves him off, unaffected. "He's supposed to be tracking our missing girl, not gallivanting around London and mowing down rogue criminals."

"Clearly, he's not! My psycho brother is here right now!"

"That's your problem. Not mine. I didn't ask him to come."

"Then what does he want from me?" Axel hisses in anger.

"I'd imagine to add your name to his list."

"His list?" I parrot.

"The Hunter operates on a strict moral code. Anyone who crosses him soon finds themselves on a list then floating in chunks at the bottom of a ravine."

In any other circumstance, seeing Axel's eyes bug out would be amusing. But not while hearing that his bounty hunter, illegal assassin of a brother holds some stupid childhood grudge.

"Wait." Warner holds up a hand. "Regardless of the infrastructure we failed to dismantle, you don't have the capital to afford this. How are you paying him?"

"Ah," Blaine hums. "The catch."

Coursing with an invisible current of ire, Axel steps closer to Blaine. Each movement shrieks of untapped violence. My eyes flit between them, the lessening distance spelling out danger. It's like watching two tornados circle each other.

"What did you offer him?" Axel implores, advancing another step.

"I did this for Ember. To end her pain and turmoil."

"What. Did. You. Offer. Him?"

"Information," Blaine admits.

"Such as?" Axel specifies.

"He wanted to know all about his lucky twin brother and the life he never got to have. The Hunter wants to hunt you next."

All hell breaks loose.

Axel pounces on Blaine, the pair coming to blows in a spectacular fashion. I'm lifted from the sofa and shoved backwards by Warner, his yelling going unheeded. Neither man stops trying to batter the other.

They slam into the TV console, sending a priceless vase flying. Crystal smashes against the hardwood floor before Blaine's dropped onto the shattered fragments. He doesn't appear to feel it, too busy smashing up Axel's face like a man possessed.

The sight of spraying blood only cheers Blaine's viciousness on. He's a ruthless whirlwind. Axel gives as good as he gets, kneeing him in the dick then clocking his barely healed nose with a powerful right hook.

They twist and roll, slamming backwards into the long wooden unit. It causes the television to waver, almost like it's listening to Hyland's warning cry, then the flat screen topples forwards on top of them.

There's an electric pop as glass and plastic fall apart, burying the two men. But it still isn't enough to halt them. Axel emerges from beneath the ruined TV first, a hand curled around Blaine's leg to drag him out too. Only to wallop him straight in the gut.

"They're going to kill each other!" I tug on Warner's grip.

"Let them get it out," he grunts in my ear.

"Forget it!"

"None of us are getting in the middle of that fight. Especially not you."

"We can't just watch them!"

"Axel betrayed the trust of our entire team, and Blaine fed private, personal information to his estranged psychopathic twin. I think they're entitled to beat the shit out of each other."

"I have a decent view from here," Hyland calls from the sofa. "The little shit owes me a new flat screen, though. Axel knows we have a no fighting in the penthouse rule."

"We've got to stop this!"

"Stay out of it." Warner winds two strong arms around my

waist. "Violence is the only language these two speak."

Hoisting Blaine around the midsection, Axel howls like some kind of deranged animal. He hauls his captive upright then batters him into the wooden coffee table, causing the structure to crack clean down the middle.

Wood splinters and collapses as the pair drop onto the middle of the debris. Even that doesn't stop their snarling punching match. Axel's a legitimate challenge to The Phantom's savage reputation.

The living room is half-destroyed by the time a loud ring disturbs the pseudo cage fight. Both men hesitate but quickly dive back in to resume beating each other. Warner releases me to check his phone, pulling up the penthouse's built-in security system.

"We have a visitor." He clicks the live video feed off. "Wait here."

"With the cavemen?" I heave.

"It's no better at our front door, love."

Hyland grimaces, attempting to wrestle himself upright and failing. I dodge the chaos being caused by the raging fight to navigate my way over, offering him a helping hand.

"Do you need anything?"

"Some peace and quiet," he complains.

"I'll lend you my cold packs. Works wonders for a headache."

"They worked?" He brightens up.

"Like a treat."

"You can apologise to my self-help book later for ever doubting it."

"Yeah, yeah."

Heaving up the massive grump takes great effort. Even I'm not strong enough to yank him fully up, especially not now with a new myriad of bruises and scrapes. I manage to turn him, enabling his feet to find the floor alone.

Shakily standing, Hyland jams two fingers into his mouth then unleashes a piercing wolf-whistle. It bounces off the high ceiling and around the trashed room, causing both idiots to freeze mid-fight.

"Are you done acting like fucking three year olds?"

Split lip dripping, Axel lowers his fist. "This fucker has ruined my life!"

"You did that all on your own," Blaine seethes.

"No! You led him straight to me!"

Another punch knocks Blaine back onto his spine, spreadeagled among splintered wood, broken glass and complete destruction. He lays there cackling like a madman with blood pouring into his eyes.

"Cheap shot, Ax."

"Do not call me that." Axel pants for air.

"Couldn't even finish the job. I'll never understand why your brother is so desperate for your life. You are pathetic."

"You're dead! Son of a—"

I release Hyland to step forward, straight into Axel's path. He halts his advance a second before his next punch would've landed directly in my face.

"Enough!" My boom carries all around us.

"Ember, move. Let me take the trash out."

"No, I'm sick of this. Whatever you've done, whatever Blaine's done… put it aside. We have a job to do, and Gracie's running out of time."

"He cannot stay! Madden can't be trusted!"

Blaine wrenches himself to a sitting position. "Says the liar."

"You're no better than the monster I've spent twenty years forgetting," Axel blasts at him. "Remember that, Madden. You will never, *ever* belong to this team or this family."

He hocks up a bloody mouthful then drops it in Blaine's lap. Wonderful. I've got a team of salivating wolves on my case and zero other options for finding Gracie. Those thugs might as well have shipped me back to Gael yesterday.

Multiple footsteps sound out as Warner returns with company. Behind him, a typically smartly dressed Kade marches into the room accompanied by another, their face open and friendly, with a shock of brightly coloured hair.

"Are we interrupting?" Kade scans over the disaster zone.

"Only these two idiots who don't know how to use actual words to communicate." I gesture towards our bleeding fighters. "What is it?"

"Sorry for barging in so soon after the attack, but this couldn't wait. I wanted you to hear it from me first."

"We left Brooke at a baby scan with Eli, Jude and Hudson." The other man speaks up, his interested gaze fixed on me. "I'm Phoenix."

"Ember," I reply.

"So I've heard." He smiles cheekily. "Couldn't you take them both? Spare the poor TV a battering?"

"I decided to sit this one out."

"Shame." He chuckles.

"Nix." Kade nudges him. "Give it a rest. This is urgent."

"Sorry. Carry on."

Pulling the leather satchel from his shoulder, Kade drops it on the back of the sectional to pull his laptop free. I help Hyland move over to get a good view, his movements stiff and awkward.

"This was sent to us three hours ago by Mexico's federal intelligence agency." Kade taps on a saved video file. "We've verified the authenticity. It's legit."

His laptop screen fills with the sight of a raging inferno. Numerous fire fighters attempt to tackle the blaze, out of control flames devouring what looks like an arched veranda with colourful Talavera tiles cracking in the heat.

"Oh." I quickly cover my mouth. "Is that…"

"What we believe to be Antonio Gael's estate," Kade confirms with grim certainty. "It's the right location and description. There's a strong possibility this was our target."

"The architecture… It's familiar."

He nods unhappily. "I'm sorry, Ember. We've been informed that it was torched before a warrant could be issued by the local judge. The whole estate is gone."

"He was tipped off," Hyland mutters.

"It would appear so."

Ignoring Blaine and Axel's staggering approach, I pull backwards, grappling for air to breathe. After all these months, countless hours of chasing leads, scouring maps, entreating agencies to search their own land… this is how it ends.

In fire and ash.

The decimation of all evidence.

Nothing left. Gone.

"The Gael estate has been destroyed." Kade sounds distant, locked in a bubble that can't reach me. "All traces of him are dust."

"There's nothing left?" Warner utters.

"Nothing but rubble… And an audio recorder left outside the front gates. The fire crew retrieved it and turned it over to the authorities."

Minimising the video, Kade clicks on another file. It brings up an image of an old-style, manual voice recorder, the kind used by law enforcement for police interviews. Another subtle jab. Using the very tools of our trade against us.

Fastened to the worn plastic, a yellow note is scrawled in neat, elegant script. I'd recognise Gael's handwriting anywhere. He signed enough shady contracts in my presence, convinced I'd never live long enough to rat on him if I escaped.

PLAY ME.

"He does love theatrics, doesn't he?" Phoenix tsks.

Nodding, Kade loads a final file. "We've been sent the transcribed text."

"Read it," Warner requests.

"The message is graphic." Kade looks up from his screen, gaze landing on me.

"Em?" Axel attempts to place a hand on me.

I duck out of his reach, needing personal space. The raging fire still plays against my eyeballs, wiping out all the evidence we need to bring the cartel down. All I can hope is that Gael emptied the holding cells before lighting the match.

"Read it." I somehow locate a calm tone. "Please."

"Very well."

Kade opens a text file from his email, so at least I don't have to endure hearing Gael's voice again. Listening to his disgusting words read in Kade's clipped, cool tone almost softens the blow.

"I gave you the chance to come home, 768. You disobeyed me. Humiliated me. Betrayed me. Your usefulness to this operation has expired."

"Love." Warner holds a hand towards me. "You don't have to listen to this."

"Yes, I do. Please continue, Kade."

He clears his throat, disregarding Warner's pinched eyes.

"There's no deal left to be struck. I will show you no mercy. I'm coming for you, 768. I'll kill everyone you love in front of you before I grant you the mercy of death. Starting with *her*."

"Gracie," I whimper.

Closing his laptop, Kade clenches his eyes shut. "It would appear that Gael's patience for games has expired. The failed hit yesterday was his final attempt to get you back."

"So what now?" Axel dares to question.

"His revenge."

No one has another word to offer. Axel studies the closed laptop while Hyland massages his forehead. Blaine flexes his swelling fists, seeming to steel himself. Warner stares off out the window, contemplating the night sky like it holds some miracle.

I lick my lips. Preparing. Steeling. Resigning myself for what must be done. We don't have time to chase a list of leads provided by the world's criminal elite. Right now, we need fast results. Before this battle escalates into a full-scale war.

"Blaine."

He looks at me, bloodied and slumping. "Yes, sweetheart?"

"Call The Hunter. Tell him we want to meet."

NFIDENTIAL
Why?
Suspect?
INDEX
A
TYPE I (NORMAL) POSITION
Play me
3
1
2
DO NOT CROSS
POLICE LI

play
me
DO NOT CROSS
Suspect?
NOT CROSS
POLICE L

22

EMBER

ALL OF HUMAN KNOWLEDGE MADE US DUMB – SOFIA ISELLA

It turns out, the Madden family empire holds even more secrets than any of us realised. There's not just one warehouse that escaped Sabre's excavation of their infrastructure but a whole host of off-the-record, abandoned haunts.

Staring down at the city, I find myself contemplating the vast wealth and power of the career criminal who has aligned himself with our cause. Blaine's thugs have sealed off all accessible routes behind a wall of armed muscle.

Only one way in.

And one way out.

After two days of silence, part of me doubted whether Gunnar Slaughter would agree to a meet. The lack of response was deafening. Particularly given Gael's very real threat against us all.

But when his text confirmation finally arrived, our plan was set in motion.

We're here to drive a new bargain with the devil. Off the record and most definitely beyond the legal confines of Sabre's operations. None of this is by the book, and if it goes wrong, we will certainly all hang for it.

"Do you think he'll show?" I whisper to Warner.

"I'd say it's unlikely."

"The Hunter wants his brother, and he knows that Axel is with us. Won't that incentivise him to come?"

"This isn't on his terms," Warner disagrees.

"How so?"

"We're in Madden's territory, and even if we're not here in a professional capacity, we still represent Sabre to him. The Hunter may not believe that we'll keep this meeting quiet."

"I think curiosity will win out." I watch the foreboding night for signs of life.

"Perhaps you're right. But something tells me that Gunnar Slaughter isn't the type of man to do anything he hasn't orchestrated personally."

"Then let's hope you're wrong."

Like me, Warner studies the eerily quiet street. Here in the outskirts, we're far from Central London's chaos. This residential area provides the perfect protection for Blaine's empty bolthole. Despite not being used in years, the old townhouse remained untouched by the authorities.

When I glance over my shoulder, the display of overt force behind us is enough to set my teeth on edge. Each member of our entourage is armed and ready for anything. Even Raye and Spyder, though neither are thrilled to be working beside Sabre agents.

It seems all battle lines have dissolved in the wake of the brewing storm. If Gael's out for revenge, no one will be left untouched. Sabre or not. Agent or criminal. We've all worked to bring the cartel's operation down, even from opposing sides. Now we're all under threat.

"If The Hunter does show up, he won't walk into a certain trap." I eye the array of guns holstered in plain sight. "We have to come in peace."

"This is as peaceful as it gets when meeting an internationally wanted criminal bounty hunter."

"Warner… he's our one shot at locating Gracie before Gael has her killed."

"And we have no guarantee that he'll help at all." He heaves an aggrieved sigh. "So excuse me for being cautious."

At the sound of Axel's voice echoing behind us, Warner tenses up. He's been a wall of carved tension ever since the extent of his teammate's deceit was revealed. Honestly, it's rare to see him so speechless.

Warner's the fixer, the steady ship, the glue that binds this dysfunctional family unit together. Without him balancing out the competing forces in this team, I doubt it would exist at all. Now it feels like we're all teetering dangerously close to an irrecoverable precipice.

"You have to talk to Axel sometime." I try to remain diplomatic.

"Leave it, Em."

"It's been days. You won't even look at him."

"How I choose to manage this team is my decision. Not yours."

"Is that so?"

"Yes. Drop it."

His clipped rejection slaps me in the face. I swallow the ball in my throat then turn to peer up at Warner properly, trying to see past his Sabre-approved mask of professionalism.

"I'm trying to help you, but by all means, continue to act like a prick. Push us all away. Punish Axel for being forced to tell a lie against his will as a child. See how that works out for you."

Warner casts a cold, icy blue shard over me, a riot of conflicting hurt and confusion cracking through his attempt to remain nonchalant. His poker face is shit when it comes to me.

"Why are you pushing this? Axel lied to you too."

"Because we don't have time to let the past tear us apart right now." I grasp hold of his bicep and squeeze. "Be mad at him when we're done fighting for our lives."

"I don't know if he can be trusted," he lays out. "Until he regains that trust, I will treat Axel the same way I treat Madden. He's an asset, not a member of this team.”

“How can you say that?”

“How could he lie to us all this time?” A vein pulses in Warner’s neck.

“He had no choice!”

“As a child, perhaps not. But he’s an adult and fully capable of choosing his own path. Instead, he chose to protect a murderer and keep an innocent locked up for a crime she didn’t commit.”

“Right.” I push him away then throw my hands up. “Because life is that black and white. We’re all just good and evil, murderers or innocent. It’s really that simple.”

His nostrils flare, conveying his annoyance. “In our world, it is. That’s how we do this job. We aren’t allowed the luxury of second chances.”

For the love of God, I really hope Axel can’t hear this. He’s unstable as it is—a pacing wreck of nerves, barely functioning or even communicating—so hearing Warner’s dismissal might just tip him over the edge.

“Then what the hell am I doing here?” I hit back at him.

“That’s different.”

“One rule for me and one for him?”

Rather than find a pitiful argument, he merely clenches his jaw shut.

“Just stop and think, Warner. You’re hurt and feeling betrayed. *I get it*. But don’t let that tear this team apart because I know for a fact you don’t believe it’s that simple.”

“I have nothing to say to him.” He hurls the words at me as if he’s tasted something unpleasant. “That’s all. Will you get off my back now?”

“No.”

“Fucking hell, Em. You can’t fix us all.”

“Axel is your family,” I implore through gritted teeth. “And family forgives each other last time I checked. Grow up, put your hurt ego aside, and be there for him. Else you’re not the man I thought you were.”

Warner looks like I’ve swept his feet out from underneath him when I storm off, unable to deal with his attitude for a moment longer. He's hurting. I get it. I'm fucking hurt too. That doesn't mean we give up on each other when shit gets real.

He knows that better than anyone.

Across the top floor of the empty terrace house, our stealth team has set up camp. Hyland looms over Rayna's shoulder, watching the live video feed of the street. Blaine speaks in low murmurs with a sour-faced Raye and Spyder. Axel lingers, the silent mountain of solitude in the corner.

Not exactly the likeliest of alliances, but we aren't here to arrest Gunnar Slaughter. No matter how long his rap sheet is. Today, we want his help. Only evil can sniff out its own, and I'm willing to sacrifice all kinds of moral high ground to end this fight.

"Anything?" I stop next to the technical setup.

"Negative." Rayna twirls a chunk of lilac hair. "No signs of movement yet."

Grimacing, Hyland rolls back his shoulders, attempting to mask his discomfort. "It's still early. He's only half an hour late."

"What's wrong?"

"I'm fine," he replies. "Just a muscle spasm."

"You should still be resting. Did you take your pain pills today?"

"Yes, ma'am." Hyland squints at me.

"Less of the bad attitude, we've got enough of it in this room."

This is precisely how I know we're in trouble. I was not cut out to be the voice of reason between four overbearing men at loggerheads with each other.

"Nothing from the outpost?" I glance off to the side.

From their huddle, Blaine's dark head lifts so his gaze can catch mine. He slips out from between his confidantes to approach our workstation, a thumb tucked into his belt loop.

"No, nothing yet."

"Isn't this guy known for being punctual?" I huff impatiently. "You know, professional assassin and all."

"Bounty hunter," Blaine corrects with an amused grin. "He doesn't kill all his marks. Well, only the ones that he charges his clients a premium to quietly dispose of on their behalf."

A cold chill crashes over me, bringing reality into sharp focus.

"Is that why you promised Axel to him?"

The sly bastard is utterly unrepentant as he shrugs like we're discussing our favourite restaurants.

"I was merely trying to solve a problem for you."

"By offering up my teammate as bait?" I blink repeatedly.

"His services demand a high price. Fortunately, I had something he wanted. It's an easy trade."

"Jesus, Blaine! You tried to have Axel killed!"

"Traded," he counters. "Not killed."

"Oh, sure. Because he was only hoping to take Axel on a little family picnic to reunite and reminisce about old times. Nothing more. Right?"

"Now that really isn't a concern of mine."

"You're as bad as the rest of these idiots!"

"Ouch." Blaine lays on a mock-pout. "Now that I take personally."

"Ditto," Hyland grumbles.

While Blaine doesn't operate with a functioning moral compass, even for him, this situation is beyond belief. I don't know whether to crash all their collective heads together or just walk away.

"Axel is going nowhere." I massage the bridge of my nose, trying to breathe through the pain brewing behind my eyes. "Whatever The Hunter's price, the previous deal is off the table."

"He won't like that." Blaine's ominous response has my fine hairs spiking.

"Well, if Gunnar Slaughter wants payment, he can bargain with Sabre Security for all the goddamn riches in the world. Members of our family are not for sale, and they never will be."

"*Your* family." His smile falters, exposing a deep wound. "Not ours."

Ignoring the multiple sets of eyes watching our exchange, I march straight into Blaine's personal space to jab a finger in his firm chest.

"Choose a side and choose it fast. You were offered the chance to belong. Nobody is stopping you from making the right choices from here on out, only you."

He captures my wrist before I can move, a thumb bearing down on my pulse point. Not even the razor-like pressure of Hyland's stare into the side of my head can wrench me from Blaine's depthless, midnight orbs.

"My choice has always been you."

Despite wanting to strangle him, I can't help but follow the trail of his tongue as it slips out to moisten his lips.

"That doesn't entail trying to barter the lives of those I care about."

"Perhaps you should revise who you allow into your heart then," he suggests. "I've never once claimed to be a good man, but I am an honest one. Can you say that about all of them?"

"Careful, Madden," Hyland cautions.

"Or what?" He peers over my head at the big grump lingering far too close. "You need me more than I need you right now."

"I've never once needed a thing from you."

"Then I can call this meeting off. Shall I?"

Moving away from the window, Warner menacingly steps into the melee. The look on his face is downright thunderous. Not a hint of the soft, reassuring soul that I've come to associate with safety.

"Ember belongs to us." Warner delivers the words with stinging disdain. "Choose her and you choose us. Our team. Our rules. It's high time you learn that lesson."

"I'm not a part of your world." Blaine narrows his black eyes.

"Then do what you do best, Madden. Just disappear."

"Blaine isn't going anywhere," I say angrily. "Nor is Axel. For once, put your egos back in their fragile little boxes, and focus on the task at hand."

When no one responds, my dwindling patience erupts.

"Now! Gracie's life depends on it!"

Warner ducks his gaze while Blaine has the decency to look chastised. I cast Hyland a penetrating glare then move my eyes to include Axel in the sentiment. Silent or not, he's still on our team.

The tension is far from defused, but each man backs down without throwing hands or making another empty threat. I wait for Blaine to stalk away and light a cigarette before looking at his people.

"Should we be calling you 'boss' now?" Spyder snickers.

"Shut it. You two are stowaways."

Raye harrumphs, her stare sour. "You're welcome."

"For what exactly?"

"Our help. None of us want to be here, so don't act like this makes us friends or whatever."

"Raye," Blaine scolds around a circle of smoke. "Back off."

"Just calling it like it is, boss. She can't talk to you like that."

"I said enough."

"Why are we even here?" She rolls her eyes. "This isn't our fight."

Blaine's on the verge of giving Raye a public dressing down when an ear-piercing shatter cracks through the entire floor. Cold air rushes in to kiss my back, rippling through shards of fast-flying glass.

The huge, crisscrossed bay windows at our backs implode at the intrusion of a quickly moving shadow swinging into the room. Warner tackles me from the side to crush me as our hideout is infiltrated.

Before I hit the floor, I see the flying figure release what looks like a grappling rope to deftly land on two feet amidst the broken glass. Muscles taut as a highwire stretched to its limit, an attack or round of bullets never comes. Not even once Warner has me protectively tucked under him.

Our intruder doesn't move. Doesn't speak. Doesn't so much as offer an explanation beyond dusting himself off then surveying the entire floor and everyone on it. Those almost-glowing, honey eyes immediately reveal his identity.

Gunnar Slaughter.

So much for our perimeter.

The Hunter is cut beneath dark jeans and a black, military-style weapons vest over a muscle tee. He's the same height and build as Axel but somehow lighter on his feet—a deft, deadly ballerina who picks through the shattered glass to get a better look at us all.

"Your security is lacking," he announces casually. "If you're going to guard the street, put men on the roof too. It's a glaringly obvious exposure point."

Once-purple hair is now a shock of spiked chocolate-brown, removing the identifiable feature he used to dupe me. But his boyish features, full lips and matching eyes are a dead giveaway. He's a breathing replica of our Axel.

Everyone has moved as one, taking attack positions and quickly drawing weapons. Warner rises above me to spin and face our newest arrival.

"Was it necessary to break into the building?" Blaine drops his lit cigarette to warily approach us.

"Yes." Gunnar cocks his head, his orange-hued gaze unsettlingly cold and appraising. "I don't answer to your patrolling guard dogs, Phantom."

A shiver snakes its way down my spine, nodule by nodule. Fuck, even his baritone is light and lilting, a carbon copy of the twin standing not so far away. Axel is ashen, stiller than a corpse while assessing his long-lost brother.

Gunnar casts an analytical look over us all, one by one. He lingers on me, the corner of his mouth twitching ever so slightly. I take the hand up that Warner offers, wincing when my bruises twinge from the hard landing.

When his icy stare touches the brother who lied to conceal his existence, Gunnar's posture changes. He doesn't seem to have much visible emotional range, but his legs spread, shoulders squaring in clear preparation.

"Brother." He nods tersely.

With a telltale gulp, Axel takes a single step forward. "Brother."

"It's been a long time."

"Not long enough. What do you want?"

Glancing between them reveals a whole roster of differences. Axel can't hide a single thought or feeling that crosses his mind. It seems his brother has the opposite problem. His identical features are disturbingly blank, failing to betray a single clue.

With a chilling smile, Gunnar slides a long, terrifyingly sharp hunting knife from his vest. Not even the guns being trained on him by Hyland, Spyder and Raye seem to provoke any hesitation. He acts like the rest of the room is invisible.

"I was summoned." His shoulder twitches in dismissal.

"In London," Axel clarifies.

"Ah. I had business to tend to."

"And that's what we'd like to discuss." Warner remains in front of me, taking over the conversation. "A business proposition."

Still, Gunnar ignores him. He may as well not even exist.

"Why didn't you listen to her?"

Inching out of his corner, Axel calmly spreads his hands. "Who?"

"Meredith."

I watch a shudder snap over Axel, almost shaking his knees. "What about her?"

"She told you to run." Gunnar's words are clipped. "Yet here you stand."

"How do you know about that?"

The twisted look of pure contempt and disgust on Gunnar's face fills me with a very bad feeling. What we're witnessing isn't the kind of hatred you can talk through. He looks physically repulsed by his twin.

"I've been privy to every conversation you've ever had with the woman who birthed us, brother mine. Every phone call. Every email. Every visitation request. Every time you neglected to mention the person you both cast aside while happily catching up."

"Cast aside?" Axel's laugh is achingly hollow.

"You abandoned me to die."

"We protected you!"

"You *erased* me."

"I did what she told me to do! I was thirteen!"

"You're as pathetic as I imagined." Gunnar steps forward, wielding the hunting knife as expertly as his name would suggest. "Killing you will have to be my warmup before Mother."

"Take one more step, and there will be three bullets in your skull," Warner booms from in front of me. "You're in a room full of trained agents, Mr Slaughter."

Looking back over us, Gunnar seems to remember that we're still here. Armed and ready. Not that it deters him in the slightest. He merely sighs like this entire scene is some minor inconvenience.

"Why did you ask me to come here?"

"Gracie Livingstone," I redirect.

His smirk spreads, oozing danger and bloodthirst. "I don't work for free."

"Name your price."

"I believe I've already done that, 768. A life for a life."

For once, the old name doesn't make me flinch. Dealing with his kind feels like familiar ground.

"Axel isn't up for grabs. Name another price."

"You have precisely six seconds before I kill every last one of you." Gunnar passes the blade back and forth in his hands. "So don't waste time bargaining for my brother's life. It's mine regardless."

"He's off limits," Warner deadpans. "Now lose the knife."

"This has been a short negotiation. Who wishes to die first?"

Everyone braces, guns raised and aimed at our assailant while Gunnar menacingly eyes his twin. One wrong move and we'll all be left to pick up the pieces.

"Just stop!" I hurriedly step in front of Axel, ignoring the protests it causes. "Axel is under our protection, so whatever issue you have with him, you take it up with us."

Gunnar's laugh is a deep, full-belly thunderclap that unnerves me.

"Believe me, you do not want that."

"Then why did you agree to meet?" I question.

His smile grows savage. "I intend to repay my twin for the neglect he's shown me all these years. When I'm done, he will know a mere ounce of my pain."

"What pain?" Axel blusters from behind me.

"You know, brother."

"No! I don't know! And I'm sorry for whatever you've been through, Gunnar, but it isn't my fault. I didn't choose to send you away, and I don't know where you've been all these years."

"You. Lied."

"I was a child!" Axel pushes me aside to shout back.

"So was I!"

The air chills, laden with irreconcilable secrets. Years worth of lies. The deceit meant to protect a child that instead doomed him to solitude. For Axel—his swirling amber orbs glistening with unshed moisture—the unbearable weight of that choice lies heavy.

His open posture, slack face and outstretched hands plead for his brother to show mercy. I must be naïve for thinking he may just get it.

But I'm not prepared for Gunnar to draw back his arm then snap his blade out faster than any of us can intercept. The hunting knife slashes through the air at speed, hissing straight past me to find its fleshy target.

THUD.

Bile creeps up my throat at the soft squelch of metal carving flesh. Axel recoils, a scream tearing from his throat as the blade lodges in his shoulder. His knees crack against the dusty floor as he's carried down in a heap.

"Axel!" I shift to intervene.

A gunshot cracks behind me, making me freeze when the room's tension detonates. Gunnar seems to anticipate the response, folding himself in half to duck before propelling himself forward to avoid the incoming shot.

Warner charges faster than I've ever seen him move, colliding hard with The Hunter to send them both hurtling downward. The men grapple in a heap of muscle, trading fists and attempting to overpower the other.

"Help Axel," I yell at Hyland.

"Ember! No!"

He can't stop me from diving into the mix in an effort to separate Warner and Gunnar. Trying to grab hold of Gunnar is like wrestling a coiled viper, bucking and twisting with incredible skill. He's so fast, locking his arms around Warner's neck to catch him in a chokehold.

I leap onto his back, driving a fist into the side of his head. The Hunter barely even flinches. I've managed to clock him in the nose when his head slams back to collide with mine, causing stars to burst behind my eyes.

My body goes limp, toppling off Gunnar's back to land in a heap. I breathe through the pain, the cobwebbed ceiling a warbling riot high above me for several stomach-turning seconds.

CRACK.

Another gunshot blasts my eardrums. The explosion precedes a loud thud. I watch Gunnar catapult backwards onto the floor, freeing Warner. To my right, a Sabre-issued pistol is clutched in a badly trembling, blood-slick hand.

Axel barely stands upright, the knife now removed his shoulder, leaving a ragged, bloody mess behind. He pays the wound no attention while keeping the gun cocked straight ahead.

"Are you okay?" His crazed eyes dart to me.

Gasping, I wrench myself upright on the floor. "You just shot your brother!"

"Bulletproof vest," a voice wheezes.

The Hunter is spreadeagled, conscious and biting back his own agonised groan. I watch Axel limp forward, the barrel of his gun pointed at his twin, ensuring he doesn't launch a fresh attack.

"Next bullet goes in your forehead," Axel warns in a tight voice. "Do not move."

"Congrats, brother." Gunnar groans in pain. "Nice aim."

"I didn't want to kill you."

"Then you're a fool."

"A fool who can end your life in a heartbeat," he retorts. "Now we have a job for you to do, and it's urgent. Are you going to behave and negotiate like a sane human being?"

Tugging at his damaged bulletproof vest, Gunnar casts a critical eye around the room. Beyond Axel, Raye and Spyder who still have weapons directed at him, Hyland looks like he's itching to break his skull, and even Blaine appears ready to call this whole thing off.

"You have nothing that I want," Gunnar scoffs.

"Me."

Axel's offer causes multiple shouts to break out. I've barely found my feet with Warner's help, yet I'm ready to smack the moron myself, even if he is keeping our assailant at bay.

"Stop!" I hurl at Axel.

He cuts me a look. "This is my deal to strike, Em."

"No! You're not thinking straight!"

"Gunnar wants to settle what he believes to be an old score? Fine. He's welcome to try. But not until we've located and rescued Gracie Livingstone."

"You're willingly surrendering to me?" Gunnar guffaws.

"I'm offering the opportunity to settle this between us once the job is done." Axel engages the safety on his pistol then shakily tucks it away. "Nobody else has to be involved. This is our fight."

"Axel." Warner tries to reach for him. "No."

"Stay out of this. I made this mess, so I'll be the one to clear it up."

"He wants to kill you!" Hyland's eyes are wide as saucers.

"Then he's welcome to give it his best shot." Axel eyes his smiling twin. "I've already explained myself. If he doesn't want to listen, then we'll deal with this the old-fashioned way."

I can't believe what I'm hearing. More worryingly, I'm astonished to see Gunnar stand up then reach out a palm towards his brother. Their hands lock, sealing the agreement in fresh blood.

"This is insane." I shake my head in disbelief.

At my side, Warner gawps at the scene. "He can't go through with this."

"Should've thought of that before you alienated him. Now he's willing to sacrifice his life to make amends."

Standing side by side, the way both twins even move similarly is disconcerting. If it wasn't for their hair and differing tattoo coverage, I wouldn't be able to tell them apart at all. It only makes the deal they're signing off even more sickening.

"Perhaps you're not as cowardly as I thought." Gunnar grins broadly.

Axel drops his hand like he's been scalded. "Ever consider that you don't know me well?"

"I know enough. If this is your offer, then I accept the terms."

"Good." Axel nods decisively. "Help us to rescue Gracie."

"There's no need."

Axel cringes as he lifts a hand to put pressure on his oozing shoulder wound. "What does that mean?"

My heart lurches into my mouth, already bone-dry from watching their little pact take shape. We all wait on tenterhooks for Gunnar's answer. He simply shrugs, barely casting us a second glance.

"I've already found her."

"Where?" Blaine demands.

Gunnar ducks to pick his red-stained hunting knife off the floor where it was discarded. He doesn't even blink while wiping it off on his vest and re-sheathing it.

"Estonia. She was purchased by an international buyer."

I step into The Hunter's line of sight. "Who?"

The glance he casts over me is contemplative, scrutinising. Full of professional curiosity. I can't decide if it makes my skin crawl or fills me with pride that he sees me as a threat at all.

Yet his next words kill my brief thrill.

"Nolan Madden."

Play me
POLICE LINE - DO NOT CROSS
Asset?
Incoming Call
Unknown
DO NOT CROSS
POLICE L
Suspect?

23

WARNER

STRONGER – THUNDERSTORM ARTIS

The stairs leading to Tom's apartment are hellish on my swollen limb, but I claw back any evidence of my pain. We're twelve hours out from leaving the country. This is not the time for my useless leg to flare up and hold our team back.

"Just take it slow." Ember stands above me, watching each stiff movement.

"I'm alright."

"I don't know why you bother to lie to me. It's never worked."

"Worth a try."

Lips mashing together, I brace a hand on the sleek metal banister while swinging my prosthetic up to tackle the next step. She always sees straight through me. It's incredibly annoying. Though, come to think of it, I'm sure she feels the same way when I read her like a book.

"We've got one team member recovering from a car accident and one being stitched up after his twin stabbed him." She runs a hand over her face. "Not exactly the A-Team, are we?"

"Price of doing business," I grunt back.

"At least Tom's out of the hospital now. I can cross one person off my list of worries."

Sure enough, he received the all-clear after weeks of agonisingly slow recovery. Tom's lungs are badly scarred from the pneumonia, but he's well enough to continue healing at home. Or rather, the impenetrable fortress that I've erected in his apartment.

"Pretty sure our list of worries extends beyond that." I catch up to her so we can ascend together. "How do we know that Gunnar is even telling us the truth?"

"I'd say he has a pretty decent motivation."

"Axel's deal is bullshit, and you know it."

Ember shoots me a glare. "I have zero intention of allowing Axel to surrender to that lunatic. But as long as he thinks that's going to happen, we will pump Gunnar for all his intel."

"He isn't a reliable source."

"We're fresh out of those."

Well, shit. I can't quite argue with that.

"Not even Dominic Pit or the other prisoners will confirm if Nolan Madden is in Estonia." Ember shakes her head. "They've all accepted their fate behind bars. No one is talking but Gunnar."

"I know, Em."

Her desperation is obvious. And I don't blame her for it. With Gael's threat looming and a possible ID on Gracie's location, Ember's racing to end this battle before there are any more lives lost.

Yet that doesn't mean we should trust an international bounty hunter with about as much credibility as the monsters we're hunting. For all we know, he's leading us straight to Gael and Nolan Madden. Not offering them up to us on a silver platter just to win his brother's head.

"Gunnar places Nolan's base of operations in Estonia's capital, Tallinn." I grab her shoulder to halt her at Tom's door. "I'm willing to go, but we will not put anyone else at risk. That includes you."

"I have to find her."

"And we will. But no more casualties."

"What else do you expect me to do?" she hisses.

"Stay safe! Follow orders! Be careful!"

Ember begs me with her big storm cloud eyes. I'd still lock her in a fucking closet to stop her from undertaking this mission. It's a high-stakes, international rescue op. Hardly a walk in the park. The reward is great, but so are the risks.

"Gael doesn't know we're working with Gunnar." I tug the end of her braid, rubbing the blonde and red strands between my fingers. "We'll use that to our advantage and hope we catch him by surprise."

"What if Gracie is already dead?" Her lip trembles the smallest amount.

Hand lifting to brush over her mouth, I smooth the tiny tic. "You can't think like that."

"I'm being realistic. What if we're too late?"

There are times when being the ultimate authority in our team sucks. Point in case. No one else has the heart to tell Ember that this could all be for nothing. Though it seems she's having the same doubts already.

"Then I'll happily hold Gael down while you take whatever pound of flesh you so desire from his corpse." Her lip shudders where I pull it free. "And I'll do the same thing for Nolan Madden."

"I don't want revenge," Ember mutters. "Only justice."

"Will you settle for an end to this nightmare?"

"Not if it doesn't involve bringing Gracie home."

Dismissing me, Ember turns to tackle Tom's new fingerprint ID scanner. It protects his steel-reinforced, Sabre-fitted door, the crown jewel in a whole host of improvements. Growling under my breath, I catch her around the waist and spin her to face me.

She makes a small squeak when I back her up into the front door, aligning our hips and bodies in perfect correlation. Her head tilts up to mine as I clasp her chin between forefinger and thumb to prevent her from looking away.

"What are you doing?"

"You're going to listen to me carefully, Ember."

Defiance barely covers the sheen of real fear roiling in the thunder-stricken skies that paint her irises. Bravado aside, I know she's scared. Terrified even. We've come so far to reach this point, and the end feels within reach.

"I will not lose you now that I've found you," I whisper harshly, pinching her chin tight. "Not for justice, revenge or whatever you want to call it."

"We have the advantage." Ember stares back at me without flinching. "Nolan Madden doesn't know that we have his location. We can extract Gracie and apprehend him in one fell swoop."

"Just like that?"

"Not exactly. But this is the lead we've been waiting for. We can't allow fear to control us now."

This fucking woman.

Only Ember can lecture me about grand, heroic gestures and still turn me harder than steel with the rough timbre of her voice. That fiery defiance is one of the first parts of her that I fell in love with.

Uncaring of our location, I frantically crush my mouth on hers. Abrupt. Heavy. A dominant display of just how hard I'll fight to keep her on the safe side of this fight. Even if she hates me for it.

At least she'll be safe.

Ember furiously kisses me back with all the rage that's kept her going until now. The sheer, unbreakable will to confront her abusers. Her need for redemption wrapped up in this teenage girl's stolen life.

We're a messy tangle of emotion, both grasping each other and trying to find some sense in the unthinkable. She can't walk away from this case. I can't protect her from it. We're on a one-way track to an ever-nearing collision, and still, she refuses to stop.

I push my hand beneath her cropped black tee, fingers splaying over soft skin. Ember winds an arm around my neck, pulling me closer so she can deepen our kiss with a hot swipe of tongue. It makes me growl down deep like some kind of wild animal.

I'm itching to touch her. To cast all final doubts aside and slide so deep within her, she can't ever hope to dig me from her veins. I want to own Ember, to love and fucking cherish her. To hold her close and share her with those I care about most.

I want her.

And I don't care who that will hurt.

If we're walking into a firefight, I refuse to do it without cementing her place at my side. No matter the complications or countless problems still to sort. I'll take the small slice of her heart she's willing to part with and charge ahead as a happy man.

Tearing my lips from hers takes great self-control, but I find the sense to do it, tucking my face into the crook of her neck and breathing her in. Her scent seeps freely, all feminine and floral. She shivers against me when I lave my tongue up the side of her neck, throat to ear.

"Fuck, love. I want to throw you against this door, spread your gorgeous legs wide open and sink my cock inside your heat."

She moans lightly, her fingernails scratching against my scalp. "You sure do choose your moments."

"Your brother's going to skin me alive for even laying a fingertip on his little sister, but I'm past the point of caring. I refuse to hide the way that I feel. We've already wasted far too much time."

"Warner…"

"No, Em." I nip her neck, tongue roving beneath her earlobe. "You. Are. Mine."

The way she shivers and mewls in response only solidifies my choice. Tomorrow could be the end of this case. Or even us. But I'm not facing it without wiping any trace of uncertainty aside.

Reluctantly, I release Ember to reposition my throbbing cock. She glances down at the bulge straining against my jeans and snorts in amusement.

"Tom really will kill you if you walk in there sporting a massive erection."

"Massive?" I waggle an eyebrow.

"Of course, that's the only part you're concerned about."

"Given the rumours I've heard from my teammates, I'm taking it as a compliment that you're willing to use the 'M' word after sleeping with them."

"Who told you that?" Ember's mouth falls open.

"You did." I tap her chin to click it shut. "You're incapable of falling apart quietly, love. I heard everything from my office while Hyland fucked you into an oblivion."

"Oh."

"And Axel isn't exactly subtle when it comes to you either."

Seeing her blush dark-pink is a pure delight. I hold that image in my head while tackling Tom's security system to access his newly reinforced apartment. I'll need something nice to think about while he breaks my face for trying to fuck his sibling.

The sound of conversing voices guides us into the kitchen living area. I offer Jamie a nod, standing in the black-and-white tiled kitchen and chopping ingredients for dinner.

"Hey. Cooking anything nice?"

"Lasagne." Jamie smiles happily. "Tom's favourite."

"Did you two finally move in together?" I gesture towards the marble counter.

He points at me with a vegetable knife. "Mind your own business, mister."

"Just saying. You seem pretty comfortable here."

"How about we discuss your love life instead?" Jamie winks salaciously. "The fancy security system you installed outside has a door camera."

"Ah," I splutter. "Yes. That."

"Indeed, that. You have some explaining to do."

"Is that what we're calling it?" Tom calls out.

Wincing at the sound of his voice, I turn to head for the sofa. Tom's resting in the corner, a laptop balanced on one knee and a half-empty beer clasped in his hand. Two frigid, angry green eyes land on me with enough impact to make my ears ring.

"Tom." I wave awkwardly.

"Where is she?"

"Right..."

"...here," Ember finishes for me, strolling into the apartment looking far too relaxed. "Sorry, couldn't untie my laces."

"Why didn't you ask Warner here to help?" Tom gently sets his laptop down on the coffee table. "He sure looked confident while trying to tie his tongue with yours out there."

"Excuse me?" Ember coughs.

"Give it up. I know how to work my own security cameras."

Seeing Tom stand up to his full height, holding the weight he's managed to gain during his time in the hospital, I back up a couple of steps. That beer is going to be in my face. I just know it.

"Listen, Tom…"

"My sister," he deadpans.

I slowly lick my suddenly dry lips. "Yeah."

"My fucking sister, Warner."

"Yes… I'm aware of who she is."

"You're a little more than aware," Tom cuts back with acid ferocity. "By the look of things, you're well acquainted with the one person I told you to protect with your life."

"I've done exactly that."

"Did I tell you to fuck her too?"

"Tom!" Jamie gasps from the kitchen.

"That's out of order." Ember protectively steps up to my side. "My relationship with Warner is none of your business. Frankly, if you acted rationally where my safety is concerned, I would've told you sooner."

"Sooner? How bloody long has this been going on?"

Ember's poised to leap into an almighty argument that we all know she'll win. Likely by having to storm out the same way she did when we hired her. This time, I save her the effort.

"I love her," I blurt out.

The apartment falls silent. Jamie has abandoned his meal prep while Tom blankly stares at me, condensation from the beer dribbling over his hand. Beside me, Ember freezes still, daring to peek a glance up at my face.

"I've been in love with your sister for a very long time. I'm sorry that it took so long to tell you, but I was terrified of jeopardising our friendship. You're family to me, Tom. You gave me a home."

"And now?" Tom interrogates. "You just decided to stop caring?"

"No, of course not. But I can't pretend like I don't love your sister. Not anymore. I've done nothing but hurt her by keeping my distance for so long, and I refuse to do it for a second longer."

"She's your co-worker! Your friend!"

"Ember's far more than that, and she always has been."

In spiralling desperation, Tom looks to his other half. I'm prepared for Jamie to join the Warner hate train when he steps out of the kitchen, looking appraisingly between us.

"What are you so tangled up about?" He laughs. "They look good together."

"Jamie!" Tom's eyes bug out. "He's my best friend!"

"And she's your sister. Who better to look after her?"

"Excuse me." Ember holds up a hand. "I don't need anyone to look after me."

"True." Jamie indulgently smiles at her. "Okay, then who better to look after Warner than your awesome, kickass, secret agent sister?"

"Better," Ember hums approvingly.

"Hilarious." I roll my eyes.

Tom whooshes out a breath. "Not funny!"

Resting a hand on the back of the sofa, he dips his head to drag a hand over his still-pale face. Despite being fit enough to leave the hospital, he still doesn't look quite like himself. Part of me worries whether this will be the final straw for the sanity he's managed to claw back.

Ember inches forward to touch his shoulder. "Please sit down. We can talk, but you should be resting up."

"We are not discussing this!" Anger ripples across Tom's features.

"Yes, we are. Now fucking sit."

He baulks but slumps as the fight drains out of him. "Fine."

"Thank you."

We end up seated on his two sofas, a fresh round of beers opened and Jamie's chopping resumed to give us time to talk alone. Tom glares daggers at me across the drinks, making me feel like I'm at the world's worst job interview.

I should've sent Hyland or Axel in here first. At least they could've taken the heat. Next to them, I'd look like a ray of fucking sunshine, saving Ember from the worst that Sabre Security has to offer.

"How long has this been going on?" Tom questions.

While I look down at my clasped hands, Ember doesn't shy away from his interrogation.

"It's complicated, but I've had feelings for a long time now," she admits. "My relationships with the guys—"

"The guys?" he repeats in a high-pitched chirp.

Ah, shit.

That skin-melting glower returns, aimed directly at me and dialled up to max. We've had our fair share of fallings out over the years, but Tom's never looked at me like *that* before.

"Guys… Plural?"

"Yes." Ember's head bobs in confirmation.

"Jesus fucking Christ!" Tom points an accusatory finger right at me. "What the hell did you do to my sister?"

"Nothing!" I quickly raise my hands. "Not me personally."

"It sure didn't look like that from the security feed. You were seconds away from throwing her over your shoulder like some kind of caveman."

"And if he was, so what?" Ember bats back. "I'm an adult. If I want to be with Warner, then I'm entitled to make that decision. Regardless of whether or not you like it."

"He grew up with us, Em!" Tom protests indignantly. "He's literally family."

"So you know exactly what kind of person Warner is."

"That doesn't mea—"

"Warner's kind. Loyal. Empathetic. Loving. He's honest and reliable. He cares about me and our team. He makes me feel safe, loved and welcome. Even in my lowest moments since returning home. What else could you possibly want?"

Stumped, Tom's mouth slams shut. He looks down at the beer rolling between his hands, taking several seconds to mull over her words. In that time, I briefly consider whether running is a viable option. He's in no shape to chase me.

"I don't want you to get hurt," Tom admits eventually. "And least of all by him. I can't hate your asshole ex if he's my best friend, Em."

"What makes you think that I'd hurt her?" I challenge.

"Besides the fact that you have one of the most dangerous jobs in the whole country and could easily die at any given moment?"

Tom pins me with a stern look.

"Uh… Yes."

"You haven't sustained a romantic relationship in all the time I've known you. Not once. If my sister's just going to be another notch on your bedpost, I'll save us all time and kill you now."

"For fuck's sake, Tom. Do I have to spell it out for you?"

"Please!" he shouts.

"Fine! Has it occurred to you why I've never been serious with someone?"

After a shameful glance in Ember's direction, I refocus on my hands. One is clasped over my rumpled jeans' leg, covering the carbon fibre joint that lies below. Another insecurity that I've kept buried.

Some would say it's a reason not to be with me. But not Ember. Not once did she show an ounce of pity or judgement in the aftermath of my amputation. Nor the turbulent years that followed. She was there for me unconditionally just like when we were kids.

"I only ever wanted her." My confession comes out hoarse. "No one else. In all my years fighting overseas, my time at Sabre, all the people I've met or worked with… all I wanted was Ember. To call her mine. To love her like she deserves to be loved."

Tom's mouth clicks open, but he remains silent. Clearly, he's stunned.

"I should've owned up to it a long time ago, and for that I'm sorry. For a long time, I thought the feelings would die. Then Ember was taken, and all I cared about was bringing her home. To you. To us. The moment I saw her… it all came crashing back ten times stronger than ever before."

When I look at Ember, her eyes are glistening.

"I've been lost ever since." I pick at the label of my beer bottle.

Tom doesn't hurl his drink at me or tell me to leave. I almost expected him to list all the reasons why us being together would make him uncomfortable. I'm sure it's a long bloody list. But he seems to be rendered speechless by all that I've revealed.

"I don't want to lose our friendship." I catch his gaze. "But I won't stand at the sidelines any longer. Not while she feels the same way. We've both been through hell to get here, and I think we should chase our chance at happiness. Together."

Sighing in exhaustion, Tom rubs his forehead then takes a very large gulp of beer. "Well… that's it then, right?"

"What is?" Ember inches forward on the sofa.

"The two people I love most in the world love each other." His laugh comes out wispy, fatigued. "Who the hell am I to tell them they can't?"

We both stare at him like he's an invading alien occupying Tom's skin. The same man who forbade Ember from joining Sabre Security, prompting her to move out of his apartment. He's never backed down from an argument.

"I'm sorry… The two you love most in the world?" Jamie crosses his arms while wandering over to us. "Thanks for dancing on my grave, darling. I love you too."

That's all it takes for laughter to envelope us all. The back-breaking, relieving kind of laughter that cracks a soul wide open and lets the light flood into each dark, dingy corner.

Tom captures Jamie's wrist to yank him closer then plants a kiss on his mouth, the pair still cackling away. Watching them laugh eases something inside me. An awful, crippling anxiety that's gripped me ever since I first looked at Ember in that way.

"Your sister's fortunate to have found someone who loves her enough to risk it all." Jamie pushes his boyfriend's arm. "Count yourself lucky that she hasn't chosen an asshole."

"Well." I clear my throat. "We all have bad days."

Wiping beneath his eyes, Tom lets out a long breath. "Look, I'm not going to pretend like this isn't weird as hell for me. But I also learned my lesson the last time that I overstepped. It isn't going to happen again."

Ember curses to herself. "Are we sure the doctors didn't give you a personality transplant while you were on the ventilator?"

"Shut up, trouble. I can take it all back."

Smiling, she saunters over to her brother's side to perch on the sofa arm. Tom rolls his eyes when she bends down to plant a kiss on his cheek.

"Love ya, big bro."

"Alright, get off me. Love you too."

I can't quite believe what I'm seeing. After all that terror. The endless, anxious fretting, convinced that I could never find the courage to take what I wanted. All for it to end in two siblings putting their differences aside.

"Just don't slam my sister up against my front door again." Tom glares at me in clear warning. "I may only be the legal counsel, but I still know some bad dudes. You'll be dead by morning."

"Do those bad dudes happen to work for me?" I smirk at him.

It's an unwelcome reminder for Tom whose smile quickly drops. He refocuses on Ember with a look that would kill any person weaker than our formidable girl.

"Speaking of... *the guys*? Which guys? What relationships? What the fuck?"

Ah, that one didn't skip straight over his head, then. I sink backwards into the sofa to nurse my beer while Ember reddens and splutters away. This should be fun to watch.

NFIDENTIAL
Why?
Suspect?
INDEX
A
Play me
TYPE I (NORMAL) POSITION
3
1
2
DO NOT CROSS
POLICE LI

PE I (NORMAL) POSITION
Compact Cassette
play
me
DO NOT CROSS
PO
Suspect?
POLICE L
NOT CROSS
4

24

EMBER

NOTHING MATTERS – THE LAST DINNER PARTY

Walking back to Warner's SUV, I feel lighter than I have in a long time. It doesn't make sense. Not with the monumental task that lies ahead or Tom's warning about the legality of working with Gunnar Slaughter ringing in our ears.

But fuck it.

My hand is wrapped up in Warner's dry palm, and I don't feel any fear. He proudly stood in front of Tom to bare all. We both did. Despite the awkwardness, I know my brother will come around. Tom would never cut Warner out of his life, and I think he finally realises that.

"We're due at HQ to go over travel arrangements with the directors." Warner clicks the key fob to unlock his car. "Hudson's

been questioning Gunnar all day to get the full picture of what we're walking into."

"And?" I prompt.

"It doesn't sound good, Em. Nolan Madden has a decent crew behind him now. He's ready for a fight. If Gael's already there... we could be up against significant firepower."

"Madden's been off the grid since you cleaned house when Blaine was arrested. How has he amassed any amount of followers since then?"

"Power and influence." Warner opens my door for me. "His two languages."

"Well, it's high time we learned to speak them too."

Waiting for him to climb in after me, I check our group chat for messages. The others are all together, making preparations with the Intelligence department and Falcon Team. Despite our differences, Archer, Oscar and Kyle have all agreed to join the op.

Warner stares ahead at the road as we wind out of Marylebone and head across the city towards Sabre HQ. With each passing mile, the countdown to our departure grows ever closer. Not even the promise of the private jet can make the four hour flight sound any more appealing.

When I squirm in my seat for the fifth time, Warner reaches a hand over the console to clasp my thigh. "Breathe."

"How can you be so calm?"

"We need to keep our heads clear if we're going to pull this off."

Fingers curling, he attempts to soothe me with gentle strokes. It has the opposite effect. Everywhere he touches starts to tingle, skin prickling beneath thick denim, making my heart race.

I let my eyes close while shifting into his hand, encouraging him to move higher up my inner thigh. Between the cool leather seat cupping my body and his fingers digging deeper into my leg, nervous anticipation melts into a pressing need for any form of relief.

He shifts behind the wheel, knuckles clenched tight. That doesn't stop his nails from scraping over the seam of my jeans, right above where my core is waking up. Each slow tease makes heat swirl inside me, filling my extremities with trickling warmth.

"You okay, love?"

"Yes," I reply breathily. "Can you pull over?"

"We're in the middle of the city, Em."

"Then hurry up and drive faster."

Warner chuckles under his breath, now rubbing circles against my denim-covered crotch. The friction is electrifying. I can feel the pressure on my clit, but it's held back by layers of fabric that I'm longing for him to tear off.

Impatience forces me to shove his hand aside, unfastening my seatbelt to click it back into place behind me so I'm freed up in the seat. Warner gives me the side eye, attempting to focus on the road but obviously distracted by me straining over the car's centre console.

"What are you doing?" he asks suspiciously.

"Just drive."

Reaching for his belt, I make short work of unfastening the thick leather to free his zipper. He's wearing boxers underneath. That doesn't stop me from stretching to slip a hand inside and feel for his already-hard length.

"Fucking hell, Em. You need to stop."

"You need to focus on the road." I slide my hand around the bulge trying to punch through his boxers.

"Little hard to do with your hand on my cock."

"Well, learn fast… My hand isn't staying here for long."

Sliding his dick free, I take a second to appreciate the thick, generous shaft. He's slightly smaller than the other two, but not by much. Still broad enough to fill my palm, the corded steel pulsating with heat.

When I replace my hand with my mouth, Warner unleashes a slew of curses. I'm folded over the console to reach his lap, allowing me to eagerly suck him in. Hearing him muttering above me is damn exhilarating, accelerating the throb between my thighs.

It isn't the most comfortable position, but I don't let that stop me from working my mouth up and down on his cock. With each pull, I take another inch between my lips, tongue swirling over the velvety head.

Not even the sound of the SUV's engine rumbling as he

accelerates can deter me. I've got Warner trapped. Pinned to his seat by my mouth worshipping the one part of him that he hasn't given me.

Yet.

I'm going to change that.

Wrapping my hand around the base of his dick, I pump his length in time to each lick and suck. He's a growling mess, veering through traffic fast enough to test my balance. On what feels like a sharp turn, I fall forwards an inch, causing him to breach the back of my throat.

"Oh, fuck," Warner hisses out. "Love, please. You're going to kill me."

After our last interruption, I'm the one feeling fit to burst. Knowing that he sat there and listened to the sound of his enforcer ploughing into me is too much. I wish he'd walked in to join Axel and Hyland.

A warm hand clasps the back of my neck and pulls, encouraging my head to lift. Warner keeps one eye on the road while guiding me back into my seat, leaving his cock bare and glistening.

"Fine. You want to play?"

"Yes," I hum.

"Then sit there and touch yourself like a good girl, Em. Get your cunt wet and dripping for me. The minute we've parked, I'm going to slide straight into it."

A rolling spasm bolts through me, sending nerve endings into overdrive. My hands shake as I reach for my waistband to work on rolling down my jeans. With the SUV's tinted windows, I don't have any qualms about kicking them off with my shoes.

I'm left in rapidly soaking panties and a cropped tee, exposing my belly. Warner spares me a hungry glance, keeping a hand on the wheel while lowering the other to grab hold of himself.

"What do you want me to do?"

"Goddammit." He licks his lips. "Put one hand beneath your shirt. I want you to find your gorgeous tits and play with your nipples. Tell me how it feels."

Breath short, I skate my fingertips over my belly then beneath my shirt. I'm wearing a stretchy sports bra underneath, the elastic soft and malleable. It easily gives to allow me access to my breast.

My head presses into the seat as I take a handful and squeeze, thumb rubbing over my firm nipple. Warner touches himself while navigating the traffic lights ahead, his hand still slicking over his length.

"I wish you were touching me," I moan.

"Are your nipples hard, love?"

"Yes. Fuck, I want you so badly."

"Not yet. You need to get yourself ready first."

This bossy, sexy Warner is going to drive me insane. I whimper under my breath while tweaking my nipple, tugging it into a stiff peak. It's still not enough to satiate me.

"Lower now," Warner commands without looking at me. "Find your pussy."

I bite down on my lower lip, releasing my breast to drop my attention downward. Gooseflesh covers my naked legs, despite the heat pouring through the cotton that imprisons my core.

When I dip a finger beneath the elastic to hover over my pussy, another moan escapes. I'm soaking. Heat trickles from my entrance onto my lips, saturating the thin panties.

"Go slow, Em. Tell me how wet it is."

"So wet," I whine in need. "Please."

"Push a finger inside for me."

I'm powerless to refuse his dominance. My hand has taken on a life of its own. Sliding a digit through sticky moisture, I swirl it over my tight hole then press inside to find some relief.

"Fuck. Warner… Please. God."

"Play with your cunt, Em. Stretch yourself open for me."

Each dirty word is like liquid endorphins pickling my brain. I pump my index finger in and out of my hole, circling with each rotation until I'm arching against the seat's soft leather.

We're deep in the city now, our faces illuminated by passing traffic. Yet no one can see that I'm spread wide open, one foot wedged against the door, giving me access to my pussy.

It feels illicit. Forbidden. The thrill only soaks my hand more as I toy with myself, easing a second finger inside then scissoring the pair to find a new level of intensity.

"That's it," Warner praises. "Good girl."

"I'm so wet for you," I confess.

"Perfect, love. Keep playing with that pretty cunt now."

My eyes flutter shut, allowing me to focus on the sound of his voice. His short, heavy breathing. The maddening sound of him getting off to my pleasure. Rumbling vibrations coming from the car's engine, intensifying each iteration of desire.

I roll my clit in teasing circles, adding pressure to the miasma of sensations saturating my bloodstream. Just performing for him is enough to make my muscles tense in delicious anticipation. I want to sit on his face again. I want to taste his cock. I want to let him make his mark on me for the first fucking time.

I want it all.

I want him.

At the sound of Warner's low growling, I feel myself clench. Every neuron misfiring in my brain synchronises in perfect agreement. Warmth floods my fingers as I cry out, revelling in the short, rapid release that getting myself off brings.

"That's my fucking girl." His sexy rasp is lighter fluid on the flames smouldering my body. "You're breathtaking when you come."

I blink past a dizzy blur, seeing HQ's towering monstrosity rising high above us. Warner tucks his straining erection away long enough to pull up to the parking garage's security system. Unashamed, I pull my hand free but make no move to cover up.

He pulls inside the structure, finds a quiet spot in the farthest corner of the garage and parks quicker than I can come down from my orgasm. Warner kills the engine then snaps off his seatbelt to grab hold of me.

Our teeth click together from the power of him yanking me into place, allowing his mouth to consume mine. When his tongue aggressively thrusts past my lips, I happily take the intrusion.

Warner clasps my throat, pressing his thumb into the hollow and lightly squeezing to command the kiss. It's an enticing power move. One that promises control. I let him grip my neck, kissing him back with a frenetic command of my own.

"Ember." Warner tears his mouth from mine. "Why did you

have to start this now?"

"We're leaving in a few hours, and I refuse to face death without branding your heart first."

"Shit, love. This isn't the right time or place."

"What happened to spreading me wide open and sinking your cock in me?" I taunt with a grin. "All talk and no action, Mr Mead?"

"You are such a little brat."

"Then get over here, and teach me a lesson."

Ravenous desire slashes through his baby blues as Warner snaps, sinking his teeth into my bottom lip. I gasp at the stinging pain, feeling blood rise to drip between our mouths. Undeterred, he licks it away in a thorough, bruising kiss that makes my toes curl.

Reaching between his legs, Warner locates the seat's controls to push it backwards, freeing up more room between him and the steering wheel. He reaches over the console to grab my waist, plucking me from the seat.

"Climb," he murmurs.

"Where? We're in a car."

"Onto my lap. I'm going to show you exactly why I'm not all talk and no action."

With his support, I excitedly clamber over the section holding us apart and position myself on his lap. My legs are bent, spread either side of his thighs, shoving my chest directly into his face.

Warner bites down on the nub where my nipple strains against my t-shirt, causing me to cry out. His palm cracks against my ass cheek, allowing fiery tingles to spread. Not that I need any further encouragement. I already feel like my mind is fraying.

"This could've been slow and romantic." He runs his nose along the column of my neck. "Just like every time I've pictured the moment when I finally get what I want."

"Please… Now." I rake my nails over his shoulders.

The sound of fabric tearing is like music to my ears. Beautiful, primitive music as he literally rips the panties from between my legs then tosses the ruins aside. God, that's hot. Far too attractive for such a carnivorous move.

He plunges two fingers into my heat, testing my arousal for

himself. "Now I'm going to fuck you fast and dirty in some damn parking garage because you couldn't wait a second longer."

"No! I can't wait. Please don't make me."

"Beg me, then. Plead for my cock to fill you up."

Undulating on his fingers, I ride the force driving up into me. "Yes… I want it. I want you to take me right here, right now. Give me everything."

"After all this time… that's what you want?"

"Yes!" I wail.

"Not even a date or a fancy restaurant first?" Warner teases.

"No… Fuck. Please, enough. Please…"

"You want to be roughly fucked behind the wheel like the brat you are?"

I don't know where my gentle, tender Warner is right now, but I'm glad he's decided to vacate the premises. That poor man doesn't need to hear what filth his possessive alter ego is taunting me with.

"Yes!" I gasp. "Do it."

Feeling him rummaging beneath me, I know when his cock has made a reappearance. The firm heat presses up into my core, sliding back and forth between soaked folds. I throw my head back, bracing my hands on his shoulders.

"I'm going to sink into this cunt." His whispered words are guttural. "You will ride me, love. Use me for your pleasure, and don't hold back."

"Yes! Now!"

The moment he enters me, the dim parking garage fades away. I don't care about the steering wheel pressing into my back or the discomfort of folding myself upright to fit in his lap.

Each minor distraction is overshadowed by the pure satisfaction of being filled by Warner. His generous length reaches the farthest depths it can find before he lifts me by the hips to withdraw.

In an instant, I'm slammed back down, impaling me on every punishing inch. My cries ricochet all around us, forming a sweet symphony with Warner's groaning. He lifts me again, almost to the point of pulling out, then pushes me back down once more.

"God, you're so hot and wet." The praise rushes from him. "So fucking tight and perfect. Take it, love. Take every inch of me."

"Yes, more. Please… more."

"Ride me, Em."

Pushing my knees into the leather seat, I lift myself on his lap to take control. I'm a trembling mess already, but I can still find a steady pace to lift and fall on him like a good fucking girl. Seeing his eyes roll back in his head only adds to the triumph.

We thrust and grind, chests pressed together while trading slow, languid kisses. Each time I sink down on Warner, he gasps into my mouth, his steel pressing up against the hidden sweet spot that makes my vision burst into stars.

I bounce on him, slow at first but gaining in speed. I want to see every smile. Each muttered gasp or intake of breath. All the evidence of the man I've long wanted finally giving in to what was always meant to be.

His fingers dig into my hips and ass, propelling each movement. Prolonging the agony of him breaching every last part of me. My thrusts are shallow, but in this position, he's at the perfect angle to snatch the oxygen from my lungs. It's exquisitely overwhelming.

"You feel so good on top of me," he grunts, panting for air.

I keep hold of his shoulders, slowing my strokes. "You do too."

"God, I want to do so many things to you."

"Everything," I moan back. "I want everything with you. All of it. Forever."

"It's yours, love. I have always been yours."

Hips rotating, I'm grinding on him when a squeal of tyres nearby precede light flooding the SUV. I duck my head to hide in Warner's shoulder, still seated on him with his cock sheathed inside me.

At that second, Warner's hips rise to piston into me. I call out in surprise, feeling full to a breaking point. I'm so riled up and over-sensitised, I can't take much more from him.

Car doors slam before the lights extinguish, and we both sigh in relief. Warner cups the back of my neck to guide my lips back down to his, exchanging breath in a fast and furious kiss.

"Get in the backseat," he says into my mouth. "Now."

"What? Why?"

"Because I want to bend your tight ass over and fuck you properly."

After pecking his lips, I'm sure it's not an elegant sight to watch me clambering from his lap. Warner slaps me on the ass again as I slide between the seats into the SUV's spacious backseat. He exits to round the car, head swivelling to check if anyone is around.

When Warner climbs into the back and slams the door shut behind him, I know all bets are off. He pushes his jeans and boxers down to unveil his metal prosthetic, fully freeing himself in preparation.

"Face down," he orders.

"Yes, boss." I smile cheekily at him.

"Faster. I want a face full of that ass."

Body still trembling from riding him, I turn over on the supple leather, pushing my chest down and backside up. Warner grabs my thigh from behind, steering it wider so my knees are spread wide apart.

I'm left exposed—bent in half, cheek pressed into the seat and ass suspended high in a vulnerable display. His breath is hot as it glides over my soaked holes, tickling swollen skin that pebbles in response.

"Such a perfect pussy." Warner lays a kiss down on my mound. "It's almost a shame to ruin it."

Fire ignites where he tightly grips my hip, splaying one hand across my lower back to deepen my arching. I whimper pathetically, needing to feel him. Or anything at all but the fear of what we must face once this is over.

"Fuck!" he roars, plunging in.

I'm rocked back and forth on the seat by several fast, almost frantic thrusts, testing my limits in this position then shattering straight through them. From here, Warner can pump into me as powerfully as he pleases, keeping me bent in submission.

The intense feeling of being overwhelmed reaches a new peak, allowing a sizzling electrical current to stream through my extremities each time he glides back inside. I greedily accept each stroke, each slap of his skin on mine, each drop of uncontrolled Warner in all his glory.

"Yes!" I cry out, gripping the edges of the seat. "God, I need to come."

"You will, love. You're so tight around me."

Another spank and I'm aroused in every cell, breath shooting past my slack lips. The pain cuts through my mental fog and sends me catapulting towards a black hole of all-consuming pleasure. His continued rutting ensures there's no turning back, leaving me a gasping wreck.

Even with its size and weight, the SUV rocks around us from Warner's commanding strokes. For the life of me, I can't find it in me to care if anyone can see what's happening. Not until I've found the end point to this torturously building climax.

"After I break this greedy little pussy, you're going to limp in there and make those idiots see who you belonged to first." Warner doesn't stop thrusting. "Ensure they understand."

"You. Always you."

"That's right. You can kiss their lips and bat those bloody lashes, but you'll have my seed running down your legs the whole time. I'll be the one soaking into your skin."

"Fuck, Warner!"

"And the next time Hyland decides to fill this cunt while I'm working in my office, I'll walk in there and make him watch while I sample it first. Only then can he dare to take a taste for himself."

This should not be so goddamn hot. It isn't hot. Not even a little bit. Only it really fucking is and my core clenches around the steely force swelling inside it, promising a hard-earned end to the onslaught.

"You can let Hyland take you," Warner continues gruffly. "Or Axel. Hell, even that dickhead Blaine if that's what gets you wet and ready for me. As long as you don't forget."

"Forget... what?"

He hits me again, harder this time. Pain radiates across my rear, melting past tingling flesh to mingle with the treacle-like heat oozing through me. I'm close. So fucking close I can almost taste the orgasm.

"That." He pummels into me, over and over. "You're." Another spank, right across my stinging ass cheek. "Still." One more forceful pump. "Mine."

We fall apart together, finding mutual destruction in each

other's climax. I feel myself clamp around him while Warner grips my hips in a vice, allowing him to sink in deep. We cry out in unison, creating a ragged chorus.

Heat rushes inside me then spreads, adding to the blissful agony of letting go. It's a monumental surrender. My torso shakes and knees burn from the force of being suspended at his mercy, a willing recipient of his shooting seed.

Each tidal wave barging through me sets off more internal fireworks. Over and over. The sensation continues to roll through me, prolonging the endless torrent. It doesn't stop even when his weight collapses onto my back, sending us both falling.

We tangle together on the backseat, no discernible space between our sweat-soaked limbs. I feel Warner slip out of me as he twists, allowing his release to spill onto my thighs. Common sense quickly rears its head at the strange feeling.

"We didn't use protection," Warner mutters.

"Yeah, I know."

"Shit! I'm so sorry, Em. I got caught up and didn't think."

"It's not just your responsibility," I pant for air. "We both forgot."

"Bloody hell. And I've trashed the backseat."

Breaking out in laughter, I roll onto my back so I can look up at him. He's half-slumped, half-braced over me, still trying to catch his breath. Seeing his baby blues so full of life makes me grin like a fucking idiot.

"You were worth the wait."

His lips hook up in a matching smile. "Oh yeah?"

"I'd say so."

"I may need a couple more rounds to make up my mind on that front. Care to volunteer?"

I run a hand over his mussed salt and pepper hair. "Believe we have a plane to catch."

"It has a bedroom."

"And non-soundproof walls."

His smile turns devious. "Even better."

"Warner!"

Both giggling, we startle when there's a light tap on the back window. Warner curses, struggling to yank his boxers and jeans into place so his ass isn't hanging out. All I can really do is cross my legs.

Pressing the window control, he lowers it an inch to peer out. His shoulders visibly relax and the window drops another few inches to reveal familiar, dirty-blonde hair, piled up in a messy bun above twinkling olive eyes.

"Could you have picked a worse spot?" Hyland greets.

"Wasn't much thought in it," Warner responds with a grin.

"Evidently. We're all waiting upstairs."

"Give us a minute?"

"I gave you thirty. Now we're out of time."

Peering into the backseat, Hyland lazily drags his gaze over my bare legs. I know the second he's spotted the warm pool that's between my thighs and slicked across the dark leather. It takes a moment for it to register, then he quirks a brow in question.

"Do I need to call the medic for the morning after pill too?"

Wonderful. Not embarrassing at all.

My head crashes against the seat as I slump. "Please."

"I expected more responsibility from you, team leader."

"Fuck off, Hy," Warner threatens.

"Very reckless." He chortles in amusement. "I'll be upstairs."

I groan up at the car's fabric ceiling. "And I'll be here pretending we weren't just caught in the backseat like two teenagers."

"Good luck with that, red," Hyland calls over his shoulder. "I'd like it known now that the next parking garage hookup is all mine."

play
me
DO NOT CROSS
POLICE
Suspect?
NOT CROSS
POLICE LI
(NORMAL) POSITION
Compact Cassette

25

EMBER

SOMEDAY – NICKELBACK

Head down.
Senses alert.
Always ready for attack.

The mantra plays in my head as bustling traffic covers the sound of me trekking through the busy market. In all directions, local residents and tourists alike barter for their wares, haggling over fresh fruit, hand-carved souvenirs and all manner of intricately woven scarves.

My chin is tucked low, red hair concealed by a dark, woolly hat to protect against the chill. In Eastern Europe, the snow falls thick, and the temperature plummets when autumn surrenders to full-blown winter. I'm learning that first-hand.

"Come in, red. Any luck?"

"Affirmative," I murmur quietly. "Electrical line secure."

"Shit. Good work."

"Did you doubt me?"

Hyland's deep chuckle echoes through my earpiece. "Not for a second."

"Well, I was trained by the best."

Weaving through the chaos of Tallinn's streets—despite the arctic weather—I keep a wary eye for any tails. We know this capital city belongs to Nolan Madden. He runs the black market behind its beautiful architecture, taking advantage of its strategic position on the northern coastline of Estonia.

Imports and exports.

That's a polite way of saying that Madden is finishing what his son tried to stop him from starting in the first place. All this time, we've been focused on hunting down Gael, but he's just one of many heads on this snake. A single spoke in a larger wheel.

I'm going to demolish that wheel.

By tooth and nail if necessary.

All this time, we've assumed Nolan Madden was squirrelled away by powerful friends. Perhaps we even feared that he would re-establish operations in a new country. After all, the web of human trafficking doesn't belong to any one country. It isn't a regional issue.

Wherever humans go, the need to exploit and profit off their suffering follows. This is a global scourge, irrespective of who comes from where. Every nation on the planet will have an underground flesh market, and it looks like Madden has established one of his own right here.

With a crackle, Fox's voice whispers down the line. "We're hacking into the fibre optic connection to access the building's electrical mainframe."

"In English?" I sigh.

"We'll have control of any security cameras inside soon," Rayna answers for her colleague. "Nice job, Ember."

"Sorry it took so long. The wires weren't easily accessible."

"I did see some crazy Tarzan action on a drainpipe when the drone flew over." Rayna giggles. "Did you almost fall?"

"Ugh. Please delete that video."

"You got it."

"Enough back slapping." Warner sounds unhappy, even as a disembodied voice. "Shift your ass and get back here now, Em. We don't have long to debrief."

"Copy that, team leader."

"You too, Madden."

"What? Blaine?" I blurt.

"Like I was going to let you wander around an unknown city alone." His suave, aristocratic drawl drills into my head. "I did enjoy watching you scale that drainpipe though, sweetheart."

"You controlling fuck. This was my task!"

"And mine is to follow you. Move faster."

"Obsessive son of a—"

"Careful," he warns. "You're supposed to be stealthy right now."

"I'll show you fucking stealthy when I kick your overbearing ass."

"Sounds intriguing." He sighs pleasurably.

It's a challenge to swallow the barrage of indignant insults I want to hurl back. Even more challenging not to whirl around and confront the invisible shadow lurking somewhere behind me. If we're being surveilled, I can't blow Blaine's cover.

"How do we know it's the right building?" I cough to cover my question.

"Shell corporation," Warner volunteers. "Gunnar gave us the coordinates his research turned up, and the deed is registered to a nesting doll of companies. Sound familiar?"

"The Madden special."

"Hey," Blaine mumbles.

"It's true."

"Still, you'll be hard-pressed to find a more elegant system. No false identities or documentation required. The companies are registered as subsidiaries that collapse into one another. Beautiful."

"Fucking lovely," Hyland grunts. "Where the hell are you both?"

"Coming," I whisper.

The backstreets form a winding maze of cobbled stone beneath tall apartment buildings, all sealed tight to protect against the chill. I'm not an expert, but I can appreciate the eclectic blend of Soviet and Scandinavian architecture.

Only a few brave souls dash down the deserted streets, likely headed for the market to stock up on weekly produce. No one stops me during the half-mile walk back to our base of operations, tucked into a private home paid for entirely in cash.

The world's least friendly welcome party awaits outside, wrapped up tight in thick, all-black layers to keep warm and conceal their weaponry. Neither Axel nor Gunnar look happy to be stuck in each other's company while playing guard.

"You two survived a few hours without killing each other," I remark jokingly.

"Barely." Axel kicks at a clump of snow. "You good?"

"Fine. Didn't know that I needed a shadow."

"Apparently, we all do." He glowers at his twin.

In response, Gunnar bares his teeth.

"See what I have to deal with?" Axel rolls his eyes.

"At least he isn't trying to stab you anymore." I lightly tap his shoulder. "How's the wound?"

"Burns like a bitch."

"Be glad I didn't remove the whole arm." Gunnar's smile is far too animalistic.

"Gee, thanks," Axel drones.

A plane ride with the pair of them trying to avoid another stabbing or going on a shooting spree was difficult enough. For a while, it looked like Axel would be willing to rip his stitches for the chance to hit his brother again.

I'm still not quite sure what to say to Axel, but I make a point of dropping a chaste kiss on his cheek. He's been isolating himself, staying away from everyone, since the revelation at the hospital. Considering his flat, lifeless demeanour, it's taking a toll. I've never seen him so sullen.

"On my way up, team leader."

"Bring the twins in too," Warner orders into my ear. "Don't let them kill each other."

"Yes, boss."

"Ember." There's a warning in his tone.

"Yes?" I reply sweetly. "Problem?"

"Just… get up here. For fuck's sake."

"On my way."

Hah. He loves being called that.

Waving for the two seething men to follow, I strip off my warm leather glove to tap in the security code then swing the building's gated door open. Kade organised secure accommodation for us in Estonia, but I've yet to see another living soul on this block.

We traipse upstairs and into the spacious three-bed home currently occupied by Sabre's might. Our two intelligence droids tap away on their laptops in the corner, surrounded by crushed energy drink cans, while the Falcon Team pour over stacks of building blueprints.

Looking up from his task, Kyle meets my eyes. I nod once, and to my relief, he nods back. We haven't spoken since he essentially denounced my presence on this case, but at least he's done arguing for my permanent expulsion. I'll take that as progress.

Warner presides over the room, bulging arms tightly folded and face set in severe lines. He tugs the earpiece free upon seeing me and quickly scans over my body, searching for any injuries.

"Told you I could do it." I twirl on the spot to give him a better look.

"Good work." He smiles faintly. "What's this about a drainpipe?"

"Ember unleashed her inner Cirque du Soleil acrobat." Blaine strolls into the apartment, pulling off his baseball cap. "It was quite enthralling."

"So you were following me." I spin around to glare at him.

"Yes, sweetheart."

"And you didn't help?"

"It looked like you had the situation perfectly under control."

"I was halfway up a damn drainpipe!"

"While I had a wonderful view of your tight backside, wiggling in the air." He winks at me.

With a spat curse, Hyland looks up at the ceiling as if searching for strength. "If I kill him abroad, I can't be prosecuted. Right?"

"That's still premeditated murder." Warner sighs wearily. "Not even Tom can argue against extradition of a foreign agent who kills one of his own."

"Great." Hyland deflates.

Sauntering past the twins, Blaine shucks off a silky-looking, navy plaid scarf then cracks his neck from side to side. God, he shouldn't look so at home in the chaos. It's hardly fair.

"Alright, focus up." Warner claps his hands together. "Let's go over the plan."

We all gather around the large, hewed wood dining table that dominates the high-ceilinged living room. It's layered with organised stacks of maps and paperwork on one end, while a heap of corrugated ammo boxes fills the other.

Given the firepower we're bringing in to get the job done, the directors needed time to clear our rescue operation with local authorities. I don't know what kind of incentive Kade offered, but I've heard he's a master negotiator.

"Thanks to our intelligence." Warner nods towards Gunnar, however reluctantly. "We know that Nolan Madden has a centralised base of operations in downtown Tallinn, disguised as a legitimate storage and freight handling business."

Rough fingers tangle with mine as a solid weight stops by my side. I look up at Hyland's stony expression, our hands curling together naturally and without question.

"It seems he was aided in escaping our last investigation by our primary target, Antonio Gael." Warner grimaces at that. "We're anticipating that Gael intends to show up in Estonia to purchase Gracie Livingstone so he can eliminate her personally."

"My sources confirmed that she is still alive and under Madden's ownership," Gunnar clarifies, lingering apart from our group. "They're well paid and trustworthy."

"With all due respect to your sources…"

"Not," Hyland murmurs almost inaudibly.

"We have to perform our own verification," Warner continues with a narrowed look in our direction. "Once we've secured the internal video feeds, I want Gracie's location confirmed before any kind of rescue operation can be launched."

"What if she's not here?" I vocalise.

From the intelligence team, Rayna clears her throat. "There's another property outside the city registered to one of the subsidiaries tied to Madden's warehouse. It's likely owned by him too."

All the reasons why he would want to take Gracie to his home and not hold her in their criminal HQ don't quite bear thinking about. But I contemplate them regardless. The swarming rage that fills my gut will come in handy when I tear his fucking head off.

"This is a shitty idea." Hyland shifts next to me, his torso brushing my shoulder. "We're in unfamiliar territory and up against an unknown amount of force. Madden will be on high alert."

"If she's in there, I refuse to leave without her." My voice catches in my spasming throat. "One way or another, Gracie comes home with us."

"Agreed." Warner nods.

"My father won't surrender what he considers to be his property without a fight," Blaine adds, bent over a survey of the building structure.

"Then we remove him."

His head lifts, two midnight shards locking on me. "Why do you think I'm here?"

We exchange a silent confirmation. I get Gracie, and Blaine gets his piece of shit father. I'm not going to begrudge him the opportunity to kill the man who made his life so miserable.

"So what's our play?" Axel motions towards the ammo boxes. "By force?"

"We have permission to be here, but let's not push our luck." Warner rubs a spot between his furrowed brows. "Infiltrate the building quickly and quietly. Locating Gracie is our top priority."

"She may need medical attention," Hyland grunts.

I clench his hand tighter, attempting to remain level-headed.

"Local hospital is on standby for medical evac with police posted at every entrance and exit." Warner rattles off the information. "Courtesy of Kade's diplomacy."

"Shit." Surprised, my eyebrows climb. "How does he do it?"

"Flirting with diplomats?" Axel suggests.

"Nah." Hyland quickly shakes his head. "Brooklyn would stab him in the kidney for even thinking about it. He must have another party trick to get clearance on these international ops."

"The Estonian authorities want the same thing that we do," Warner clarifies. "They're just glad that we're here to remove Nolan Madden. It saves them from doing it."

Releasing Hyland's paw, I inch closer to the table to peer over Blaine's shoulder. Rayna pulled detailed blueprint plans of Madden's bolthole from the city hall's offline backup system. We've got a decent idea of how the building is laid out.

"Here." Blaine points at an emergency exit to the back street. "It's logistically difficult to bring a large team through this road, but it will likely be less reinforced. My father will concentrate his men on the main floors to protect any wares."

"Wares?" I repeat.

"Drugs, weapons, people."

"Right." My body recoils at the thought.

"I doubt he has enough people to cover the whole building." He traces the route inside the building. "Our real concern is whether Antonio Gael has skipped across the continent to join his pal."

"Got the video feeds!" Rayna announces.

Straightening up, I briefly touch Blaine's arm. "Let's find out, shall we?"

The tight smile he flashes me is all kinds of wrong. So unlike the confident crook I've come to both love and hate. Beneath his bravado, Blaine's afraid of his father. Perhaps more than any of us.

Rayna carries her laptop over to the table, taking the far corner so we can all see the screen. It's been split into six boxes, all showing grainy, black and white video feeds. Despite the shit quality, an average looking factory operation is clear.

"There." I point towards a moving black dot.

"And more," Warner adds grimly.

Across the different levels, multiple figures seem to operate patrols. They walk up and down, all packing guns. Clearly, they're guards. It seems Madden has recruited a new crew. His money must pay well.

"I'm counting fourteen," Hyland mutters.

"That we know of." Warner studies the live feed. "If we split into two teams to penetrate each wing, we have an even dispersal of assailants to target. Lethal force is to be avoided."

When Axel opens his mouth to object, Warner raises a hand to cut him off.

"This isn't our country or laws, Ax. If local authorities want to prosecute, we will respect their wishes. Self-defence is permissible, but we don't need to piss off the Estonian government today."

"Understood." Axel bobs his head.

"Good."

Shifting between the different feeds to take a closer look, Rayna studies each frame. The quality really is terrible. Better than nothing but still a far cry from the clear picture we'd hoped for.

"I'm not seeing any signs of a prisoner." She squints at the screen. "There are what look like multiple rooms which could be holding cells. Hard to say from here, though."

"Bollocks." Warner slams his palm onto the table.

"It was a long shot." Hyland studies the laptop screen, his neck muscles twitching. "We can't be sure that Gracie is being held here without infiltrating the building."

"It's a huge risk."

"We've faced worse odds." He grins at our team leader.

"One day, our luck will run out." Warner fails to summon a matching response.

My gaze bounces between the two men. Neither are enthused by our odds. Fear coils around my insides, watching them internally debate. When Warner's shoulders drop, I feel myself release a breath.

"Let's hope that day isn't today. This is our shot—we have to take it. If Gracie isn't here, we clean house to weaken Madden's operation then move to the secondary location."

Hyland's chin dips in solidarity. "Agreed."

Dividing up our numbers takes a great deal of arguing. With our injured members evenly dispersed, I end up paired with Warner and Axel. Naturally, his asshole brother insists on accompanying us. God forbid he let his prize out of sight.

Blaine opts to accompany Hyland, Archer and Oscar on the Beta Team, leaving Kyle to hold the emergency exit from above for our quick getaway. The surly sniper manages to hold back a comment about the last time he watched chaos unfold below him.

"Alpha Team will approach from the west entrance, taking this fire escape." Warner's pointer finger trails over the plans. "Beta Team, secure the eastern exit then ascend from there. Any remaining targets will be boxed in between us."

Everyone hums their understanding, the mood turning frosty with anxious anticipation. Tension fills the air, and suddenly, our surroundings feel a hell of a lot more threatening.

"This is fun and all." Gunnar eyes us all disdainfully. "But I do have other places to be. Can we stop standing around with our dicks in our hands and get this done?"

"No dick here," Rayna combats.

I roll my eyes. "Nor here."

"Yes, hilarious." Gunnar moves to rest a hand over the knife sheathed in his vest. "I can clear that whole building myself in three minutes. If you wish to be a part of it, let's move out."

Warner eyes him. "Get ready. We leave in ten."

The team disperses to fasten Kevlar and distribute weapons, leaving me lingering at the table's edge. I stare at the video feed of Madden's lair, a sickening twinge curling in my stomach.

"Em?" Axel shifts to my side.

"Last time we did this, I lost myself." My voice weakens to a croak. "I don't want to become that person again. I want to let 768 go."

"You're not her, Em," he whispers tenderly.

"Aren't I?"

Placing his hands on my hips, he pushes me backwards to step into my direct line of sight. I peer up at Axel, the vivid flames that stain his honey-dewed eyes and all the love that fuels them.

"No. You're my Em. Nothing more and nothing less."

"You saw what happened in that dockyard," I utter quietly. "Ax, I didn't kill Carlos's men because I had to. Some twisted, broken part of me wanted to tear them down. She enjoyed it."

"What's so wrong with that?" He shrugs.

"I don't want to be the kind of person who enjoys killing people."

"We all have a shadow." He cups my cheek, a thumb stroking over healing scrapes and bruises. "That little voice whispering every last thought we pretend doesn't belong to us. No one is all good, Ember. Not even the people we idolise."

"I doubt everyone walks around thinking about killing their enemies."

"You wanna bet?" He grins, resembling the old Axel for a heart-stopping flash. "You're allowed to have rage. It's what you do with all your anger that will define you. Not your shadow."

"And if I choose to hurt people with it?"

Axel's forehead touches mine. "Then I'll be right behind you to pick up the pieces and ensure none of it ties back to you. I'm here for *all* of you. Not just the good parts."

Noses nudging, I let my mouth ghost over his. It's a wordless plea for some external comfort. Nothing can cure the niggling fear in the back of my mind, but Axel's acceptance comes pretty damn close.

"Don't let me lose myself again," I plead into his lips.

"Never, babe. I'm here to catch you when you fall."

His mouth secures itself onto mine more possessively. The kiss is everything I need. Affirming. Full of unconditional acceptance, regardless of my terror. Axel cradles me close, including all the awful parts that I can't keep hidden.

"I love you, Ember."

Lungs squeezing with equal parts surprise and jubilation, I run a hand over his silky faux hawk. My broken boy, hiding grief behind big smiles and bad jokes. My Axel. My home.

"I love you," I return simply.

Our lips trade fast kisses, expressing all that words cannot say. Axel cups the back of my head to take what reassurance he needs, and I steal it all right back. His promises curl up into themselves in a small, protective corner of my heart, ensuring I can't forget what he said.

He loves all of me. Not just the good parts.

Truthfully, I'm relieved.

Because I'll need the bad parts to end this war tonight.

Location?
Suspect?
LINE – DO NOT CROSS
CONFIDENTIAL
DO NOT CROSS
POLICE

26

AXEL

EMERGENCE – SLEEP TOKEN

Moisture dripping and the distant whirr of a ventilation system fills the otherwise lifeless silence. For a clandestine criminal lair, this nondescript storage facility fulfils every last stereotype. I expected more from the infamous Nolan Madden, despite his forced retirement from London's criminal world.

"Three assailants gagged and bound on the roof." Warner taps his earpiece, keeping his voice low. "We're inside and descending. Status report?"

"In progress." Hyland's reply is strained with exertion.

"What does that mean?"

Silence is the only response.

We all exchange worried looks, save for the bored-looking dick hovering on the outside of our trio. Being lumped with Gunnar wouldn't be my first choice, but my twin seems determined to ensure that his grand prize doesn't slip out of sight.

Accessing the fire escape was relatively easy. All the buildings in Tallinn are in close proximity, the city growing on top of each other to compete with rising demand. It was child's play to scale a nearby residential block and move across to Madden's rooftop.

"Rayna?" Ember taps her comms. "Can you see them?"

"Four guards at the rear exit, two down and two still standing," she replies quickly. "Archer's handling it. No cause for concern."

Warner heaves a tense breath. "Let's advance."

"I hate this," Ember mutters.

Keeping my semi-automatic locked and upright, I flash her what I hope is a reassuring look. "We have to split up sometimes."

"You're only saying that because I'm on your team."

"Last time I let you out of my sight, you were beaten within an inch of your life," I say unapologetically.

Fist balled, Warner waves for us to be quiet. "Hear that?"

We halt in the middle of a long, echoing corridor, surrounded by sealed storage rooms. Warner already cracked a couple open. Hidden in plain sight, Madden has a smorgasbord of illegal narcotics packed and ready for immediate export.

If the authorities knew about this place before we turned up, they'd have enough to hang his hide from the port's front gates. It's bordering on absurd how he's running a criminal regime in the heart of Estonia's capital city.

"What is it?" I strain my ears.

Ember cocks her head to the side. "Crying."

"Close by," Warner confirms.

We follow close behind him and Gunnar, taking the lead deeper into the dimly lit structure. It's so cold, I can see my breath fogging in front of me. No one could live for long in this hellish prison. Not without succumbing to hypothermia.

It's a thought that I don't vocalise. Ember's on edge as it is. With no sign of Gracie, Madden or Gael, each step onwards feels like inching into the belly of the beast. I can only hope its jaws haven't closed behind us.

The sound of faint whimpering becomes a treasure trail, leading us farther into oblivion. The more storerooms full of all manner of substances we pass, the more my shock settles in. If Madden's dabbling in the skin trade, he certainly isn't doing it for profit. This drug operation is huge on its own.

"Incoming!" Rayna warns. "Straight ahead, seven o'clock."

Right on time, multiple encroaching feet cover the sound of crying. Gunnar moves in a vicious whirlwind, charging ahead of us to intercept our attackers before they can swarm. He meets the burly, over-muscled shadows at the end of the corridor.

I bar an arm over Ember's chest to hold her back from joining in. She hisses at me but soon realises that Gunnar has it handled. Apparently, four on one is meagre odds for someone of his extensive skill set.

The three of us watch in awe and mild horror while my twin brother mows through human beings faster than a meat grinder. He seems almost reluctant to drop their unconscious bodies, lip curled in a look of derision.

"Keeping them alive is a waste of my talent," Gunnar calls to us.

"Bloody hell." Warner adjusts the gun trapped in his grip. "Are we certain he's sane?"

"You're asking that question now?" I glance at him.

"Perhaps a little too late."

"And stupid. He's clearly not."

Watching the monstrous whirlwind, I decide his brutality is a little much even for me to swallow. Two of the guards now boast matching pulpy messes where their faces should be, one's collapsed in a pool of blood, and the last is still breathing but with a leg resembling snapped dried spaghetti.

I can inflict some horrific damage when the need arises, but that was a new level of violence for a mere thirty second beating. The worst parts of my nature seem to be magnified to an extreme extent in my less-than-stable twin brother.

"Onwards?" Gunnar steps over one of the sentries, disregarding his mess.

"Did you even break a sweat?" I gawp at him.

"Why would I? They're overpaid thugs. Child's play."

Shit. He broke that poor fuck's leg without blinking. I'm starting to understand why my mother told me to run. If I have any hope of escaping this bargain, I'll need to make the first move and kill my twin before he kills me.

In the stillness, the crying sound resumes. We're getting closer to its source. Walking onwards, the thin metal door at the end of the corridor leads to a larger space, almost resembling a mess hall. Empty tables and chairs are spread throughout, all strewn about like their occupants fled fast.

"Fan out," Warner commands, his head flicking on a swivel.

The first door tucked into the corner of the room leads to a bare-bones kitchen. Rusted metal appliances boast no signs of use. Even the fridge is empty, save for a few stale sandwiches. Madden must run this place on a minimal crew.

Emerging from the kitchen, we congregate in the centre of the big room. Warner holds a finger to his lips, causing a hush to fall. The crying continues, closer but still muffled. Ember surveys the space then nods towards an ajar door in the farthest corner.

"That way."

"Behind me." Warner gestures ahead, taking the lead with his finger on the trigger.

We're all marble-carved columns of tension. Not even the deserted corridors loosen the anxiety strangling my windpipe. The only person who looks remotely relaxed is Gunnar.

"We're in and ascending," Hyland reports through the comms. "Four perps subjugated."

"Copy," I murmur back.

With each step deeper into the facility, pained weeping escalates to a keening, ever-worsening sob. It sets my teeth on edge. Only wounded animals caught in a hunter's trap make that kind of desperate noise.

The next room beyond another empty corridor is much smaller. A disgusting stench marks its main difference from the previous rooms. The scent smacks us all in the face and coats our skin in the scent of rancid human waste, causing me to gag.

It's gloomy as hell without any windows to illuminate the obvious filth. Ember and Warner pull their flashlights, the bright beams cutting through thick plumes of dust.

"Christ," Warner exclaims in horror.

A handful of tiny metal cells seem to be built into each of the four walls, the bars clumsily cemented in place to form makeshift holding pens. My stomach fights against the noxious smell of rotting bodies, filth and decay, causing vomit to rise.

"Bodies?" I choke out.

"It's a morgue," Warner agrees.

The revolting smell is almost to the point of overwhelming. I can feel it crawling all over me. Multiple people were imprisoned in here and left to rot. It's the only explanation for such a hideous stench.

A rustling movement on our left causes us all to tense up. When a single, dirt-caked hand slams against one of the barred doors, Ember shudders all over.

"No." She's turned white as a sheet. "They're alive."

The sobbing comes from the nearest cell where two bloodshot eyes and a swollen, badly beaten face joins the small hand. Young. Male. Lips trembling, he strains to reach us, barely visible in his cell.

"H-H-Help me."

Ember drops her flashlight to the floor in front of the cell, collapsing onto her knees to peer inside. She stares at the creature for a long second then starts to survey the crudely built prison cell.

"You're okay." She attempts to sound reassuring, but her voice is edged with very real panic. "We're going to get you out of here."

"H-Help," he weeps.

"I know. You're safe now."

"C-C-Cold. Please."

"Shh, it's okay. We've got you."

We huddle around her, casting more light on the cage door's shitty mechanism. Warner curses, eyeing the thick bars and messy welding with a frown. Hardly a high-tech prison cell.

"Whoever built these don't give two shits about the people they're stuffing inside. It's barely big enough to fit a child."

"Eight cells." I gulp down the sickness bubbling in my throat. "Are they all full?"

"Sold," the boy gasps. "Just m-me."

Ember's head bows low, her entire body shaking. But I know she's not crying. It's taking all her willpower to remain calm for the sake of this poor kid instead of tearing this room apart brick by fucking brick.

"Rayna?" I depress the comms piece. "Do you have our location?"

There's a pause before she responds.

"Looks like the fourth floor? The heat signatures aren't registering well. I'm flying low overhead, but there's a lot of interference."

"We have a live victim." I study the boy's gaunt face. "Young male, perhaps eleven or twelve. We're going to need something to jimmy this cell door open to get him out."

"Did you say live?" Hyland joins the exchange.

"Yes."

No one else tunes in to offer a reply. I'd imagine they're all picturing the horrors that we're seeing in real time. We expected there may be evidence of trafficking, but nothing like this. Not a starved, innocent child, rotting in a frozen wasteland.

"We're two floors below you," Blaine eventually says. "I think I saw a crowbar in one of the storage rooms."

"That should do it." I fight to keep my tone level.

"Sit tight, and let us find you."

"There could be more." Ember rattles the cage bars in frustration. "We need to be fast."

"Please don't leave me!" The boy bursts into more agonising sobs. "P-Please."

"Hey, hey." She reaches between the bars to outstretch a trembling hand. "No one is going to leave you. What's your name?"

Those big, tearful eyes cast over us all. Fuck, he looks petrified of us. Lord only knows what's been done to him or how long he's been held captive.

"I d-don't remember," the poor kid warbles.

"That's okay." Ember lays on the fake comfort in great, heaping doses. "I'm Ember. That's Warner and Axel. We're here to help you, kid."

"I'm so c-cold." His teeth clack together, chattering uncontrollably.

"I know. Hold tight, we're going to get you out of there soon."

Warner has to turn his back for a second to collect himself. He faces Gunnar instead, a palm on his chest as he works on evening out his breathing. At the back of our group, my twin wears a perplexed expression, staring far too intently at the imprisoned boy.

There's something in his cold, dead stare. A glimmer of unbidden pain, maybe. Shadows writhing and dancing like twin flames, seeing the past echoing right before his very eyes. He looks… haunted. Excruciatingly so.

"Can you get this open?" I ask him.

He visibly recoils, seeming to shake off whatever had rattled him. "Without the key, we need that crowbar. Otherwise we're screwed."

"Shit!" I crash the heel of my palm against my head then return to the comms. "Get here quickly, Blaine. We're exposed, and the kid's terrified."

"I'm on the move," Blaine replies.

With a loud exhale, Warner turns back to face our predicament. Eyes ping-ponging everywhere but the cage, it's clear that he can't bring himself to look at the child. I wonder if, like me, he's picturing Ember locked in a similar setup.

"Fuck, I hope there aren't more."

Concern pouring off her in waves, Ember looks up at his words. "He said they were sold."

"Not here," Warner adds. "Elsewhere in the factory."

She nods, crouching lower to meet the child at eye level. "Help's coming, I promise. But I need to know if there are more rooms like this one. Can you tell me?"

"My s-sister." The kid hugs his bony, stick-thin legs. "They took her."

"When? Is she here?"

He sobs so hard, it's a wonder he hasn't passed out. "D-Don't know."

"Motherfucker," Warner spits. "We have to keep looking just in case. Wherever Nolan Madden is, he won't be away from his base for long. I won't risk leaving anyone behind if we have to split."

"Stay with the kid." I draw upright, gut clenched tight. "I'll continue searching. Clear this floor."

"Gracie," Ember wheezes. "She could be here. I'm coming."

"Stay, Em. Wait for Blaine."

"She'll be terrified! It has to be me!"

"It isn't safe," I try to argue. "You're better off waiting here. The kid needs protection too."

"Then why don't you stay, and I'll go? Because either way, I'm finding Gracie tonight."

This is shaping up to be a nightmare. We're wasting precious time bickering about it and scaring the kid further in the process. Reluctantly, I nod and give her a helping hand up.

"We go together."

"Great." Ember adjusts her earpiece. "Come on."

"Blaine and the others will be here soon." I meet Warner's fearful eyes. "Hold down the fort."

"This is ridiculous." He puffs out air.

"We don't have time to waste!"

"I know, fuck! Go fast. Protect her with your life, Axel. If a single hair on her head is harmed, I'll be removing yours."

Ignoring his threat, I whirl on Gunnar. "Stay with him."

"Attempting to renege on our bargain, brother?" His eyes squint in suspicion.

"Clearly not! We're coming straight back. But if you get my team leader killed, I'll be shoving that bargain somewhere very unpleasant for you."

Gunnar smirks like this is all a big joke. "Sure."

"When Blaine and the others arrive, follow us. We may need help too."

With the plan agreed upon, I snatch up Ember's discarded flashlight then check that my weapons are in order. Ember spares the crying child one last look before striding ahead, her shoulders squared like she's frantically clinging to why she has to leave him behind.

We roam deeper into the maze, coming to a sharp bend down the next short corridor. The metal door screams in protest as I swing it open, plunging ahead with Ember hot on my heels. It leads to a deserted, brick-lined room with a winding staircase at the back.

"Dead end." I spin around the space.

"The only way is down."

"Beta Team is ascending." I turn the flashlight on each corner, ensuring that there's nothing hidden. "They can clear this section. We should turn back."

"We're in the western wing now, they're in the east." Ember anxiously bounces on her feet. "Blaine and the others won't come this direction first—we have to clear the rooms below."

"Shit! This is a bad idea with just two of us."

"What if there are more?" Her eyes coast over my face in a frenzy. "We can't leave them!"

"You think I don't know that?"

"Please, Ax. Gracie could still be here."

Clenching the flashlight tightly, I turn it on the staircase. It descends into a hole in the floor, creating another access point to the level below. No sound emanates from downstairs. Not a single shout nor sign of movement.

"Fuck this," I growl in frustration. "Alright, come on."

"Want me to take the light?"

"Yes. Keep alert, there may be more guards."

"You too." Ember holds her hand out for the flashlight.

Passing it over, I wait for her to light the staircase better then take the first steps down. Together, we tackle the spindly metal guiding us into the next circle of hell.

The air is cold and stagnant, bereft of any life. Dirt-coated floorboards are illuminated by grimy windows and Ember's light, unveiling the lower level. Immediately, toxic chemicals burn my nostrils.

The room is huge, filled with workbenches not unlike the setup of Blaine's base. But rather than being wiped of all evidence like his, this place looks like it was abandoned mid-session.

All manner of drug paraphernalia litters each bench. From burnt out pans to stained test tubes and crumpled packets of household ingredients, there's no questioning where Madden got his extensive hoard upstairs from. All cooked and assembled in house.

"What is that smell?" Ember's nose crunches up.

"Ammonia." I cough into my hand.

"Like… a meth lab?"

"It's cheap and easy to batch create. I'm not surprised Madden's dabbling in the trade."

We creep into the middle of the room, surrounded by a mounting pile of evidence. Honestly, it's fucking sloppy. I really expected better. Either he wants to get caught or he doesn't care enough about this portion of the business to cover his tracks.

"It's like he has the place divided up by business function." I look around the huge mess. "Preparation, storage and transport."

"Transport?" Ember repeats.

"Most victims aren't taken to be sent into illegal fighting pits, Em. Drug trafficking goes hand in hand with the skin trade."

"Jesus. You think Madden's trafficking people to transport his narcotics?"

"I'd bet my life on it."

From what I understand, it's the one step he wasn't able to take while running his operation from London. Blaine prevented his father from securing that final expansion. It seems he's perfected his illegal trade since setting up shop alone, without his son's oversight.

We quietly traipse onwards, clearing another large room set up near identically. Big enough to house an operation that would feed a whole country's underground drug trade. At the head of the room, a desk seems to preside in a position of authority, granting its occupant a view of all the benches.

"The boss's throne." I wave towards it.

"You think Madden handles this personally?"

"I doubt he'd outsource ever again after losing Blaine and his stake in the empire. You don't rebuild this level of infrastructure in a matter of years without fighting for your place in the market."

"He has help too," she adds. "Gael."

"I'd imagine he's the ideal friend if this is your legacy."

Another glance around and it's clear that we've reached a dead end. There isn't another door to push through, leading us deeper into Madden's evil labyrinth. No more starving children left behind in this wing.

And no Gracie.

"Dead end." I sigh.

"Apparently."

"I'm sorry, Em. We'll keep looking."

"I really thought she'd be here." She kicks an empty cardboard box, dislodging stacks of clean plastic baggies.

"We still have Madden's residence to investigate. We'll regroup and plan our next move. This isn't the end."

Ember creeps on silent feet to approach the desk. When her flashlight skims over the surface, we both stop dead. In the centre, an old-fashioned audio device rests ominously.

"It's the same type of recorder." She eyes the clunky plastic. "His handwriting too."

Yet another scrawled message on a scrap of paper, containing the same basic command as Gael's last taunt.

PLAY ME.

The endless theatrics are getting tiresome. I'm starting to think that Gael is bored.

"Do you think it's a bomb?" She studies the note.

"I'd say that it's unlikely. Not his style."

"I'm going to play it."

"Em…"

She reaches out to press the well-worn button, causing a tinny crackle to fill the room. The audio recorder flickers with a blinking red light to commence playing the message.

I'm braced for Gael's voice.

Perhaps Nolan Madden's.

Not a tiny, weak-sounding female whisper.

"I w-want to go home, Ember… Please. You p-promised to take me home."

My arm snaps out to curl around Ember's waist, stopping her from stumbling forward into the desk. She turns translucent, stricken by the fragile whimper of a lost girl.

"You l-left me," the voice cries. "Left me h-here to die."

"Gracie," Ember keens.

"Breathe, Em. She's alive. We're going to find her."

Breaking free from my hold, Ember seizes the audio recorder. She cradles it close to her chest, rocking back and forth to the sound of Gracie's crying. It damn near breaks my heart.

"It's y-your fault." Gracie heaves between broken sobs.

"I know… I know. It's my fault."

"It's your f-fault!"

"It's all my fault," Ember replies to the recording. "It's my fault!"

"Dimples," I beg. "Put it down. Let's go."

"You heard her, Ax. It's all my fault."

"Don't do this. Don't let them get inside your head."

"You left me to die." Gracie's accusatory voice forms a cruel lash. "I hate you."

In a fit of rage, Ember hurls the device at the wall. It shatters upon impact with the solid brick, raining down in jagged shards to cut off Gracie's cries.

"I did this to her!" Ember clutches her head. "I left her there."

"Em… No. Don't believe that, babe. This is what they want."

Wrapping my arms around her from behind does little to calm her tremors. I'm shaking hard too. All I can hear is Gracie's terrified voice, coming from those goddamn speakers.

"I'll never find her." Ember trembles against my chest. "She's gone, Ax!"

"Shh, babe. Deep breaths. Gael's messing with your head."

"You heard her—"

"I heard a scared girl saying whatever she was told to. He's taunting you."

"I still left her there!"

My arms tighten, attempting to squeeze the self-hatred out before it swallows her in one greedy gulp.

"You were torn apart," I whisper into her ear. "There was no choice in it. They took you away from her, Em. They did this. Hate the right people."

"She's all alone… I can't find her…"

"We will. I swear on my life, we will find Gracie."

"Your life, brother mine? It isn't worth much."

Gunnar's vocal whip scares us both, causing me to surrender

Ember and spin on the spot to face him. Neither of us heard the invisible Hunter following our tracks. He steps into the room, a pistol aimed ahead in his right hand.

"What's going on?" I ask uneasily.

Gunnar cocks the gun. "Did you receive the message?"

"What fucking message?"

"I'm not usually one to play the role of running errands, but I wanted to make sure you'd find it at the right time." His gaze travels to the shattered plastic. "I see it was well received."

"You," Ember howls. "You're one of them."

"Never." Gunnar seethes at her.

"Then what the fuck is this?" I shout back.

"I'm a contractor. Consider this your team being outbid for a higher price."

Measuring the distance between us, I try to calculate how long it'll take to draw the gun I holstered and empty it into my twin's useless hide. He'd likely shoot me first.

"I know that you have zero intention of fulfilling your end of the deal." Gunnar snickers haughtily. "That's why I negotiated a better offer. They get the girl, and I get you."

Slowly, I inch in front of Ember. "Over my dead body."

"That's rather the point."

"What about Warner?" My gaze homes in on his weapon.

Gunnar laughs, a skin-crawling sound of pure delight. "You set me up rather nicely to slip away from them and follow you. It was awfully shortsighted of you to put so much trust in me."

Fingers twitching, I long to tap the piece still tucked in my ear to call for help. On our current system, we have to press the device to speak, keeping communication lines clear. Our backup is likely with Warner by now, unaware we're in deep shit.

I hear Ember shift behind me, stepping closer to us. Gunnar fires off a warning shot that blasts my ears, the bullet lodging itself in the wall just to our left.

"Don't move."

"You're seriously going to hand us over?" Ember glares daggers at my twin. "You saw that child, Gunnar. He was nearly starved to death. Are you going to help the monsters who hurt him?"

"Those monsters sign my paycheck, and I get to walk away. I'm not helping anyone but myself." Gunnar juts his chin towards me. "A lesson this one taught me long ago."

"It isn't too late—" I begin.

"It's eighteen years too late!"

The next shot hits directly in front of me, mere inches from our feet. Ember sucks in a breath while I try to implore my brother with wide, begging eyes.

"You can stop this. Help us bring down Madden and Gael."

"Why do you think I care?" He hurls a laugh.

"Because I saw your face when we discovered that poor kid," I continue knowingly. "I saw the pain and the loneliness. I saw the ghosts that haunt you."

"Enough."

"What happened, Gunnar? Who hurt you?"

"I said enough!"

"You've been that child," I press on, noting the way his hands shake wildly. "You were lost and alone. Begging for a home. Hurt, terrified. Hungry. You know how that feels."

Just as the gun wavers, he looks ready to relent. Gunnar clamps his eyes shut and snarls, teeth bared in a pained scowl. I've lifted my finger to hit the earpiece when he re-trains the pistol on me, eyes flinging open and burning bright.

"I do," he sneers. "Because of you."

In all my years of service, I've often felt death's cold breath. Far more times than I can count. Each encounter lessens the impact when it comes back around until the fear feels practically normal.

But at the sound of his gun firing, a new level of fear ignites and races through every single part of me. It should happen in a flash. A mere heartbeat. In reality, it's agonisingly slow. So slow I can feel my life slipping between my fingers.

Then… pain.

The kind of pain that leaves no room for thought or reason tears through me at close range, hitting beneath the vest to penetrate my lower abdomen. Ember's scream mirrors my own. She seizes hold of me as the bullet rips a hole in my body.

It feels like being punched by a sledgehammer. Wet, scalding heat pours from my abdomen like molten metal is tearing into my flesh and chewing it up. When I look down and see how much blood I'm losing, my knees fail me.

Time stutters, carrying my consciousness in disjointed flashes. Hitting the floor. Nerves wailing. Broken glass slicing my intestines up then spitting them back out the hole that's been carved in me by a laser point. Warmth gushing between my fingers.

Blood.

Everywhere… hot, sticky, endlessly pouring from me.

All I can do is peer up at the white spots forming above me, causing my vision to blur at the edges. Then a face. Pale and horrified. Eyes glistening. Tears splashing my cheeks. Lips moving to form words that I can't focus on.

Ember.

"R-R-Run," I wheeze out.

She shakes her head, hands clamping down on top of mine. The pressure causes more searing agony to melt me from the inside out. Something is burrowing into me. A terrifying, animalistic realisation. I can't fight. I can't run.

I'm going to die.

My mouth flops open but fails me when I try to warn Ember. She's shadowed by a looming presence. Face slack and stare lifeless. Not even triumphant. My brother dominates over her without a single speck of emotion as he taps the bubbles from the liquid in a syringe.

Where…? How did he…

Her shriek fails to penetrate my cotton wool brain as the needle buries in her neck. Ember spasms, mouth forming an 'O' as the dosage is delivered. Then Gunnar wrenches the needle free, grabbing her red braid to pull her from me.

"No," I whisper weakly.

She's tossed across the room to land in a heap. I'm left with the image of my brother's identical face braced over mine, lips curled back to flash menacing teeth.

"You never should've asked to meet me."

Then his booted foot lifts to bear down on my screaming abdomen, and the entire room whites out.

play
me
DO NOT CROSS
PO
Suspect?
NOT CROSS
POLICE L

27

EMBER

I WILL NOT BOW – BREAKING BENJAMIN

"**D**on't tug, Mum."
"Hush, Ember. I have to get the knots out."
I bite my cheek through another painful stroke of the brush. As rushed and forceful as the first. She tuts at my little whimper, pulling on the ends of my long, flaming-red hair.

"Sit still! I can't do it if you keep wriggling."

"You're hurting me!"

"No I'm not."

"Excuse me, Ms Lawson? Can I help?"

Relief comes in the form of his soft voice. The lonely boy with sad eyes and no home of his own to go back to. When he does, I get excited. I like playing in the garden with him.

"You always seem to have better luck than me." Mum huffs in annoyance. "Here."

"Thank you, ma'am."

My eyes are clamped shut to hide the tears. I don't want Warner to see me crying again. He's older than me and far cooler than any of my school friends. He'll think that I'm a baby.

"Hey, little Em. Can I try?"

"Be gentle," I whisper in embarrassment.

"Always am. Keep still for me."

Soothing fingertips comb through my hair, nails barely scraping against my scalp. It doesn't hurt. Without the plastic brush jerking on my knots, he can easily separate the strands with his fingers alone.

"You need to wake up, Em."

"Hmm?" I startle.

The gentle touch grows more urgent. "I need you."

"Who...? I don't understand."

"Wake up!"

A firm yank on my hair causes fire to race over my scalp, interrupting the dream world with the cold, harsh bite of reality. My eyes fling open, but I'm no longer sitting cross-legged on my bedroom floor.

Mum isn't here. Neither is a young, sad-looking Warner. My childhood home doesn't have rusted bars or a low ceiling. It's warm. Dusty. Full of framed photographs and dog-eared TV magazines.

Not blood.

Not a used bedpan.

Not two terrified blue eyes locked on mine.

I must still be in a dream. Or a nightmare. She features in them regularly enough. My Gracie doesn't look like this—bony, blood-splattered and dirt-streaked. She's smiling. Healthy. Living a happy life at home with her parents.

"Ember. Are you with me?"

Another hair tug. Crap, that hurts.

"Wake up, we don't have much time."

"G-Gracie?"

"In the flesh," the girl drawls with a sad smile. "Snap out of it."

"You're not... Where? Where am I?"

"You slept through the car ride. They must've given you the strong stuff."

Attempting to lick my lips, I can't quite clear the acrid, chemical tang from my mouth. It's the same furry grossness that covered my tongue each time we were shot with sedatives then hauled around like branded cattle.

Fuck!

This is very real.

The ghost hanging over me with a concerned frown isn't some manifestation of my worst nightmares. She's breathing. Blinking. Lips wrinkled in a hopeless kind of smile.

"Gracie," I gasp. "You're here."

"Didn't we already establish that?" She scrapes a fleck of dried blood from the back of her hand.

"Oh my God."

My limbs feel leaden, but I still snag her elbow to haul her into a tight, awkward hug. Gracie has to bend down to hug me back, hiding her face in my loose braid. She trembles with each inhale.

God, she's little more than skin and bones. I can practically feel the blood swimming in her veins, her skin is stretched so tight over her skeleton. Uncontrollable tears well up and spill over, causing me to hiccup.

"Hey." She sniffles.

"Hi."

"You came back."

"That was the plan." I push her back so I can wipe my face. "Although not the part about getting drugged and kidnapped too."

With those choked words, it all comes flooding back. Nolan Madden's house of horrors. Welded cages and a ghostly child behind bars. The audio recorder. Gunnar. Gunshots… And Axel.

"Oh, no." The tears come faster. "Axel's… he… Oh, no. Shot. He got shot, and now—"

"Ember, breathe." Gracie slides a hand beneath my neck. "He's right there. You were brought in together."

She guides me to a sitting position in the cramped cage, allowing me to see an identical setup a couple of metres to our left. Passed out in a matching metal prison, Axel lies sprawled in a lifeless mound.

"Ax!" I clutch the bars, longing to go to him.

"He's been out of it for a while," Gracie murmurs. "Since the medic dug that bullet out of him and cauterised the wound. It was bad. He screamed a lot before blacking out again."

"Medic? What medic?"

"He works for Nolan." She shrugs.

My mouth falls open. "Madden?"

"He likes to be called Nolan. Or master."

Yep, I'm definitely going to puke.

The vomit rises in a fast-moving spew to erupt from my throat. Gracie pulls loose hair from my face while I twist to hurl into the corner of our shared cage, needing to purge the chemical remnants from inside me.

When I've made it to the dry heaving stage, I bat her away to sort myself out. I'm still dressed in my full assault gear, but some of my hair has escaped its braid, sticking to my face in sweaty clumps. I try not to think too hard about the crispy, dried blood soaked into my sleeve.

"Is he here too?" I fight to breathe normally.

"He was." Gracie's eyes drop to study the dirty floor.

"Where? Is Madden alone?"

"No… there was another." Her voice trembles. "The man who bought you before is here to meet him."

My stomach heaves again. "Gael."

"I've seen him a lot. They're friends, I think. Business partners. Sometimes he brings more girls over for Madden to purchase."

"Fuck! Okay… I need to focus."

Pinching my cheeks does little to alleviate my fogginess. I slap myself in the face then twist to look back at Axel. From here, I can see his chest rhythmically rising and falling.

His Kevlar is gone, and his undershirt shirt is shredded, revealing fresh white bandaging. Other than that, he looks unharmed. Just far too still and deathly for my liking.

"Was there someone else who looks like him?" I ask her.

"His twin." She nods. "He was upset."

"Upset? With Madden?"

"No, with his brother. Axel's heart stopped, and it made him freak out."

"It stopped?" I bite back a screech.

"The medic did CPR after he finished cauterising the wound. He wanted to do more, but the brother shoved him out then started screaming at Nolan about some kind of deal. They left a while ago, still arguing."

I'm not sure if I have the mental capacity to fathom exactly why Gunnar shot his brother then proceeded to panic and save his life. That's a question for a trained mental health professional. Even then I doubt it would be an easy feat.

Focusing instead on surveying our surroundings, it reveals a grim outlook. We're not being held in the factory that Sabre infiltrated. Gunnar must've removed us somehow. This building looks barer, a concrete husk with no identifiable features.

Other than our two cages, there's a variety of wooden crates stacked around us. All stamped with various destinations. No prizes for guessing the legality of the contents. We've been bagged and tagged with the rest of Madden's exports.

"How long was I out?"

"I don't know." Gracie winces while cracking her neck. "A few hours?"

"Shit. You arrived with us?"

"They tossed you both into the van with me. I couldn't believe it when I saw your face. He's thrown other girls in with me before during transport, but I never thought I'd see you here."

"Transport where?"

"Parties," she says vaguely.

Her tone is matter of fact. A little too flat and nonplussed. I wasn't sure what I'd find, but this older, hardened version of Gracie isn't it. She's far from the hysterical girl I was torn from.

"We've been looking for you ever since I got home." I try to clear my aching throat. "Your parents too. Nobody ever forgot about you."

"My parents?" Her blue eyes fill with tears.

"Yeah, I met them not too long ago. You look a lot like your dad."

The moisture swells then flows over, streaking down her cheeks to leave clean lines in the dirt. I cup her jaw and swipe the tears aside with my thumb.

"I promised to get you home, Gracie. I'm going to get us out of here."

"Home," she dares to whisper. "No more parties?"

"No, honey. No more parties."

Biting her chapped bottom lip, she pulls away from me but holds back a full breakdown. I can see it battling to escape.

"I think they're just holding us here." She gulps down a lungful of air and shakes herself, burying her hysteria. "I... I heard them talking about some kind of police in the area. Nolan wants to leave the country."

"That'll be our team."

"What team?" Gracie tilts her head in confusion.

"I work for a private security company now. We're investigating the trafficking ring."

It takes a second for her to digest that.

"Ember... they said they're going to kill them."

"Let them try." I laugh hollowly.

We fall into silence, broken only by the sound of yelling in the distance. I focus on stretching out my limbs, ankles rotating and knees flexing, attempting to work blood back into my body. The cage is too low for me to stand, but I can warm my muscles up.

Every time I glance over at Axel, terror attempts to inch into my mind. His chest is still pumping, but he has yet to rouse. I have to look every few seconds just to remind myself that he isn't dead.

"Your hair's red." Gracie squints at me across the cage. "Since when?"

"It always was. It was dyed when we met."

She chuckles forlornly. "Has it been that long?"

"I was held for six years." I watch her reaction for signs of a meltdown. "The Anaconda Team found me in Mexico about six months ago."

Her expression cycles through several different emotions, landing on a look of numb shock. "That would make me nearly twenty-three now."

"I guess so."

Gracie drops her gaze to stare at the dirty concrete. "Years of my life… Gone."

"I'm sorry." My apology sounds weak, irrelevant.

Curling her knees up to her chest, she covers the torn, white sundress that barely covers her modesty. Like the rest of her, it's bloodstained and streaked with all manner of filth. I can still make out the twisted skin that warps her inner elbow.

777.

A brand matching my own.

Three numbers dooming us both.

"We're not going to die in here," I announce, stretching myself out the best I can. "When they return, stay quiet and behind me. I'll handle it."

"You can't take them, Ember!"

Little does she know, fighting was my punishment instead of disgusting parties.

With some careful manoeuvring, I manage to position myself in a crouch. My feet are tucked beneath my butt, allowing me to spring up at a moment's notice. I'm flexing my knuckles to alleviate the tingles when a loud bang echoes from elsewhere.

More shouting. Another bang. The voices spar in a passionate torrent. I don't know who is outside the door to this room, but it doesn't sound like a particularly happy conversation.

"Stay back," I warn her.

"Ember… Please. We should just go with them."

"Forget it. You're going home."

More crashing escalates my heart rate. I'm counting my inhales and exhales to hold my nerve when thudding footsteps near, drawing closer to us. With a final look at Axel, I focus on the door that hides our captors.

CRASH.

It slams back against the wall loud enough to make Gracie cower in the corner of our cage. I don't flinch. The heavy-set, finely dressed stature of none other than Antonio Gael doesn't deserve to enjoy that sight.

His razor-sharp, yellowing eyes crawl over my skin like fire ants, taking in the details that have changed. He smiles thinly, adjusting the thick gold signet ring that encircles his pinkie finger.

"You look well, 768."

"Señor Gael." I keep my reply short and clipped.

"I had wondered what it would feel like to look into those traitorous eyes again." He steps into the room, forehead wrinkling. "You've caused great pain to my business these past few months."

"I like to think so."

"Quite."

Gael spares Axel a disinterested look, too occupied with studying me like I'm a piece of regurgitated meat that now turns his stomach.

"I imagined how I'd take you over my knee and crack your spine myself. Or have my men hold you down while I slice that back open with my whip again. Perhaps I'd even cut your wicked tongue free and make you eat it for daring to humiliate me. Really, the possibilities are endless."

Behind me, Gracie bursts into tears.

"I hear this one went for a pretty penny." Gael motions towards her.

"Didn't fancy expanding your own collection?"

"Jealous, 768?" He sneers. "Nobody could ever fill your shoes."

"Jealousy is the furthest thing from what I feel."

"No need to be bitter. We'll be home together soon enough."

Horror stabs through me, carving a gaping chasm. "What happened to wanting revenge?"

"Ah," he hums. "That was before I laid eyes on you. Now I'm feeling more remorseful. After a period of correction for your recent behaviour, I'm sure we can find a new role for you."

I'll crack my skull against these bars and join Axel on death's door before taking whatever job offer Gael's conjuring up. From the sick, happy leer on his face, it won't involve the fighting pits this time.

"777 here is leaving with her master to parts unknown now that you've brought the authorities to his door. So say your goodbyes. We'll be leaving too once I've paid that belligerent bounty hunter."

"I'm not going anywhere with you."

"My dear friend, Nolan, gave me permission to sample his plaything if you dared to question me. So by all means, protest. I'll make you watch as I take poor little Gracie for a ride."

"Don't leave me again." Gracie grabs my wrist, still weeping. "Please, Ember."

"I rather think she wants it. Don't you?" Gael grins at us.

Frustration threatens to suffocate me, knowing that the odds of breaking his neck from behind these bars are nil. It's been six years, but I still find myself in the same conundrum. I have no choice but to play along to get him within reach.

"Leave her alone. I'll come."

"No!" Gracie wails panickily.

Still I ignore her, cutting off all emotion.

"Ah." His smile fades. "Disappointing."

"What happens to Axel? He needs to go to a hospital."

"That isn't my concern. The Hunter can do what he pleases with his kill."

Pulling a sheath of keys from his suit pocket, Gael searches for the wrought gold one then bends down to unlock the cage. He holds a silvery brow up in invitation. No handcuffs. The threat against Gracie is enough.

"Let me say goodbye," I blurt, rising to exit the cage. "To him."

"You've grown soft. We'll be having none of that."

"Please… I'll come quietly. Whatever you want. Just let me say goodbye one last time."

Keeping my arms and fists relaxed at my sides, I stop in front of him with the same obedience that his trainer beat into me. It isn't hard to find that mental prison. Stuff myself inside of it. Bite my tongue. All the things that once kept me alive.

Gael slides a finger along my jaw, tilting my head up to peer down at me with those calculating eyes. Malice writhes in the pale yellow hue, unveiling the devil who hides behind his handsome mask.

"Say goodbye, 768. You will never be permitted to look at or speak to another soul again. If I decide to let you out of my bedroom in the next ten years, it will be to source a replacement when I grow tired of ripping you open each night."

Real fear snakes through me, almost causing my act to falter.

"Do you understand?"

"Yes," I confirm.

"Yes, what?"

"Yes… Señor Gael."

"Good. Make it quick."

He keeps a keen eye on me while unlocking Axel's cage. I deliberately don't look at Gracie, a curled-up, crying wreck left behind in our cell. My whole focus is on getting to Axel.

Gael lingers in the doorway while I limp inside, crouching down to rest a hand over his heart. The beating is present but uneven. A quick peek under his ruined shirt reveals blood spots soaking the bandage wound around his abdomen.

"Axel." I carefully touch his cheek. "Wake up, Ax."

Not a peep.

"You were right. We should've all stayed together. In the future, I promise to keep my mouth shut and never question your decision making."

The smile I long for doesn't appear.

"Gunnar could've let you die. I don't know why he saved your life, but I'm thankful. I thought I'd lost you, and I couldn't bear to see a world without you in it, Axel Slaughter."

Lowering my head, I press it into his clavicle, needing to hear his breathing for just a moment longer. My hand inches over his still-sticky shirt, brushing across bandaging and cold skin. Feeling around his waistband, I press the slight bump in the fabric.

Bingo.

"Ax, if I don't survive this… save her. Save Gracie."

Leaving the man I love behind devastates a part of me that won't ever click back into place. Pain swims through every brain cell, causing my eyes to sear. I avoid looking at Gael while he re-locks the cage then spares Gracie one last look.

"Until next time, 777."

"Ember!" Her wails pierce my heart. "Stop! No!"

I keep my teeth clenched to hold myself back. Tears flood my cheeks at the look of complete devastation on her face, sending me catapulting back into the past. Only this time, I'm choosing to walk away.

"Go ahead, 768." Gael gestures for me to lead. "I'll be right behind you."

I'm unsurprised by the feel of a cold barrel nudging into my lower back. His trust only extends so far. Leaving the room filled with the sound of Gracie's screams shatters me, making each step unbearable.

On the other side of the door, I almost laugh at what awaits. We're in a closed restaurant. If I had to guess, Nolan had the cages installed in some kind of storage room. We emerge from behind a wooden bar into the main serving floor.

Only one chair is occupied. A single, solitary shadow. Even with his brown hair and lack of tattoos, my broken heart splits into another dozen pieces. Gunnar looks far too much like the lifeless body I left behind.

"Where is Nolan?" Gael barks.

Shrugging, Gunnar rises to stand. "Gone."

"What?" He jerks in shock. "Gone where?"

"I don't know."

"What does that mean, Hunter? Explain yourself."

"He left. I didn't care to ask where he was going."

In a string of colourful Spanish, Gael shoves me forward with his gun. "I don't have time to waste. Your payment is downstairs. Leave the girl for Nolan to deal with when he returns."

Two glowing, sunshine-bright eyes find mine. Flickering with life. Grief. A hint of regret. It's like watching a tide sweep in to erase the shoreline and each disturbed grain of sand. Wiping at his drawn face, Gunnar physically shoves the feelings down to reveal a stoic expression.

"Your brother's going to die," I announce, holding his stare. "Why did you bother to save him? To prolong his agony? Or did you realise how it would feel to watch him die?"

His Adam's apple bobs without a word.

"You can't do it, Gunnar. You won't kill him."

"Enough, 768." Gael pushes me harder. "We're out of time."

"His mother told him to run, but he didn't do it!" I shout in desperation. "He told us the truth and agreed to meet you. Axel never gave up on you, and you're a fucking coward for giving up on him!"

"Move!" Gael roars.

"Fuck you!" I yell back.

Blistering pain explodes in the back of my head where Gael loses patience, smacking the butt of his gun into my skull. I trip and stumble, collapsing against one of the empty tables.

"Enough!" Gael stomps his foot in an uncontrollable fit. "Come quietly or unconscious. Your choice."

"Do what you'd like to me, Gael. I won't ever follow orders again. I won't be quiet. You can whip every last bit of unmarked skin I have left, and I still won't bow to you!"

Feet kick my legs out, sending me plummeting to the cheap, scratchy carpet. I kick against Gael's weight sinking on top of me, one hand capturing my hair while the other flips me over to slap me in the face.

"You disobedient *puta*! Stop fighting me!"

"You taught me to fight!"

"Then I'll pluck those memories from your brain with my bare fingers and start fresh!"

He clobbers me with another brutally strong slap, this one carrying more force. My teeth clack together, causing fresh blood to seep across my tongue. I blink past tears to laugh in Gael's rapidly darkening face.

"Nolan's gone because that's what rats do on a sinking ship. He knows your time is up and he left you behind for the wolves to tear apart, Antonio."

"You will *not* call me that!"

"Once you're dead, it won't matter what you're called." I hawk blood in his face. "I'm going to erase your stain from this planet until everyone forgets that you ever existed."

His skin is nearing purple, turning the handsome, suave businessman into an enraged demon who would frighten even a grown man. It's fitting. The true Gael finally shows himself to get his hands dirty for the first time.

The next punch makes my ears ring. I gasp through shockwaves of pain, trying to find air that seems determined to evade me. Another series of strikes hit my kidneys and rib cage, worsening my ability to breathe.

"Do I need to march back there and kill the girl myself?" Gael threatens.

"Leave h-her alone!"

"Then learn your place. It'll be little hardship for me to cover her purchase fee just for the pleasure of bleeding her dry in front of you."

"No!"

Muscles locked tight, I abruptly smash my head forward to crack into his. A shit move that hurts me as much as it hurts him, but the effect is tremendous. Gael hisses and slumps, now bent low over me.

I twist my head to sink my teeth into his earlobe. Cartilage battles against me, causing him to howl like a wounded lion caught in a trap. With my teeth sunk deeply into his skin, I jerk my head to create a delightful, skin-popping tear.

"Argh!" Gael's hands fly to his damaged ear.

Blood sprays across my mouth and face, pouring from the deep wound. My fist sails into the side of his head, making his screams amplify. Then I deliver another. Over and over. Crunching bone and splitting skin to create a picture of human destruction.

Shoving Gael's heft off me, I scurry upright to continue my attack. He's writhing on the carpet in a frenzied attempt to locate his gun. But it skidded just out of reach, leaving him with no choice but to fight me bare handed.

"Ember."

The light baritone freezes me, overcome with surprise at his use of my actual name. I halt halfway to Gael's body to look up at Gunnar. His hand is mid-air, clasping a familiar hunting knife by the blade to offer me the handle.

"I..." His voice seizes, prompting him to hesitate. "You were right. I was that boy in the cage. And I know exactly how it felt."

Gunnar waves the blade, urging me to take it.

"You sold us out," I manage through gulps of air.

His shoulder lifts in his usual shrug. "I'll pay the price for that. Please make this right."

That flash of brokenness in his honeyed shards emerges again. I take the blade then adjust my grip, turning to face the half-scrambling man who dared to lock me in a cage. Just like Gracie. Just like Gunnar. Just like all of us.

Gael hisses and kicks a foot out, colliding with my stomach. I groan at the impact but push onwards, prising his legs apart so I can straddle his wide, flat stomach. He halts at the twinkling blade hovering a breath from his throat.

"You took my freedom." I search his face for the reward of his terror. "You took my choice. My life. My voice. You took it all and more from all the others who did not escape."

"Ember—"

"No. You don't get to call me that."

"Perhaps we can—"

I cut off his bargaining with one fell swoop to the throat. Ear to ear. Easier than slicing melting butter left out in the sun. His skin parts beneath the deadly sharp blade without a single complaint from my muscles.

Bone scrapes against the knife, Gael's throat resembling a comical smiley face peppered with muscle and veins. Copper-scented death sprays over me, a torrential misting that hits every bit of skin in range. Yet I don't balk at the dousing.

Because I'm not 768.

I'm not enjoying it.

I'm Ember... and I'm fucking *loving it.*

The knife clatters beside me as I relish in the sight of Antonio Gael choking on his own lifeblood. He spits and gargles, those hateful yellow eyes filled with existential dread. I'm an angel of death taking every last second of consciousness from him for my own glee.

All I offer is his own words back to him.

"There's no deal left to be struck. I will show you no mercy."

Caught beneath me, Gael suffocates in a puddle of his own blood, unable to strike any more deals or bargains. Only his entrance through the gates of hell.

As his gaze grows glassy, I let myself slide sideways through sticky warmth. His blood trickles over my mouth, neck and chest as I scoot my aching body up against the nearby wall to stop myself from collapsing.

"Better?" I ask the sullen shadow.

Wearing nothing but pain and misery, Gunnar lowers his head. "Yes."

"Then you can go ahead and help your brother. There's a tracker stitched into his waistband. I activated it before we came out. Backup will be here any moment now."

"A… tracker?" Gunnar's eyes widen.

"Did you really think we were going to let you take him?"

He stares. Blinks. Falters.

"Well, yes."

Pulling my sleeve cuff down, I wipe it over my eyes to clear the layer of blood.

"Gunnar… You have a lot to learn about family. We never leave anyone behind. Not even those who lie or take the wrong path. We forgive. *We forget.*"

His eyes fill with tears, that tiny crack in his armour growing to a full-blown mountain crevasse. I've broken the famous Hunter. At last. All it took was showing him what he'll never have.

A team.

A fucking family.

And together, a future.

When the restaurant's windows collapse inwards, I find the energy to tilt my head to watch the broad shoulders of a violently vengeful angel storming inside. Olive malachites seek me out, blowing wide as he takes in the scene all around.

"Red?" Hyland exclaims.

Stretching out a trembling hand towards him, it drips with blood.

"I found her, Hy. I found Gracie."

POLICE LINE
DO NOT CROSS
E LINE - DO NOT CROSS
Weapon?
CONFIDENTIAL
DO NO

EPILOGUE

HYLAND

HOW TO BE ME – REN & CHINCHILLA

Unloading Sabre's jet on a private landing strip in the barren expanse of Wales's endless countryside is no easy feat. At least we're a smaller group after separating in Estonia, sending the Falcon Team and intelligence department on a flight to London.

I hold the bag of fluids connected to Axel's IV line high enough to avoid getting tangled while his wheelchair is carried down the metal steps. He's groggy, thankfully. Unaware of the fact that Blaine Madden of all people is carrying him to safety.

"Easy," I mutter.

Blaine sets the chair down with Warner's help. "He's fine."

"He will be. Get Ember, please?"

Nodding, Blaine ascends the steps back up into the private jet. The fact that he doesn't question my delegation of Ember's safety to him speaks volumes of all we've survived together in the past forty-eight hours.

Warner fusses over Axel, checking that his feet are seated in the footrest and the IV lines aren't tangled around him. All Axel can summon is a lopsided, drug-addled smile.

"You're so pretty," he coos.

I burst out laughing. "Oh, damn."

"Shut up," Warner snips back. "Thanks, Ax."

"Such big, beautiful blue eyes…"

Axel trails off in a round of semi-lucid laughter. I'm fighting back a hysterical fit of my own. The doctor we paid handsomely with Sabre's funds did his best to patch up Axel's badly cauterised wound, but he faces a long road ahead.

Arguably, not much longer than the trauma we all must live with. I'm not sure any of us can scrub the image of crashing into a random, deserted restaurant only to find Ember slumped on the floor, covered head to toe in blood.

Next to a corpse.

Antonio Gael's *very dead* corpse.

My body shivers at the mere thought. Sure, I'm fucking proud of our girl. She didn't need to wait for our tracking beacon to kick in and backup to arrive. Oh no. Not our Ember. That woman had it all handled long before we arrived in a panic.

Waiting for Blaine and Ember to emerge into the cool winter morning, I rest a hand on Warner's shoulder. "Did you get some rest?"

"Nah." He shakes his head.

"We can't track Madden in this state. Leave it to the Falcon Team and everyone back at HQ. He can't have gone far."

"Nolan Madden abandoned his residence and slipped away. That's unacceptable to me, Hy. This case isn't over until he's dead or behind bars."

My head pounds just thinking about it.

"Can we take a small win?" I sigh. "Please?"

"Is there much to celebrate here?" He gestures at Axel.

"Injuries aside, I think there is. Our prime target is in a body bag. Gunnar Slaughter's on his way to a holding cell in the bowels of Sabre HQ to be torn apart by Hudson. Gracie is going home. Even Nolan's victim is alive in the ICU, set to be reunited with his parents."

"Hy—"

"No. Cut the shit and take a win for once. Take multiple fucking wins, you stubborn idiot."

Warner manages a tiny smile. "We're running away from our enemies to hide in the middle of nowhere rather than facing them. Is that a good result?"

"We both know that Nolan Madden won't take our assault lying down. He'll attack and attack hard. The safest place for Ember and our team right now is off grid until we can regroup."

"There's nowhere we can hide from that man," Warner disagrees. "He'll tear London apart to find Ember and Blaine. This is just a short-term solution."

"You have to run with it for now. We need to lie low. Ember needs time to rest and heal. You do too. We can't fight Madden if we're dead on our feet."

Squeezing his shoulder, I release him with a final back slap. He rolls his eyes at me then refocuses on the jet's steps. Blaine reappears with our flame-haired goddess curled beneath his arm.

Convincing Ember to let the Falcon Team take Gracie with Rayna and Fox was an hour-long screaming match. She was set on going with them. It was Gracie herself who convinced Ember to relent, pleading with her to go so she could return to her family.

Then Ember locked herself in the plane's bedroom and didn't emerge for the entire flight. Judging by her blotchy, red-spotted face and swollen eyes, she needed time alone to come to terms with all that's happened.

"Where are we?" she croaks at the base of the steps.

Warner leans into Blaine's space to lightly touch Ember's cheek, careful of the fresh swelling.

"About thirty miles east of Briar Valley, love."

She wriggles out from under Blaine's arm to stretch. "Gotcha."

"Come on, we should take cover." I grab hold of the handles on Axel's wheelchair. "They're expecting us."

Warner seizes Ember's hand while Blaine hooks an arm around

her shoulders, keeping her upright between them. For days, none of us have slept much. I'm sure we all look as exhausted as Ember does right now.

Pushing the chair towards the small hangar on the other side of the landing strip, we greet the border officials who have already been told to stand down by a well-placed call from the one and only Kade Knight. The master diplomat strikes again.

Axel yelps when we hit a bump in the accessible ramp, head flopping so he can glare up at me. "Careful with my sweet ride, man."

"Apologies. Didn't mean to harm your Ferrari."

"She's a Lamborghini." He blows a raspberry. "Canary yellow and oh-so sexy."

"What have the doctors got him on?" Warner mutters.

"I'm not sure." Blaine chuckles. "But I'd very much like some of it."

The tinkle of Ember's tired laughter is music to my ears. I look over my shoulder to peek at her smile, however faint and brief. It chases some of the new shadows from her eyes. Ones that weren't there before this operation.

If I have one task ahead of me, it's to erase those goddamn shadows for good. They have no place there. We saw some harrowing shit, but Ember took her life back into her own hands. She eliminated Gael. That alone is reason for her to smile again.

Inside the hangar, our welcome party almost causes me to pull up short. It takes a second to overcome the surprise of seeing Ethan's warm smile after all this time. He doesn't hesitate, just grasps my hand as he bundles Warner into a hug.

"You guys look like absolute shit."

"We missed you too." I grin at our missing team member.

"It's been a quiet couple of years." He scrubs a hand over Warner's silver-streaked hair. "When did you get so old?"

"Piss off." Warner bats him away.

"All that stress is showing, old man. Glad you've come around to my way of life. Maybe we can shave a few years off with a couple weeks hiding out in the mountains."

"You are old." Axel chooses that moment to slur.

Snickering, Ethan takes a look over him. "This the patient?"

"Soon to be corpse," Warner supplies. "He's flatlining. Think we should call it."

"Shh!" Axel presses a finger to his lips. "It's past your bedtime, Grandpa!"

I'd throttle the pup on Warner's behalf if we hadn't found him on death's door in a locked cage. He's earned himself some leeway before his next beating for being a blabbermouth.

"Ember, this is Ethan." Warner nods towards him. "Our ex-team leader. He retired and lives in Briar Valley with his partner now."

"Hey." She waves a limp hand.

"Hi, Em. Glad you're safe."

"Me too."

"And it's fiancé now," Ethan corrects with a glance around our circle.

I give him the side eye. "When were you going to mention that?"

"Ryder got me drunk one night and popped the question. I couldn't exactly refuse."

Punching him in the shoulder, I leave the wheelchair to grab him around the waist. "You sly shit! I don't know whether to be happy or mad."

"Alright, alright." Ethan playfully shoves me away. "Enough celebrating. Ryder's playing the role of bride to be. Go fawn over him and his wedding plans instead."

"Congrats." Warner beams at him.

"Thanks. So who else do we have coming along?"

Clearing his throat, Blaine shifts uncomfortably on his feet. Ethan casts him a perplexed look as if he can't figure out how to place him. Then shock and disbelief take hold. After all, we did dismantle the Madden empire together.

"Are you… Blaine fucking Madden?"

"Hello again, Ethan." Blaine avoids making eye contact. "You know that isn't actually my name. Just Blaine Madden will suffice. Less of the fucking part. Or failing that, Blaine."

"Right." Ethan blinks rapidly. "What the fuck?"

"It's a long story," Warner hedges.

"Clearly. What the hell have I missed? We put this guy behind bars."

I plaster on a weak smile. "Actually… it's a fun story."

"Fun?" Warner splutters.

Ethan fights to compose himself. "Let's get you all somewhere safe. Then I'll raid Killian's homemade whiskey supply, and we can dive into this fun story that involves a wanted criminal standing on my doorstep."

"Can't wait," Blaine murmurs.

Leaving us to gather the few belongings we travelled with, Ethan walks over to the other side of the hangar where the bathrooms are located. I frown while watching him rap on the ladies' door.

After a long pause, the door swings open. My breath catches at the golden-olive skin of the woman who emerges. It's been almost three years since I last visited Briar Valley to help Ethan move after the Sanchez case was wrapped.

In that time, Willow hasn't changed. She still radiates joyful optimism with her effortless smile and warm, open nature. Even her midnight-black curls and full curves haven't changed a bit.

"Look what the cat dragged in." She saunters over to us.

"Come here, you." I drag her into a bear hug. "Hey."

"Hi. Glad you're safe."

"Me too."

Willow sinks against me, her soft curls smelling of pine and fir trees mixed with her floral shampoo. I hold her close for several seconds then let go so she can breathe again.

"Thanks for the wakeup call." Willow's radiant hazel eyes search over me.

"Sorry, I didn't mean to wake you. Just figured we should call ahead."

"I'm joking, Hy. Where's the trouble?"

"Behind us, hopefully," Warner inserts. "But it's coming our way."

She casts Ethan a look. "Then it sounds like you need a place to disappear. Thankfully, helping people vanish is what Briar Valley does best."

Enveloped in a hug, Warner thanks her again. Willow pats him on the back as she whispers assurances. In her mind, she owes her life to Sabre. I don't think it's quite as clean cut as that. She fought damn hard for her own justice not so long ago.

When they separate, Ember lifts her head to greet Willow. I spot the moment that the pair lock eyes, a strange sort of tension rippling between them. Ember stiffens into stone, suddenly looking wide awake with huge pupils.

"Em?" I reach for her.

She seems to shake herself, still trapped in a stunned stare off. Willow almost stumbles on her feet, a hand flying up to rest at the base of her rapidly bobbing throat.

"Oh my… Ember?" she whispers in awe. "Is that really you?"

Much to our disbelief, the pair gawp at each other like reunited friends.

"Hello again, Willow."

THE END

TO BE CONTINUED IN…
TRAPPED TRUTH (ANACONDA TALES #3)

PLAYLIST

LISTEN HERE:
HTTPS://BIT.LY/RAVAGEDSOUL

makes me want you – sombr
Staring at the Sun – TV On The Radio
Cold – Chris Stapleton
Fitzpleasure – alt-J
Johnny Wants To Fight – Badflower
One Last Breath – Creed
Fine Again – Seether
southbound – Artemas
Goddess – Xana
Will You Love Me When I'm Dead – Amira Elfeky
hostage – Billie Eilish
Zombie – YUNGBLUD
Doctor Doctor – LOWBORN
Which Witch – Florence + The Machine
What I Need – High June
2005 – South Arcade
Be Good – Roseburg
Oil and Water – Incubus
Black Chandelier – Biffy Clyro
Redemption – Jevon
Chalk Outlines – Ren & CHINCHILLA
who are you – mehro
All of Human Knowledge Made Us Dumb – SOFIA ISELLA
Stronger – Thunderstorm Artis
Nothing Matters – The Last Dinner Party
Someday – Nickelback
Emergence – Sleep Token
I Will Not Bow – Breaking Benjamin
How to Be Me – Ren & CHINCHILLA

ACKNOWLEDGEMENTS

Another book baby done and dusted! It's always such a blessing to type those magical words and close a manuscript after months of drafting.

Writing Ravaged Soul in the middle of planning a wedding then getting married was quite possibly one of the most stressful experiences I've had yet, but it was worth it to dive into this deliciously angsty sequel. I hope you loved reading it as much as I did writing it.

I'd like to thank my *new* husband, Eddie, for bearing with me while I was a ball of stress for the past few months. I feel truly blessed to finally be able to call you mine… forever. Love you always.

As usual, the army of incredible people supporting me make this career possible. Thank you to Kristen for being my number one cheerleader and source of support. And to my wonderful friends—Lilith, Lola, Nat, Kaya and so many more—who all keep me going on those hard days.

An extra-special mention goes to my phenomenal PA and friend, Zoe, for running my chaos on a daily basis. Thank you for being my second brain and cheering me on when life gets tough.

Of course, I'd be lost without my talented editor, Kim, and the amazing team at Valentine PR who help with each book I release. You're all superstars.

Finally, I'd like to save the biggest thank you for the beautiful souls reading these words. Thanks to you, I'm able to wake up every single day and write these stories for a living. So much has changed since I first published nearly five years ago and the biggest changes are yet to come. But I'll never stop being eternally grateful for this privilege. You've made my dreams come true.

Stay wild,
J Rose xxx

WANT MORE FROM THIS UNIVERSE?

Begin this shared world in Blackwood Institute. Learn more about Brooklyn, Hudson, Kade, Eli and Phoenix by diving into the dark and twisted world of an experimental psychiatric institute.

TWISTED HEATHENS
SACRIFICIAL SINNERS
DESECRATED SAINTS
OMNIBUS

Dive into Sabre next. Set in the same shared universe, the Sabre Security series follows Harlow and the hunt for a violent, bloodthirsty serial killer. Featuring cameos from all your favourite Blackwood Institute characters.

CORPSE ROADS
SKELETAL HEARTS
HOLLOW VEINS
OMNIBUS

Follow Willow's story next as she flees an abusive marriage and takes refuge in the small mountain town of Briar Valley, assisted in her hunt for justice by Sabre Security.

WHERE BROKEN WINGS FLY
WHERE WILD THINGS GROW
OMNIBUS

Explore Warner's early days in the Harrowdean Manor duet. Follow Ripley, our morally grey antihero lead, as she wages war on a corrupt corporation with the help of her sworn enemies.

SIN LIKE THE DEVIL
BURN LIKE AN ANGEL
OMNIBUS

NEWSLETTER

Want more madness? Sign up to J Rose's newsletter for monthly announcements, exclusive content, sneak peeks, giveaways and more!

Sign up: www.jroseauthor.com/newsletter

ABOUT THE AUTHOR

J Rose is an independent dark romance author from the United Kingdom. She writes challenging, plot-driven stories packed full of angst, heartbreak and broken characters fighting for their happily ever afters.

She's an introverted bookworm at heart with a caffeine addiction, penchant for cursing and an unhealthy attachment to fictional characters.

Feel free to reach out on social media. J Rose loves talking to her readers!

For exclusive insights, updates and general mayhem, join J Rose's Bleeding Thorns on Facebook.

Business enquiries: j_roseauthor@yahoo.com

Come join the chaos. Stalk J Rose here...
www.jroseauthor.com/socials

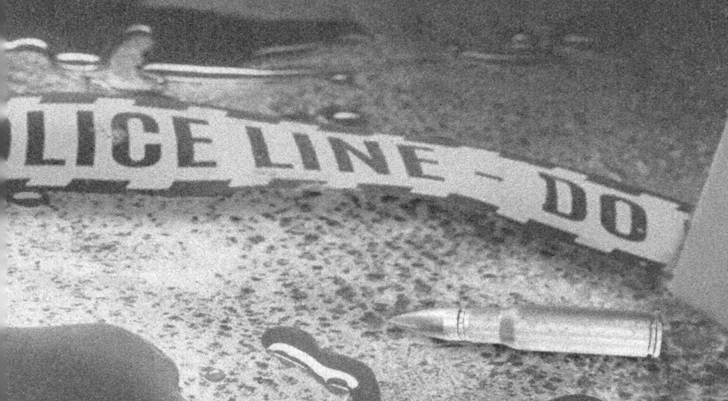

ALSO BY J ROSE

Read Here: www.jroseauthor.com/books

Recommended Reading Order: www.jroseauthor.com/
readingorder

BLACKWOOD INSTITUTE

Twisted Heathens
Sacrificial Sinners
Desecrated Saints

SABRE SECURITY

Corpse Roads
Skeletal Hearts
Hollow Veins

BRIAR VALLEY

Where Broken Wings Fly
Where Wild Things Grow

HARROWDEAN MANOR

Sin Like The Devil
Burn Like An Angel

ANACONDA TALES

Fractured Future
Ravaged Soul
Trapped Truth

STANDALONES

Forever Ago
Drown in You
A Crimson Carol

WRITING AS JESSALYN THORN

Departed Whispers
If You Break